First Person

RICHARD FLANAGAN

First Person

Chatto & Windus

LONDON

1 3 5 7 9 10 8 6 4 2

Chatto & Windus, an imprint of Vintage,
20 Vauxhall Bridge Road,
London SW1V 2SA

Chatto & Windus is part of the Penguin Random House group of companies
whose addresses can be found at global.penguinrandomhouse.com.

Penguin
Random House
UK

Published in the UK by Chatto & Windus in 2017
First published in Australia by Knopf Australia 2017

penguin.co.uk/vintage

A CIP catalogue record for this book is available from the British Library

HB ISBN 9781784742195
TPB 9781784742201

Printed and bound in Great Britain by Clays Ltd, St Ives PLC

Penguin Random House is committed to a sustainable future
for our business, our readers and our planet. This book is made
from Forest Stewardship Council® certified paper.

For Nikki Christer

Minutes of Evidence
Select Committee on Transportation of Convicts
London, 5 May 1837

Question—Are there many booksellers' shops?

James Mudie, Esq.—I should think there are about half-a-dozen in Sydney.

Question—What kind of books do you see sold in those shops; is the class of books different from what you see sold in booksellers' shops in London?

James Mudie, Esq.—Inferior certainly; there are many novels, for instance. I have attended what they call book sales myself, and I have always found that books really valuable have sold for much less than they could have cost in England, and I remember on one occasion there was a regular noise in the room when the Newgate Calendar was put up, and every person said, 'Ah, I shall have that!'

I forget what it brought, but it brought something enormous . . . Then they are fond of the history of highwaymen or anything of that kind.

British Parliamentary Papers

1

1

OUR FIRST BATTLE WAS BIRTH. I wanted it in, he wanted it out. All that day and half of the next we argued. He said it had nothing to do with him. Later I began to see his point, but at the time it seemed bloody-mindedness and evidence of an inexplicable obstruction—as though he didn't actually want any memoir ever written. Of course, he *didn't* want a memoir written, but that wasn't his point. Or the point. But I only realised this later, much later, when I came to fear that the beginning of that book was also the end of me.

Too late, in other words.

These days I content myself with reality TV. There is a void, a loneliness that aches and rattles. That frightens. That terrifies me that I should have lived and never did. Reality TV doesn't have this effect on me.

Back then though, all this was confusing. It was feared by others that I might relapse into literature. By which I mean allegory, symbol, the tropes of time dancing; of books that didn't have a particular beginning or end, or at least not in that order. By whom I mean the publisher, a man by the unexpected name of Gene Paley. He had been quite specific in this regard: I was to tell a simple story simply, and where it was not simple—when it dealt with the complexities of the spectacular crime—simplify, illustrate by way of anecdote, and never have a sentence that lingered longer than two lines.

It was whispered around the publishing house that Gene Paley was frightened of literature. And not without good reason. For one thing, it doesn't sell. For another, it can fairly be said that it asks questions that it can't answer. It astonishes people with themselves, which, on balance, is rarely a good thing. It reminds them that the business of life is failure, and that the failure to know this is true ignorance. Maybe there is transcendence in all this, or wisdom in some of it, but Gene Paley didn't see himself in the transcendence game. Gene Paley was all for books telling you one or two things over and over again. But preferably only one.

Selling, Gene Paley would say, is telling.

I opened the manuscript again and re-read the opening lines.

On 17 May 1983, I signed my application letter for the position of Acting Safety Officer (supervisor) (Acting Class 4/5) at the Australian Safety Organisation, with two words, Siegfried Heidl, and my new life began.

Only much later did I discover that Siegfried Heidl had never existed until that day he signed the letter, so—strictly speaking—it was an honest account. But the past is always unpredictable and, as I was to learn, not his least gift as a con man was that he rarely lied.

Ziggy Heidl's point of view was that his twelve-thousand-word manuscript—the thin pile of stacked papers on which he would frequently press down with his outstretched hand as if it were a basketball to be bounced and put back into play—said everything that anyone would ever be interested in reading about Ziggy Heidl. My job as a writer, he went on, was simply to sharpen his sentences, and perhaps elaborate here and there a little on his account.

He said this, as he said so much else, with such belief, with such confidence and such conviction, that I found it very difficult to point out, as I had to, that his manuscript made no mention of his childhood, his parents or even, for that matter, his year of birth. His reply has remained with me, even after all these years.

A life isn't an onion to be peeled, a palimpsest to be scraped back to some original, truer meaning. It's an invention that never ends.

And when I must have looked struck by his elaborate turn of phrase, Heidl added, as if giving directions to a public toilet: Tebbe. It's one of his aphorisms.

What he lacked in facts, he made up for with an understated conviction; and what he lacked in conviction he made up for with facts, albeit mostly invented, and rendered all the more plausible because they were so lightly thrown up from an unexpected angle.

The great German installationist, Heidl said. Tomas Tebbe.

I had no idea what a palimpsest might be. Or who Tebbe was, or what an installationist did, or was, and said so. Heidl made no reply. Maybe, as he told me another time, we take from our past and the past of others to make ourselves anew, and the something new is our memory too. Tebbe, whom I only read many years later, put it best: It may be someone else's blood soaking into the dust, he wrote, but I am that dust.

I looked up.

Out of interest, I said, whereabouts *in* Germany did you grow up?

Germany? Ziggy Heidl said, looking out the window. I never went there until I was twenty-six. I told you. I grew up in South Australia.

Your accent is German.

Roger that, Ziggy Heidl said. And when he turned his fleshy face back to me I tried not to stare at the small muscle in his otherwise puffy cheek that twitched when he smiled, a knot of tautness amidst the slackness, a single tight muscle pulsing in and out.

I know it's odd, but there you are—I grew up with German-speaking parents and no one to play with. But I was happy. Write that.

He was smiling.

His smile: an undertow of sinister complicity.

What? I said.

That.

What?

Write: I was happy.

That terrible smile. That twitching cheek.

Boom-boom, it silently went. Boom-boom.

2

We were working in a publishing executive's corner office in a publishing company's headquarters in Port Melbourne. Perhaps it had been the office of an editorial director or a sales manager, recently retired or lately sacked. Who knows? We were never told, but the office made Ziggy Heidl feel important and that was important, and if I felt embarrassed, that wasn't. It was 1992, that time so close and now so far away when publishing executives still had such rooms and liquor cabinets; before Amazon and e-books; before phrases like *granular analytics, customer fulfilment,* and *supply chain alignment* had connected like tightening coils in a hangman's noose; before the relentless rise of property values and the collapse of publishing saw publishers' offices morph into abattoir-like assembly lines, where all staff sat cheek by jowl at long benches reminiscent of, say, a Red Army canteen in Kabul, circa 1979.

And like the Red Army then, publishing was entering a crisis of stagnation not yet understood as either a crisis or as terminal. And beneath where the publishing people sat were so many little holes being bored by redundancies slowly coming together into one large sink hole through which, a few years hence, the several floors of the publishing house would suddenly and unexpectedly fall until they landed with a crash and compressed into just one floor. Then that floor, in turn, would begin to shrink as a rising sea of start-ups, finance companies and net businesses flooded over the publisher's office space—an encroaching ocean of *disruption*—until the floor was now only half a floor, and on that vanishing island books were now only content and writers only content providers, sandbag fillers, but of an ever lower and lower caste, if such a thing were possible. All of which may suggest I write with some nostalgia, that the Port Melbourne office had charm or character.

I don't.

It didn't.

If it was bookcase lined, the bookcases were, on closer examination, like the world of publishing then, dispiriting. The shelving was particleboard covered with a hokey teak veneer, an uncomfortably faecal brown, more plasticised than varnished. And the books! The books that house—the then mighty Schlegel TransPacific (or as it was variously known, TransPac or STP)—published were the only books on those shelves. Books on chocolate, gardening, furniture, military history, tired celebrities; tedious memoirs and pulp novels—a small part of the profits from which paid for the publication of the few books that I thought books were—novels, essays, poems, stories—none of which lived on those glossy shelves. In addition to these and the cookbooks, pictorials, and reference books that still had a market, were the collected works of Jez Dempster, each Jez Dempster tome a cinder block blinged with the words JEZ DEMPSTER picked out in great gold lettering. What junk they were. How dispiriting they seemed. It was my first intimation that my idea of books, of writing, was a very small and largely unsuccessful subset of what at STP was known—in a cod-craft mystery-like way—as *the trade*.

The trade explained all things. While phrases such as 'that's how it *is* in the trade' or 'the trade's *tight*' told you nothing, they were understood to explain everything. And from my first day I understood that *the trade* somehow thought my telling of Heidl's story was far more real a book than the real book I had until that time thought I had been writing, that real book being my own unfinished first novel.

This made no sense to me, but then *the trade* made no sense. It made no sense, for example, that Heidl's memoirs were—for reasons I never could divine—secret. No one was meant to know at the publishing house, other than the handful working with us on the book—Gene Paley himself, though as publisher he left most of the work to the editor, Pia Carnevale, and one or two others. We were to tell everyone else we were co-editing an anthology of mediaeval Westphalian folk verse. I am not sure whose lie this was—Ziggy Heidl's or Gene Paley's then, or mine later—but it was as impressive as it was ludicrous. Why such a project would be undertaken within the house was, to my knowledge, never questioned. In a line of work full of perplexity, it was just one more oddity—but wasn't that just how it was in *the trade*?

The furniture matched the tone of shoddy bombast—the executive's faux Edwardian Laminex desk behind which Ziggy Heidl made his unceasing calls was too big, while the conference table at which I worked was too small for its real purpose of hosting meetings. The slightly soiled tub chairs in which we sat were upholstered in a nylon jacquard beset by a salmon and grey weave. When your fingers touched the fabric, it felt half-melted. The tormented colouring for no good reason always put me in mind of a Francis Bacon painting. I felt as if I were sitting in a muted scream.

3

Gene would like to see you, Kif, said a young woman at our office door. Needs you to sign a contract.

Gene Paley wanted no such thing—I'd signed my contract on the very first day already so long ago it was hard to believe it had been only Monday and it was now just Wednesday. Gene Paley, I knew, wanted to know how it was going.

Slowly, I said as I stood before Gene Paley in his office suite, while he stared down at tractor feed spreadsheets papering his desk. He just won't *give* . . . detail.

Early life?

Vague stories about being born in a remote South Australian mining town called Jaggamyurra to German parents.

That's it? Gene Paley said, still not looking up.

More or less.

Mmm.

Mostly less.

The con? As I was saying, he's not a criminal celebrity for no reason. Seven hundred million dollars. It's the biggest con job in Australian history. Has he explained how he did it?

Vaguely.

CIA?

Even vaguer.

Mmm, Gene Paley said and fell silent. Much of his conversation was punctuated with this slight downward falling murmur, as if every sentence were a judgement of failure. That, or the repetition of the phrase, As I was saying. His whole manner of speech was unusual, clipped sentences delivered quickly then slowly, such that he often sounded like a dying telex machine.

Good—, I said, but I could hear myself faltering.

On one of the spreadsheets, as wide as a small suburban road, Gene Paley made some precise marks, the wet black ink of his fountain pen vivid against the pale blue and white striped paper and ash blur of dot matrix printed numbers.

Good stories, I said. Just a little . . .

Vague?

Vague? Possibly.

As I was saying, you can write, Gene Paley said, eyes continuing to track the numbers arrayed below. But we need him to talk.

His eyes were oddly hooded, and that, and his small face, his beak of a nose, the suggestion of a powdery odour, the sense he might bite deeply and unexpectedly, all put me in mind of Suzy's pet Indian ringneck parrot that missed no opportunity to bite me.

I need him to tell me something, I said. He's—*he's* just not interested in the book.

Gene Paley raised his eyes and caught mine with an unforgiving stare.

Mmm, he said, and with a quizzical gesture he held out at arm's-length his oversize fountain pen, as elaborate and nonsensical as a piece of chromed agricultural pipe, and dropped it on the several kilometres of numbers on the spreadsheets below. Decades of living through numbers such as these—the *numbers* printed, the *numbers* sold in, the *numbers* sold through, returned, and remaindered, the *numbers* he gave away as margin to booksellers, the *numbers* he lied about to other publishers and journalists, hellish real *numbers*, dreamt-of *numbers*, true *numbers*, false *numbers*, *numbers* lost to rapacious book chains, *numbers* clawed back off witless authors and vainglorious agents, the despair and beauty and sheer alchemy of *numbers*—their *numbers*, our *numbers*, bad *numbers*, good *numbers*, even, for God's sake, *numbers* on *numbers*—all these innumerable *numbers* had over time honed in Gene Paley a sensitivity so great it verged on a sixth sense: to the possibility of profit and the terror of loss. And that sense was even then twitching with concern, perhaps fear.

Your contract is not just to write, he said, his voice still kindly but somehow firmer—somehow resolute. It is to write with *him* for *us*. Your job is to make *him* talk. Without him talking there is no book. Without a book at the end of six weeks, there is no money for you. None. No. Yes?

No, I replied. Yes.

No, Gene Paley said. None.

Yes, I replied. No.

As he talked, Gene Paley folded the spreadsheets into a neat rectangular mound, stood up, and took off his shirt without shame or concern to reveal a white singlet, slack on his scrawny white body.

They say there are only three rules for writing a book, Gene Paley said in what felt an anecdote greasy with retelling. Only no one can remember what they are.

The slightly sagging undersides of his skinny arms were scored with a few bright red moles not much bigger than odd biro marks, approximately attached to a body that gave the impression of never having done any manual work. A man as seemingly unconcerned about being named Gene as Gene Paley, was, I realised, a man beyond the conventions of masculine self-doubt as I had been brought up to understand them. And after only three days of working on the Heidl memoir I was beginning to understand this narrowness in my own thinking as only one of my many limitations. Still, I could not help but think it a shameful body to reveal, the torso of a dachshund topped with the head of a cockatiel. You would need to have been Arcimboldo to do such a body justice.

He opened a cupboard door from which he took out a freshly ironed shirt.

But try finishing a first draft, Gene Paley said. Quickly. That's my advice.

Without any concern as to my presence, or as to what I might think, he put the shirt on, offering a single sentence that was apparently sufficient as explanation.

Lunch, he said as he did up his buttons, with Jez Dempster.

Jez Dempster's books sold in the hundreds of thousands. Perhaps millions. Jez Dempster was *big in the trade.*

As I was saying, a writer like you can learn a great deal from the Jez Dempsters of this world, Gene Paley said. Yes?

Yes, I replied, or repeated—it seemed to amount to the same thing. Such as—?

Such as, if you can only learn to write badly enough you can make a great deal of money. You live the alternative.

I write well?

You make no money.

Although there was in Gene Paley's slightly hooded gaze and his faint smile gentleness and even—perhaps—kindness, there hid in that skinny body, those flaccid arms, a stiletto-like instinct that was highly attuned to status and money. But above all, money. Perhaps that was what was most developed in him: his almost shamanic feeling for money—its needs and its demands, its ecstasies and torments, the supplication and the acts it required of him as an intermediary between its world and ours. There was about him a resolve that I understood even then could easily shade into cruelty, because a man who didn't care what another man thought of his body was a man who didn't care what any other man thought about anything or, for that matter, what fate might befall that other man.

Jez Dempster tells me, he said, unbuttoning his trousers and easing his fly to half-mast, that a classic is a book that never finishes what it wants to say.

He tucked his shirt flaps in and buttoned his trousers back up.

You're not writing a classic, he said. You're writing a bestseller. And I want you to say everything that anyone would ever want to read in a book about Siegfried Heidl. And I want that book finished in six weeks.

I must confess that the sight of Gene Paley changing shirts

unnerved me. Something in his behaviour—like the kings who dealt with their courtiers and supplicants and matters of state while shitting—made our respective positions far clearer than anything he ever said to me. There was in him an absence of so many things that I understood men were meant to be, and yet it was clear that he thought himself superior. And much as I hated it in myself, I found myself in my awkward posture, my nervous replies, seeming, though I told myself I did not believe it, to somehow agree.

Not thought, Ray said later, when I told him about the changing of shirts. *Knows*. Knows he's better. And people like him are brought up to know it.

Your shoes, said Gene Paley, now dressed and ushering me with extended arm to the door.

His eyes dropped to my feet to where the leather of my right Adidas Vienna runner was tearing away from the sole. The shoe wasn't exactly falling apart, or not just yet anyway, and if I lifted rather than rolled off my foot as I walked I had hopes of it lasting the full six weeks.

Don't you have another pair?

All that time I had been looking at him he had been examining me and he had, I realised, found me wanting. And the truth was I didn't have another pair, and I could afford none, but I was too ashamed to say that, or to say anything. All I could do was try harder to get Heidl to talk in order that I'd get paid and have some money for, among other things, a new pair of runners.

4

I went back down that long corridor, walking with a slight limp as I tried to preserve my Adidas Vienna a few days longer, and turned into the increasingly oppressive executive's office where

Heidl was standing behind the executive's desk talking on the executive's phone. He waved at me in a way that might best be described as *managerial*—at once dismissive, controlling, at ease; a gesture of power. I sat back down at the small conference table, with its three simple chairs, perhaps, I thought now, not so much complex Francis Bacon portraits as straightforward Edvard Munch screams, and as I booted up the Mac Classic I watched Heidl. He put the phone down and immediately began talking once more about toxoplasmosis, or *the toxo*, as he called it.

The toxo fascinated Ziggy Heidl, or Ziggy Heidl said the toxo fascinated him. Either way, it was for him a frequent topic of conversation—how the toxoplasmosis parasite affected rats' brains in such a way that rats lost their instinctive fear of cats. The newly emboldened rats would then be eaten by the cats, a carrier the toxoplasmosis parasite used to reproduce in during the next stage of their breeding cycle. The cats, in turn, would cultivate humans, on to whom they passed the parasite through faecal contamination.

And what fascinated Heidl above all was exactly how the toxo—which fatally altered rats' behaviour—might affect humans. He would speculate for hours on the way mad people so often had so many cats. Was the toxo using these people to care for the cats in order to maximise the chances of the toxo surviving in the cats? Were the mad people mad always or had the toxo made them so? He would talk of how the toxo had been strongly implicated in suicides and schizophrenia. The question no one could answer was this: why would the parasite manipulate human beings to such extreme acts?

If you could only stand listening to him he was, in his way, a beautiful talker, yet almost nothing of what he said was of any use to me. And as he talked of how dolphins were now being infected with the parasite from farm run-off, I began to worry that he was like the toxo that so fascinated him. I momentarily had the ridiculous notion that something might take hold of my mind and make it act against its own will, against its own interests. And with that, I realised how fearful I already had become, and how crazy my fear was.

I resolved to focus on just getting a few more words done for the day. He told me the kid goat story a second time—or was it the first?—only this time he shot the kid in the head in such a way that the kid died very slowly and he just had to watch.

This too you learnt from Heidl: how easy it is to remember; how hard to know if there is truth in even one memory. How candour aids the necessary lie and how the lie allows us to live.

5

I remember I went to the window after the goat story for the first or last time and looked out. In the distance, some cranes were hunching wearily, and behind them, there on the horizon, a red sun rolled low, spilling grey and bloody light on the world beneath. On the street three storeys below some khaki-clad workmen kicked a football to each other. I envied them their odd freedom. I didn't know that I was still free. My gaze dropped to the entrance to STP Publishing where, standing far below, I saw Ray, leather bomber-jacketed, strapping up a rollie, looking bored.

When I turned around, Heidl was still on the phone. I gestured that I was having a break and left the room, taking the stairs the three flights down to the foyer and the main entrance.

Outside, as inside, everything was new. The instant turf strip along the pavement was without filth and cigarette butts. No graffiti had yet flowered on the grey concrete of the tilt-slab warehouses, nor damasked the umber and olive renders of the low-rise office buildings, the startling sameness of which filled the street and beyond as far as you could see. Everything was ordered and bright, waiting to be eroded into a uniform drabness, and it was all so new that some windows on a building opposite still had their protective film, twisted tails of blue plastic wagging here and there.

The word shithole, Ray said, is too interesting for a shithole like this.

It was all so new and yet something was already over. That's how it felt. I longed to feel so many other things—excitement, ideas, emotions I might use to imagine Heidl's imaginary childhood. But I just felt an enormous boredom. If I had been a real writer I might have found post-modern beauty or at least a few lines that pretended I did. But I was an islander from an island at world's end where the measure of all things that mattered was not man-made, and such sights that moved modern literature did not move me. I came from what I had been told was a dull and provincial backwater, and I did not even know how to correctly see, and so how could I properly write?

It's just shit, Ray said.

He was leaning on a long concrete planter box that was chest high. Along it ran an aluminium sheet on which was screen-printed the words STP PUBLISHING and the company's celebrated colophon, a stylised breaching white whale.

I said Heidl was back on the phone.

The wind blew in erratic gusts, and when it hit my face it was gritty. The day smelled of damp stone. I suppose there were sounds but I don't remember any. Maybe distant traffic. Maybe not. It was that sort of place where nothing made an impression, not noise, not silence.

Well, this time we made it to Australia without nearly dying, Ray said.

I was Australian, but I didn't really know anything about Australia, having grown up in Tasmania, about which no one knows anything, least of all Tasmanians to whom it is only ever a growing mystery. Melbourne was a confident town, by its own estimate, if few others, a great city, which believed it was born out of gold rushes rather than an invasion by Van Diemonian settlers a few years prior to the discovery of gold, men who had made their mark running death squads on the Tasmanian frontier hunting down remnant Tasmanian Aboriginals and massacring them at night around their campfires.

Some Tasmanians said Melbourne was like Tasmania, only bigger, which now struck me as stupid as saying Tasmania was like New York, only smaller, which was just as true and just as stupid. Really, the world was full of stupid things yet without them what would we have to talk about? Perhaps the only difference between man and animals is man's capacity to fill his days and life with a universe of stupid things until the only real thing, death, finally arrives to end the nonsense. These days I envy anyone who has been told that they have this or that terminal disease. In my more hopeful moments I pray for cancer.

I'm going for a walk, I said.

The road's bitumen was black and clean as a luxury apartment's kitchen benchtop, fresh concrete dust dulled the still light grey kerbing, and the galvanised grates gleamed a silvery pearlescence. I could see, as Gene Paley had pointed out at our first meeting, how everything around these streets was about how the country was booming, how—in spite of the recession, in spite of interest rates—the nation was growing, or at least the economy was turning the corner. There was a lot of talk about the economy in those days, it was like Christ the Redeemer; people still believed in the economy like they had in politics before and God before that, mug punters would even talk about J-curves and floating exchange rates over a smoke, as though these words somehow explained them and their lives.

But as I stood at the first intersection—wondering if I should take smoking back up if just for the duration of this book—the

17

only curve I was conscious of was the growing bulge of loose leather that had torn away a little more from the sole of my right Adidas Vienna runner. Everywhere were more streets that were more of the same, a labyrinth of monotony so total that for a moment I was confused as to where I was and how I would get back to the publishers, which was, after all, only two hundred metres behind me. I limped back with my Vienna-prolonging gait and asked Ray for a smoke.

Fuck me, Ray said, you need a hip replacement before a durrie.

He was watching the workmen playing football on the street. One wore a cowboy hat: when he marked the ball he would stop, straighten up, lean down, pull up his socks, toss gravel into the wind, and, with great solemnity, kick back to his mate. As his mate marked he would run around in a small circle, waving a victory finger in the air.

Fuck what? I said.

Shit, Ray said slowly. He could invest a single meaningless word with the gravitas and mystery of a Nobel laureate glossing string theory.

What?

That's it, mate.

What's it?

It, he repeated.

I had no idea what he was on about, but I rarely did.

You know, mate, Ray said, leaning in.

He was smiling now, rolling me a cigarette with his Champion Ruby tobacco, looking through me as if he had won another pub brawl. Or was about to start one.

You fuckn know, Ray said and winked. Handing me the durrie, he leant further in so that our foreheads were nearly butting. He looked furtively around, and hissed.

He thinks they want to *kill* him.

6

They want to say things, the dead. Ordinary things, everyday things. Of a night they return to me and I allow them in. I let them their tongue. They talk of what we watch, what we see, what we hear and touch, free as the moon to wander the true night. The unbodied air, wrote Melville. But there is no Ziggy Heidl. No Ray. No others. Back then, before I had written anything, I knew everything about writing. Now I know nothing. Living? Nothing. Life? Nothing. Nothing at all.

2

1

THE BANKS, HEIDL SAID on the fourth day, as if in answer to my persistent thoughts. They want to kill me.

After the fluster and hope and excitement of the first three days, things had ground to a halt. At best, Heidl answered in irritating riddles and, at worst, was distracted or, worse yet, entirely uninterested. His principal concern was how he might get Gene Paley to pay him the next instalment of his advance.

You? I said. Why on earth would they want to kill *you*?

Because of what I've done. And what I know. I know a lot that could cause—*well*—damage. Prominent people. Powerful people.

He was almost droning, transfixed by the romance of his own destiny, when, as was his way, another thought seemed to strike him and he grew suddenly animated.

Do you think Paley would pay me half the instalment if you could show him some pages now?

I said there were no pages.

Isn't that your job?

I shook my head.

Make the pages? Isn't that what you do? What you're here for?

I suggested that if he might just tell me something about his life I might just turn it into some pages and Gene Paley might just turn that into some money.

Heidl ignored this, if for that matter he heard it.

No bank would want to kill you, I said, seeking any form of engagement. They have you about to go to jail anyway.

At such times he would look about conspiratorially, and, leaning forward, seem to be taking me into his confidence.

Things I know they wouldn't want you to know. Who can say what I might say in court?

Like?

Heidl laughed. His cheek dimpled furiously.

I am not going to tell you anything. But that's what they think—that I am going to tell you. And there are *people* feeding their fears.

People?

People like Eric Knowles. He knows about my links. My connections.

Connections with whom?

People.

What people?

People, he hissed. He blew a derisory breath out of his nose and shook his head at my naivety in not knowing exactly who *people* were.

And, somehow, it was embarrassing for me not to be up to speed with things such as *people* the same way I wasn't up to speed with so many things.

I am not saying that these *people* exist in your world, Heidl went on. But they exist nevertheless. And in our world, the real world, you have to deal with them, or you have to have someone who deals with them for you.

So?

So, maybe I was that someone.

If you mean the CIA, Siegfried, I need you to say the CIA.

I only directly worked for them in the early '70s. Laos. The FRG. Not later. Not here in Australia.

So, what did you do for them in Laos, I asked, and off he went again with his euphemisms, his riddles, his rhetorical formulations that could mean everything or nothing.

Or both.

In Chile, he said, as if to torment me further.

Chile?

My codename, he said, was Iago.

But his tone was once more unsure, as if he was uncertain of what he should know and how much he did know. He always seemed able to evoke a mystery, but the moment you sought to penetrate the mystery, he sought to escape what it was he had just suggested. His first feint was to go with your building of the mystery, seeking to draw you in with agreement and encouragement. To have you invent his lies. And at the beginning I fell for it every time. At the end, perhaps not enough. Perhaps I became it.

I am not what I am, I said.

What?

Iago.

That's what I said.

That's what Iago said. *Othello*. But I will wear my heart upon my sleeve for daws to peck at: I am not what I am, I said.

Roger that, Heidl said. That's me.

A great character, I replied.

A great novel!

And we were back, lost again, whirling in that vortex of it may have been or it may not yet be; it wasn't or it is; it was or it isn't.

I am not saying we have to know everything about your private life, I said.

No, Heidl said.

But it would be good if we could just see a little of it from your viewpoint.

Yes, Heidl said. But I don't have a viewpoint.

Your life, then. For one thing, readers want that. And for another it makes you look more sympathetic. As someone who thinks about life, his life. The unexamined life is not worth living—

Socrates.

—far less reading, I added, surprised that Heidl had spotted the allusion.

The problem, Heidl said, is that the examined life is not worth contemplating.

There was a knock on the door, and Pia Carnevale put her head in.

Gene would like to see you, Kif, she said. Needs you to go over some copy with him.

2

Gene Paley wanted no such thing. Once more, he wanted to know how it was going.

Worse, I said.

I stood with Gene Paley in TransPac's basement car park where he was showing me one of his executive's cars, soon to be sold off, a recent model Nissan Skyline GT-R, a much-coveted car of its era. It would be mine for so long as I was working in Melbourne.

This is how we'll work it, Gene Paley said, his very white, very tiny fingers that put me in mind of the paws of a marsupial softly drumming the car's roof. I want a first chapter from you by Friday. Until then consider yourself on probation. If the chapter isn't what we're after, we'll consider our experiment at an end. As you'll have read in your contract, you'll be paid a quit fee of five hundred dollars. If, as we all hope, the chapter passes muster, we will continue on.

It wasn't what I had expected. Nor had I read that or anything else in the contract. I had presumed when I began that some cheque or bulky envelope of banknotes would welcome me. But that was not to be.

I wanted to ask for some cash up front, as Suzy and I had only $220 left in our bank account and I didn't dare touch it. I didn't know how you might go about such things without being rude. In any case, it was all starting to feel academic, as I had no idea how I'd get even a chapter out of Heidl by Friday. I felt my tongue moving in my mouth as I tried to find a way of telling Gene Paley, making what I felt was the very reasonable case for something to live on. But the publisher was so knowing, so definite—he was so *many* things and who and what was I?

And so I said nothing.

Gene Paley picked up on my confused silence as enthusiasm for the car. He picked up on many things. He asked what car I drove at home.

An EH Holden wagon, I said.

He laughed. Who wouldn't? A near thirty-year-old car too commonplace to be loved, too old to be anything other than unsafe; the mechanics were so primitive even I could work on them. I didn't tell Gene Paley of having to fibreglass a new floor in to replace the one that had rusted out. I didn't tell him of how it leaked in the rain, how there was no heater to demist the car in winter, nor how dangerous the car was in the wet.

Hop in, Gene Paley said, patting the gleaming roof of the Nissan Skyline. Try it out.

Sitting in the bucket seat felt like being in the cockpit of an airliner. Gene Paley sat in the passenger seat, leaning forward, swaying slightly, eyes fixed on something or nothing, and I saw in him the pale indifference of a secret policeman, a serial murderer, a hedge fund manager.

If you want, Gene Paley said, I could pay you with this car rather than in cash. Yes?

Suzy and I had talked of what we could do with the ten thousand dollars—use half to make a big payment on the mortgage, buy a twin pram, a second bassinet, the hundred and one things a baby needed and of which we would need two hundred and two.

It's not a car I'm after, I said, though not without regret. It's cash.

Mmm, Gene Paley said, flexing his lips into what may have been a smile or may have been a threat. His gaze dropped as if gravity or boredom had defeated what small interest he had initially taken in me.

It's not literature I'm after, he said, and his sad eyes looked up at me. It's a page turner, Kif. And for such a book this car is a good swap.

We returned to Gene Paley's office. He was searching his bookcases for some footballer memoirs he wanted to give me as a form of instruction and example when his phone rang. He picked up the receiver. As a distant voice crackled, Gene Paley's face gripped in a sudden contortion.

Jez Dempster! he cried, enunciating each syllable as if he had just confronted an excruciating horror he had hoped to avoid.

With his free hand he waved me to the door.

3

At the small conference table where we worked Heidl was diminished, exhausted, prevaricating. He seemed physically small and personally insignificant. I must have seen images of Heidl a hundred times or more on TV and in the papers, but I couldn't really recall anything about him. And even working with him it was hard to *see* him. I remember he didn't have much hair and he was of indeterminate age, small, slightly stout, but apart from that—and his twitching cheek—it's hard to say what he was. Ray sometimes called him the hobgoblin. It's as good a description of the little sorcerer as any I can offer. From the beginning, he was always there and never to be found.

But when I returned from Gene Paley's office and found him sitting behind the large executive's desk he was another man. He seemed bigger, taller, more authoritative, and somehow certain. It was as if the intimations of power that the desk suggested allowed him to behave as if he himself were powerful, while I, sitting in the tub chair at the conference table, was no longer an equal, but a wretched minion, a stenographer, a subservient clerk. If it was a charade, it was one that I thought might at least be put to some good.

Heidl stood up and was about to walk back around to his place at the conference table when I suggested he just stay where he was.

That's a much more comfortable chair than the ones here, I said, which was true. And, besides, it's easier for you to get your other work done.

He smiled, turned, and without any further consideration sat back down in the executive's chair behind the executive's desk. I realised that it was the first time I had seen him so at ease. His body stretched, his language changed, his diction grew more informal, and he seemed able to balance both small talk and the harder matter of answering my questions. And he somehow stayed larger. Not that he wasn't still evasive—in a way that's all he ever was—but he seemed to be finally behaving as he wanted to be behaving; being what he wished to be—which was, I suppose, someone of note, but also a conformist, a man you might miss in any crowd.

You're doing an excellent job, Kif, he said, leaning back in the executive's chair. I've told Gene how impressed I am.

Thank you, Siegfried, I said, typing as I spoke, adopting the tone of an inferior.

Behind the executive's desk, Heidl brought his hands together and crossing his fingers cracked his knuckles as he slowly rocked in his chair. It's not that a dog looks a king on a throne, I thought. It is that everyone agrees it is no longer a dog. Perhaps some hatred of him was already growing in my heart.

Now we really need to work, I said.

Of course. Why else would I be here?

The CIA? Tell me what that was like.

I told you.

Laos. The secret war. Tell me about that.

I was never in Laos. Who told you that?

Langley?

You expect me to tell *you*?

Well—*yes*, I said, I do. For the two hundred and fifty grand they're paying you I do. Not all of it, but some of it. Maybe. What about Germany?

As I talked, I was desperately searching my inadequate knowledge of early 1970s Germany.

I guess you were working on Baader-Meinhof? I asked.

I knew the Jackal. Carlo, they called him. But that's off the record. We were focused on Stasi mainly.

The Jackal is good.

What? Heidl said, and I knew that too, whatever it was, was gone.

Heidl walked over to a light switch and looked at it suspiciously.

You do know what they do if you tell? he said.

Tell me.

Laughing, he went to the executive's desk and lifted the phone handset.

You have to understand, Ziggy Heidl said. The life doesn't account for the achievement. Look at Papa Doc, say, he said.

Augusto Pinochet, Walt Disney. The achievement invents the life it needs in way of explanation.

Walt Disney?

Exactly. That's what I'm saying.

Why? I asked.

Why? Heidl suddenly shouted, slamming the phone down. Why! Why! It's an age that thinks for every act there is an explanation. But there isn't. Why this? Why that?

What do you mean?

There is no why! Heidl screamed.

4

And the great necromancer that he was, his rage vanished as abruptly as it had arisen, and in its place there appeared, as if by magic, a seeming gift.

Okay. I'll tell you one thing, Heidl said. Just one thing. Because it's known.

I waited. And he told me the baby goat story for the second or the first or the last time.

The goat, he said. A baby goat—what do you call it?

A kid.

He pointed a finger at me. That's it. A kid! Well, they give you a kid to hand raise.

The CIA gave you a goat?

Roger that, Heidl said, his tone more confident. Crazy, eh? But it's so you learn.

You have to hand feed it?

Heidl looked at me, as if in surprise.

They're nice animals, baby goats. Smart.

Kids.

Kids? Kids are very smart. For a goat. And they bond with

you. And you grow fond of them. Then one day they order you to shoot it.

To teach you to kill?

No. Well, perhaps. But that's not the point.

Where do they tell you to shoot it? The head?

The head, he said.

He seemed unsure.

Or somewhere else?

He pondered this matter of exactly where *somewhere else* was for some time. His cheek twitched. Time passed. Finally, he spoke.

The stomach.

Why the stomach?

Heidl said nothing. He ran a finger up and down the desk top. He seemed to be thinking of something else, but whether it was a memory or another idea it was hard to say. With Heidl it was always hard to say. He was always working something out—you, the world, another story. Mostly another story.

So it . . . it dies, he said.

Slowly?

Slowly? Yes, Heidl said hesitantly. The stomach. So it dies slowly.

He seemed to be tasting his words rather than saying them. And, abruptly, his tone grew confident, even assertive.

And you have to watch.

That's awful, I suggested.

Yes. Awful! Heidl smiled. Awful! And the baby goat makes these noises as it's dying. Atrocious noises. And the smell! Shit, goat shit. Piss.

When was this?

Horrific noises. Like a human child in agony.

I didn't know what to say. I couldn't think of a question that seemed appropriate.

It's an awful thing, Heidl said. I can't tell you how—

When did they make you do this?

Heidl put his hands up in the air.

I've already said too much.

Dates.

The thing is, you know, you listen to that goat die. It sounds like—

Was it '70? '71?

—like . . . *somebody* who has all the skin peeled off them and you are witnessing their death. If you can imagine such a thing.

Or the late '60s?

I can't tell you that.

Where did they train you? Tell me that.

What does it matter where it was? he said, momentarily adopting anger. The point is there is a goat, a baby goat—

A kid.

A kid, yes, and you hear it die, and every so often the officer who has ordered you to shoot it comes in.

The US?

How's the goat going? he asks. It's a test, you see.

Laos?

They wouldn't get a goat in Laos. Laos was fully ops, not training. You see, they're monitoring you.

Germany?

They don't want psychopaths—not for my job anyway—they don't want people who don't feel. They want you to feel and to understand you must conquer those feelings.

I gave up with my line of questioning—with hoping to get the slightest detail that might lend the anecdote a shred of authenticity. I gave up, as I was already giving up on so many things that a real ghost writer should never give up on. But I hadn't *given up*.

And at that moment Heidl looked up, looked me in the eye,

and I believed. Maybe it was only a brief moment, but for that moment I did believe. And though I couldn't have told you what I believed exactly I tried to run with what Heidl was saying, which, perhaps, I reasoned, might lead to something.

So you know everyone to them is a goat, Heidl told me. So you know that there is no one who can't die slowly if they give the order.

The Philippines?

You don't want to be that kid.

He paused, his pupils two black buttons stitched into his face.

And you don't want to be the one made to watch.

5

The goat story was great. Or maybe it wasn't that great, but it was something. But when I wrote it up, as Pia Carnevale pointed out when I showed her, it didn't work. She said nothing seemed to anchor it. And I could see that she was right.

That it seemed untruthful when I described it yet truthful the way Heidl had told it was of no help. So many of his stories were like that, building through a strange accretion of your suggestions, your hopes and your fears, into his story—a sort of reverse charades—and yet not one of them could I make work on the page. There, his stories floated and never seemed to quite come to earth; there was no dirt, no detail. And in the paper-lined grotto that was her office, stalagmites of manuscripts rising around her, Pia held up her long, dark fingers and wiggling them said, A good writer needs dirty hands, Kif.

When I returned to our office, I felt it was beyond me. I stood by the window and looked out over the industrial estate below and the sorrowful boulevards of Port Melbourne beyond. A truck whooshed by one way, a motor scooter another. Mostly there was little traffic. The city went on, as cities do, disappearing into the dirty light, blocks, suburbs, aeons away.

You're a phony, I said, turning back around late that first Thursday afternoon to see Heidl sitting there, at what was now his desk, doing the crossword.

Really?

I said nothing. What else was there to say?

We're all phonies, Heidl said. We all know that who we pretend to be isn't who we are. How am I any different?

He flirted like that with destruction, daring me to push him further.

Having fought him all week for some basic details of his early life and failed, I decided a better way was not to bother with any such back story and tell him so.

I don't care where you were born, I said.

Predictably unpredictable, he took offence. His head jerked around, only a little, but quickly.

You don't care?

No.

Surely you want to know?

I said I didn't. And I realised I didn't.

He struck an attitude of astonishment. He struck many attitudes, sometimes so heavily they broke into pieces. Astonishment was one of his less successful. His face gurned like a junkyard dog's straining at the end of its chain.

But surely you want to know where I was born? You do, don't you?

Maybe he felt it as a challenge to his authority. Maybe he just wanted to see what he could do with me, to know how far he could push me, having argued until that moment that his birth was irrelevant, and now insisting I know.

I've got a new idea for the beginning, I said, though I had no ideas at all. I was out of ideas.

But *you* want to know, don't you?

I don't care, Siegfried.

And it was true. I was weary with Heidl, exhausted by his games.

But you must put it in. My birth, you have to.

Not any more, I don't. Gene Paley just told me to get the book done.

I was born—

You know what?

Born, he said, pressing on regardless, in a South Australian mining town in the desert. Jaggamyurra.

I'm not actually that interested in you, I said, hoping insult might excite some response. I find you boring, if truth be told.

No one lives there now. Ghost town.

He had told me this story before and I had checked it out.

The last recorded birth in Jaggamyurra, I said, was in 1909.

Heidl said nothing. Perhaps he hadn't heard.

You've aged well, I said.

It wasn't recorded, Heidl said, looking up from the newspaper to finally look at me, a slight sad smile on his face. How could it be? Hundreds of miles from anywhere. It was awful for my poor parents.

I said nothing as he went on with what I felt to be inspired improvising.

He said, How can you not believe me? He raised both his hands in an outstretched and upward manner, as though he were a priest bestowing a blessing. How can you not?

Jaggamyurra?

Amazing place, Heidl said.

You ever been there? I asked.

1978, Heidl said.

Realising his error, he hastily added, I'd gone back to show my family.

So you want Jaggamyurra in?

Heidl looked at me incredulously. Well . . . I *was* born there.

Of course, I said. What was it like?

Dusty.

Dusty?

Yes.

Anything else? Friends? Stories? Family life?

Just dust.

It was all to no good end. He would tell me nothing I could use. And out of his dust I was expected to somehow conjure up a childhood and a book. With a growing horror I realised I had no idea how I was to write Heidl's memoir and collect my fee; no idea how to begin far less finish the book if I wanted a new pair of runners and to return home to Suzy and our growing family with something to tide us over while I finished my unfinishable novel; even less idea who my subject was and no idea what to do next. There was a long silence in which I felt a paralysis of the soul and mind so complete that for a time I was unable to speak. But I had to try one last time with Heidl.

What sort of child were you? I asked.

Child? replied Heidl, leafing through the latest *Woman's Day*. And without looking up he said, Child, yes. Child? I have no idea. I have been missing since I was born.

He went back to reading.

I typed: *I have been missing since I was born.*

I stared at that line. And then I cut it from the end of my document, scrolled upwards, and pasted it at the top, immediately below the words *Chapter 1*. And sitting there at the beginning of what I still dared hope might yet be a book, I read it again.

It read like something, but what that something was wasn't clear. It felt like a voice in the desert. Lacking anything else, I resolved to follow it. I felt it move something within me, or, more precisely, I heard the line and that line, that sentence, led me to start hearing other sentences, at first one or two, then more, and finally so many that my head began to crowd with them.

I erased everything I had previously written. Realising I had both the opening line and possibly the key I needed to the entire book, I began typing the sentences as I heard them. While some were amalgams of things I had previously made up but now told afresh and aslant, as if they had always happened, much was of necessity fresh invention. And in this way I began writing the true story of Siegfried Heidl, Australia's most notorious con man.

6

The following day, on Friday afternoon, a little after 4 pm, I walked down the corridor and into Gene Paley's office. I handed his secretary a laser-printed manuscript of the first chapter. What he would make of it I had no idea. But I already knew. I would meet myself writing Heidl. There was no other way to write the book. I and I. Me and me. Did I know, at the very beginning, the crimes I would commit? If I did, it's not that I didn't tell others, it's that I didn't even admit them to myself. But I think even then Heidl knew. Being the first person, perhaps that's what I hated in him most.

3

1

I WAS THIRTY-ONE when the magic vanished and the phone rang, though, as you will come to see, not in that order. I heard Ray at the other end, asking how things were.

You know, I said. Good.

Maybe I said I was getting by. It doesn't really matter what I said. Maybe I asked him how he was going, and he told me how he had only just got off the work he'd been doing in the remote tropical country of Cape York. It doesn't matter what Ray said either, but it reads better if he is given some words too. The point of the story is *what* Ray was going to say, but first he said, You still want to be a writer, right?

Ray felt being a writer was like doing the dive masters course he had taken some years before to work as a scuba diving guide on the Great Barrier Reef: a short explanation of theoretical issues, some technical matters to be learnt and practised before you took to fucking English backpackers ten metres down amidst schools of gropers and fairy fish.

I remember that it was night, and a winter's night, when Ray asked me his real question. But memories are like cancers, they spread until they are impossibly entwined with everything else, the bad and the good, the true and the false. Do I remember listening to Ray in the closeness of the small lounge room into which we had retreated for those long dark nights, with its cheap Taiwanese cast-iron wood heater I'd installed myself and which kept that much of our home warm, or do I just imagine it was so? The point is that I was trying to write a novel on no money, and I was failing. And I didn't know it, or if I did know it, I ignored it.

But something—a feeling like the grim world outside that night—was taking hold of me. I stood with my ear to the phone receiver, back to the wood heater. Its cast iron groaned as it expanded with the heat of the log fire inside and burnt into the back of my legs. It was unclear where I was going and where we—by which I mean me, Suzy, and Bo, our three-year-old daughter whose real name was Brigid—would end up.

If I am to be honest, things weren't going great. I wasn't panicked, but it's fair to say I could feel a shadow lengthening and I was doing all I could to stay away from it. It's also fair to say that we were, after our fashion, happy within the aspirations of our place and time, determined to have a family, to make a life on our island home which we persuaded ourselves we loved. Ray was more sanguine.

Loving Tassie is like loving a beautiful junkie, Ray would say, and Ray would know. *It's always going to let you down with bad habits.*

Though we didn't know it they were the good years. So much that was unknown to us lay in the future, so much unbelievable and bad, and we didn't worry about any of it. We were broke, without prospects and with no possessions of worth, and yet we were right to think life was *sweet*. We had so little we didn't even know how little we had. We didn't care. All that we didn't have was uninteresting and irrelevant. The future was an infinite horizon over which the sun still glimmered its early-morning promise. Everything had a smell and every smell was fresh—the morning air, the sun on the bitumen, the evening rain. There was just today and that felt more than enough.

The idea of *bad*, of all the bad that waits just out there, all the bad that will one day, sooner than you think, be inside here, inside you—well, that was just the stuff of the fairytales I read each night to Bo. German fairytales of wolves in disguise bearing gifts.

Will we turn the page and see what happens next? I'd ask Bo. BOO! I'd say, and Bo would close her eyes and instinctively grab me. And look! The wolf is disguised as the woodcutter! Look! The woodcutter is pretending to help the little boy! Look! The wolf is eating him all up! And Bo would squeal and laugh and I'd turn over to the next page.

Later in the night, spooned into Suzy's back, I would close my eyes and see us as a couple floating, bending, flying, entwining around each other, holding each other while there swirled below us a wild world, as if in a Chagall painting, wolves and beasts and flames. But as long as we held together we were free of gravity; we were safe from all that waited outside. Chagall's early genius slimed over time into a cheerful high kitsch. Perhaps, given half a chance, we might have also.

In any case, we weren't in a Chagall painting, we were in Hobart, Tasmania, and flying and wrapping around each other like ribbons in the wind was no longer a straightforward matter because Suzy was pregnant with twins. We were astonished to know that we might soon be the parents of something so extraordinary, so miraculous as twins. And having had one child and seen all that it meant with work and money and living, we were also a little terrified. Suzy was heavily pregnant, and, to be frank, hugely pregnant.

We had looked at the books—it was still a time when you might, as we did, visit a library and borrow books on a subject that pressed on you as the impending birth of twins now pressed on us—and we had gasped and laughed at the illustrations and the badly printed photographs of women pregnant with twins, women who looked, to be honest, like whales, so distended were their poor bellies. That might be them, we told each other, but that won't be *us*. You see, we still talked that way then, still thought of us as, well, *us*. And *we* were never going to be that big, but Suzy soon enough was, and improbably, amazingly, kept on growing even bigger.

We.

That glorious, sweet first-person plural.

Of a night when Suzy woke and tried to turn over I had to get both my arms beneath her and bulldozer-blade-like lift and roll her belly of twins as she followed. So big was Suzy that of a day we put the front bench seat of the EH Holden wagon back as far as it would go, and still her stomach jammed up against the steering wheel. So big, she had had to give up her work as a typist in her seventh month of pregnancy, and now had three weeks left to term.

We were making do on what I earnt labouring a few days a week and being a doorman for the council on some others. It wasn't much and it was becoming clear that it wasn't enough. On days when work fell through, on nights when I wasn't too tired, and early in the morning when I could force myself, I wrote, trying to turn a confusion of notes, ideas, and stories into something coherent that might be a novel. It wasn't that I wanted to be a writer. It was that I *knew* I was a writer. It wasn't the least of my vanities, but it was the most breathtaking.

I had so many opinions, certainties and verities about writing, that, in another age and in another country, I may well have been a star product of an MFA creative writing course, or several MFA courses, or, for that matter, a professor teaching MFAs. I could have been anything.

But I would not have been a writer.

For I faced the inconvenient dilemma of not knowing how to write a novel, and the growing unspoken terror that perhaps I couldn't. Written I had words. Written I had anecdotes, theories, lyrical passages of prose that seemed, in moments of delusion, good. But only when deluded. The rest of the time I knew they were rubbish. Written I had nothing. Yet unwritten I had a life, feelings, memories, dreams—a universe! How had I made of this universe of everything a nothing of words? I had imagined that there might be some getting of wisdom in the struggle, but it felt only a quickening of idiocy. My writing was only *words*. There was no story. There was no soul. And whatever gave a novel its soul was a mystery to me.

If by some miracle I ever were to find that soul, I didn't know how I might get the book published. And if, by a second miracle, I somehow were to get it published, I had even less idea how I might subsequently make a living from writing that would lift us out of poverty. It wasn't that I didn't have a Plan B. It was that I didn't even have a Plan A.

2

Still, they were the good years. A great global party had started, the Wall fell, History ended, and everything was beginning. Including, it seemed, me. And if the nation was, for a moment, temporarily thrown from its trajectory of growth by a short, sharp recession in the early '90s, things were still soon going to be good again. The recession's consequence was spiralling interest rates that left a nation in a mood of vindictive rage. As it turned out, the party of prosperity would have another two decades to run. The recession was but a blip, a blown fuse in the amp; the party was going to go on for far longer, but nothing is as unwelcome to a party than feeling it is being shut down just as it's starting.

Australia was particularly bitter about the '80s entrepreneurs who only a few short years before had been national heroes, winning global yacht races and buying up Hollywood studios. But by 1992 the moguls were on the skids, their once much-admired commercial chutzpah revealed as a criminal web of deceit, fraud and theft. Banks were collapsing over the exorbitant loans they had given, and every Australian with a mortgage—and for a short time every Australian seemed to have a mortgage—viewed it as a personal affront that interest rates kept rising. It was as if the entrepreneurs had personally robbed them of their property-owning rights as Australians and willed the recession. That everyone was buying into the same Ponzi scheme at higher rates of absurdity was not a point anyone much wanted to hear.

We were no different. We had bought our home—a run-down terrace—with a deposit cobbled out of credit card debt and money borrowed from friends. Every month another letter came from the solicitors—who ran the sort of mortgage rackets that later got the US into such trouble, lending to the lowest at the highest rates—to say our repayments had to go up again. Yet each month we somehow found the growing sum we needed to stay in our home. Each month I would walk across town to the solicitors' *chambers*—as their dowdy, oppressive office was grandiosely called. Each month I would wait for the receptionist to flick through a sticky-taped shoebox of grimy index cards searching for our particular pink cardboard rectangle, and each month I would pass the necessary notes and coins across the counter.

But that night the phone rang, the latest letter on the kitchen table was saying interest rates were now up to 19.5 per cent and our repayment had increased to a sum that was beyond us. Suzy wasn't earning anything, I wasn't earning enough for the three of us, and with every passing day I was finding it harder to ignore my failure to finish my novel.

And if I did finish it, what then? I had read some books. But Borges and Kafka and Cortázar had none of the answers

I needed. None of them had mortgage payments they feared every month they would not make. They played games with time and infinity, made myths of dreams and nightmares. They didn't even know the questions I tried not to ask, so unliterary did my questions seem.

Such as how to afford ten litres of paint? How to pay off the nappies that were on lay-by? How to finish a novel between hanging out unspun wet washing and taking the washing machine apart to fix a clutch assembly? How to find enough dollar notes to stuff in my wallet and walk across town, feeling them pressing on my buttock, before handing them over to the young woman in the solicitor's office to once more count out, with me watching?

Ashamed.

Humiliated.

Fearful I had the amount wrong. To make sure, I would count it out before I left home. There was a world and my writing and nothing joined the two. How to make money? How to make a story work? How to afford a double pram? How to get a character out of a room? Sometimes I'd run my hand down the back of our old couch for the coins I needed to make up the total owed. I spent evenings and weekends fixing up old furniture found on the tip face, repainting a chest of drawers, working out how we might fit three kids in a single, cramped bedroom. I counted and I counted, but writing was ever the second person and life always the first, and there was sometimes nothing left to buy food and we would live on lentils or pea soup until the next bit of cash turned up.

I wrote in a room so small it only just fitted my desk, a chair jammed beneath it, its back against the far wall, while facing me on the opposite side was the room's sole decoration: a postcard of Caravaggio's painting of David brandishing Goliath's severed head, the face of which, in a gruesome joke, is Caravaggio's self-portrait. To get in or out I had to climb up onto the table. Everything was pressing in, and Caravaggio's sad, unseeing eyes stared down as I counted our mortgage money and my novel's words and either way, no matter how I figured it, there was never enough of either.

And then that night the phone rang.

Kif, Ray continued. You do, right? Don't you?

I was slow in replying.

That's what I said to him. That you want to be a writer, right?

Sure, I said.

I got someone who wants to talk to you, Ray said.

And a German-accented voice came on the line.

Hello, Kif, it said.

3

Ray was given to violence and drugs and women, and violence and drugs and women were given to him. Maybe I liked all that. Maybe I liked the violence. I certainly liked the women, the frisson of excitement. There were fights, police, car chases. Parties. Petty crime. Stealing cars and joy-riding with the one cassette we always carried with us and played as we sped away: The Saints' 'Stranded'. Sometimes Ray would bring his welding mask along—he was a boilermaker–welder by trade—and we'd take it in turns wearing it after spotting hash off the cigarette lighter, dreamily staring out through its Ned Kelly visor of smoked glass at the world dissolving into streaks of car and streetlights—that's one image of our youth.

Another is of us in a Valiant station wagon we had stolen. It was an older car that had been hotted up, replete with an Impala floor shift, a brutal piece of chromed iron bar that was installed by home mechanics to replace the domestic column shift. Befitting its jerry-rigged purpose, the Impala floor shift had an unusual placement for each gear, meaning first was where reverse was meant to be and so on. But we were blind to such shortcomings, seeing only a cool four on the floor with a furry roo scrotum stretched tight over the eight ball to replace the Australian suburban verity of the three on the column shift—so suburban, so safe, so middle-aged. Ray had a particular loathing of the office workers who would catch the bus in front of his home when he was a kid, their slack suits, their tufted cardigans, their slumping flesh, which he was convinced came from eating endless stews of grey meat.

Fuck fuckn two-tooth! he'd cry. Fuck hogget, fuck brisket, fuck corn beef, fuck the fuckn clerks.

His hatred of their purported meats extended to his name for the sorry drones of clerkdom: silversiders. Any evidence of silversiders—such as a column shift—tended to bring on bad behaviour in Ray.

Late that night we turned at some speed from a city street into an alley to park prior to going to another bar. At the alley's far end the darkness suddenly lit up with flashing blue and red lights—a police car waiting in hiding for just some quarry as us. The stolen Valiant, a space capsule of hashish fumes and forgotten '70s songs, filled with their spotlight and an accompanying sudden panic. As the police car began advancing towards us, Ray crashed the unfamiliar floor shift with its odd gear placements into what he thought was reverse.

He hit the accelerator, and the Valiant roared as Ray dropped the clutch. But instead of reversing at high speed out of the alley, the car, its Impala floor shift mistakenly jammed hard into first gear, reared up like a wild beast and flew straight at the police car. The police, fearing a maddened frontal attack, braked hard, threw their car into reverse and began heading back up the alley with us now in seeming pursuit. We careered after them,

Ray madly braking while attempting to crash the floor shift out of forward, our heads whiplashing backwards, the Valiant fishtailing, brakes and tyres shrieking, gearbox cogs and flywheels grinding.

Ray found reverse, the car roared and shuddered once more, and, our heads whiplashing forwards, we backed at high speed out of the alley and into the lights of oncoming cars. Somehow we missed a collision, and had already crashed through our first red light when we saw the police car now out on the street, lit up, siren blaring, and in pursuit. Ray switched off his headlights and we ran several more red lights, slaloming our way through late-night traffic. We lost the police car near the wharves. We dumped the Valiant behind the old jam factory there and walked back to the bar, where Ray promptly lost a fight with three bouncers. When I took him to the hospital to be stitched up, he demanded we swap pants. His were bloodied and torn, and he worried that he might not look respectable.

Ray beat up his enemies, strangers and people who met him when they shouldn't have met him, which is to say any time after ten in the evening, except on Sunday when he had a roast at his mother's. There was some open wound in him that was also for women a beauty that frequently dazzled them. And when they discovered that he wasn't what they had thought; when he sought escape through betrayal, in bed with their flatmate, friend, sister, or, once, mother; when they saw him—as he did one night—put two nightclub bouncers through plateglass windows, they finally understood. He was not mouldable. He was nice but he was not nice.

He was like that and he was like all the stories told about him, and he was not like that, for he was also fun, and kind, and oddly gentle. Life was to him a constant source of wonder. He wanted to touch, fuck, hit, lick, taste everything. His fridge freezer was full of dead birds—booboks, hawks, pardalotes—that he had found and kept to look at when he was bored. He was moved by the fine quilting of feathers, the slow merging dapple of colour, the form of a beak, and what it all might mean. He longed to be able to fly. He would sit at his kitchen table, thawing owl or eagle before him, searching their defrosting wings, their dewy tails and their chill torsos for a key to that mystery, as if he had lost something precious that he might yet still recover.

There was goodness in Ray. I am not sure exactly how much, but it was there. He just didn't like it all that much—what he was and how he wasn't. I was reading Jung, who said that inside every alcoholic is a seeker. Inside Ray, though, was only more Ray. And it was hard to say what Ray was when he had no idea himself. Maybe he was a seeker, sort of, when he wasn't pissed or stoned or whacked out on everything he could swallow and sniff and snort and mainline. He was a boilermaker–welder who read Hermann Hesse. He was a man who thought he could fly. He was a hypocrite and a bastard. He was, in the final analysis, inexplicable.

And he was my friend. My best friend.

Sometimes he would moan how his head felt as if he'd lost a live electrode in it, the type that went white-hot when he welded with them.

Can you smell it? he would say, abruptly grabbing me by the shirt with both hands clenched. It's ripping back and forth inside my brain. *Can you smell it?* he would snarl. And then, flushed face up against mine, he'd yell, *CAN'T YOU FUCKN SMELL IT?*

4

What did Ray want? Suzy asked when I got off the phone. I remember I took a few moments to understand what had been said, and what on earth it might mean.

Ray wanted me to talk to his boss, I said.

Australia's most wanted?

Yeah. That one.

The crook?

I guess so.

The crook wanted to talk to you?

Yeah.

Isn't he in jail? After that huge manhunt?

Not yet. I mean he was, and now he's out on bail.

What's the most wanted want with us?

He wants me to write his memoirs. Ten grand.

Suzy seemed unimpressed.

He's a crim, she said.

It's a job.

What's that mean?

Ten grand, I repeated. Six weeks to write it.

Ghost write?

I guess so.

And you said no?

No.

Good.

No, I mean, I didn't say no.

What did you say then?

I said get your publisher to ring. I'll talk to them. I mean, I wasn't talking money with a con man who ripped the banks off seven hundred million dollars.

So you'll do it?

How could I say I was flattered? Excited? That I felt, well, alive? For the first time in so long: alive.

I don't know, I said.

And I didn't. I was just buying time. Was ghost writing a good look for someone who wanted to be taken seriously as a writer? I had no idea. I waited up till midnight for the publisher to call, but no call came. I didn't know what to think. My novel had reached the point where it needed form, but day after day at that desk in that narrow corridor of a room no form presented itself. It was a jellyfish pretending to be a white pointer. Suzy had gone to bed some hours before, but she was still awake when I finally went to bed.

He was what I thought, I said, rolling her belly over for her. Just a con man talking shit.

What Ray always said he was.

I guess so.

So why's Ray still his minder, then? That's as crazy as you two trying to kayak Bass Strait.

From downstairs came the sound of the phone ringing.

God, who could that be at this time of night? Suzy said.

It was Ray.

I can only speak for a minute, he said when I finally got downstairs and picked up. I gotta get back to him. You going to do it?

Is it for real?

For sure it's for fuckn real, Ray said.

I don't know, I said. If his publisher rings I'll know he wasn't full of shit.

You should do it, mate. Be good for—

There was the sound of the mouthpiece being muffled, Ray yelling something to somebody, and then he was back on the line.

Gotta go, Kif, he said. I just wanted to say one thing. Do it, but just don't trust him. You understand?

No. Not really.

Don't tell him anything about yourself. You understand?

No. Ray—

Give him nothing. *Don't let him in.*

And before I could ask one of the several questions that now came racing into my mind, the line went dead.

5

We did these things to see what lay beyond fear. We discovered an addiction that was hard to break. We discovered the meaninglessness of physical courage, along with its ease and its wild pleasures. We found within ourselves a certain cruelty, the cruelty of the strong, one more illusion that would be finally shattered by Siegfried Heidl. We lived like reptiles, sleeping, resting, waiting for those moments when we could be fully alive. The rest was feigned nonchalance, drink, drugs, sex, pushing the night.

A Tasmanian newspaper ran a photo of us kayaking Cataract Gorge in full flood with the caption, *The Suicide Twins*. It was a joke, albeit one consistent with our behaviour to that point, which had established us as people who would shoot any rapid on any river, no matter how big and frightening. That's how we ended up lost in the New Guinea Highlands.

I was twenty-one and Ray twenty-two when Ray organised—if that is not too strong a word for Ray's capacities in this regard—an exploratory kayaking expedition on a wild, remote river in the New Guinea Highlands that was known as the Colorado of the South Seas. No one had ever attempted running it. The trip was funded largely by the third member of the expedition, Ronnie McNeep, who at the time was doing okay running dope for the Trimbole family, driving a Monaro with a bootload of weed fifteen hundred kilometres from Grafton to Melbourne and back once a week. Ray assured me and Ronnie of three things: that in the far New Guinea Highlands it would be the dry season and the river thus low and the rapids not too large, that the trip would take seven days, and that he had all the maps we needed. When we finally made our way to the top of the river it was the middle of the monsoon, the river was flooding, and the rapids huge.

On the ninth day, having somehow survived the largest rapids any of us had ever seen, two days after our food had run out, Ronnie and I demanded to see the maps. We were standing on a gigantic boulder scree above a large waterfall into which the entire river vanished, perplexed as to what we might do next, smoking the last of our New Guinea cigarettes, nine-inch durries tailor-made from pages of old *Sydney Morning Herald*s. The tobacco was coarsely shredded and tended to flare wildly on the first few puffs. Behind gouts of flame, wreathed by our smoke, a vast jungled gorge shimmered. It was one of the most beautiful places on earth. And I would have given anything to be somewhere else, anywhere else, that might be safe.

Ray produced a single greasy photostated page. Its header read 'Jacaranda Schoolboy Atlas'. It showed at an absurdly reduced scale an entire country. At such a scale it was more an idea of a country, a visual notion, than a map you could use to determine place and distance and likely time left on the river. But still, in the straits we now found ourselves, even an idea would have been helpful, bar one detail.

Ray? Ronnie McNeep said, tapping a finger on the bottom of the page. It says here—Irian Jaya.

Two large jungle trees—roots, trunks, canopy—washed over the waterfall and emerged in pieces far below.

So? Ray said, flames rising around his nostrils as he lit up and inhaled.

Ray, Ronnie McNeep said, we were—last time I looked—in the New Guinea Highlands.

Yeah—well?

Ray, Irian Jaya is the left-hand side of the atlas. New Guinea is on the right.

So?

It's like, you know, next door.

Ray stared at Ronnie.

Breathe, Ronnie, Ray said, exhaling a dark smoke wreath.

The country next door, Ray.

I understand that, McNeep. But so fuckn what?

Ray, you photocopied the wrong half of the atlas.

And? Ray said.

I am not sure how to explain something that is explained, Ray. We are not in the same fucking country as the fucking country we're fucking in.

But Ray on occasion wasn't even on the same planet.

We made it out fifteen days later, having survived by begging sweet potato and corn from Stone Age villagers for whom we had to perform demeaning tricks in return, humiliations such as leaping off rope bridges high above river gorges in our kayaks; singing for their amusement; letting their children touch our white skin, something they had only ever heard of in stories; or letting their old people wear our plastic whitewater helmets and gaudy lifejackets. The villagers were gracious, generous, and bemused. We were desperate, stupid, and stunned by their kindness. Without it we would have been dead. By the time we finished I nevertheless had tropical ulcers and malaria; McNeep, malaria, hepatitis and giardia; and Ray a rising good humour.

A few days after we escaped that river alive, Ray and I were, late in the evening, walking out of the Chimbu Lodge Disco in Mount Hagen—a large, grass-roofed hut in the New Guinea Highlands guarded by bouncers bearing pump-action shotguns, something others may have interpreted as a worrying augury. We had been befriended by a Chimbu called Michael who had taken us there. It was a purely local nightspot, which is to say no whites ever went.

Inside the Chimbu Lodge Disco was a carefully stratified confusion of tribal and late-twentieth-century mating rituals. Along one wall stood Chimbu women, along the other Chimbu men. The dance floor was largely empty. A DJ played a melange that segued from Scottish bagpipe music to 'Ave Maria' to

Madonna and back to more bagpipes. The only common denominator seemed to be that all the music was western. Michael, Ray and I left with some Chimbu women.

We walked straight out into three near-naked Chimbu men holding axes and dressed, as they frequently were, as Stone Age warriors, with painted faces, feathered headgear, and wearing only what was known locally as arse grass. When we went to walk through them they blocked our way. They stood there before us immobile, implacable, their painted faces expressionless. We smiled, we muttered a few words of greeting, but they said nothing. Instead they just kept chewing betel nut, their fiery red-stained mouths occasionally opening to reveal an ochry hell inside.

We turned to our right but four more warriors with axes materialised out of the darkness to block our escape. And when we turned to the left, several more had appeared on that side. We were surrounded. Ray smiled. The exotic nature of the evening was finally devolving into the more familiar contours of a Friday night at a Tasmanian pub, replete with the customary late-evening brawl. The idea seemed to hearten him immensely. For me, it bespoke a not unreasonable terror.

I don't think they like us being with their women, I whispered.

The difference in place and culture—the difference being that here people were routinely, or customarily, killed—eluded Ray.

So?

Maybe we should tell the girls to go.

No, Ray said. I want a fuck. *And* I want a fight.

The circle began tightening around us in what felt an inexorable noose. More warriors assembled, so that the circle was now two deep. Not for the first time in Ray's company I sensed the likely prospect of imminent death. The girls—wiser than Ray—had meanwhile melted away, and Michael with them. Ray seemed not displeased though to have at least half of what he regarded as an ideal evening come to fulfilment. He turned to me, face flushed with excitement.

Get your back up against mine, Kif, he said. You take the four on the side, I'll—

It's not fucking Friday night in Hobart, I began—but I was cut short by a wild roar. Out of the darkness, revving hard and driving at accelerating speed straight at the ring of warriors there appeared a pair of dim headlights, and sitting above them in the cabin of an old Toyota six-ton flat tray truck was Michael waving wildly to us. One warrior went down as the truck glanced him, and the others momentarily scattered. We saw Michael's terrified face in the truck cabin yelling at us to jump on the back as he sped by. Ray—abruptly ripped to his senses—and I threw ourselves onto the flat tray and hugged its splintering boards.

Some of the warriors gave chase and began catching up. Michael dropped the low-revving diesel into second gear, but our speed was too slow for the change and the truck too low geared, and in consequence, rather than picking up speed, we lost it, and the warriors gained more ground. One Chimbu man was within touching distance and only Ray getting to his feet and kicking him away stopped him clambering on board. We hit a downhill slope, the truck finally accelerated, and we sped away into the night as rocks thrown by the warriors bounced off the cabin, one hitting Ray on the head on a ricochet.

The rest of that evening and the next two days we spent hiding in a hut twenty kilometres distant from Mount Hagen, watching a tribal war play out in a valley not far below. At one point a man went to the river with a bucket. A dozen warriors followed him and, from our distance, seemed with their axes to have hacked him to death.

6

We should have taken all these things as warnings, but we were young and read them otherwise: as incentives, as proofs, as charms.

And so when Ben Coors, a mate, was getting married in Sydney and we couldn't afford plane tickets, it seemed obvious to us that we would kayak Bass Strait, the three hundred or so kilometres of ocean between Tasmania and Australia, and, on making it to Australia, hitch from Victoria up to the wedding in Sydney. Really though, we wanted to do it because no one ever had and everyone said it was impossible, that it was a death wish.

And that seemed the grandest joke of all, and therefore irresistible.

But what happened in Bass Strait wasn't a joke. A Force-Nine gale blew up, our boats sank, and for fourteen hours we were alone, tossed around a huge, wild sea clad only in lifejackets and t-shirts. We tried to hold on to each other, but the waves— moving mountains—just picked us up and tore us apart. The last I saw of Ray was a dot vanishing over a distant wave crest.

Later, people said we looked like idiots. We did. But what does anyone who didn't live it know? We also nearly died out there, and out there is really out there, so far fucking out I wasn't sure if I'd ever make it back, so far out that maybe I went over to the other side for a time and maybe—truth be told—*maybe* I never made it back.

To die alone?

To die alone.

As waves shrieked around me, as I was swept up and down a vertical sea fighting to keep my head above water, I found myself in the land of visions, of derangement, of transcendence and a solitude so terrible, a terror of dying alone so overwhelming, that it still brings on in me a prickly panic thinking about it.

It was just on nightfall when a fishing boat finally found and rescued me. Later that night I was transferred onto a police boat which had rescued Ray shortly before I had been found, miles away from where the fishing boat had discovered me. Ray came up to me, his eyes murderous, his tone demented, demanding.

Where's Kif? he said. We've got to find him. We can't give up.

He didn't know who I was. I heard him say that Kif was dead, that Kif was not dead, that Kif was. The truth was we both thought by not holding together we were somehow responsible for the other's fate, that we had each killed the other.

Years later I met one of the policemen who had been on that boat. He said that Ray had been in the final stages of hypothermia. They had expected him to die and had the body bag out ready for him.

A lot of people found it funny, but I didn't laugh for a year or more after it happened. When I thought no one was looking I'd cling to the earth like a lunatic, ear pressed to the ground, and I knew the earth was turning and me with it. I would clutch it harder so that I might not be spun off. I would hold it until I could hear it breathe beneath me, and only then relax, and only then a little. It was in that time I met Suzy and conflated her and the planet in my affections. I clung to her for as long as I could.

4

1

THE MORNING AFTER RAY'S CALL I had four hours' work as a doorman at the city council's civic square exhibition. It was my one regular job, four mornings a week in an otherwise empty building that had once been a public library. I sat at the top of a long flight of stairs at the entrance of the old reading room in which a few desultory models, plans, and interpretation panels formed an exhibition which purported to encourage informed civic debate. I had two tasks: to keep count of the visitors with a click-counter and to make sure no one walked out with one of the models.

No one came to be counted. Most of the time I was able to work away in an exercise book hidden on my lap beneath the table, writing what I hoped would be my novel. But as I sat there that day all I could think of was Heidl's tormenting offer. On the one hand, it would be money—and a published book. A book I would write. It was astonishing. Unbelievable. I would finally become what I had always said I was going to be—a writer. Admittedly, a ghost writer, but that was a small thing. After years of poverty and increasing frustration, if not outright depression, at my failure to write a novel, it seemed the fast track to authorial integrity. And with the money I could pay bills, buy time, *and* finish my novel.

But fears flew around that dusty, forsaken foyer and muddied my mind. I worried that I would somehow be tainted, not simply publicly, but in my heart, having abandoned some sacred trust for a Faustian deal involving money. Because money was the only reason I would ever do such a thing. Fuck the money, I thought. *Damn the money!* I scribbled in my exercise book, a typically false transposition of my own feelings. If it was money I wanted I'd be anywhere else in the world, I told myself, not sitting as a doorman at the Hobart City Council exhibition.

I worried once more about my literary reputation. After a time, I realised I had no literary reputation to worry about. For that matter, I had no novel. Some years earlier there had been my art history honours thesis, which had been published to a screaming silence by a Brisbane publishing co-operative, Hoppy Head Press—not so much a publishing house as a share house got lucky, first through a commercial connection with Ronnie McNeep, and later by making a great deal of money out of a Pritikin diet cookbook. A little of this it then lost on a far less lucrative McNeep suggestion: my *Quiet Currents: A History of Tasmanian Modernism, 1922–1939*.

There had, in addition, been two short stories, one of which won the Wangaratta City Council Edith Langley Award, the citation for which had meant even more than the five-hundred-dollar cheque, extolling me as 'possibly a new voice in Australian literature'. The adverb was, as I felt adverbs were, hopefully redundant.

I resolved to stay with literature. I would stick with the novel and I wouldn't take the ghost-writing job. It was an insult and worse to a real writer, even a real writer like me who had not really written anything real.

I returned to writing in the exercise book balanced on my knees. The few who had seen gobbets of my work found it hard to say anything. It wasn't that praise was beyond them. It was that even contempt was difficult. Ray, to whom I showed a dozen pages, and who had been excited to read it—honoured, he said—came back into our kitchen, put the pages down on the table, and looked up.

Lot of words, mate. Thousands?

The drowning . . . I said. Is it—

Amazing, Ray said. His voice was without enthusiasm.

You think—

There'd be thousands there, right?

I don't really know what I wanted Ray to say. Nor did Ray. Genius? Masterpiece?

Words, Ray said after some time. I mean. Like. How many are there in what I just read? Thirty thousand? Forty?

Three, I said. Three thousand. Or so.

Well, mate, that's fuckn amazing. I thought it was a lot longer. They all seem to work too, Ray said. The words, I mean.

And that was that. Like a piece of PVC pipe or a tap, a fork, a sewer or serviette, the words seemed to work. The only thing left was to go on writing, yet writing had become an agony. Simple words grew impossibly complex. I spent one morning listening to myself sounding out the ever stranger, more mysterious word 'and'. It assumed a connection could be made and should be made. But in my mind no connection was. Every sentence seemed false, and my suspicion about language crept into conversation: everything disintegrated into meaninglessness the moment I said even the most obvious thing to Suzy or Bo.

Hang in, I told myself. You're not the first to despair. It will get better. I tried to persuade myself that one word follows another, and in that way sentences, paragraphs, love affairs, wars, nations and novels come into being.

Or so I had imagined.

But the words didn't come, and they wouldn't. And so to gee them along I had tried, to name but a few muses, dissipation, industry, asceticism, marathons, masturbation, meditation, tantric denial, cheap beer, home-made slivovitz, hashish, and speed. For a time, I deliberately avoided writing, to let ideas ferment and arise through some organic mystery. No ideas rose, writing wasn't dough or yoghurt, all things and every sentence kept sinking. My mind was as empty as the exhibition room. Yet for me, the only thing worse than writing was not writing.

2

Lost behind my table in the council foyer I thought of Suzy, the impending birth, this matter of twins that suddenly seemed to me far more extraordinary and far more pressing than the exercise book that lay on my lap full of forced sentiments and stolen ideas, words that had once seemed profound, even brilliant, but which now struck me as trivial and embarrassing.

I tried to console myself that it was okay to write rubbish, a necessary prelude, an inevitable bad patch. All of which suggested I was capable of a subsequent good patch. For that, though, there was no evidence whatsoever. I was caught between the fear of not finishing my novel and looking a fool, or finishing a rubbish book and looking an even greater fool— worse, a deluded fool, a mediocre and vain pretender. The art, I read, was to find your centre and write from that. It wasn't that I worried I couldn't reach my centre. It was that I feared I had. And there was nothing there.

In all this Suzy was an enigma. She neither believed nor disbelieved in my talent. That's you, she would simply say. As the evidence of my failings as a writer mounted I resented this more and more. Surely she should love me, I thought, for my talent. But what was everything to me—whether I had this kernel, this essence, this *thing* that might mean something beyond me—was irrelevant to Suzy. The problem was this, I realised: Suzy loved me whether I had talent or not. Suzy loved me right or wrong, good or bad, *thing* or no thing; she loved something beyond and separate of whatever I might or might not be. Such a love made no sense to me. At times, I perhaps even hated her for it, because it did not admit to its logic the one thing I hoped was not mediocre in me: my talent.

For my fear was greater than any gratitude, my growing failure was more important than her unconditional love, and, try as I might to hide from Suzy my growing terror, my anger, its surest messenger, I couldn't. So when Suzy had that morning told me she knew I would write the novel and that the novel would be a success, I told her she was a fool for believing such nonsense. When she started crying, saying she only believed in me, I grew so angry I threw a chair across our kitchen where it hit the wall and snapped a leg, because I felt she wasn't listening when I said I had nothing to write.

Don't you see, I yelled, there's nothing to believe in?

Great loves are worth destroying in order to remind us how ordinary we really are. Or so Tebbe says. I don't know whether our love was great, but it took some wrecking. We had begun to fight more during the pregnancy. Our poverty didn't feel oppressive, or rather we didn't see it for the oppression it was. Yet every day it was leaving us a little less.

We couldn't see what it added up to: the food we couldn't afford, the home we couldn't heat, the car that kept breaking down, the petrol we couldn't pay for, the time expended on making good the innumerable small things that were bad— the dilapidated junk-shop furniture, an electric toaster that needed rewiring, the external door that had to be rehung, the car brakes. To which may be added the refrigerator that no longer worked, the stove with only one hotplate, the ever-tormenting washing machine, the second-hand clothes, the steady erosion of joys and the creeping glacier of worry. And though we lived it every day, what was hidden behind it all, even from us, was our mounting, unspoken despair.

Suzy grew dreamy and seemed ever more focused on her enormous belly. While walking she would rest her hand on the top of it, as if escorting strangers into the new world. It reminded me of the way people on horses in the movies rested their hand on the horse's neck as they chatted before they rode away. There was something about the gesture that drove me crazy, and that was because there was something about the pregnancy that felt exclusive and excluding. It was taking Suzy somewhere new and leaving me behind, marooned, condemned to playing a part for which I could find no real feeling. Much as I strived to discover it, other than a biological fact I felt no connection. It wasn't my belly. What I had was more poverty, growing worries, a new fear—all of it congealing into a fetid desperation.

I was ashamed that I felt such things.

But I felt them.

And when my anger came on me now it was as something new, as a rage and as a madness. I felt powerless against its sudden eruptions. But I felt powerless generally and perhaps that was the problem. I kicked a side panel of our car in when the recon-ditioned gearbox seized; I put my fist through a glass sliding door when the washing machine broke down irretrievably and there was no money for that as our total savings had been spent on the gearbox. Suzy, I felt, ignored our true situation by seeking to reassure me we would cope just fine when the twins arrived. But it wasn't that. It was that she rested her hand on her belly when she said it, as though even while saying it she was riding ever further away from me, and I had yelled, How? How can we look after them, Suzy? Because I could no longer see a way, and though I had to have forty stitches in consequence, the wound inside only grew worse.

At such times I frightened Suzy. I frightened myself. The night after the sliding-door incident we again fought. She called me a monster; she said she didn't recognise who I was becoming. In truth, I didn't either. She railed against *the book* as if it were a person, a thing, a force that had come to destroy us.

And perhaps it had.

Suzy said a word I had never heard her use, in a way she didn't normally speak but used with such force and clarity that I had to believe her.

I am *aggrieved*, she said slowly, growling the word as if it were made of moving metal parts. And I have cause to be *aggrieved*.

She said nothing more but had somehow said everything. And like a fool I began to try to justify the way everything had to be sacrificed for the book, why I worked on the book seemingly every waking hour, why I had no time to get a real job, why the book mattered more than anything else. I filled the air with empty words in the same way I filled the screen with empty words, and I suddenly realised not one word meant anything.

I stopped talking.

In that terrifying void I heard Suzy ask if I loved her.

I didn't say anything and I couldn't think what I should say. Instead, I wearily waved my arm and mumbled something about it not mattering. And with that Suzy ran her hand along our only bookcase, pushing several shelves of books to the floor, the falling books smashing a coffee mug and breaking a record player's perspex cover. She was yelling that I'd changed, that something had got into me, that she hated the book, that she didn't understand me any more. And with that she collapsed onto the mess of scattered paper on the floor, where I could hear her sobbing over and over:

The fucking book is killing us.

At other times the whole wonder of the pregnancy would seize me with an almost violent force; I would grab Suzy and push my face to her weather-balloon belly and feel both panic and wonder. That taut hemisphere was a miracle, and whether

I wanted it or not, whether it seemed to exclude me or include me, I felt as I heard distant heartbeats from within that this was also me, no matter how much it wasn't; *this was me*, or it was allowing me in, that there was a place where you could be nothing and something at the same time. But I didn't know how to reach that place. As she cradled my head, all I could do was reassure her that the book would soon end.

It will never end, Kif, Suzy said in a distant voice. Never.

3

Still, as every other morning I worked at the council, I kept furtively writing, exercise book hidden below the table on my lap. It was my last, my only, my remaining and irreducible belief—that somehow in the writing the writing would emerge. If the con man's publisher ever rang, I resolved I would take the call. It was, after all, flattering for someone who in the deepest part of their being feared he could not write to be rung by a real publisher and asked if he would write a real book for a real publishing company. That would be something that the world owed me, paid up.

And I would say no.

Though I did not dare think it, I understood I would later retail the story around those few friends I had left, how I, Kif Kehlmann, had been asked to ghost write a book and turned it and the money down, in order to concentrate on my real work as a writer, the finishing of my first novel.

In this spirit, I readied myself to be an immortal writer in the manner of de Maupassant, who put a pistol to his head, spun the barrel, and when he failed to kill himself saw it as proof of his own immortality. My pistol would be the call from the publisher—I needed the money, I needed the sense of purpose it

might give me, I needed to publish a book, any book; I needed—
for fuck's sake—the *chance*. I would talk to the publisher as an
equal, I would talk as a man who could pull the pistol's trigger.
And that was why when he called I would prove I was willing to
risk death by saying, No!

Kif?

I looked up from my exercise book. It was council's Corporate
Services and Equal Opportunities Manager, Jen Birmingham, a
large woman by turns bullying, pitiful and drunk. But mostly
drunk. It was said of Jen Birmingham that she had been a great
beauty. Her grand face bespoke the ruin of ravaged empires. She
wore ruby red lipstick applied in only an approximate relation
to her lips. It was also said of her that she either wanted to lick
you or kick you. The last time she had come by she had talked at
length about a daughter who no longer spoke to her. But I could
tell from her voice—slightly brittle, sharp—that today was not a
day for a licking.

Are you?

It was unclear as to what was the right answer. I was on my
last warning about wasting council time by using it to write a
novel. How I might use my pointless hours in an empty foyer
standing guard over an empty exhibition in a manner that prof-
ited council had never been explained.

Are you working on—here Jen Birmingham paused—*that
book*?

It was even unclear to me if it was a book or a grave error.

Again? Kif? After our warning?

I was staring at my knees, at an exercise book of twenty-six
symbols chaotically arrayed into many patterns. Was that what
a book was?

No, I said.

I am sorry, Kif. You've been warned *again* and *again* about—

Mrs—, I pleaded.

But I was stopped by the sight of Jen Birmingham's real lips and perhaps sixty per cent of her trompe l'oeil lips seeking a word that might give adequate expression to her disgust. It was possible to sense in her cruelty a comparable wound, but it didn't make her cruelty any less cruel nor my situation any better. And when Jen Birmingham's lips finally found the word, they opened, and she cried—

WRITING!

I clutched my exercise book tight.

See out your shift today, Kif. There's no need to return tomorrow. We are letting you go.

After Jen Birmingham left the foyer, I was alone once more in front of the empty exhibition room. I reopened the exercise book and began another sentence. But it was no good. There was neither flow nor dance; neither pause nor movement. Filled with dread at the thought of even getting a character to stand up and leave a room, I instead stood up and left the building.

That afternoon I spent labouring for a builder was welcome in its mindlessness. I could forget that our last regular income was gone and all we had left to live on was this casual work. My first hour was taken up digging and barrowing out clay from the side of a house in preparation for a foundation; the next, exhausted, carrying steel up a steep drive; the final two hours mixing concrete for footings in a wheelbarrow. It was a clear winter's day, my body hot until I stopped, and then it chilled rapidly.

4

We lived halfway up an old, steep street. With its rotting colonial cottages, the street always seemed on the brink of a gentrification that never came and never would come. No one much in the street seemed to work. Our next-door neighbour was a junkie family, the father of whom was up on eighty-three separate drug charges. They survived by dealing, and an unmarked police car sat outside most days watching who came and went. Occasionally, Meredith, one half of the junkie couple, would come out with a mug of tea, smoke quietly, enjoying the day, the air, the cars and people who passed. When her tea was drained and fag finished, she would straighten up, lean out over the low, cracked concrete fence, tense with a sudden rage, and scream, Fuck off pig cunts! And two figures in the car opposite would slump downwards.

That night, chatting with Suzy after tea, both of us watching Bo playing in a cardboard box, I felt something unexpected: such an enormity of emotion that it seemed more had passed among the three of us in five minutes than could be described in a thousand-page novel.

It was an overwhelming feeling, a transcendent few moments that was also an eternity, in which all was one—the sound of Bo's breathing, the rustle of the bark and leaves she had collected from the park and was playing with, a toy black bird that Suzy circled Bo's head with, Suzy's smile, Bo's laughter, the doll thrown under the table, its head half-gone, grey flock stuffing spilling onto the lino floor and some Argentinian ants crawling around it—yes, all was one, and even the smallest things seemed pregnant with revelation.

And I knew that if I could just get a fraction of what I had just seen and felt into words and onto the monitor, I would have my book. I rushed up the stairs to my tiny writing room, climbed over the desk and slid down into my chair, jammed between the desk and the wall with just enough space that I could shimmy into it.

But the Mac Plus froze almost immediately. I manually ejected the floppy disk with a paperclip I kept solely for that daily purpose, switched the machine off and on and reinserted the disk. As I waited for it to boot back up there came through the wall the sound of screaming as the junkie couple fought. I had a cassette player that I turned on at such times. Its sound, thin and crumpled, seemed only to amplify the thick noise of a world collapsing a wall away.

After several more reboots the Mac Plus seemed to find its necessary equilibrium. But the words that I now typed conveyed not a speck of what I had felt. Not a jot, not a glimmer. When I went to write, all the things I had known so strongly and completely just before lost all feeling. They became nothing.

Some cement dust appeared on the keyboard, shaken out from my fingernails by the tapping of keys. I flicked the keyboard upside down, drummed its back, and righted it. I tried to re-enter the dream, the drift I had known only a few minutes before with Bo and Suzy. But it was gone. I swept the cement dust off the desk and into the beer carton I kept for waste paper. The screen froze once more. When I went to eject the floppy disk and reboot the machine, the paperclip snapped from metal fatigue. From behind the wall came the sound of a bottle smashing, Meredith's sobbing, then silence. I found a notebook and went to write, but when the pen touched the paper the words vanished. There had been a moment but the moment had gone.

5

I was still staring at a taunting cursor and empty screen when Suzy called from downstairs, saying there was a phone call for me. I went back down to the lounge room, the lazy heat of the fire, and picked up the receiver. The speaker didn't introduce himself immediately but asked if I was Kif Kehlmann. The accent was private school Anglo-Australian, superior. On my saying I was, he introduced himself as Gene Paley, the head of Schlegel TransPacific Publishing and Siegfried Heidl's publisher.

I was dumbstruck.

He asked what I had written. I told him about my history of Tasmanian modernism and the Wangaratta City Council short story prize. He fell silent for some moments, and in that silence I felt the full insignificance of my autobiography.

Nothing else? he said finally.

A novel, I said. Almost done. Just tidying up a few loose ends.

I've looked at *Dead Tide*. Good title.

Quiet Currents, I corrected. *A History of—*

Mmm, Gene Paley said over the top of me. Well done. Titles are important. But can you ghost write a memoir?

In the silence that followed silence followed.

What do you think? Gene Paley said after some time, as Suzy pointed to the phone and I mouthed shock and mimed writing. You understand that if I was to employ you, you must accept our advice. Me. Editors. So on. If we say that must go, or this needs more work, you have to do what we say.

I had no idea what editing entailed. Hoppy Head Press proved assiduous, even pedantic proofreaders. But that was all. I also felt confused: I hadn't said I would be taking the job; I had readied myself to tell Gene Paley with what I felt was the easygoing casualness of a real writer who has a lot on his plate that I too had plenty on mine. I realised I needed to state my refusal quickly, as Gene Paley continued on about how it would involve working closely with Heidl, that I would need to come to Melbourne, that—

I haven't, I said, said yes.

No? Gene Paley said.

Yes.

Good, Gene Paley said. You'll be paid ten thousand dollars on delivery of an edited manuscript. No royalties. No rights. Just ten thousand dollars. It's a lot of work, I'm the first to admit it. But it's good money.

Ten? I said, shocked, because I guess I hadn't really believed

Heidl, and the way I said it seemed in a strange way assent, or agreement.

Yes.

Expenses, I said, not knowing why I was saying such a thing. I had no experience of this sort of dealing, but I felt I had to push now. I would be in Melbourne, there's accommodation, travel, food, and—

How much?

Sorry?

How much do you want?

This was an unexpected question to which I had no answer. I imagined that there would be tram fares, lunch—a pie or salad roll or some such—perhaps a coffee or two. I could sleep on the floor at Sully's place—Sully was an old family friend, and was always welcoming when I visited the mainland—so that would more or less be it. I quickly calculated my daily costs would be in the vicinity of nine dollars.

Eleven fifty, I said. But—

I couldn't finish the sentence. Even in 1992 eleven dollars fifty was an insignificant sum. It didn't seem quite the right moment to say I was refusing the offer. And in not finishing the sentence, I sensed something was happening that I hadn't intended, some shift in an unspoken balance of power, and I was not in control.

Eleven dollars fifty? I heard Gene Paley say.

Yes, I said, growing uncomfortable.

Mmm, Gene Paley said.

I wasn't really arguing about expenses, I realised, but something fundamental: my dignity as a writer. And I was using a ludicrous demand for pie money to assert the very fact I was a writer, however dubious a fact that might have been. My dilemma was Gene Paley seemed to be agreeing I was a writer. And at that remarkable point I could have no argument with him and had to agree—

Yes, I said. That's it.

I was already regretting not going in harder and pushing for a round fifteen dollars, when I sensed that was equally stupid and that I was very far out of my depth.

Total? Gene Paley asked, the slightest tone of incredulity in his voice. He was relieving me of the painful charade of pretending I had a difficult choice. He understood my needs far better than me, but he wasn't, as I was to discover, alone in that.

I need to think, I said.

Mmm, Gene Paley said.

I sensed, wrongly, that this urbane-sounding publisher may have calculated that a salad roll, coffee and tram fare would be lucky to come to nine dollars, and now suspected me of shameful deceit. I heard what I feared was a stifled laugh.

I can bring tea bags, I said. Or—

Kif—may I call you Kif? Kif, let's forget expenses. I'll give you a work car while you're here. How does that sound?

Amazing, I said, and regretted it immediately. I was so naive I was still impressed by such things; worse, Gene Paley now knew it.

And you can eat at our canteen free of charge.

I need to think about it, I said, trying to steady, seeking to ready him for my refusal while striving for the correct tone and failing.

I'll throw in a staff petrol card, Gene Paley said. That way you don't pay for fuel.

I haven't said—I began, but for a second time I didn't know how to finish. The words just drifted away. I hadn't said—what? No? Yes? I want more money? I could hear my breath in the receiver.

Kif, can I take you into my confidence? Did Siegfried give you any sense of a timetable?

He said we'd need to do it fairly quickly.

As I was saying, Siegfried Heidl goes to court in six and a half weeks' time. He'll be going to jail for a very, very long time. The book has to be finished before the trial.

Six weeks to write a first draft?

To finish a book.

Mr Paley—

Gene. Please.

Gene. I don't think I—

Don't think now, Kif. Take all the time you need to think in the next twenty-four hours, and just give me your answer tomorrow night.

And to this I agreed, because it's always easier to agree than not. And besides, it played to my vanity to think that I had this momentous decision to make, when in my heart the decision had been long ago made: I would not be ghost writing any book. The only book I was going to make up was my own. The world begins with a yes. And so too hell.

5

1

MR PALEY?

Gene, please.

There was a pause. A day had passed, my resolve not to sell out had only strengthened, and Suzy—though a little disappointed about the money we were forsaking—supported me in my implacable stand. And yet, somehow, I had started my second call with the publisher badly.

It's a very generous offer, Gene, I said. But—

It is, he said, *handsome*.

I was trying to think how I could phrase my refusal but retain some connection with Gene Paley—the only real publisher who had ever spoken to me—that might lead to his publishing my novel when I finished it. But it wasn't simply that this necessary politeness was leading me astray. It was also as if there was an inevitability about the conversation that I hadn't understood. Gene Paley, of course, knew what he wanted. I just hadn't realised he also knew what I wanted.

Gene, I was working on my novel last night—

Yes! Your novel! he said, dragging out the word *novel* as though I were offering him the prospect of the original manuscript of *Ulysses*. I have had my secretary take the liberty of booking you a morning flight tomorrow to Melbourne.

This took my breath away. I had been about to say no, and here it was, everything finally happening—the flight, work, a book.

Money. All mine, if I just said yes. I didn't say yes. But nor did I say no. I parried, I paused, I argued, thinking it was for time.

You did say ten thousand dollars? I heard myself ask in a tone I didn't recognise, as if seeking confirmation of a deal I still thought I was going to reject.

Yes. Ten thousand.

I heard myself say that my wife was eight months pregnant with twins and I heard myself insist that I wanted flights home every weekend, and, to my astonishment, I heard Gene Paley agree to my conditions.

I drew breath, and, emboldened, continued.

And if she goes into labour while I'm working in Melbourne, I want a flight home immediately, I said, albeit with a slight nervous stammer.

Absolutely.

And two thousand up front?

I couldn't believe what I was saying, but the idea of finally being a writer and, even more incredibly, being paid, was infinitely seductive.

Those sort of details, Kif, we can sort out when you arrive— agree a plan, meet Siegfried, and you two can be at work by lunchtime.

Okay, I heard myself agreeing although I didn't really agree at all. Perhaps I just wanted to savour it all a few moments more.

Some minutes later I put down the phone. I went to the kitchen, poured a glass of water, and put it down.

What happened? Suzy asked. Did you say yes?

No, I said. No, I didn't.

And I hadn't. Instead I had felt a riptide grabbing me, taking me out, and rather than fight it I had swum with it.

And here I was.

For the first time in twenty-four hours I did what I'd said I'd spend the last twenty-four hours doing—thinking. Some people later said that I should have had moral qualms about working with a criminal; perhaps I said I did, but really what did I know about him other than vague memories of news items on TV and in the papers? I remembered a smile, some accusations, more rumours, nothing that would bring on outrage or make me feel he was morally beneath me. Wasn't I a writer, after all? Nothing was beneath me.

The only concern I can recall having was this: how on earth did you ghost write a book? I was a Kehlmann of all trades, a jack hammerer and a doorman, occasional roof painter, and a Bartleby of writing, forever saying No to finishing my own book. Now, in some way I didn't understand, I found myself fully committed to writing another book for someone else. Yet there was no evidence I was capable of such a task. My presumption was that because I could do so many other things— admittedly menial, even trivial—well, surely, I reassured myself, I could write a book. It wasn't the sort of idea writers confessed to in the *Paris Review*. But it was the only idea I had, and for no explicable reason I took comfort from it. I headed upstairs to pack the small duffle bag that was all I had for travel.

What are you doing? I heard Suzy say from the bedroom door. I thought—

And when I looked up and saw her, huge as a battleship with our two children inside her, ridiculous as it sounds, I laughed with joy.

I'm going to be a writer, I said.

2

STP Publishing was a six-storey complex set in the wastelands of Port Melbourne amidst other such purpose-built bunkers, out of which poked black glass rectangles at irregular intervals. The landscaping was of the brutish bush banal then in vogue with aged-care facilities and other sundry reposes of last hope—state schools, warehouses, outer-suburban supermarkets—concrete planter boxes rendered in beige acrylics, bedecked with spiky grasses arranged like bouquets of olive-green stilettoes.

As I drove up in a cab I saw Ray standing next to one such concrete garden bed, his tall figure stooping over a short, bearded man wearing sunglasses, a red baseball jacket and a baseball cap. Ray came over to the cab as I was paying the driver. His mood was at once conspiratorial and furtive, unlike anything I had ever known in him.

Good you're here, mate. Come and meet Ziggy.

He's inside already? I said, surprised.

No, that's him there, he said, gesturing with a tilt of the head in the direction of the short man in the baseball cap.

Is that a false beard?

He's worried there might be a hit on him. He's in disguise.

It's a false beard.

Ray halted, as if confused, then his mind seemed to clear. Perhaps sensing the oddity of his own situation, he laughed.

Could be anyone, mate—the hitman could be you!

Me for sure, I said.

The sky was flat, the street devoid of shadows, and there was something welcoming, even reassuring in such uniform mediocrity where everything had been reduced to the need to make money and only make money or otherwise not exist. I felt strangely moved. It looked like the future, and for a short time yet I felt part of it.

In this transcendent frame of mind I wasn't looking where I was going. As we walked over to Heidl I trod in a fluoro-green puddle of what I assume was leaked coolant. I felt the fluid wash in the torn gap between my Adidas Vienna's sole and upper, and dampen my sock so badly it squelched.

It wasn't how I wanted to meet Heidl, to be introduced to a publishing company, to begin work, with one soggy foot slowly growing cold through the day. I took the runner off, tipped out what fluid wasn't absorbed in my sock and felt my good spirits run away with the gritty green liquid. It was while so balanced on one leg, stooped in a semi-crouch, that I heard a voice say my name.

On looking up I saw my distorted reflection in a set of mirrored sunglasses. The impression of my cringing self lasted only a moment and then the dull epoxy stucco, the tinted windows, the black track marks of silicon joining the tilt-slabs of STP Publishing came into view and, in front, there stood a short, slightly flabby man in aviator sunglasses wearing a ridiculous fake beard staring down at me. As disguises went, the beard, along with the American baseball jacket—an oddity in Australia— seemed to be about drawing attention rather than evading it.

These days I take comfort from photoshopped images in cookbooks, or advertisements for watches which rise to an idea of serene hope watches can never attain. That, and instagram- ming food. But in those days, my better days, I guess, optimistic as they were for us all, I hoped to like people. Still, I felt surprised to meet in one of Australia's greatest criminals somebody so mundane. But what human being ever is the equal of their works? As if reading my mind Heidl said in a soft voice, his accent a light German, less stilted than it sounded on the phone:

All human contact is a form of disappointment. Adding, as he smiled: Tebbe.

Only later did I realise he was talking about me.

Ray made the introductions. Heidl called me Kif; I called him Siegfried. He had about him the unsettling manners of an unctuous undertaker, the sudden reforming of the mouth into an empty smile, the firm taking of your hand in his, the fixed staring into your eyes while his remained hidden behind his gold- framed sunglasses.

Kif, I must ask of you that you respect the secrecy of our project.

This was unexpected news, and all the time he kept holding my hand, as if I were being inducted into some secret order, and all the time he continued to smile. It was one of those smiles that fixes like a palsy or rictus grin on a face and demands agreement with its certainty and good humour—a smile which, when I think about it, was the smile of the era. But I never saw it focus with such compelling force as it did when visited on you by Ziggy Heidl, and it would not depart until you acquiesced. It was a vehicle for domination, an expression of power, and my only response was to look away, but you could only do that for so long. Ziggy Heidl, as I was to discover, could smile forever.

Nobody knows, Kif, he said. Nobody *is* to know. It's very important. I have—he turned his head this way and that, as though scanning the road and warehouses and offices for apex predators—*reasons*.

And as he spoke I wasn't so much listening as looking, trying to get a feel for Heidl. But I couldn't. I tried not to stare at the twitching muscle caught like a fish in that otherwise empty net of his fleshy face. For he was more a lack of features, a mystery of conventionality, a face of odd emptiness. He never stopped smiling while he spoke, as though everything he was telling me was wonderful news for us both.

Nobody in this building, Heidl was saying—other than the managing director, the publisher, and the editor—is to know who we are and why we are here. You see, Heidl said, we have to keep this secret.

Why?

Because, Heidl said, looking astonished, *we do.*

I glanced at Ray, who nodded his agreement.

It has to be, Heidl said. He rolled his hands out in a gesture of expanse, as though to cup a beach ball, a cheesy evangelist of sinister mystery. There are things, he continued so quietly that I had to lean in to hear. *People.*

People?

He looked around as if someone had been eavesdropping, and nodded.

People.

Why are we here then, Siegfried? I asked.

Call me Ziggy. You're my friend now.

I mean, Siegfried, what do I say when they ask me questions about what we're doing?

People ask me all sorts of questions, Kif. If I tell them the truth, they call me a liar. But if I tell them a lie, they're happy.

Again that smile, that noxious smile. In the manner of an abbot inducting a novice into the sorrowful mysteries, he continued:

It's baffling to me why anyone thinks the truth matters. It's unclear why we invented it when to survive we need to deceive, tell white lies, and wear masks. You understand?

Not exactly.

Tebbe says words are just crude metaphors that people forgot are just crude metaphors. Roger that?

Roger what? No. Not really.

But that's the thing, Kif, Heidl said, smiling on and on and on. Words take us away from the truth, not towards it. Like madmen walking backwards.

I looked away to avoid his eternal smile, that intolerable certainty.

That's why there is no truth, only interpretations. That's why we do better liberated from the truth, he went on. Believe me. That's why we're here to do a book of poetry.

Poetry? I said.

Roger that. An anthology. That's why we're here.

An anthology of what? I asked.

Westphalian folk verse, fifteenth century to be precise. We're the editors. That's our cover.

We need a cover?

Everyone needs a cover.

And Ray? I asked.

For in all this Ray seemed a sudden liability. He had read Hermann Hesse, it was true. Why, I can't say, nor yet what he derived from it, for he was not a man who could hold a conversation for a minute about anything literary. For that matter, he was not really a man who could hold a conversation, full stop.

Consultant.

I said nothing.

Assistant, said Heidl, who seemed to have reconsidered. It seemed a better story, a half-truth, because as minder of Heidl Ray was a sort of assistant. It was just that in my experience, admittedly highly limited, Heidl didn't come across as any sort of poet or editor. On the other hand, I had never met an editor of mediaeval German poetry, and I sensed even in a publishing house I wouldn't be alone in this.

I don't know anything about German poetry, I said. Far less mediaeval Westphalian folk verse. Do you?

I am the forest, Heidl said. And a night of dark trees.

For the first and not the last time, I found myself unexpectedly impressed.

But he who is not afraid of my darkness, Heidl continued, will find banks of roses underneath my cypresses.

Perhaps I was already falling under his spell.

That's a mediaeval Westphalian poem?

No, Heidl said, his smile tautening into something else—contempt? victory? No, he said, that's Nietzsche.

He kept on talking, and he kept on smiling, and the muscle of his cheek kept twitching, a strange metronome counting in my acquiescence as we headed up the steps into STP's offices.

3

Heidl's manner now became that of the CEO he had once been; the confident swagger as we walked to the lifts, the seeming familiarity with all people and all things and Ray and me following behind, already an entourage, not equals but accessories to power. On another floor we strode down the corridor, past a secretary and straight into a large office in which a tall, thin man was quickly getting to his feet. Buttoning his suit jacket with one hand he brought his other round to clap Heidl on the shoulder, in a welcome of necessary and insincere complicity.

As they made small talk, I looked around the office, a tired nod to something I later came to learn no one really believed at TransPac: their tradition. A large bookcase of French-polished Huon pine, unlike any other in that building, old, grand, overly ornate, chipped and inkstained, ran the length and height of one wall; its wearied, slightly sagging shelves housing a small museum of Australian literary history.

There was what appeared to be a near complete set of the early Pacific Library paperbacks with their laughing kooka-burra colophon that had revolutionised the Australian market and reading habits in the 1940s and 1950s, and four shelves devoted to the hefty hardbacks of the 1970s when Pacific had merged with the once glorious powerhouse of the 1890s nationalist revival and by 1971 nearly defunct Schneider & O'Leary to create TransPacific Publishing and pioneer the 1970's Australian literary renaissance. There were the international blockbusters that had come with their acquisition by the German media conglomerate Schlegel in the 1980s to form Schlegel Trans-Pacific. Posters of Nobel Prize winners who had no knowledge of Australia other than the rights agreement they had signed in New York or London or Barcelona sat cheek by jowl in equal size with local contemporary bards such as Jez Dempster, whose fate would very soon be that of the walrus moustachioed profiles of the nineteenth-century balladeers who had once made Schneider & O'Leary a household name. Perhaps books still lived, but the publishing house seemed like a soon-to-be-abandoned gold-mining shaft that had almost exhausted all its profitable veins and in which odd skeletons rattled and timber props groaned.

I've brought you our ghost, Heidl said, extending an arm towards me in a gesture that is still sometimes described in books as avuncular, but by anyone else as creepy.

Ah, Kif, said the executive. So very good to meet you. Gene. Gene Paley.

He shook my hand, said hello to Ray, whom he seemed to acknowledge as one might a dog, say, or a shopping bag.

He pressed a button on the intercom, softly asked for something or somebody, and a moment later a woman of perhaps thirty joined us.

Kif, let me introduce you. Your editor, Pia Carnevale.

When I remember Pia Carnevale the first thing I think of is her laugh. Throat open throttle, nothing polite or feigned. And yet I can't have heard her laugh until later. What I do recall is, oddly, her long fingers, and her face, one of strong lines, olive in colour and shape, which, framed by the gold brocaded upturned collar of the dark maroon jacket she was wearing, put me in mind of a Byzantine icon. Later I discovered this was somewhat misleading. She was very far from a Byzantine saint, delighting in vulgarity and gossip, and was in her way far more assertive than accepting, but the impression remained.

Gene Paley asked Pia to take Heidl and Ray to the office we would be using to work in, while I was to stay back to sort out 'the boring paperwork'.

4

Why me? Gene Paley asked after the others had left. Why have I been chosen? That's what you're asking yourself, I know.

It wasn't, but I agreed it was. Gene Paley leant back in his chair. He seemed to be appraising me. He raised a hand as if he were a traffic policeman halting traffic in an empty street.

Hold that thought, Kif.

He stared at me a few moments more, and sighed.

I always say it's a mistake to write your own autobiography. Far better to let a professional pen a good story well. But Siegfried insisted that he write it himself. Months went by. Produced nothing. Well—one thing. A twelve-thousand-word press clipping file. He called it a memoir. And why do more? Whole life built on not leaving a paper record. Said he had writer's block. One after another we sent three of our top editors to work with him. Each gave up within half a day.

Why? I asked.

To say they ran out of the room screaming is too colourful, Gene Paley said.

So?

They crawled out of the room weeping. No! Joking! But he did intimidate them. Bully them. He ignored them, he was impossible to work with. He was awful. He worked hard at being awful so that they would give up. After that, we insisted he work with a proper ghost writer. Best in the business. This ghost has worked with some of the biggest names. Sports stars. Politicians. Movie stars. Monsters! He knows how to deal with the biggest egos. But Siegfried isn't an ego, or at least not in that way. The ghost writer lasted two and a half days. When he gave up, he said he would happily work with Pol Pot or Vlad the Impaler. But he had limits. Joking!

Comprehending Gene Paley sometimes felt like reassembling

Finnegans Wake after it had been put through a paper shredder. Still, if I was confused, I did now want to know.

Why me, then? I ventured.

I said to Siegfried, if you won't work with one of our writers, *you* find a writer you will work with. He said he didn't know any writers. And his bodyguard—

Ray.

Right. Anyway, the bodyguard piped up, I've got a mate in Tasmania. He wants to be a writer. So, I got *Dead Tide*. Read *Dead Tide*. Have to tell you I wasn't really keen, but Siegfried was. To be frank, we had no alternative.

At this point Gene Paley seemed to revert to the publisher's more traditional technique of gloving the fist with flattery.

And besides, you're impressive. A young writer of obvious promise. Yes?

I didn't know if it would look presumptuous or arrogant if I agreed, and so instead I said nothing.

Gene Paley changed tack.

Somewhere in Siegfried is a book. Yes?

Yes.

Mmm, Gene Paley said.

His gaze was drifting to his bookcases, he seemed unsure for a moment what a book was: he swivelled on his chair, reached out to a shelf, half-grabbed a volume only to push it back in.

I would like—

Mmm, Gene Paley said, swivelling back to his desk.

Well, a credit. On the cover page.

As the writer?

Writer, I said, though I sensed a chasm of divided interpretation opening up in that simple word. Yes.

Hold that thought, Kif. I always say don't insult the public. Don't pretend that there wasn't a little professional help. Not an easy task. We can talk about that later. For now, a few formalities.

Here, he said, sliding a small stack of papers across his desk. We pay you five thousand dollars when the book goes to the printer, and five thousand on the day of publication. No royalties.

He handed me his fountain pen.

Sign here, he said, flicking through the pages to where an arrow-shaped stick-it note pointed to dotted lines.

As I tried to make sense of what I realised was my contract, Gene Paley grew reflective.

As I was saying, a ghost writer exists somewhere between a courtesan and a cleaner. Privy to much, revealing only what is appropriate.

I looked up. Gene Paley was glancing at his watch, trying not to show his impatience. I felt it would be rude to read the contract, taking up so much of such an important man's time.

You know what they call ghost writers in France?

I didn't.

Nègres. And here, he said, after I signed the first page, turning the contract to another page and pointing. And here.

I signed and I signed and as I signed again, I felt gratitude, even pride.

Blacks?

Slaves, Gene Paley said softly, turning the page. And here.

6

1

WHEN I ENTERED OUR OFFICE on the first day of our first week, Heidl—in a pattern that would quickly become familiar—was already leaving.

I have a lunchtime meeting, he said, picking up his cap, sunglasses and beard from the large executive's desk. You'll need to get organised here.

For a moment we both looked at the overwhelming order of the room, the chairs that were only for us to sit on, the conference table only for us to talk over and a Mac Classic only for me to type on, the room only for us to write the book in, replete with a side table on which sat Heidl's manuscript in one neat pile and research notes on Heidl in another, alongside which was a tray of club sandwiches—everything, in short, that existed in defiance of what Heidl had just said.

There was nothing to organise.

Please settle in, he said in an avuncular manner, as if he were the host and TransPac his home. I'll be back to start in the afternoon.

I was going to suggest perhaps we could get a few hours' work in, when for the first time I saw his eyes. I almost never can remember with certainty the colour of someone's eyes, even my own children's. Heidl's I never forgot. They had the depthless calm of black water in fatal rivers. Later I noticed that on some days his eyes were like those of a wild dog, the pupils preternaturally dilated. At such times, he seemed almost to circle his prey like a wolf. Mostly though, his eyes had the glaze of road kill. Without hope, they both terrified and mesmerised me. As I helplessly stared, his face lifted his mouth into its rictus smile, half-mockery, half-triumph; it was as if all the skin had been peeled away and all that moved in the horror was the twitching nerve in his cheek.

2

Heidl returned late afternoon with Ray. I put down the research notes I had been reading and suggested that I was happy to stay back late and work on. Without saying a word, Heidl turned to Ray and with a slight movement of his head indicated the open door. As if he were a trained animal, Ray rose from his seat in the corner and shut it. So little was ever said between the two, and yet Heidl only had to point, to look, and Ray would rise to do his bidding. With the door closed, Heidl sat and smiled. He always made the simplest of human transactions feel conspiratorial.

Roger that, Kif. And I think the best way of working is us getting to know each other over dinner.

And so we left. There were drinks in a bar. There was dinner in Chinatown and more drinks. There was awkward conversation, where I was intent on asking Heidl about his life, and Heidl was intent on not answering and instead questioned me about my life, questions I in turn evaded by asking him further questions.

A night of hapless negations ended as abruptly as it had begun with Heidl standing, saying we all needed an early evening as there was much work to be done. We came out of the restaurant into a drizzly side street. A waiting photographer began snapping away. Heidl took out his wallet, handed Ray a wad of fifty-dollar notes, and smiled. As if he were a puppet, Ray turned and went back to the photographer. Heidl continued walking and gestured I follow. The fading sound of Ray and the photographer arguing gave way to the sound of something smashing.

No need to look, Heidl said, hailing a cab, and opening its door for me, he smiled. No need to worry about Ray.

As my cab was driving off I saw through the rear window Heidl hail a second taxi for himself, abandoning Ray. It took me some moments to realise that I was doing the very same thing, that I was not doing what I wished, but what Heidl wanted. I told the cab driver to go back, and we found Ray wandering up the street. He got in, swearing about the photographer as he did. With Heidl Ray was ominous. Without Heidl Ray was Ray.

I asked what happened.

He shouldn't be taking photos without Ziggy's permission, was all Ray would say for some time. He let slip that he had asked for the film. When the photographer refused Ray had grabbed the camera, exposed the film, and smashed the camera on the pavement.

I asked what would happen if the photographer went to the police.

He won't do anything, Ray said. I threw more cash on the ground than his camera and the photo were worth combined. And told him if he ever tried again more than his camera would end up broken.

I asked why he would do that for Heidl when he said he couldn't stand the prick.

Fuck knows, Ray said.

I don't.

You will.

Outside it was a Melbourne winter, benign and imme-morable in equal measure. And looking out the window at the mizzle and the cars and the lights that couldn't stay still in the dazzle of nocturnal bitumen, Ray brightened at the possibilities of the night.

Where are we going? he asked.

But I had no idea. No idea at all.

3

In the end, we went to a pub Ray knew called the Gutter and the Stars. With Heidl out of the way we were as we had always been. But something was different, something that felt less obvious and more deeply etched than the odd manner he had shown towards me at the publishers, something more than the faux vigilance he adopted whenever Heidl was around.

He talked wistfully of working with Heidl in far north Queensland. They had spent the best part of the fifteen months since Heidl had been released on bail getting about the frequently inaccessible parts of tropical Cape York in helicopters and four-wheel drives.

When I asked him what they'd been doing up there, Ray was suddenly furtive, muttering something about it being secret. When I asked why, he said it was commercial-in-confidence.

What are you talking about, Ray? Commercial-in-fucking-what?

Ray was both evasive and, I began to think, ignorant of key details.

It's not for the book, right? Ray said finally. You can't tell anyone.

Ray lowered his voice to a point of near inaudibility.

We were looking for a place to build a rocket launch site.

What?

It's a big deal. Crazy shit. NASA.

NASA employed Heidl and you to find a rocket launch site?

Not exactly. It's not like that.

But it is. That's what—

No. Look. I can't say any more. But . . . apparently . . . there's a need for a satellite launch facility in the southern hemisphere. For special satellites.

How special?

Spy special. That Star Wars thing, you know, that Reagan got going.

And NASA paid for you and Heidl to go on this jolly for a year and a half?

Maybe. I can't say. Ask Ziggy. I don't know.

I wouldn't trust him as far as I could kick him.

Well, you'd be right not to, Ray said.

He cursed Heidl, bought a jug of beer and six Southern Comforts, and grabbed some glasses. We leant in on a small bar table, perched on stools, sloping in as if buttressing each other, and Ray repeated how I was not to tell Heidl anything about my family. He poured the Southern Comfort into each beer glass and topped them with beer. It made the beer taste manky, but taste was never Ray's primary interest in drink.

You're a friendly bloke, Kif. Don't be a friendly bloke. He'll want to be one of your mates. Don't be his mate.

He's your mate.

I know. Why do you think I'm telling you this?

He says you're his best mate.

Ray looked at me blankly.

There are stories about Brett Garrett in the research notes.

Ray seemed to suddenly awaken. What sort of stories? he said.

The book keeper who disappeared, I said.

I know who Brett Garrett was. What sort of stories?

Kept asking questions. Wouldn't let Heidl expand. He was holding the whole show back.

Weird guy, Ray said. So?

And then he disappears.

Weird guy, like I said.

Heidl said something similar. He's quoted in a profile saying Garrett was one of those blokes who you find twenty years later hanging around the Kakadu rainforest.

Ray made a strange choking noise, as if he was trying to both vomit and swallow something at the same time, then blamed it on the beer.

There was a story that Ziggy did for him, I began.

Killed Garrett? What sort of story?

A contract killing, I said. A rumour.

You believe that shit, you'd believe anything, Ray said; suddenly, strangely angry. Who told you this crap? Ziggy?

I told you. The research notes the publishers gave me.

Ray seemed to think about this, or perhaps he wasn't thinking about it, but something else that was at once very far away and so close he could see and think of nothing else.

So do you believe Heidl would go that far? I asked.

Ray downed his beer, poured another, skolled that, and looked at me. His eyes momentarily had the same dying wombat look as Heidl's.

The thing is it gets inside you after a time, his *talk-talk-talk*, all of it. It takes over something in you.

Listening to Ray, I realised that he, whom I'd never known to be fearful of anybody or anything, was frightened.

Let him *talk-talk-talk*, but just tell him nothing, that's all I'm saying. Nothing about Suzy. Nothing about Bo.

I went to make a joke, but stopped.

Don't tell him Suzy's pregnant. And if he calls you at home, don't let him talk to her.

Ray was staring into the swirling foam lines of his half-full glass of beer and Southern Comfort. It smelt like stale underarm deodorant. Maybe he was seeing the same whorls of wind spume and sea fear that so nearly did for us both in Bass Strait.

He's like slime, Ray said, looking into the sea wrack of his glass. He covers you. And you can't get him off. That's my dream. He's all over me, this slime, this fuckn awful green slime, dragging me under, and I scrub and I scrub, but I can't get him off.

4

After I got home to Sully's place later that night I read Heidl's manuscript. It didn't take long. It was a mashup of quotes from newspaper stories about the growth of the Australian Safety Organisation—or ASO as he mostly called it—supplemented by extracts from annual reports, memoranda, letters of praise from various politicians and thanks from public figures—ambassadors, police and fire chiefs, big-name businessmen, retired American generals—linked by the occasional unenlightening paragraph by Heidl. It was in its way as extraordinary as it was almost unreadable. One example will suffice to give the general tone. Describing Heidl as *a truly great Australian*, the prime minister of the day went on to hail Heidl as *an inspiring example of caring, corporate Australia.*

I understood why they needed a writer. There was nothing about Heidl's background, nothing of his private life, nor anything about the collapse of the ASO, the missing millions, the banks and businesses and jobs and lives that went down in consequence, the manhunt and his subsequent arrest and pending trial. Nothing, in short, that might make a book.

Next, I finished reading the research folder, a compilation of the extensive media coverage the ASO had received. For Ray, working at the ASO had been like belonging to an elite military unit, with its uniforms, martial discipline, and its expensive toys. The newspaper reports told a similar tale: the ASO had a sophistication in logistics, technology and equipment, unmatched by either government or business, capabilities no one had ever thought of, far less achieved. They were the first in the country to have firefighting helicopters. The first with specialised sea search vessels with mini-subs and helicopters attached.

As well as undertaking the more conventional jobs training workers in the oil and mining industry in safety, searching for missing walkers and fishermen, and specialist bushfire fighting, there had been some spectacular successes—the putting out of an oil rig fire in the Timor Sea that was threatening an ecological catastrophe; the daring rescue of the world-famous French solo sailor, Olivier Espaze, when his yacht overturned fifteen hundred kilometres south of Australia in huge seas and he was trapped inside; the nation-stopping saving of the 'Barrington 17' when seventeen Hunter Valley coalminers were trapped for ten days a kilometre below the earth's surface after a tunnel collapse.

But ASO's rapid rise to an organisation of such size and with such capacities had always been mysterious and frequently controversial. The clippings divided on the matter: right-wing newspapers praising the ASO as a new model for twenty-first-century business, left-wing newspapers condemning the ASO as a covert CIA-funded front like the notorious Nugan Hand Bank, pointing to the shadowy paramilitary organisation Heidl had built.

Sully was still up when I finished, sitting in his lounge room in a ripped russet recliner, reading. He seemed to know about such things, and between sips of his eccentric nightly drop, cheap sparkling shiraz, empty bottles of which littered his makeshift bookcases, he said that it had been the '80s, that government was suddenly out, business was in, outsourcing was the god, and even business stripped out costs by paying others for services now deemed *non-core*. And everything other than being a politician or CEO was suddenly *non-core*—from welfare to jails to search and rescue. Really, the only mystery was why parliament itself hadn't been outsourced. In any case, any business opening up in these areas was going to explode with growth. The ASO, according to Sully, just coincided with a new stupidity in public life.

And having explained everything, I was at a loss to understand why none of it seemed to add up to an explanation.

5

The following morning, determined to make a good start, I arrived early to find Heidl there before me. He was standing at one of the hideous bookcases looking at the hideous books publishers published. As I entered, he was pulling a book out, adding it to a pile he was making on the sideboard.

He glanced around as I went to the table and we exchanged greetings. For the first time I was able to properly take in his face. I don't think I saw another like it until the invention of HD TV. You could see multiple imperfections—crooked teeth, an errant hair rising above a highly arched eyebrow. Small details that seemed mistakes, that featured too strongly as though I was looking at a face through binoculars, both far away and very close. Perhaps that's why it's hard to say exactly what his face looked like without risking inaccuracy, for it was at once so infinitely vague and mysteriously precise that a child could draw a reasonable likeness, like the moon, and yet the likeness would tell you nothing. Sometimes, it was almost as if he wasn't really there.

Siegfried, how do you . . . how would you like us to do this? I asked.

You do it, Heidl said, his voice particularly gentle. That's how.

Not without you, I said, thinking he was joking.

That's what they're paying you for, he said, returning to his browsing.

I was taken aback. I pointed out that I could only order his thoughts; write up whatever he might wish to have written up about him, but that I couldn't exactly *make it up*.

This seemed to strike Heidl as news that was both unexpected and unwelcome. He looked at his watch, and asked if I had seen Gene Paley on my way in.

I hadn't.

It's my advance, he said. They've only paid me a third.

And, in an instant, his mood changed from one of placid serenity to a ferocious rage as his voice built from a low register to a near scream.

How the fuck? How exactly the fuck am I expected to get done all that I need to get done, if they *fucking* won't pay me?

That's the system, I said. A third on contract signature, a third on delivery of finished manuscript, a third on publication.

Heidl muttered something about it being his money; pointing at me, he said that, thanks to him, I was there so the finished book was a given and now Paley should pay up.

I tried to change the mood by changing the subject, asking him about his childhood.

As abruptly as he had begun raging, he stopped, said nothing more, and went back to browsing his glossy picture book.

I asked a general question about his parents.

Heidl put the book in its shelf and pulled another out.

I asked if he was close to his mother.

Here, he said, walking over to me with *The Chocolate Lover's Guide to Tuscany* held open. Why don't you take this home?

They're not our books.

Heidl smiled.

Take it.

It'd be theft.

You're a writer.

I am not a thief.

Maybe. But you like books.

That's not a book. It's a joke.

Oh, Heidl said, looking around as if someone were watching. I see. What sort of book would *you* like then?

I don't want any book here, Siegfried. If I wanted one, I'd ask. I'm sure they'd happily give me or you whatever we want.

Take it then, Heidl said, smiling. If they don't care, you can't either. You want it. Take it.

I don't want it, I said.

If you don't want it, take it for your wife. What's her name again?

Suzy, I said.

Suzy, he said, and as he said it, I remembered Ray's warnings. Suzy likes chocolate, right?

I tried to answer with another question about his parents but Heidl cut in.

She does, doesn't she? Ray told me all about her. And twins? That's right, isn't it? She's due to have twins any day now. She'd crave some chocolate, wouldn't she?

I was unsure what to say—with how I might divert this spilling river back to within its own banks.

She would, Heidl continued. Who wouldn't? Ray says she's lovely. Maybe I should come to Tasmania and we can work on the book closer to Suzy. That'd be so much better for you, surely?

As he continued talking, the book remained open in front of us, a large photo of molten chocolate pouring out of a beaten copper pot into a mould. For the first time, I felt an odd panic seize hold of me.

We need to get back to work, I said.

6

I began my work with Heidl with the intention of taking notes of our conversations, assuming in this way I would amass the necessary material for the autobiography, my job then to order and personalise Heidl's memories in the form of a book. But I got nowhere. I may as well have used a pair of scissors to pick up spilt mercury. My method changed. I would pursue a direct line of questioning with him on this or that subject. When I had gleaned what I could from his ramblings and riddles—at best fifteen or twenty minutes—I would halt the conversation and suggest he make some calls while I typed up the next few pages.

After I had worked away for half an hour or so, I would seek his attention, always beginning with the necessary fiction—*Can I just check a few facts with you, Siegfried?* When I could get him off the phone, always a difficult task, I would read out what I had created out of his delusions and evasions. He would lean forward on his desk, face resting on a right-hand fist. The more outlandish, the less related my story was to the few, vague facts he had outlined, the more ludicrous I was, the more pleased Heidl seemed, and the more he would claim that it accorded *exactly* with his own memory. Within five minutes he would be on the phone to Charlie at *60 Minutes* or Greg at the *Herald* or Margot at *Seven*. In that first week he cut three deals for paid interviews about himself on the basis of such inventions.

Because birth had proved impossible and childhood vexed, I thought that we might move on to what, presumably, was something easier: adolescence. It wasn't. Other than a single mention of the city of Adelaide, which may or may not have amounted to a fact, it was an hour of increasingly tortuous evasions, after which I said I had had enough and he could get on with his work. For several minutes I stared at the blinking cursor and strobing screen.

I stared—

—and stared.

But there was no other way. I would have to make it up. After another half-hour of Heidl reading the newspaper, Ray dozing and me working, I asked Heidl if I could check some details. Without looking up from his paper, he nodded, licked a finger, and turned a page.

I began to read out a lacklustre invention in which I described a Heidl adolescence in '60s Adelaide. I had done the best I could with some hoary clichés about monstrous heat, the solitude of adolescence and excessively wide streets, describing a place and time about which I knew nothing. *Speak, Memory* it wasn't. But as an explanation of Heidl's otherwise absent youth it was the best I could do. Bizarrely, Heidl seemed to like it.

I read on.

Yes, Heidl murmured in a distracted way, yes.

I read on. The high point of these teenage years for the young Heidl was, elongating the only other fact I knew about mid-twentieth-century Adelaide, the Beatles visiting in 1964.

Absolutely, Heidl said, now more attentive.

The Beatles' example had woken in the young Heidl—who I claimed saw them from a distance while working as a bellboy in the hotel in which they stayed—a desire to make something of himself.

Heidl put the newspaper down, lifted his arm, pointed at me and, jabbing his finger for emphasis, gave a reptilian hiss.

Yes, exactly! Exactly! That's *exactly* how it was.

And smiling as if he had just spotted a lost credit card, he leant forward, picked up the phone, dialled a number, and began talking. Within moments, he was cutting a deal for a paid inter-view about his adolescence, the high point of which he described as the Beatles visiting Adelaide. He was telling the journalist what I had just told him as if it were some forgotten piece of his own personal history, which, I could hear, it was quickly becoming. Only in Heidl's telling the story was replete with details I had never mentioned, as if my version was a poor gloss of the truth.

Heidl told of how a fight had erupted when a photographer had sneaked onto the Beatles' floor. John Lennon smashed the photographer's camera, punched him, and flushed his head down a toilet. Heidl, then a young bellboy, had been called to the floor to clean up the incriminating smashed camera. Lennon, who he remembered had chewed fingernails, was drunk, and there were several young women, including two topless in bed with Ringo, with whom they were drinking tea.

His storytelling was an astonishing performance, a master-class, but better was still to come.

It was close to midnight, Heidl continued, and when he went to leave, Lennon asked him what time he had started work and Heidl told him noon.

That's a tough day, the Beatle said, giving the bellboy a five-pound note.

And not knowing what to say, Heidl said, I blurted out that it'd been a hard day's evening. I remember Lennon laughed, saying it would make for a great song title. And then one day I hear this new song on the radio . . .

At that point, what little sense I had left of my own worth as a writer evaporated even further. I didn't even know if I knew what I was doing, working with a man who wasn't even sure if the life we were writing was the one he had lived, but who— nevertheless—was happy to sell on subsidiary rights to chapters as I made them up, in the process making of my dreary inventions something infinitely more interesting.

A depression came on me.

Writing had once been passion, ambition, hope. Dreams. Now I no longer knew if I was a writer or if Heidl was me, or several other even more disturbing possibilities. And yet the more I doubted myself the more I had to make sense of him and his quixotic ramblings.

Still, I told myself, it was a job. And all those things that went with a job—patterns, timetables, schedules, rituals, and work-mates—I found not unpleasant. As I met others in the tea room, or corridor, I persisted with the lie of the poetry anthology. The ruse was a burden, a joke, and an excitement, but looking back it's hard to believe anyone would have been interested enough to care whether it was true.

A book of mediaeval German folk verse was admittedly an odd project, but for a few years yet, publishing could still be an assort-ment of odd projects and make money. Within the house people each had their own books and their own worries—books to edit, design, market, sell, distribute. What did they care about an arcane project some transient editors were working on that would be published to simultaneous acclaim and oblivion? In a culture of follies, it loomed smaller than most. Now I look back on it and I think, of course, people there knew our cover was rubbish. The only person who truly believed in the deceit was me. Heidl had me from the beginning.

7

I hadn't felt good leaving Suzy alone in Hobart, heavily pregnant, and with Bo to look after. But from the moment that I accepted the job, it was clear to us both that it would be the only way we could keep our home. It wasn't a matter of what was best, but what was necessary. And this seemed of a piece with the preg-nancy, which was a force spinning me both into Suzy and wildly spinning me away from her, a violent power at once centripetal and centrifugal. We became cruel to each other for reasons that were never clear, and our fights grew more frequent. Perhaps that was because there was from the beginning something wrong about us, though we were unable to see what it was, as we were unable to see so many things.

And after we fought there was often intense sex. What had become erratic and perfunctory had returned with an odd desperate ferocity, the more so perhaps because Suzy seemed almost entirely fixated on her own pleasure. It was as if sex was all we had to explain and understand all that was inexplicable and beyond understanding. Her jolting body. Her soft lips after. Her command: Love me. I heard people say that she was beautiful. They had no idea. Yet what brought us momentarily together somehow only succeeded in leaving us more divided, and empty, and alone. Each time it only confirmed something that neither of us wanted to express.

We covered the opening abyss and our own eyes with rice-paper words: love, mostly. Family, often. Those sorts of words. The lies that blind, you could say. And yet, the words were as true as they were false. Raised by an alcoholic father, Suzy wanted a family, stability, a home. Perhaps I wanted similar things. Certainly, I used similar words to keep fear at bay. Like Suzy, I wanted a family, some peace; yet behind it all lurked death, my fear of death, a fear driven deep within me in the middle of a wild sea when death kept wanting me, when death kept dragging me down. And now my desire to taunt death, to remind death I was still alive, to taste if only a little of life before I was gone was an overwhelming force within me.

But how to live?

That was what haunted me. And Heidl made me think I answered the question wrongly. For I also wanted, with a force almost violent, to be free, alone, and, beyond all that, to escape what I could feel was coming to me and enshrouding me like a spider's web. Perhaps I was always planning my escape. It would be unfair and wrong to say I lied to myself. I lied to myself completely.

Yet sometimes when I was alone of a night in Melbourne lying on a foam mattress on Sully's floor and thought of Suzy, of our children born and unborn, of that strange necessity which joined us, I would feel a pain grip my stomach with such agonising force it would leave me panting.

8

I made it home for the weekend mid-Saturday. Suzy picked me up from the airport, and though weary was in unexpectedly good health. We had again and again been warned to expect the worst, but other than the practical difficulties of vastness, which were not inconsiderable, Suzy suffered no ill health beyond lack of sleep and occasional indigestion. She was also extraordinarily serene, as if the carrying of twins had led to a double dose of whatever soothing hormones a woman's body releases at such times. Mostly she smiled and laughed.

The doctors had said that Suzy might go into labour at any time from the six-month mark. But the sixth month had calmly given way to the seventh through which we had waited anxiously, and then the eighth came and still we waited for the waters to break, still we waited for the first contraction, for all the strange unknown unknowable things that signalled birth. Yet, amazingly, week after week passed, and now the ninth month was upon us, and the health of both Suzy and the unborn twins remained excellent. We scried Suzy's body for signs of the beginning of birth. But other than Suzy growing even larger than she already was, nothing happened.

To prepare us for the likelihood of a premature birth the hospital had a few months earlier arranged a special tour of the neonatal intensive care unit. A midwife had taken us through the humming and clicking machines, the tubes, the bright fluorescent lights, the air of heightened efficiency, to a humidicrib. There a tiny neo-reptilian creature lay encased, translucent skin beneath which florettes of fine capillaries sustained life.

This is Jo-Anne, she said. She's our pin-up girl. Nine weeks prem, and now three weeks old.

Jo-Anne seemed too much of a name for so small a puckered thing, two rash-red bulbs, one slashed with eyes, the other, larger, sprouting four tiny tendril limbs occasionally spasming. The most distinctly human thing about the baby were her wisps of fingers clutched in defiant fists.

Everything that can happen has happened to Jo-Anne, the nurse said. But she boxes on.

Twins, we were told, invariably come not just early but mostly far too early, the simple reality of the combined mass of two embryos tripping the body into contractions. The consequences were unpredictable. Many bad things, which other parents in the modern world no longer considered possibilities, were of real concern to us. And these things were mostly about death, or the cruel price that must be paid if you escape death.

As we gazed at the stomach-clutching sight of tiny babies twitching inside slightly opaque perspex humidicribs—kept levitating above death by a tangled vermicelli of monitor wires and feeding and draining and breathing tubes—we were told that twins, one or both, could die in the course of labour. And if they survived birth their struggles were far from over.

The risks were outlined in dreary, forbidding detail by a cheery woman in her late twenties. Feeding difficulties. Breathing difficulties. Developmental difficulties. Once, death of both twins common. No longer. Now death of one not uncommon. Lifelong health problems for the survivor. Impaired intellectual development. Therapy. Prem death, early death, maternal death.

We seemed to have walked out of life into a war zone, where there were no longer guarantees, happiness, the simple joys—if they were that—of parenthood and family; but rather trauma, triage, at best survival. And everywhere there still lurked death, death's possibility, death's likelihood. In consequence, the new breeze of more intimate birthing—with far less medical intervention, in low-lit rooms—which was sweeping the western world in the late twentieth century, was not to be ours.

The reality of twins pushed us back to another time, another era when the men in white coats called all the shots. We were powerless, fearful for our unborn children, and we said yes to all their rules and all their injunctions. What choice had we?

9

Early on the Sunday afternoon, a few hours before my flight back to Melbourne, Gene Paley rang to say he had read the draft chapter. He declared it good *as far as it went*. Though he felt I had conveyed something of the psychology of Heidl, what he needed now was a story. Readers need a story. *The trade*, he went on, needs a story.

So, as I was saying, he said, we build on what you have, and you forward me an outline for the entire book by Thursday.

It was the first time he'd said anything like this.

But . . . the chapter? I asked, irritated that having demanded it, Gene Paley now seemed to find it of almost no consequence. I am not sure what I had expected as feedback. The letters of Rainer Maria Rilke to a young poet? All that, I guess. And more. But I had Gene Paley, and Gene Paley paused, as if having been asked to explain an empty plate.

Oh, he said. But that's done. What we really need now is an outline.

It was becoming clear to me that I would have to pass several hurdles before I was safe as the writer of the book. What wasn't clear then but what I can see now was that Gene Paley was as desperate as Heidl and me. We had all gone too far with something we all regretted, as if the three of us now stood in front of a shallow grave that had to be filled. Trying to repress a growing resentment, I asked what sort of an outline.

You know, Gene Paley said—a rough outline. That sort of thing. Something of each chapter. CIA? Banks? Sales are pressing me for something concrete, and they're right to press me. Twenty or thirty pages are plenty. But I'll need it by Thursday so we can know whether we have a book.

After the call ended I felt angry and sick at the same time. What sort of thing was *that sort of thing*? Twenty pages wasn't much. It was also a mountain. When it came to Heidl's life, I didn't even have enough to fill a page. Over the week Heidl had talked much and told me next to nothing. By some miracle, I'd concocted a chapter out of tone, voice, the oddities of intonation and a handful of concrete details. It seemed a cruel joke to think that a further few days would produce substantially more.

I told Suzy what Gene Paley's next demand was. I said I didn't know how I might meet it, how it felt beyond me. She told me she knew that I would do it, that I always did. I was in despair and her consolations infuriated me. How could she know when I didn't? She just did, she said. How stupid was she not to see how impossible it was? It wasn't impossible for me, she replied. And in this way we began arguing.

My growing anger with Heidl, my deepest fear of failure, all grew into a rage with Suzy. I was fiddling with a kitchen knife on the sink. I was yelling how I couldn't do what Gene Paley expected of me, couldn't she understand? Using my hand to emphasise a point, without thinking about it, I drew the knife up above shoulder height, blade in, angling down.

Don't you see! I was shouting when I saw Suzy's expression change. She was staring above my head. I looked up to see a knife hovering over us, angled ready to cut and hack. And I was holding it. I don't know what I meant to do with the knife. I never had such a terrible feeling.

Kif?

And in rage, in demonstration of something I even now don't care to give words to, or in terror, or shame, I slammed that knife down in front of Suzy with such brutal force that I drove it through the stainless-steel trough.

The knife sat there upright, tip jammed hard into the steel, shivering with the slightest thrum, an accusation awaiting its crime. A vibration seemed to swirl out from that knife long after it was still, its whirlpool-like rings enveloping me. Against my will, I could feel myself beginning to be pulled down and becoming someone else, a stranger who, nevertheless, seemed familiar.

Perhaps we hurt each other in the hope of discovery, only to discover all the things we wish we had never known. I turned to Suzy. I heard myself talking. I heard myself trying to defend the book, my hours, my ambition to be a writer, my neglect of her. And with each word I uttered I felt the emptiness of everything I was saying.

And lacking words that might matter I walked out of the kitchen and went up the stairs to return to writing words that didn't matter at all.

7

1

IF MY FIRST WEEK HAD, in spite of its difficulties, proved modestly productive, the second week began badly and, as far as Heidl's interest in the memoir went, only worsened. My questions elicited nothing beyond the curtest of responses from Heidl, who sat behind his desk, quiet, absorbed in the newspaper, or making phone calls.

I remember, for example, asking him about Brett Garrett, the long-time ASO book keeper who had disappeared in 1987. I spoke of how distressing that must have been for what was still a small staff, as Garrett was said to have been much liked. I was hoping it might spark some memories.

Sad? Heidl said. He went back to reading the paper—he was fond of newspapers—and some time later, without looking up from the page, as though he were asking for help with the crossword, two words for *satisfaction* in eight letters, he said, Very sad.

I began to wonder if Heidl felt any real emotion. Or, if rather than emotions he had a gallery of poses in his mind, and when he felt it appropriate he could go to that gallery and cloak his mind in whatever was needed—sympathy, say; or anger; rage or affection. Or perhaps he felt nothing, perhaps he lived in some world beyond love, beyond grief, beyond pain. Perhaps he watched the world and he played with the evil he found in it as he played with us—Ray, Gene Paley, me.

He pointed to an article he was reading about the Queensland government denying media reports that it was working on a clandestine rocket launch project with NASA that employed Siegfried Heidl. He shook his head, dismissing the claim as wrong in its details, the statement of idiots who knew nothing about *the shadow world*. It was all said in such a way that it implied there *was* a NASA connection, the existence of which, along with the space station, he had denied when I had previously asked him about it.

At lunch he impressed on me that Cape York was *a big project* financed by a venture capital firm out of Seattle, while an hour later he said it was all a ridiculous media beat-up. By mid-afternoon it was the pet project of a Singapore media mogul whose anonymity he needed to protect.

He contradicted his own lies with fresh lies, and then he contradicted his contradictions. It was as if he couldn't exist except in the tumult of self-denial. The necessarily incomplete nature of Heidl's stories, rather than denying their supposed truth, instead confirmed it. I am not saying Heidl consciously made sure his slow-drip stories never quite matched, and were often entirely opposed. But as an instinctive ruse it was more than effective. For the challenge to reconcile such outrageous lies lay not with him, but with you, the listener.

There was so much in this that I could see might help me as a writer—so much that I hadn't known; so much that confirmed to me that I hadn't understood my craft at all. I was now with a man who had no interest in books other than stealing as many as he could, yet who instinctively understood so much more about them than I ever had.

When I began questioning Heidl once more about who the real backers were of his launch station scheme he switched again. He hinted that he had worked with the CIA on the deposing of Whitlam as the Australian prime minister in 1975, learning from the mistakes *we* had made deposing Allende in Chile.

Chile was another incantory refrain of Heidl's, not as frequently intoned as the toxo, but more disturbing. Sometimes it was as if he wished to claim as his own legacy all the tortured bodies and bloating corpses that were the Santiago national stadium and its aftermath— to say nothing of the secret war on Laos and the forgotten Laotian dead, to which he also alluded; and on and on, the incinerated and butchered and forgotten dead of Indonesia, of Haiti, of Nicaragua, of so many other countries, the endless forever forgotten dead—so many dead, in fact, so much so abhorrent and wrong, and all of which he seemed to need to proudly imply was in some way his own handiwork, but about which he would never say anything.

Sometimes when he talked like this, so softly, so reasonably, I wondered if there was no evil in which he did not wish to be implicated. It was almost as though he saw himself as a being who could multiply infinitely to visit a universal horror on the world. It was in equal measure ludicrous, laughable, and disturbing. And yet the moment you pressed him for a detail he could spin away from such nonsense, seguing into a run of questions that often felt malevolent. At such times, he talked simply, in the way the best writers write simply; his words nothing, the undertow of them everything, and I felt the weight of something cold, and cruel.

Do you love your wife? he asked that Monday in reply to my pressing him about the space station, his soft voice the voice of a priest, of a confessor, of a cop working patiently to entrap you in a crime you never committed.

And when I made no reply, a silence which also somehow felt a betrayal, he grinned slyly.

Do you, Kif?

2

Siegfried, I said (I was still respectful in those first weeks), if you know something about the CIA's involvement with deposing Whitlam, just say it.

I was thinking more on my idea, Heidl replied. How perhaps it would be better for you—and, to be frank, the book—if I came to Tasmania.

Just one fact, I said.

We could work at your home.

Just say it.

And you'd be there to help your wife.

But don't bother me about my private life.

What's her name again? Suzy?

That's not the subject of this book, Siegfried.

Suzy, he said. That's it. You know, Kif, you'd make a lousy CEO.

You'd make a great novelist.

A good CEO *shares*. That ability to open up with colleagues.

His terrifying smile. His pulsing cheek. His corpse eyes.

How can I, Heidl said, be loyal to someone who won't even tell me his child's name?

That was too much for me.

How can your wife be loyal to her husband, I said, who won't even tell her his real name?

This aggression of yours, Kif, Heidl went on, it is *so* unnecessary. If you were working at home you wouldn't feel so stressed. I'll speak to Paley about it.

I said nothing, forlornly hoping, perhaps, that he might weary. He didn't. He couldn't.

You shouldn't take their side, Kif, accusing me of wicked things.

Whose side?

The banks. You're meant to be helping me tell my story.

Your story doesn't have a side. It's got more angles than a smashed mirror.

What is it then?

He had me. I had no idea.

It's a novel, I said.

There was perhaps a touch of admiration I couldn't disguise within what I said. He had something I doubted I'd ever have; that cold pleasure that maybe was necessary to finish a novel. To steal. To kill, perhaps.

Heidl leant back, his executive's leather chair wearily flatulent.

I mean it's something, isn't it, I said. Some people rob banks with sawn-off shotguns and balaclavas. No one sees their face. After, if they get away, they hide. They're careful how they spend the stolen money.

But you—*you* rob a bank out in the open. You rob banks with handshakes, with photographers and TV crews in tow. Then you spend their millions in front of their eyes on madness. Your face is everywhere. They even give you an Order of fucking Australia.

The suggestion that the theft of seven hundred million dollars might in any way be a criminal act was sometimes taken by Heidl as a vicious and unfounded slur. But I was losing my fear of giving offence, and that day, in any case, he seemed in an affable mood.

Madness after madness, I went on. Armed troops—

PJs, Heidl corrected me. Parachute jumpers. Emergency workers trained with paramilitary structure and discipline. And we were proud of that discipline. They were the best, all five hundred of them.

A submarine then—I mean, *a sub*?

Heidl smiled. *Two* mini-subs and one submersible, he said.

A sub's something, I said.

Heidl laughed.

It is, he said. Nasty inside though. So confined. We employed a psychologist part-time to deal with the issues our submariners had. And that's because health and safety were always primary drivers for us. Kif, that's too easily forgotten. Put that in, it's important that be noted.

And that set him off for some time, as if he were still the CEO dictating an annual report, pointing out industry best standards, award conditions, professional development programs, strategic goal setting, and so on, and so forth, and soon enough he was back talking toxo. Ray called such gabble *heidling*. While Heidl could, on occasion, be charming, even interesting, and once or twice—as when he told me that ghost writing a memoir was simply a case of an I for an I—even witty, his talk was mostly a ceaseless nonsense. I sought, yet again, to take us back to the autobiography.

3

What I don't get, I said, was why ASO's board went along with it all. They're legally responsible. Why didn't they ever ask any questions?

The board? he said, and shook his head slowly, as if recalling a wistful memory.

He went over to a dozen archive boxes of documentary material that had accumulated in a corner of our office, opened one, sorted through some papers and finally produced a photograph that he handed to me.

Here's why, he said.

The back of the photograph was a typed sheet, sticky-taped on, which read 'ASO Council, 1986' and contained a list of names.

At first, as I scanned the conceited faces of the ovine dozen that formed the ASO's governing board, I was at a loss to understand.

He pointed to one blue-blazered, silver-haired figure, replete with bow-tie.

Eric Knowles, he said. Chairman.

He riffled through another box, lifted out a framed photograph and passed it to me. It was a photo of a moored mini-submarine.

The ASO *Eric Knowles*, Heidl said. Every council member had a boat or plane named after him or her. Some had a boat *and* a plane. Knowles had the lot—a sub, a towboat, a helicopter ship *as well as* a chopper, a yacht. And our biggest plane. I just had to keep them coming, keep them feeling important. It wasn't so hard.

He showed me more photos of board members at launches and events in their honour.

Didn't they think—I began, but he cut me off with a smirk.

Think? Most people are other people's opinions, Kif. As long as I supplied them with theirs they were perfectly happy.

He ran his finger along a row of people till he picked himself out.

That's me. Just another bloke, he said.

In those weary photos of corporate record I first began to grasp the genius of Heidl's method, the reduction of himself to the claustrophobic smallness of the mythic Australian everyman. *Just another bloke*, one more Australian conformist, as unremarkable as he was elusive.

Heidl handed me a large cupped glossy of a smiling Eric Knowles about to swing a champagne bottle on the bow of another ship named after him.

Flattery, he said. So obvious, so easy. It's not foolproof, but it is proof of fools.

He looked at me wistfully.

You'll make a wonderful book out of all this, he said, as if I were launching one more spurious vessel.

4

That *fucker* Knowles, Heidl said when he walked in at 11.50 am on Tuesday, almost four hours past the time he had appointed as our start that day. His hatreds were unexpected. He strove for a benign tone in conversation that often came close to simpering. But occasionally he could seem almost murderous were it not that after declaring his homicidal intent he would immediately smile, and return to the tone of mealy-mouthed platitudes that were more his stock in trade. But that morning he was angry in a way I hadn't before seen.

Look at this, Heidl said, dropping a newspaper next to my keyboard. Look!

The headline read—

LOCK HEIDL AWAY FOR LIFE, SAYS KNOWLES

Giving interviews everywhere, Heidl snarled, his hand shaking, as if he had *nothing* to do with it!

Today's adopted emotion seemed to be disgust.

The trial's only weeks away and he's saying I was clearly some fucking criminal genius who deceived him as much as the banks.

With a movement at once apathetic and aggressive he dropped himself into his executive's seat, and just as abruptly stood back up.

Well, I said, I guess we really do need to sort the book as quickly as—

I need to speak to Gene Paley, he said, his gaze skidding around the room as if something was hiding from him behind the tawdry bookcases. I need twenty grand to keep going. It's a fraction of what he owes me.

Heidl went to the door and turned to me as he was leaving.

How can he expect I waste my life sitting here when he won't pay me my advance?

And with that he was gone, only—and uncharacteristically—to

return a few minutes later. He slumped in his chair, staring straight ahead, drumming his fingers on his desk. His fluttering lips were, I realised, forming silent sentences.

Why does any of it matter? he finally said out loud.

I asked him if he got his money.

If a face can be said to be one of despair, his was as he spoke.

He wants that outline before he'll give me a cent more, Heidl said, and his voice grew agitated. Have you done it yet?

I pointed out that it wasn't so easy to write anything if he was never about.

In a series of elaborate gestures so overwrought it suggested a kabuki performance, Heidl rolled his executive's chair forward, rested his elbows on the desk, unfurled his hands outwards, and after several moments slowly dropped his weary, lost face into them. Head cradled so, he massaged his face as if it were heavy clay. This went on for a good minute or more, until, with a sudden jolt, his head jerked up with an entirely different face—a smiling, energised face. Disgust was gone, though what had arrived in its place was uncertain.

Enough small talk, he said, though nothing had been said for some time. *Enough!*

With a clap he brought his hands together in an executive's clasp.

We really need to get you to work, he said, smiling a thin executive's smile.

And so, after a week of prevarication, presumably mindful of needing another advance from Gene Paley, we—after a fashion—began.

You know people criticise the ASO, he began, but we employed hundreds of people. Hundreds! At our peak, just over 840—no—838 full-time positions and another ninety-six part-time. And that's without the small businesses in Bendigo we kept going with engineering works and other things. What do they call that? The magnification effect? That has to be a good thing. And that's what we did. Good things. Write that.

You didn't make money, I said, feeling irritated that he was telling me nothing that wasn't on the public record.

Does the government make money?

You weren't the government. You were a business.

Roger that. We were a model business. We won an export award.

You didn't export anything.

That was a mystery to me as well. But we were a successful business. That's why they gave me the Order of Australia.

You weren't Australian.

I didn't have a passport. There's a difference.

Mostly there isn't.

Roger that. The citation for my Order of Australia speaks of 'the innovative reinvention of a late-twentieth-century business'. It—

Businesses have to stand the test of the market.

Well, we stood that test well. The market gave us seven hundred million dollars.

You never gave it back.

The market never worried about that. It seemed like the future.

You lied to the banks.

I told the truth about our abilities. Showed them our shipping containers. We created jobs. Saved lives. Fought fires. We rescued sailors. Mineworkers. Took industrial training to another level. Set new levels of excellence. And the banks endorsed us, backed us all the way.

With other people's money.

All the way. Besides, what company uses its own money? I can't see how I am any different. And if we had more time, we might have been a global success story.

How?

How? We might have made money, that's how. Why is what we did wrong, but when others do it, it's okay? I don't see the difference.

They're honest.

You believe that? Really?

How could you convince the banks you did earn money?

Heidl looked up at me while he spoke and for once his black eyes were bright and glittered with some conviction that was at the same time a question.

I turned their money into a magic circle. They gave, they received. That's all business is, isn't it? That's why the world loved me. Isn't it?

5

I had just made it home to Sully's place that evening when Ray rang to say the train was leaving and we had to be on it. In other circumstances, other nights, I would have refused. But I needed a drink badly. I met him at the Beast, and after an hour there we went on to the Gutter and the Stars, and from there to a night-club somewhere in the city that Ray promised was all the good things nightclubs never are. It wasn't. But by then it was too late to leave.

Just as the Melbourne dawn began melting like dripping through the crowded back seat of our taxi, over me, Ray and two women Ray called Pink and Purple because of the colours of their dresses, I asked Ray about the containers Heidl kept mentioning.

I don't get it, I said. Hundreds of containers packed with millions of dollars of gear, and the ASO still couldn't make money.

I lifesurf, Pink said.

Yeah, Purple agreed. That's what we do. We just, you know, whoosh! Wherever.

Whoosh! giggled Pink. Whooshy-whoosh!

Pink and Purple were both there for Ray, or for each other, or because they, like us, were too far gone to be anywhere else.

They were empty, Ray said, one hand sliding under Purple's miniskirt.

It was a great idea, I said. All that gear and expertise.

The containers were empty, Ray said in an affected accent, as if he had a mouth full of marbles.

It just didn't make money, I said.

Where you from again? Purple asked.

Norway, Pink said. They already told us. He's a Norwegian writer.

I'm a Jez Dempster girl myself, Purple said. Not that I've read him, but I know I will.

That's why he talks funny, Pink said. Say something, Rayban.

Olly-bolly, Ray said.

Wow, Purple said.

Really, Ray said, his voice even more ridiculous. Empty.

What? Purple asked. What are you doing, cheeky boy?

I turned to Ray, who seemed to be licking Purple's ear.

What?

Heidl said I wasn't to tell you, Ray said into Purple's lobe.

There was nothing in them?

Maybe some spiders.

Speak some Danish stuff, Purple said.

Nothing?

Yeah, nothing, Ray said, pushing and playing with Purple as he spoke. Two hundred empty fuckn shipping containers.

That's not Danish, Pink said. I'd know if it was fucking Danish.

Outside the taxi Melbourne was slopping around in the ceaseless Melbourne rain, dissolving tail lights and traffic lights.

Things drifted and floated and nothing was fixed, and still we went on into that kaleidoscope of suppurating red and green wounds. Pink said they had to stop the taxi because she was going to vomit.

The cab driver slammed on his brakes, and ordered us all out.

Empty? I said.

Get the fuck out! the cab driver screamed.

We stood on the edge of St Kilda Esplanade, as Pink vomited and Ray laughed, and when I looked up I saw shaping out of the darkness and sheets of rain a great gaping mouth, a smile perhaps five metres high, framed within a giant white face, replete with staring, satanic blue eyes, above which red and yellow rays radiated into a vaguely oriental proscenium.

It was Mr Moon, the celebrated entrance to the famed Luna Park. There was something hellish about his vast, blood-red lips, the deeply etched lines of his cheeks, his odd arched plucked eyebrows—a grubby, grinning Mephisto.

He's a bloody funhouse mirror, Ray said. Look at Heidl long enough and all you can see is yourself.

Purple took offence and said they were going home now and we could fuck off back to the North Pole.

Only uglier, Ray said.

We watched the two women stagger across the highway to flag a taxi going in the opposite direction to us.

I learnt things just watching him using a fork, Ray said.

Shit-eating two-head Tasmanians! Pink yelled out at us as a cab pulled up for them and Purple gave us the bird.

Fuck off, one-heads! Ray yelled back, giving them a cheerful wave.

What did you learn?

I can't tell you, Ray said, blowing a kiss to the departing cab.

What?

Lots.

6

I had slept two hours, my tongue was a seatbelt buckle and I had arrived late to work to discover Heidl already behind his executive's desk, his back to me, talking on the phone.

That's *what* I said, he was saying in a hushed, if agitated way. Knowles. Eric Knowles.

Not wanting to disturb his call, I quietly set up for the day's work, arranging paper, notes and notebooks, as Heidl went on.

Blown away. Ten thousand. Okay?

I booted up the Mac Classic, and as it whirred and clattered he swung his chair back round.

Thank you, he said, giving me a long stare. Great to chat.

I looked away and when I looked back he smiled his dreadful smile.

Big night, I said, and, by way of explanation, added, *Ray.*

I hit the keyboard at random to give the impression I was back at work. Thinking: Blown away? Eric Knowles?

I thought so many things about Siegfried Heidl—but this!—the ordering, perhaps, of a murder!—*this* chilled me. But almost immediately, I was unsure. What exactly had I heard? Heidl stood up and said he had to go to a meeting with a celebrity agent who wanted to represent him.

I thought Tommy Hiller represented you?

I know that, Heidl said. But what does he know?

I waited for ten minutes after Heidl left, then I went to his desk. I noticed how he had over the days personalised it with some executive toys, papers, and two photographs of him and his family, one formal, and recent; the other a faded Instamatic shot showing them camping years before when their kids were babies, sitting around a campfire in front of a pied red and white 55 series LandCruiser. I picked up the phone and pressed redial. As I waited for someone to pick up, there was a knock on the door.

Hello, a recorded message answered in my ear. Bertie's Pizza 'n' Pasta Takeaways, Glen Huntly.

The door opened and Gene Paley came in—the first time he had ever visited our office. I was holding the phone out from my ear, in, I felt, a picture of shock, as though I had been caught midway through some social call.

Saw Siegfried leaving, Gene Paley said. Just wanted to say how much I'm looking forward to reading your outline tomorrow.

Our shop is closed and will reopen at—

That's very helpful, I said to Bertie's Pizza 'n' Pasta Takeaways answering machine. Thank you. I put Heidl's phone down.

It's going well? Gene Paley asked.

I think I'm finally onto the truth.

Great, Gene Paley said. Gene Paley made a clicking noise with his mouth and winked. Outside the primacy of his office he seemed to cultivate this odd nervous affectation.

Yes, I said. Really great.

Siegfried doesn't seem to be here that much.

He says I need my space to write.

Without him here though, Gene Paley said, there isn't that much you can write *about*.

It was a warning. As Gene Paley went to leave, I blurted out a question. I asked him what length an *ideal* memoir should be, as if that might wildly diverge from the length of any other memoir.

Well, he said, pausing at the door, with a celebrity memoir it's more weight than length. Heavy always helps. Look at American novels—six hundred pages and more and who reads them? We say they're substantial but a lot of people are frightened to lift them. I'm terrified I'll dislocate an arm in bed if I open one. But they get great reviews because no reviewer can be bothered getting to the end, so they have to say it's good. Australian memoir is the same as American novels. Big is the bluff that always works.

So . . . six hundred pages? I said, a cud of despair rising, thinking surely not every American novel was that long or that bad. How many words is that?

Oh, look, for this, one hundred to one hundred and twenty-five thousand words would be fine.

I confessed I didn't think there was a hundred thousand words in Siegfried Heidl. To be frank, I felt like saying I didn't think there was a sentence in him.

What, I asked, might be the minimum?

Gene Paley pulled a face.

Seventy-five thousand, I guess.

The maths seemed not worth pondering. Still, I pondered it. A good day for me on my novel had been three hundred words. Times the twenty-three days I had left equalled 6,900 words. Which was a short story. Or less than one tenth of Gene Paley's minimum memoir. And, as well, there still remained unwritten the outline Gene Paley had previously requested. I suddenly felt very cold.

We can put in a lot of white space, Gene Paley said, thinking it through. There are tricks we can use. Make the typeface larger. Increase the leading. Use heavy paper stock to help with the illusion. There's a danger with that approach though.

Sorry? I said. I hadn't really heard anything since 75,000 words.

People might read it. But I'm confident, Gene Paley said as he opened the door, that you're going to give us something even readers will like. By the way, he said with a sudden grimace, have you seen the latest *Woman's Day*? Heidl talking about meeting John Lennon. Great story. Except it's ours, not theirs. We have him exclusively. I wasn't pleased, but Siegfried's given me his word it won't happen again.

He waved a meek hand in farewell.

I look forward to reading your outline tomorrow, Kif.

The full horror of my situation swept over me. The outline

had until now defeated me. I hadn't a clue how to write even that. I was surfing a mudslide and trying not to fall off.

Gene, I stammered. I don't think tomorrow will be possible.

You don't?

I'm sorry. You can see there are . . . absences. That take time to fill. That need—

Gene Paley lifted his arm in the traffic cop gesture.

Hold that thought, Kif, he said. The sales and marketing meeting is next Wednesday. I can give you until ten that morning, but no later.

And with a final click and wink he was gone.

7

After Gene Paley left, I sat at the conference table. Seeing no alternative, I thought more on the maths. It was never my strong suit. Heidl left me feeling much the same as mathematics. The combination of calculation and his character were numbers less than reassuring. I had a little over four weeks left. Allowing a week each for the second and third drafts—ludicrous, I thought, and frankly, whatever way you looked at it, perhaps impossible—I had under three weeks to finish the first draft, which, on balance, was probably even more insane. For the first draft, I somewhat generously subtracted the confusion of notes that I had made, designating them, in a moment of optimism, as 8,000 words of finished manuscript. With this wishful arithmetic as my only compass I divided 75,000 by twenty-one days and realised I had henceforth to get 3,571 words written each day. 3,571! Still, nothing mattered now in the face of this almost impossible target—not my failings nor Heidl's.

I typed:

HEIDL MEMOIR: SCHEDULE
(daily total 3,571 wds)

Week 1	25,000 wds (draft 1) (2 days gone)
Week 2	25,000 wds (draft 1)
Week 3	25,000 wds (draft 1)
Week 4	Draft 2 75,000 wds (rewrite)
Week 5	Draft 3 (*fin*) 75,000 wds (revise)

Plan A, at which I was now staring, was clear and definite in demanding of me an industry that was beyond reason. 3,571 words a day? 3,571 words *every* day? 3,571 words *seven days a week*? I tried to think of a Plan B. Murder?

Perhaps—just perhaps—if I had a willing collaborator—someone who was prepared to do the work, to answer my questions and fill out the details—I could do it. I hit the Delete key and watched the cursor unzip my timetable of infinite hope.

I started typing again.

HEIDL MEMOIR: SCHEDULE

Week 1	grow feathers
Week 2	fly to the moon
Week 3	cure motor neurone disease
Week 4	run fastest 100 metres in human history
Week 5	write a book (*fin*)

Then I deleted that too. I stared at the nightmare of the blank screen and the panting cursor. The most I had ever managed in a single day working on my novel were 562 words, and many of them had veered dangerously close to plagiarism. There again, I reassured myself, this job was solely plagiarism, for what was ghost writing but robbing from the life of someone else and calling it a book?

I rechecked my figures. Perhaps I had it wrong. I mostly did. And once again I did the long division and once again I got the same number, the same answer, the same question: how was it possible? Because every way I looked at it, it wasn't.

8

Heidl returned from his meeting a little after lunch, a subdued, silent Ray in tow. He heidled some more and none of it to any point or any use. And not five minutes later he announced that he was off again: another meeting, another journalist, he said.

Another lie.

More out of perversity than curiosity I asked who he was meeting.

It's secret, he said.

I asked him why everything was a secret, and he shot me a look that might have been plaintive or might have been mocking, or both.

Without secrets how are we to live? he said.

And, with that, he was gone.

I felt utter defeat. Exhausted by Heidl, hungover, I lay on the floor and almost immediately fell into a heavy sleep, without dreams. I woke at dusk to an extreme sunset. The sky was a series of bruises and purple welts. I watched the red sun drop like a beaten head into a gutter.

9

Over the last two days of that second week—as Heidl continued to bluster and prevaricate—it was as if I had finally accepted the heaviest of burdens, taken the full measure of its weight across my back and shoulders, and bracing every fibre of my being begun to stagger forward. In my more optimistic moments I thought I might even possibly make it.

I now took down very little of what Heidl said. I was too poor a typist for that, and, in any case, most of what he said was babble. I found myself less and less interested in what Heidl might say and instead concentrated on the way he said it. To help me reach my word count for the day I took to drinking in the sound of him, straining to grasp the music of his voice on the phone in the background; striving to catch the odd clip of his sentences, a beat from which I might begin cantilevering out a flying buttress of clauses that could bear the weight of a sentence, and in turn begin building up a page with paragraphs of invention. My prose began rumpling into new shapes—those allusive, elusive arches of sentences composed of two opposing questions reaching out over emptiness: Maybe if I tell you this, or perhaps if I were to say that . . .

They were arabesques of nonsense but there was a music in them. It was almost jazz. He was Thelonious Monk and I just tried to hang in, playing around his parts, filling in all the notes and beats that he didn't bother with, rough inventions of childhood and career he needed me to find to make him whole.

And in this way, I found the ludicrous figure of 3,571 words bringing on in me a capacity for invention I had never known writing my novel.

But now I can see that all the time I thought I was simply mimicking a tone, catching a rhythm, something more was being deeply etched into me. For I was learning from him the power of suggestion rather than demonstration; of evasion rather than enlightenment; of giving only one fact—or really, just the rumour of a fact—and then letting the reader invent everything else around it.

I was, without being aware of it, learning to distract from

the truth by amusing the reader; to flatter the reader by playing on what they believed to be their virtues—their ideas of goodness and decency—whilst leading them ever further into an alien darkness that was the real world and, perhaps, the real them; and, on occasion, I feared, the real me.

And the more I saw of him, the more I found every smile, every gesture full of falsity, and each day the more frightened of him I grew. I would drive home in the Nissan Skyline, grateful to have escaped that room and him, but I hadn't really escaped anything, for as soon as I was at Sully's place I'd get in the shower, turn the taps hard on, and once more run Sully's boiler out of hot water, too ashamed to tell him that I was all that long time simply trying to wash Heidl off me.

And every night when I thought I was washing him away I was deluding myself. For he was entering me, and there was nothing I could do about it. I sensed it, how could I not? But I ignored it because the words were beginning to come. He was entering me and there were more and more words, and with each word somehow less and less of me. I was a man unmoored, once more adrift in a wild sea. Only this time, I did not know it. I had let him in. I did not know it, and all that time Heidl did.

10

If I were a better writer I'd reimagine this whole story as a vampire novel. But I am just reporting what happened. It's not that I didn't resist. I did. It's just that I wasn't as good at resisting as I thought. And that's why the words *con man* always struck me as inadequate in describing Heidl. Con men are after your money. Perhaps that was true of him. Given his long list of criminal charges, I guess it *was* true of him. But Heidl was also after something more. *Heidl was after your soul.*

And at first Heidl offered me friendship, warmth, a certain camaraderie—or as much as a man like Heidl could pretend to such things—and, in addition, what I perhaps craved more than anything else, respect as a writer. He even asked me to help him write a speech, a keynote address he told me he had been asked to deliver in a few weeks' time at a national conference of auditors in Albury-Wodonga. Their theme, he told me, was 'Auditing: Be Seen, Be Recognised'.

Taken aback though I was that such an invitation would ever be made, incredulous as I felt when I read his speech 'notes'— scatterings of words that only occasionally threatened to form a coherent sentence, I confess I found his drivel about integrity, the collapse of ethics in modern life and the criminality of contemporary society not without its own magnificence. To be frank, I felt it impossible to better his opening line: 'Bleating sheep should not seek to howl with wolves.'

That it was stolen from a '70s New Age bestseller about a Basque shepherd I only discovered years later. There was, though, something almost admirably audacious in beginning a talk fraudulently to a conference of those whose job it is to root out fraud. A man of unexpected shallows, in another life he may have risen to be a self-help expert, topping the *New York Times* bestseller lists and giving absurdly priced motivational lectures. And who knows what else? Personal branding. Perhaps even fragrance lines. As it was, his prospects were sadly reduced to me, a memoir, and a gathering of auditors.

I could see that for others he seemed aglow with some indefinable aura, a wickedness that was also a glamour; a conspiratorial mystery that somehow you and you alone felt invited to join, and at its apex, a gorgeous darkness that wasn't quite evil and wasn't quite not evil. No—I felt none of that, or at least not at first, perhaps because Ray had so frightened me with his warnings that I didn't dare see any of Heidl's exotic charm as other than subterfuge, deceit, manipulation. But I sensed that it was something more than these things, something else—the chance to submit and subjugate yourself to another, and, after all, isn't that what so many of us secretly crave? To be told what to do, and what not to do? To not be alone? Who does not feel the immense attraction of being led?

If I had been a reasonable man I might have liked him reasonably well and done a reasonable job in writing his story. But, much as I pretended to others and myself, I was very far from reasonable. And as the second week drew to its close, though there was growing within me a feeling towards him that was compounded of loyalty, sympathy, and complicity, there was also arising in me, and maybe in even stronger measure, a different, opposed emotion. And this other emotion made me shudder. Does hatred always begin in recognition?

8

1

THE BEAST AT EIGHT on a Friday evening had about it the fetid languor of pubs of the era; that sticky fug of smoke and yeast and sweet acridity of odour, the ease in the early evening of a battlefield between bombardments. Ray drank steadily, with the grim efficacy of a kitchen appliance that existed solely to empty glasses.

Heidl's bullshitting you again, I said to Ray as he downed another pot.

Even before I met Heidl, I had known from Ray that they had been working together on some project in Cape York for an extended period of time. Yet I had found it hard to believe Ray's story of them searching there for a site for a rocket launch facility. It had seemed too far-fetched until the Queensland government's refutation of it, which was, somehow, in the topsy-turvy view of Heidl that I was increasingly taking on, weird confirmation. But what Ray had just said left me once more in a state of disbelief.

Heidl didn't tell me, Ray said. I was at a party a few weeks ago and bumped into Pedro Morgan. The old ops manager at the ASO. There were a few other of the ASO senior commanders there. They were all close to Heidl. Best mates. And we got talking about Spaceportal.

Spaceportal?

The company that's behind the proposal to build the rocket

launching facility in Cape York. Ziggy set it up after he was let out on bail.

I never got that Cape York thing. It's a thousand ks from anywhere.

Exactly—that's why it's perfect. But because Heidl's a bankrupt, and facing further charges, he can't be a director or CEO of Spaceportal. He's not allowed to borrow money.

So?

So, he gets six of the senior ex-ASO guys; he says if you're mates—if you're *real* mates—you'll come in on this with me, because this thing is going to be worth a fortune. Satellites are where the world is going—communications, TV, you name it.

But Heidl runs it.

Not officially. He's a bankrupt. He's not allowed by law.

But unofficially?

Well, Ray said. Sure. He's Ziggy Heidl. And he persuades them to remortgage their homes and put their money into capitalising Spaceportal. In return, they become the directors.

So you're telling me the Cape York thing isn't financed by Singapore millionaires or NASA?

What?

Or the CIA?

I'm just telling you what I know.

It's paid for by ex-ASO employees out of their life savings.

If you want to put it that way. It sounded a good deal.

So Heidl's just scamming off his mates, I said.

I dunno, Ray said, and went to the bar.

It's his last big con job, I said when he came back.

I mean it could be, Ray said. But I don't think so. They're smart guys. They wouldn't be putting their money in, risking their homes if they didn't think it was a good idea to build a rocket launching station in Cape York.

But why do they think it's a good idea?

Well, there's a lot of evidence. It's closer to the moon there.

Ray looked to me as if I might reassure him on this point.

Isn't it?

What? Australia?

Cape York, Ray said. With less certainty, he mumbled, The equator? It's . . . fatter there. Right?

Fatter?

Or something. He coughed, readied himself as if for a recital, and told me that the scientific consensus was that it was one of the best places in the world from which to launch rockets.

Really, I said. Says who?

The . . . eh, the *consensus*.

What consensus, Ray?

Ray looked at me quizzically and murmured, Scientists?

What scientists, Ray?

I don't fuckn know. I'm not the expert, mate. But there's a lot out there about it all.

Have you seen any scientific papers saying this?

Not exactly.

No?

Not personally. Okay? But Ziggy has. He told me.

Heidl told you?

Several thoughts, all irreconcilable, seemed to hit Ray at once.

Did he show you? I asked. Ray?

He raised an empty glass to his lips and, realising his error, swore. When he next spoke his voice was furtive.

He had these . . . *papers* . . . scientific *papers* in his briefcase.

Did you read them?

Ray thought about this. His mouth went to form several different words, as though there were a dozen fish hooks in his lips pulling them in opposing directions. It was as if he were once more in a remote New Guinea river gorge looking at a damp map of Irian Jaya.

Well, not exactly.

Not exactly?

He told me then.

And you believed him?

His mouth did the fish hook thing again.

I did. But when you put it . . . like that. I dunno.

And his old friends were paying for all this?

Mates. Well. Yeah.

It was never going to happen, Ray.

I dunno, mate. Besides, even if it didn't, that doesn't make it a bad idea.

Can't you see? It's just another lie.

Don't you think it'd be an unreal thing for Australia? Its own Houston?

It's a good idea for Ziggy.

What's wrong with having good ideas? Anyway, the atmosphere is thinner up there in the tropics. Isn't it?

Is it?

I think Ziggy told me that. I don't know. Or Pedro.

How would Pedro Morgan know?

I guess Ziggy told him. I told you. He had the research.

Heidl?

Heidl, yeah. But wouldn't it be great? I mean Australia having its own rocket launching base.

Heidl? The only guarantee they've got is Heidl's word?

I suppose so, Ray said, a little deflated. I know that was all bullshit what happened in the Queensland parliament though.

When the government denied it had anything to do with the proposal?

Yeah.

But that would have suited Heidl, I said. Because once the government denied it, other people thought that they were covering up and that there must be something in it. Or that if our government wasn't, then another government, the Americans, were. And that made Heidl look far bigger and more important than he was.

Ray went quiet a second time.

2

And then he said:

It was beautiful up there, you know. Just landing where we wanted. The night sky.

He went on talking like that, about swimming with dugongs, about hunting with local blackfellas, the taste of goanna cooked on a fire, sweet and full, the particular odour of a mangrove swamp halfway between stench and perfume and how he rubbed the mud into his body so he could work out exactly what the smell was and how it was something different again, how one day with the blackfellas they caught a big leatherback turtle, and the blackfellas broke its legs so that it would neither wander off nor die quickly and its meat would not go off in the tropical heat. They killed it two days later.

The taste was unreal, he said. Great meat. But you know what was amazing. I was looking into that turtle's eyes and it just wanted to live. It wouldn't die. Two days before we ate it and it wouldn't die. It wanted to live, he said. It's an incredible thing.

I remember that night, he went on, on this beach, just staring into that sky. Like the world was new. It was—

He stopped, searching for words.

—*free.*

Maybe that was all it was.

Maybe.

Ray took a swig from his beer, belched, and wiped his wet mouth with the back of his hand.

Maybe that's something, he said, maybe it's everything. I dunno. It was fuckn great, that's all I know.

We both went quiet for a moment.

The thing is, Ray said, the turtle wanted *to live*. That's what I remember. Looking at its eyes. It was in agony. But it wouldn't stop living.

Ray seemed to have drifted back to some other memory. He ran a thumb up and down the condensation on his beer glass.

Pedro and them don't know, he said.

Don't know what?

The money's all gone.

Their money?

Heidl blew it all on us frigging around in choppers for a year and a half. That new LandCruiser of his. A few other toys.

You didn't tell them?

You fuckn joking?

So they'll lose their houses?

Well, I don't know about that. Ziggy will—he'll get their money back.

You just said their money's gone.

I don't know. Probably. Maybe. That's what Heidl told me. That's why—I'm guessing—why he rang you. He needed to look like he was going to deliver the book to pay them back a bit.

I might have felt angry if I wasn't so despairing, and I might have given in to my despair if I wasn't so angry. As it was, the effect was to leave me numb.

So I'm just another con?

I didn't say that, Ray said.

It was my turn to be quiet.

I mean, he's doing the right thing, isn't he? Ray said, screwing up a beer coaster. He's using the advance to give them a bit of their money back?

He is?

Well, what did he tell you then?

I told Ray how I thought I had overheard Heidl on the phone ordering a hit on Eric Knowles. Maybe the money was for that, I said. And I told him how when I'd rung the number I had got a pizza parlour answering machine. I laughed, but Ray seemed to take a more serious view.

You think you know him, and then you find out you don't know anything. You think he's telling the truth and it turns out to be all lies. You think he's telling the most outrageous bullshit and it turns out to be all true.

I think he just lies. Maybe he doesn't even care about the money and it's just a game.

Or maybe, Ray said, he needs the advance to quieten Pedro Morgan. Or maybe he just wants it to pay for our hotel. We've been there two months now.

There is no book, is there?

Ray looked away.

Is there, Ray?

Fucked if I know, Ray said, staring down at his drink. You tell me. You're the writer.

There is no fucking book. It's just a new scam to pay something off the old scam, and Heidl just keeps moving on.

Just finish the thing and then there will be a book. That's what you want to be, isn't it? A writer? To be a fuckn writer? So just write the book. Heidl doesn't care what you do. Write or don't write. It's up to you.

We drank on.

The hours passed, Ray flirting unsuccessfully with a goth, and after midnight we found ourselves leaning against a wall, shouting to be heard over the band and the crowd.

Why hang with the prick? I asked Ray.

What? Ray yelled.

Heidl, I said.

Heidl? *Fuck* him.

Why?

Because he's got into me, Ray said. That's why.

What do you—?

He gets into you, Kif, that's what I fuckn mean.

Ray pinched two fingers together and holding them close to my forehead twisted them back and forth like an auger.

He gets into you and he gets into you, he bores into you and you just . . . just . . .

What?

Can't, Ray said, dropping his hand. Just *can't* escape.

And he began babbling on about slimy mud.

I couldn't see Ray. What was standing next to me was an ordinary man; perhaps of all things, a weak man, a weak man whom I had made the mistake of for too long thinking was a strong man.

What's he got over you, Ray?

What do you mean? He hasn't got—

It's like he's got you scared.

And having said it, I immediately regretted saying what I thought Ray would take as the greatest insult.

He took out his pouch of Champion Ruby and started rolling a cigarette, eyes determinedly fixed on the tobacco and paper.

Maybe I am, Ray said quietly and licked a paper. Maybe I am, mate.

I thought it was only about the book.

Ray laughed.

Oh, mate, he said, and looking up from his durrie, shook his head.

And then we talked of other things, and after a further time my stories were once more his stories, we again agreed on all things, and later when we left the bar everything was as it always had been between us, as natural and close as if we were brothers.

154

3

When we were young, sometimes I'd drive over to the remote
Tasmanian west coast, to where Ray was working as a welder
on the last of the great hydro-electric construction schemes,
the damming of the Pieman River, said to be named after a
Tasmanian convict, a pieman, who, on escaping, had killed and
eaten his fellow escapees. Five hours up into the empty ache
of the highlands then plunging back down into the wild rainforested gorges of the west, until I hit the dying mining towns,
spectral ruins in a moonscape of desolation, wounded blues and
greens and bright bronze rock glistening in the forever rain and
lonely yellow headlight trails, turning north past the last of the
rusting ripple iron shanties, seven stubbies down, maybe more,
gunning it up the green-walled mountain passes until I finally
reached the last great dam construction village of Tullah.

Listening to Ray in the St Kilda bar, I could see he was
engaged in a mysterious battle between his desire to be free and
where that desire had now led him—servitude to a monster. Ray
seemed suddenly childlike, defenceless; he, the man who had
first made his name as a pub brawler in that mountain camp;
he, who had strutted his stuff there, claiming to be a French aris-
tocrat, daring anyone to laugh at him, to throw the first punch,
going up to the bar in the Tullah camp and, in what everyone
else in Tullah thought was French, asking for a beer.

Je suis more drinko.

Daring someone to laugh, because it was funny, to acknowledge the absurd joke that it was and he was and the whole
world of the Tasmanian mountain camps were, the world of
men pretending to be something that wouldn't quickly be
consumed and transformed into broken bodies collecting
pension cheques and queuing for medicines for their emphy-
sema, their diabetes, their ruinous hearts and broken backs

and increasingly confused minds; pretending to be immortal, ferocious, unbreakable; these, the most brittle and easily broken of human beings, working-class men.

Jay swee more fucking *drinko*? repeated the canteen's number two cook, reputedly Tullah's toughest man, if not its leading francophone.

The number two cook was built like a road train, his head an angry red balloon stuffed full of gravel. He was inclined in rage to speak sentences of one word or make of many words one sentence, spat out like broken teeth.

You! Fuckn! Arrogant! *Froggycuntfucker*!

They went outside, the bar following them, leaving the three-metre-long fire in which they burnt logs the diameter of telegraph poles. And in a wet gravel car park, in the sodium-lit rain, they watched the two men brutally beat each other.

It went on for perhaps a quarter of an hour.

The cook could take punishment. He could also inflict it, and his methods—knees, trips, kicks—were pitiless. In some fighters there is a grace, aesthetic, or even a charm. There was none of that in the number two cook. He was a beast—a rhinoceros, a crocodile, a prehistoric thing more commonly found in tar pits. The cook's blows swung Ray's head wildly this way and that.

Ray was smaller, but fast. He managed to keep the number two cook mostly at bay with a rapid series of left jabs, until the big man was puffing and slowing. A right blow from Ray in the middle of the cook's chest oddly halted the big man—he wheezed, he barked; and Ray saw his chance, moving in on the cook's unprotected face, snapping his head back with a blow to his jaw. When the cook fell to the ground, Ray kicked hard at his head to keep him down. No one moved. The cook was no longer trying to fight, his bloodied pudgy head and ginger hair strange jetsam in the large puddle where they floated icon-like in the gilded reflection of a sodium street lamp. His body was shuddering in strange convulsions.

He's retaliating! Ray yelled at me as I went to pull him off. The lousy cunt! he cried, throwing a wild punch at me to leave him, so that he might continue beating the cook. He pointed at the spasming body. He's still fuckn wanting to go me, *the CUNT!*

I grabbed Ray again, twisting his arm behind his back, but he broke free, throwing me against a parked car. He stood above the number two cook, fists out, not kicking, yelling.

Tell me now! he cried as much to the primeval forests and the mountains beyond as to the number two cook, as much to the moon as to the mountains. Tell me fuckn now! he roared. *What is it? What! What the fuck is it?*

But the number two cook could make no answer; no one could as the mob—realising it was raining and cold, and that the bar was dry and warm—dissolved into the night and that distant night into another and the city bar in which we now stood. Had Ray, in Heidl, for the first time in his life come up against some sort of limit that he could not adequately apprehend, far less surmount, flee, and escape? Something that he could not beat into the gravel and puddles, could not reduce to an umber-hued groaning animal felled in a dirty bowl of yellow water at the base of rainforested mountains? For some gravity of life was now reaching for us, pulling us back into the terrible void we both for a short time had had the vanity of thinking we might escape, he with his body and adventures, me with my books and my writing. His violence, my words: two aspects of the same doomed revolt.

And perhaps for the first time I felt his fear, that everything we did, everything we had done, would not be enough to prevail against the island that was still strong within us—the burghers and political hacks, the small-town businessmen and assorted silversides who had thrown us out, his family and my family, descendants of convicts in whom the sluggish, tormented blood of slavery still pulsed, the jailed and the jailers and their torturous games, the way in which some essence of oppression had for two hundred years confounded the bitter, mad, beautiful island.

I remembered that wild rage, the desire to hate and be hated and spit in the face of it all, kick it until it stopped moving, a mad violence that was also an act of liberation. It was wrong. That was its attraction. It was wrong, because the world is always right, and we would break before it, and it would roll over us. But not before Ray and I went up to that bar in Tullah one last time, and Ray called out to the barman in a most absurd voice,

Je suis more drinko!

Then looking up and down the bar, meeting each man's eyes until they looked down or turned away, daring all of them, any of them, to back the world against him.

And it was only at that moment, leaning against a sticky bar wall in St Kilda, that I realised that the Ray I had for so long known had disappeared. Ray, who was always certain and never fearful, was somehow at once lost and frightened. And if he was frightened, then, I thought, I should be terrified. I looked at him again, and tried to see once more that same man hammering a stolen Valiant through red light after red light, slewing around cars, full of a wild exhilaration, because we were finally living.

But it was no good. He was gone.

9

1

THE WEEKEND AT HOME with Suzy and Bo came and went too quickly. I was back at work, and behind his executive's desk Heidl was, more than ever, all evasion and faux irritation with my questions. Who could blame him? I was bored with them too, bored with the persona he insisted I work to create: a tepid technocrat; a diligent family man; an accidental leader so subsumed in his own humility that the great successes of the ASO simply happened like Topsy. Heidl could now rarely pass more than a few minutes before beginning a song cycle of demands—for better morning teas, for another instalment on his advance, for the heating to be turned up or turned down, for sealed windows to be opened, or a nearby executive's door to be closed.

But the *rorts*—that marvellous Australian word for robberies done with sufficient chutzpah as to approach human virtue— the *rorts* demanded something more in the memoir; something approaching, well, honesty. Very occasionally he opened up, if only a little, and spoke in the manner of a tradesman describing his craft, which was to him so simple, so obvious, as to be everyday. But just at such a moment early that Monday when I felt revelation was imminent, when I was almost hopeful that a book might remain possible, Heidl stood up, put his jacket on, and quietly said he had to go to a meeting with his lawyers and wouldn't be back until late afternoon.

Pia Carnevale, looking in later and seeing me alone and despondent, offered to take me out for lunch to cheer me up. We went to what was for me an exotic, even alien location: the inner-city restaurant. The welcome of the owner—an old friend of Pia—the ease of the waitress, Pia's familiarity with the many dishes that were not even words I knew—all this was novel for me. If I felt an awkward ingénue, a provincial in his cheap clothes and torn runners, Pia gave no sign she noticed, and every word and every gesture suggested she saw me as nothing other than an equal. She was dressed, as ever, strikingly, which is not to say I remember what she wore. What I recall was her spiky charm, that ease of someone who was confident in themselves and comfortable in their world, things I was acutely conscious of not being.

At first, Pia wandered off into salacious tales of the famous, stories delivered straight-faced and invariably ended by a short, salty cackle. The multi-millionaire Scandinavian thriller writer who, at seventy-eight, had married a twenty-seven-year-old, insisting on sex after writing his daily five hundred words, and who, while touring Australia, had to be revived by an ambulance crew after having had a creative outburst of sixteen hundred words in a single morning; the English Booker winner who always had to have two prostitutes waiting for him after an event; the celebrated American poet who phoned her publicist in the adjacent hotel room, demanding the publicist ring room service for her to order a boiled egg; writers who passed out from drink and drugs before major TV interviews, on and on Pia regaled me with the whole glorious, raucous panoply of errant behaviour, of demons and madnesses private and public.

And when she finished a story, Pia would ever so slightly tilt her head back and blink two or three times, a gesture halfway between a nervous tic and the shutter click of a camera—as they were then—that captured that moment of your response, as if with those two or three blinks she knew you but didn't judge.

Punctuating her anecdotes were asides. About her mother dying of dementia. Her ambitions. The hopes she had had as an editor of working with great writers, the reality of making rubbish that the trade could sell. The terror of old age, of losing her mind. How she had made a name for herself transforming the hastily collated nonsenses of celebrities into bestsellers. The enormous labour of rewriting Jez Dempster's annual tomes, the *rubbish* dialogue she had to reinvent. She asked me about my marriage which was, I understood, another way of telling me about her own private life. She was unmarried, seemed not to lack admirers, and confessed to *the malign attraction* of having a partner.

Do you think, she said, you can be in love with being in love?

Beneath her confidence, her ease, I began to be aware of a diffidence, a nervousness, a fear. Pia Carnevale's details began to build in a strange haste leading to some unknown point, as we rushed from topic to topic, until there we suddenly were—there, at our true destination, the point of our lunch.

Kif . . . *Kif*—does Siegfried ever call you at home?

I told Pia he didn't have my number and I wasn't in the book.

Nor me, Pia said. But somehow he got hold of my number. Should I be worried?

But like all people who ask questions she didn't want an answer, and I didn't bother giving one. Pia had been overseeing Heidl's memoirs from the beginning, working with the earlier editors and ghost writers whom Heidl had so quickly demoralised to the point of resignation. Heidl and Pia had seemed like old friends the first time I had seen them together in Gene Paley's office. But clearly it wasn't so. She dipped the tip of a sugar cube into her espresso.

He calls me at home. Says he wants to talk about the book but says nothing.

The black liquid seeped upwards into the sugar cube.

What would you do? she asked.

I didn't know. I felt too embarrassed to say that I had been warned by Ray, how I had told Heidl nothing even when it went against my nature. I asked her what Heidl said, saying maybe it didn't really matter.

She held the sugar cube in front of her, watching the black fluid wick through its entirety.

No, Pia said, I guess it doesn't matter.

She looked away, and when she turned back she leant in, face looking down, eyes up. So close, I could smell her fragrance.

It's just—he knows things, Kif. It's odd.

I asked Pia what she meant.

Things he shouldn't know, he knows, Pia said. I had a cat. It was very old. It, well, lost control. Started pissing everywhere. Poor little thing. I mean I couldn't stand it, but what could I do? And I mentioned it to Siegfried a few weeks ago. And the day after we spoke the cat disappeared.

The sugar cube she held had turned black and was beginning to dissolve into syrup. She dropped it into her coffee.

Cats do that, don't they?

I didn't know.

I guess so, I said. They wander off.

They wander off, Pia said. Yes. But then the next night Heidl rang me and—

Heidl rang?

He asked if it was better now the cat was gone.

Pia made small circles on the table top with her coffee spoon as if searching for something.

The thing is, no one knew. And then another night he calls just after a friend had left my place. He says, did you have a nice evening with your visitor? in that weird fucking accent. *Did you have a nice evening?* No, not now you've rung, I wanted to say.

I said something which she ignored. Her gaze drifted for a

few moments and then she looked back at me. She put her coffee spoon down, and pushed her cup away.

What do you make of it? she said, before quickly adding: I don't want to make anything of it.

I asked if she had told Gene Paley.

I can't, Kif. Heidl's worth a lot of money to the company. There's big numbers against this book.

I tried to suggest that it might not mean anything, that someone may have told Heidl.

Even if it's creepy, I said, it doesn't make him a cat-killer.

No, Pia said. I'm not suggesting anything like that.

There was a long silence. Finally, I said that I was lost with Heidl too. I felt I could trust Pia with my own despair. I told her how I'd only taken the job—a job I thought would be easy—to get money to finish my novel. But having to date been unable to write a *real* novel, I now worried I might not even have the ability to ghost write a third-rate celebrity memoir.

Pia Carnevale laughed. She reassured me that I would, how it would all come together, that it would be first rate, and all this was normal. Don't fight him, she advised, go with him. And then Pia came back to her cat, how strange it was, where could it be?

I couldn't say that my confidence was beginning to crumble. I said that I was sure her cat would come back, that it was fine. And as my mouth continued making words without consequence, Pia tilted her head back and blinked.

2

Once back from the lunch I used the time I was Heidl-less to what advantage I could. I set to work structuring the outline Gene Paley wanted from a confusion of notes, half-formed gobbets of prose, and research. But whenever I tried to get to the nub of

Heidl I had nothing. Growing within me was the fear that he had nothing to give. Like a dementia sufferer, like a Californian feel-good poster, today was always the first day of the rest of Ziggy Heidl's life, and there were no yesterdays.

Characteristically, Heidl failed to keep his word and was back in the office not long after my return.

Gene Paley, I said, wants this outline sorted by—

I know what Paley fucking wants, Heidl snapped, walking over to the windows. He looked out, and shook his head. You're worse than my lawyers, he said without turning around, as if addressing the world outside.

For some time he stared into nothing.

My lawyers were confident we could get at least a six-month's postponement, he said quietly. At worst—at worst!—they said three months. And now the judge won't give us even a week.

Meaning? I asked.

Meaning? he said.

But he was distracted. It was as if he was seeing everything from a great distance, that he had already left where we were and would not be coming back, as though some final fateful decision had been made.

Well, he said, no postponement, that's what it means. And that means I'll have to start trial preparations in two weeks' time.

Not three?

Not three. Not twenty-four either. Just two. Maybe a little less. Then I'll have to work with my lawyers full time for a week before the trial begins. Excuse me, he said. Picking up the phone he rang a journalist from, of all things, *Vogue*. When that call was finished, he said he had a late lunch appointment and left.

The moment the door shut I rang Gene Paley's secretary, asking that she take an urgent message to her boss. I said Heidl had miscalculated and we now only had two weeks left with him on the book.

I worked for an hour or more alone, then walked to a nearby café for a coffee. On the way back I spotted Heidl down an unfinished side street. He was leaning against a concrete water main pipe that was waiting to be laid. He seemed lost in thought and never saw me. When later he returned to the office I asked how the lunch had gone.

Wonderful, but TV people! They bang on! I had to make it very clear I will be auctioning the rights for any mini-series based on the book.

I pointed out he had grey concrete dust all over the back of his jacket. He ran a hand across a shoulderblade, and when he saw his dusty palm, he laughed.

Can you believe it? The restaurant had been polishing their concrete floors before they opened and they sat me in a chair that was still covered in dust!

I was overcome with a sudden rage—with his lies, with him, and worse, the ease with which lying came to him, with me, with the folly of having agreed to write an unwritable book. Above all things in the universe, I wanted to tell Ziggy Heidl to go fuck himself.

Ray told me the containers were empty, I said.

The shipping containers? Heidl asked.

Yes.

Heidl shook his head sadly as if I were the greatest fool he had ever met.

Of course they were empty, he said.

3

The shipping containers were known in ASO parlance as Critical Incident Response and Inter-Liaison Support Units—or CIRILs for short. These were the much-publicised heart of ASO's disaster and emergency response *capability*. The clippings file bulged with stories of how each CIRIL contained the technology and equipment needed for any particular catastrophe. The CIRILs were, inevitably, called not steel boxes but a *system*—you could have as few or as many as you needed for a crisis—one, two, a dozen, and alone or together they became the nerve centre for the rescue of trapped mineworkers or crashed jet airliners. Being housed in shipping containers meant they could be easily freighted to wherever—trucked and shipped when time didn't matter; and when it did, they could be flown in ASO's own Hercules aircraft to the natural disaster—the flood, the fire, the tsunami—and be operational there both as a store and an operations command centre within thirty minutes of arrival. Or such was the stuff of the puff pieces. With the parachute jumpers who manned them, CIRILs formed the vaunted nexus that was ASO's promise and creed: *After disaster, before anyone else: we are there for you.*

After Heidl's confession, I couldn't stop staring at him.

If the containers were empty, I said, then they couldn't be used on any jobs?

Roger that.

Then the ASO couldn't earn any money—is that right?

Obviously, Heidl said. We didn't have the resources to do half those things people thought we did.

Or that you said you did, I said.

Heidl laughed.

Or even a hundredth. That would have cost millions.

I pointed out that they had millions.

But not for those things.

But you said you did those things.

I just told you—people *thought* we did. People wanted to believe we did those things.

I asked how he persuaded the banks to give him so much when they wouldn't even give Suzy and me our tiny mortgage, and we had to go begging to a slimy solicitor who demanded an extra two per cent interest on top of the going rate.

A small mortgage is hard, Heidl said. A thirty-million-dollar business loan is easy. When I'd run out of cash, I'd call a bank saying I wanted to expand.

It seemed impossible that he had scammed so much with only empty boxes. I began to see Heidl as a magician, a sorcerer.

I'm sorry, I said. I still don't get how it worked.

Trust, Heidl said.

I could feel the gritty dust of the car seats as I put my hand between them searching for lost change, the long walk across town to save petrol, the solicitor's dank dun-coloured room, grimed with greed. And listening to Heidl, thinking of where honesty and trust had got me, I couldn't fathom what he was on about.

That doesn't explain anything, I said, as I saw before me the solicitor's weary receptionist reach for the sad shoebox of indexed despair and hope, pull up our thumbed mortgage repayment card before checking every dollar, every cent I passed over in case I tried to cheat her employer of a single penny.

Trust me, Kif: trust explains most things, Heidl said. Trust is the oil that greases the machine of the world. Even people we hate we trust. That's how it is. And, amazingly, mostly it works. The bankers trusted that the CIRILs were real, that ASO was real, until finally it was real. Like you trust the mechanic did service the car or that the bank is honest; like you trust that the people who run the world know what they're doing. But what if you discovered that they didn't? What if their theatre is just a far bigger farce than my empty shipping containers? What if they—and here Heidl looked up and around, laughed, his cheek pitter-pattering, and in a mock-conspiratorial voice said—if *they* are the real con men?

And with that he leaned back, performance done, puddles of arguments drowned in a sea of nonsense. To somehow segue from his own crime to suggesting the people he defrauded were actually the real criminals was a marvel. These days I'm less sure, and any certainty simply waits, as Tebbe says, for uncertain times to prove it wrong.

I am looking at my notes from that time as I type this. I never used them for the book. Even then I understood it was a revelation beyond what his memoir could contain. Perhaps it was too much the truth and the world can only stand a little of such things, and a memoir, if it is to work, none. I needed only revelation, another matter altogether, and that was the empty containers. And that was enough.

4

I returned to the mechanics of his scam, asking again how he actually did it.

I'm telling you how, Heidl said. Say I owe Bank A seven million and Bank B three million dollars each in interest repayments. So, I ask Bank C for a loan of, say, twenty million. And they give me the twenty million.

But how does going into more debt help?

Stay with me, Kif! Next I create invoices: BP for fighting a fire on an oil rig in the Mexico Gulf. Department of Defence for training SAS troops in deepwater rescue techniques. And, let's say, the Queensland Department of National Parks, I bill them for firefighting. Until I have invoiced out twenty million dollars.

And they pay?

Why would they pay? They never get the bill. Because—

Because?

—because we never did the work.

You never fought any fires?

Just enough to have a few newspaper clippings.

Never saved lost sailors in the southern oceans?

We saved one yachtsman. One! And we had a media field day with it.

Heidl drew a circle on his desk with a finger and sighed.

I just drip the latest loan into our main account from a hidden account as if it is paying those invoices.

Not as debt but as income?

He pointed a finger at me.

Now you're getting it. And with that twenty million *income* now ours, we can pay off the interest we have to pay, maybe even a bit off the principal debt. We were honourable.

I asked if the banks were happy with this.

Sure. They give; they receive. That's what banks do. Legally we were a charity. The auditing rules were a lot looser. Our books looked good as long as you were willing to believe. The banks wanted to believe, and there was plenty to believe in. Like God, they just needed you to supplicate. I was an altar boy, you know. And I was good at getting down on my knees, offering up the mystery of the magic circle—invoice made out, copy kept, original destroyed, income received, income receipted, income spent paying back the banks' ten million interest, plus four million off the principal. And ASO is left with six million to keep going on with—salaries, expenses, training. A few more shipping containers. Our training, he added proudly, was second to none.

That was your plan?

Plan? Heidl laughed. There was *no* plan.

It couldn't last, though, I said.

Why not? So much does.

Your plan was to borrow more to pay for your borrowings?

Roger that.

That's like paying off your mortgage with your credit card.

Except after I had maxxed out the last credit card the banks would give me a new one.

It's pure greed.

Is there any other kind?

In the end, though, wouldn't you owe more than you can borrow?

Roger that.

I tried to drag him back to the details of the scam.

Finally, the banks started going broke because of your debts, I said. Questnoc bankrupt. Tantalus in receivership.

We did theatre. They did due negligence. We only had one shipping container.

You had hundreds of CIRILs, I said.

One—only one CIRIL. And that was our star.

5

Well, it was that sort of time, I guess, Ray had told me that dawn after Pink and Purple left us, as we stood in the rain trying to hail a cab in front of Mr Moon's mouth. Heidl would tell me he was running low on cash and we had to get the bankers back to tidy things up. The suits'd fly in, and there'd be this whole big show we'd have to put on—fly them down to Geelong in one of our planes, he'd take them out on our helicopter ship, show them our sub—that fuckn sub, I never knew what the point of that was other than taking bankers on a jolly.

You had three subs, I said, holding a shopping bag over my head as the rain grew heavier.

We had a fuckn navy. It was fun, I guess. I liked it. Heidl liked it. He'd buy more and more of this shit—boats, ships, planes, choppers—then he'd maybe show them a few letters for big new contracts with government agencies and big companies—oil, mining, you name it. There was a bloke he had here in Melbourne—Geordie something—anyway, he was good at

knocking up that sort of stuff. His title was 'corporate communications consultant'—I always remember that—but forging was
his job. Anyway, after the port, they'd fly back to HQ in Bendigo,
a couple of hundred PJs would do a march past, a few of us jump
out of one of our planes with dogs strapped to us, or some stunt
like that.

And then there was the moment Heidl would always love.
He'd show them the one CIRIL he had jam-packed with all
the most amazing search-and-rescue gear. State-of-the-art stuff.
Worth millions—high tech, incredible. That container was
always getting new and better gear put into it. It was fuckn something. And as they came out of the CIRIL a chopper would land.
And the suits just loved that chopper. Ziggy would tell them
how it had been Idi Amin's helicopter and how he had survived
several assassination attempts in it. And as evidence he'd point
to the bullet holes I'd shot in it for him. Then the suits would
curl up like fuckn tacos ready to be eaten as they scrambled into
that chopper.

A taxi pulled up, and as we got in I turned and saw staring at
us through the sheets of rain the strange dead eyes of Mr Moon
keeping patient sentry on the collapsing night.

10

1

ARE YOU WITH ME STILL, Kif? Heidl said.

And trying to avoid Heidl's terrible eyes I said I was, coming back to the office, to my senses, trying to jettison my vivid memory of Mr Moon as Heidl talked.

So we'd bank to the north in the helicopter, still staying low, fly over a small clump of bush and there, on an old football oval, there they would be. All of them.

All of what? I asked.

The shipping containers, what else? Dozens and dozens of them in the end, stacked up like Lego blocks. Like Singapore harbour! As we started circling I explained to the bankers how the CIRIL they'd just seen was worth in excess of a million dollars—which was true—and how what they were looking at now below them was the very backbone of the ASO, a spectacular investment that was generating great returns. Which was also true. And they'd be staring down at those containers painted in ASO colours, orange and blue—

But the CIRILs were empty, I interrupted.

Roger that, Heidl said, as if I had pointed out air is invisible, or that water is wet.

The whole two hundred of them?

Two hundred and seven, I think. I had a Croatian down Geelong welding them up for me. Otto. Not a very Croatian name, really, but Otto used to knock them up for us, two grand a pop. They weren't CIRILs, they weren't even real shipping containers, much too flimsy, just cheap copies for set dressing.

And you told the bankers each container was full of the same gear as the CIRIL you took them through?

No. No, I never said that. I didn't need to. They wanted to *think* that. They wanted to think that they were looking at over two hundred million dollars in big long boxes. I showed them up close one full steel box, and then at a distance two hundred and seven empty ones. And as we circled in the chopper, helmeted and earphoned and miked-up, I'd say through the chopper's wireless, *There*—they're all ours! Which was true. They would say, So you put them to similar use? And I'd reply, We put them to *excellent* use. They're a wonderful source of income, I'd say, and give a thumbs-up. And up would come their thumbs like a row of pulled carrots.

Back on the ground, jolly over, they'd open their briefcases, delighted to hand over the papers that gave me another multi-million-dollar line of credit. We'd sign, and have a drink. And always they'd talk about how the most impressive thing was the sight of those orange and blue shipping containers on the football field.

When I said I still didn't get how it could have gone on for so long, Siegfried Heidl fixed me with an expression of surprise as though I were the stupidest man on earth.

Don't you see? he said, leaning forward onto his desk. *I made it up.* Every day, just like you. *Like a writer.*

He rapped the desktop with his knuckles.

I'd go to the office. Each and every morning. Again, and again, and again. Make it up, and then make it up some more. And that was enough. More than enough. It just kept on growing. And you know what happened? People began flowing through my door—more and more people—bankers, journalists, TV crews, politicians, police commissioners, ex-generals,

CEOs, ambassadors, academics. And I learnt the less I told them, *the more they made it up*. In the end, I didn't have to make up anything. I was a prophet to them. And you know what Tebbe says about prophets?

I had no idea what Tebbe said about anything.

The greatest of prophets has but the vaguest of messages, Heidl said. The vaguer the message, the greater the prophet.

2

I halted my typing. For once, I almost believed him. Was it possible that there really was no CIA, no large myth, but rather something so obvious it couldn't exist in a book?

There are two realities, really, aren't there? Heidl said, holding up a finger to lend his words the illusion of conviction.

There's this office made of concrete and glass, and there's a story called STP. And you know what? The story of STP is more real, more powerful than this concrete. Because the concrete can't destroy STP but STP can demolish the concrete. And that's because people believe in the story of STP. Around the world there are accountants and editors and CEOs and sales people, and all that unites them is this belief that STP exists. And that belief is a story.

I was, I admit, lost. Heidl, on the other hand, was just finding his theme for the day.

Look, Heidl said. There are seas and lands and animals and plants, and there's a story called the Cold War. And I tell you, *that* story nearly destroyed those seas and lands and plants and animals.

The screen had frozen.

What do you think a businessman is? A politician? They're sorcerers—they make things up. Stories are all that we have to hold us together. Religion, science, money—they're all just stories. Australia is a story, politics is a story, religion is a story, money is a story and the ASO was a story. The banks just stopped believing in my story. And when belief dies, nothing is left.

You lied, I said, as I switched the Mac Classic off and on and waited for it to reboot.

But he was doing that odd awful thing he sometimes did with his tongue, running it over his lips as his cheek tick-ticked away like some fantastic diaphragm.

I told stories, he said.

Not everything, Siegfried, is a story.

And people wanted them.

You lied, I said.

Truth is a story. But good wine needs cheap glass to hold it. Truth needs lies so we can grasp it.

The truth is you're going to go down in the courts for lies.

I don't think so, Heidl said.

It was hopeless. I was typing but no characters were appearing. I realised none of what he was saying would ever make it into his memoir, because a memoir was a series of selected lies, and Heidl was again, bizarrely, speaking to something that approached truth. And I felt sick with bewilderment, or vertigo, I don't know what, I just felt sick, as if I were falling through some portal into another life, because somehow I had begun to think like Heidl, and something of Heidl was becoming—

We are the miracle, I heard Heidl say. God created the world, but man creates himself every day. And our stories bring us together for as long as we believe in them.

And, for the briefest instant, I had the strange sense I saw everything, my life to that point, my life to come, all of it in that poor, hapless executive's office, amidst the veneered chipboard and glossy pictorials that were even in that bright fluorescent light already fading into the colours of nostalgia—the yellow of rotting viscera and the lost green of aged rot, the russet of dried blood—like the spilled brains of some dying monster.

And then? I asked.

And then you sit down with a ghost writer and look for a new story.

3

To the extent he was at work, Heidl tended to keep conventional office hours, mostly arriving about 10 am and leaving by 5 pm. Because interstate calls were still a matter of some expense, when Heidl was not about I would call Suzy on the work phone. The morning following I called home before Heidl arrived. As I waited for Suzy to answer, the odour of the work phone—scented as it always was with Heidl's aftershave, halfway between cleaning spirits and baby powder, the smell of a mortician—was so strong I had to hold it away from my face.

It was Bo who answered. She sang for me over the phone, then tearfully asked when I would be home. I heard Suzy saying four sleeps, and promise her they would go to the park later that morning if she would let Mummy now speak.

Suzy told me her visit the previous day to the obstetrician had scared her. Small things. Nothing, really. But scary. She cried when I asked her why she hadn't rung me straight away. She said I'd seemed so busy. She was worried about the phone bill. She hadn't wanted to trouble me. Some early signs that might indicate pre-eclampsia. Nothing, really.

I jotted down the name of the condition, so that I could look it up later.

Nothing too worrying yet, Suzy had said; the doctor wasn't concerned and nor was she.

And she began crying again.

When Heidl and Ray arrived I said nothing about Suzy's call as I said nothing ever about myself or my family to Heidl. It was late morning—I was typing and Heidl was reading the paper— when there was a knock on the office door and Gene Paley's secretary delivered a folded message for me.

I opened it. It was a handwritten note from Gene Paley.

Kif, Got your message about trial. Forget delivering outline tomorrow. Just write best book quick as you can. GP

What does Gene want? Heidl asked, putting his newspaper down.

It's not Gene, I said.

He stared at me. I panicked.

It's my wife, I stupidly said.

You know, one day, he said as he picked up a piece of paper from his desk and stared at it, I think I'd enjoy meeting Suzy and—he paused, and, as he put the paper down, his lips formed a round smile before popping the word out as if it were a bullet—*Bo*.

I involuntarily shuddered. How did he know her nickname? How?

Yes, I heard him saying.

In spite of my wariness, in spite of working hard to deny Heidl any access to my private life, I realised Heidl had slowly, relentlessly accumulated knowledge about me.

I think that would be so very interesting, he said.

I didn't allow my face to show any recognition or emotion.

To meet *your* daughter.

I broke. Out of fear, or anger, I can't say.

Brigid, I said coldly. Her name is Brigid.

A beautiful name, Heidl said. And Suzy? How far away now are the twins? I mean, it must be so very close. And hard, what with you being here and she being . . . *there*.

I had had enough. Two weeks of what was now a five-week project had already vanished and I had little more than a few notes, some incoherent pages, but nothing approaching coherence as to what the book was about either in my mind or on paper. For no good reason, I thought of the dark stories of his book keeper, Brett Garrett, the shadow of whose unsolved disappearance hung over Heidl and which he did not seem to discourage hanging over him.

I've been thinking, Kif—well, more than thinking. I spoke to Paley earlier today about me coming to Tasmania rather than you coming here. That way you can be close to Suzy.

There's no need, I said. Suzy's fine.

Oh, she's not fine, Heidl said. Is she, Kif?

I felt panicked. What did he know?

You've a lot on your plate, Kif. Gene agrees.

Agrees what? I said.

That perhaps I should come to Tasmania to finish the book.

It's not necessary, I said.

Oh, it is. Believe me, Kif. *It is*. We can work where you're comfortable—my hotel room, your home, wherever feels easiest.

That's very kind, I said. But I'm comfortable here.

And it would be good for me to meet your family, to get to know you better, Heidl went on. How was Suzy this morning when you called?

I kept typing.

The obstetrician, Heidl said. A few worries?

I stared at the screen so he wouldn't see my face. *He couldn't know.* And yet whether I said something or nothing, whether I met his gaze or avoided it, it was as though every gesture of mine further helped create a sinister complicity between us, sweeping us towards some doom I could only vaguely apprehend.

Pre-eclampsia, Heidl said. *Nasty*.

It had begun.

It's a worrying condition, he said.

His slow taking over of me.

I began a new line of questions: I need to get this clear, I said, even if it doesn't go in the book.

Of course, Heidl said.

I could think of nothing to stop him, but I tried.

Did you ever have anyone blown away?

I don't know why I asked that question. I don't know why I used the euphemism *blown away* rather than killed. It sounded melodramatic, stolen from movies, and I felt foolish. Yet my embarrassment only made me angrier with Heidl.

Is that the sort of thing you think my memoir should be? Heidl said.

That wasn't my question, I said, my voice shrill. Answer me!

Inside me I felt something nameless. Swelling. Growing. I couldn't control it.

Answer me! I suddenly yelled. *Answer me! Answer me!*

Heidl leaned back in his chair and surveyed me as if I were a specimen in a zoo, almost as if it were he who was composing a book about me.

Because I need to know! I heard myself shrieking. *Answer me! I have to know!*

For God's sake, Kif, Heidl said, smiling. I was a CEO. Not Don Corleone.

But, as ever, he'd persuaded me to answer my question for him.

4

And that was his way: to let *you* create your lie from his truth. And confronted with my own complicity, I gave up and stopped talking. Besides, I had run out of energy, questions, the will to press on. In spite of Gene Paley's urgings and my own desperation, I would never finish the book. It was becoming clear to me that Heidl's procuring of me in no way meant any commitment on his part to finishing the memoir. If anything, it meant the opposite. I feared it was solely to give Gene Paley the impression that he was now working on finishing the book on time, whereas the very opposite was true. Heidl was, I had come to realise, criminally indisposed to fixing detail on paper. Besides which it was work, which bored him, and a book and history and posterity, so many things that I had learnt meant nothing to him.

Whatever he *had* told me was, in any case, mostly unusable. Less experienced liars would have sought consistency in their untruths. But life is never consistent, and at some point, long before I met him, he had realised that the vast ineptitude of his illusions was by some alchemy their most convincing proof. My problem was how to impose order on these unorderable recollections. Heidl, like God, got all the great stories, but a book had to make do with the merely plausible and possible.

I sat there, silent. And almost as if knowing what I was thinking, Heidl stepped into this abyss that had opened up between us. Finally, he began to tell tales of what had happened. They weren't the most revealing stories, but they were beguiling, even a little useful, and he kept telling them. He talked like a creek flooding after a drought, and the room swam with his stories as the clock hands began moving faster and faster, until it was mid-afternoon, until it was late afternoon, until through the curtainless windows there came upon us the ochre cataclysm of dusk, transforming into catastrophes of colour and shadow as night fell and that kitsch room became a place of transcendent wonder.

And still Ziggy Heidl talked on.

Some people tell stories lightly, a trotter with a light sulky racing along behind. Others are like an elephant slowly dragging a train, but slowly the train moves. And then there are the truly great storyteller like Heidl. They ride you, and you gallop faster and faster, thinking only ever *that* is what you want and you are never aware—until it is too late, far too late—that on your back is a rider, that you are being ridden to your death, and that there is now no way of stopping the story becoming you.

5

I stood in the city's night light readying myself to leave the office, and I remembered when Ray and I were young and we would go hunting with .22 rifles, traps, snares, and ferrets. Kids ten and eleven we were. We killed birds, rabbits, possums, wombats, and any other poor creature that happened into our rifle sights. It was amazing what we killed and made suffer. When we could find nothing to kill we shot up cows, which presumably suffered greatly from the wounds we inflicted on them. We had a vague sense of wrongness, but it was very vague and frequently absent; and when it was there it was exciting, another adult taboo we might break. Mostly we were fascinated by the world, the way we lived, the freedom we had, and the ways things died—the many ways—blood dribbling out of mouth corners, dulling dark eyes, twitching legs, spasming bodies. We often stood over dying things, mesmerised.

That we were lords of death never occurred to us as we ran and laughed, making our way through paddocks and woodlands. Watching something die was often fascinating, but how quickly it was also forgotten until those nights lying on Sully's floor feeling Melbourne rising up within me. Mostly though I remembered the sense of freedom.

How beautiful! It's vanished now and it's like it never happened. I can see the sun those days, rising over what was still a new planet as we set off at dawn, lighting the white mist into which we walked until it glowed and then gave way and abruptly vanished, leaving the light so brilliant against the frost-rimed paddocks that we would close our eyes and just keep advancing into that light. I can still feel the wetness of the long grass slowly dampen my shoes and chill my feet as the sun warms my face, the green of the bush, the redness of the oily soil, like a food you might eat, the overwhelming wonder of a rivulet we are wading up. That sound of water spilling in a perfect line over a diagonal log. I can hear it. Beautiful things, holy things, but I did not know it. What happened?

If killing was a form of knowledge, it also at a certain point offered no more interest and grew boring, and we would walk off, leaving a twitching dying thing outside of itself. Not always though—I recall once I shot a wombat that had been waddling across a paddock. We rushed over to its wounded body, gazed in awe at the blood matting its dense fur, the fine slag of blood drooling from its mouth, the still-sentient eyes, aware or unaware of us it was hard to say, but conscious perhaps of something infinitely larger.

We watched, silent. It would not die.

I'm off, Ray said. I don't like this one.

I stayed, staring at the wet leather of its large nose working hard to breathe, pinching in and out in an unnatural rhythm. Its large black eyes now fixed on the earth below. And still it would not die.

Cmon, Ray yelled.

It was a mystery that we had reduced to something commensurate with our need to know. And what we needed to know above all things even at that age was death, for there was a loud blast and simultaneous jerk and I looked up to see Ray had shot it through its head at close range.

For fuck's sake, he said, let the poor fuckn cunt die. You sick or what?

6

Sometimes I think about all those terminated lives thinking about me. Standing over them, staring as they die. Sometimes I see them gathering over me. But I try not to. They crowd all around me, birds, animals and fish, and I have an ever-greater fear of enclosure, of small spaces, of lifts, of aircraft seats, of crowds, with these creatures folding over me, pushing me down, smothering me, staring dully into the earth as they do so.

Of a night now the bedroom furniture moves, it lives, it transforms into them and they are coming for me once more. Suzy wanted to live with me. I just had trouble living with myself. You know, there's always something left. Something alive. Always. What that thing is you can't say. But it's real. This is why you keep going. People always ask me that: Why? Why do you keep on doing what you're doing? You know, making all these shows, always a new series, another project, when you could just retire. Why? And I say: I love it—who wouldn't want to do this?

But the truth is that if I stopped for even a moment and thought about the things I'd done I'd have to kill myself.

And maybe that was Heidl's fear too.

I was standing at the office window staring at the endless lights when it began to rain. I realised it had grown late. The lights blurred and my thoughts were lost with them. The dreary flat-lands of Port Melbourne passed from a monotone to a voluptuous wash of gold and red, and then to a dizzying black speckled with car lights and building lights and crane lights, vivid whites and reds and blues and yellows, a shock of motion as colour, as beauty, like an underworld of the dead where dark and light, good and evil, were all finally reconciled. I felt lost in a way I never had, and at the same time intoxicated by something that felt seductive and beautiful, something that was at once my fate, the executive's kitsch office, and the night-time city, and yet was also beyond explanation. I felt the warm wash of air rising from the central heating, a slightly sweet, slightly sickly smell of something rotting, as below me occasional figures moved along the street with the unwavering and certain mystery of ghosts.

I realised Heidl had gone some time ago.

I turned, went to his desk, picked up the phone, held it away from my face so I didn't have to drink too deeply of Heidl—of Heidl's scent and the scent and sound of all the horror of the world that might well up and smother me at any moment—and I was about to call Suzy when I noticed next to Heidl's neatly folded newspaper a single piece of paper. I picked it up. Scrawled on it was a single word: *pre-eclampsia*. Next to it, in a separate hand, was an exuberant tick.

I was about to put it down when I noticed something had been written on the back. *Brett Garrett*. And through those two words there ran, in the same green ink, a single line.

11

1

AT TIMES AT SULLY'S PLACE, though it was evening and Heidl was far away, I would stand up, walk to the windows, peek through the curtains, and only when I was sure no one was watching, return to the kitchen chair, the lounge suite, to talk in whispers, the tones of the conspirator against power. Had Heidl killed? Would he kill? One night I told Sully I thought Heidl was a coward, though I had no evidence that he was any such thing.

A coward? Sully said, long body leaning back on the old torn and stained recliner that was his favourite chair, joint smouldering between his fingers, an unruly white eyebrow hair arcing out over his left eye, finely cracking his crumpled face. He pondered his own question for some time before answering himself. He said that a coward was the most terrifying man, because there was no end to the things he might do to prove both to himself and others that he had courage.

I couldn't help wondering if he was describing Heidl or me.

Late of a night, when I was done with writing up my notes, I'd drink with Sully, beer and wine, blow a number or two, and when that was done and I was lying on his living room floor on my foam mattress on a threadbare rug, I'd take down a book from his shallow homebuilt shelves which surrounded me and were, like all good bookshelves, a rickety amalgam of scattered books, cards, fading mementoes and vanishing memories that briefly flared like a dying ember being blown on when picked up.

On Sully's shelves I found Nietzsche, for whom I had gone searching after Heidl kept quoting him. I would fall asleep reading him in the shadows and light thrown by the belly-dancing flame of a candle in a sparkling shiraz bottle. The night was wonderfully dark then and the dead lived in me when I read. Some things seemed possible that would never be possible again and occasionally in the darkness I hit up against something and felt it, and I knew I was alive.

Sully had been a poet of a particular minor note that had been the fate of a young man suffering the malign influence of Baudelaire, Burroughs and Brautigan in early '70s Melbourne. He used words like *lachrymose* and *crapulent*, and eked out a living as an archivist at the Melbourne City Council. Sully felt no one appreciated how funny Nietzsche was.

No one ever writes that, he said. 'After coming into contact with a religious man I always feel I must wash my hands.' That's not bad, is it? 'Is man one of God's blunders? Or is God one of man's blunders?' Good, eh?

Sully thought Nietzsche was like the most outrageous stand-up, always pushing it beyond good taste to see how far he could go.

I said being a philosopher in late-nineteenth-century Germany wasn't—I guessed—the same thing as appearing as a stand-up comic in a Melbourne pub.

Sully thought people didn't realise Nietzsche was being funny.

I said perhaps Nietzsche didn't realise himself.

And away Sully went spouting aphorisms as if they were gags.

'A casual stroll through the lunatic asylum shows that faith does not prove anything.' 'The living is only a species of the dead, and a very rare species.' 'The lie is a condition of life.' 'I would believe only in a God that knows how to dance.' 'In heaven, all the interesting people are missing.'

I wonder if he went mad and started talking to horses just

because no one realised what a seriously funny man he really was, Sully concluded.

Sully was much older than me; he had told me he had these days a sense of vertigo, that his arse had gone, that he couldn't go anywhere now without a wad of paper stuck between his buttocks. His voice was excessively calm as he spoke.

If I laugh I shit myself, if I cry I shit myself, if I meet a woman I have to leave before I start laughing and crying all at once for fear of completely fucking humiliating myself. I feel I am falling and falling. There is so much so terrible in this world, and my work has amounted to nothing; it hasn't altered one thing for the better. What do you make of that, Kif?

I made nothing of it, there was nothing to make of it. I offered bland assurances, lies, comforts thin as his threadbare rugs. As I lay in the darkness I saw Sully as the future I didn't want, the ghost of creativity spurned. Sully's world had proven finally an illusion. Heidl's world seemed the only real world. God didn't dance after all. The interesting people were all in hell.

2

I would wake to the thrumming of the city coming alive, rising up through the wooden stumps and floor and foam mattress, and soon enough there would be the dazed drive past trams, along crowded streets, and onto the Esplanade where another world momentarily shaped out of the Melbourne winter grey-ness, a world of sea and sand and palm trees, and near its end the abyss of Mr Moon's open mouth and his giant dead eyes that I felt following me to work.

There, in the office, Heidl passed his time making calls, cutting deals with *Woman's Day* or breakfast television for interviews in which he promised fresh revelations, or meeting journalists and anyone else he was seeking to impress in our office as if he were still a man of substance, rather than what he was, a crook on bail about to go down.

Put a corpse behind a desk and people will see their superior, he told me brightly as he put the phone down from another call to the media. I must have been staring at him, because he added:

No need to mention these calls to Gene.

He was only a few weeks away from a trial and jail, and being in breach of his publishing contract probably didn't mean much to him. Still, he must have read something in my expression, for he smiled, and with a seeming pride that felt out of character he told me that for every con man born so too are a thousand fools willing to be deceived.

If this project is so secret, I said, why are you doing interviews with every second journalist in the country?

I'm not telling them about our project. They tell *me* things and I agree. Besides, it's my life.

It wasn't really, or at least that's how I felt, but it was my task, and I returned to it. My time with Heidl began taking on a strange hallucinatory atmosphere as one day oozed into the next and it became hard to know if it was the third day of the second week or the second day of the third, as Heidl performed, paraded, evaded, grew bored, played dumb, angry, annoyed, or just did the crossword. Instead of returning to Hobart, at Gene Paley's insistence we worked through the weekend and into our fourth week, or, more accurately, I tried to write and Heidl yo-yoed in and out, leaving me and the book becalmed in the shadow line of the small monochrome sea of the Mac Classic monitor.

Sometimes Heidl would grin with some inner knowledge he had happened on but would never share. Sometimes he seemed lost in some impenetrable thought. In spite of my misgivings, I felt a wisdom about him at such times that I would never know but wished to hear. I found him insufferable in his many stupidities and pointless distractions. Yet I couldn't quite deny it to myself: his self-satisfied silences, his sly smugness, all bespoke a mystery I found myself wanting to enter and share.

3

During one of those dream-days, when we had been talking about—or I had been trying to talk about—ASO's collapse, Heidl asked me if I had ever seen a dead man; the sort of non sequitur he sometimes made and to which no real reply was possible.

We now had less than two weeks left. Time wasn't so much running out for the book as disappearing at the speed of light. Heidl's conversation had begun taking on a different, harder edge. The toxo and other obsessions had faded to be replaced by talk about the impending crash, undercover ruses and front companies, Cold War spookery, '80s junk-bond trading tales, and a figure—Siegfried Heidl—who was always and ever a lone wolf acting for good.

Looked at a man who has just died in agony? Heidl pressed further.

Listening to him, I realised how much I knew nothing. I tried to reassure myself I was only there to chronicle, but it seemed wrong that I had no intimacy with the world of which he spoke; a world manipulated by some terrible darkness that might manifest itself as a secret police organisation, a tyrannical government, an international corporation, or a shadowy merchant bank. Its forms, finally, were not the point. It was this animating spirit of darkness that seemed to determine his world, and which was beginning to seep into my own thinking.

At times, I had caught myself trying to join in the conversation. If there were a thousand and one things about which I knew nothing—the Hmong alliance, hot-money laundering, or the favoured pistol of Carlos the Jackal—it wasn't that which was so pathetic about my posturing.

No; it was my fawning gratitude when Heidl—adopting the tone of a mentor inducting me into the arcane craft mysteries of the shadow world of espionage, arms, and violence—would add a small detail in such a way as to make me feel that he was in some way a gracious superior.

I told myself he had never watched a man die. But his dead eyes caught mine and I realised he was watching me, looking into me, and I was no longer so sure who was bluffing, him or me. I was trying to bring him into a book, but he wanted me to think he had stared at dead men and he was having none of it. Heidl's mouth formed a smile, gap teeth tombstoning out, as my sentences began to sputter and I lost my way in them as I was lost in my thoughts. I heard Heidl saying how he understood, how he could see books were important to me.

But watch a man die slowly, he said, and you'll never see a book the same way. You think this world is about victories, progress. It's not. It's about defeat. The only purpose in life is to be defeated by ever greater things until your own death becomes inevitable.

He had a sly look and I marvelled at him yet again. I felt as I so often did with Heidl: voiceless, bewildered, outplayed. Worse: stupid. Every time he spoke like he just had, I worried that there was within all this, in spite of his endless deceit, a genuine experience, or more, or less than that—an essence— that I should be capturing in the memoir.

But that essence, along with my belief in my own ability, vanished the moment I tried to find words to capture it on the page. In the face of his mad intransigence, the book seemed further away than ever. I pointed out to him how if there was no workable manuscript by the end of the fifth week there could be no book and therefore no final payment of his advance.

Heidl refused to believe me.

Gene will pay me.

Do you understand? No more money.

Gene will pay.

If it's not clear to you, I said, it's clear to me. He won't.

4

I was finding it ever harder to be physically near Heidl. Everything about him revolted me, even the least offensive: the black-haired puffy fingers, his nose, his ears, the mouth that might swallow the moon. There was about him that intolerable sensuality you sometimes see in an animal. He made me uneasy with the way he leant in close. I didn't have the confidence or whatever it was, the courage or contempt, to take a step backwards out of that strange aura of '80s aftershave and low, slightly feminine voice that always led me to agree, no matter how much I disagreed. It was as if he might lick you like a pet, or kiss you.

I know this makes him sound sexual in some distorted, closet way. But it wasn't that, or that was only an aspect of something much larger which terrified me. It was more than his depthless eyes, always elsewhere and always on you; the way being with him felt like being locked in a room with a mad dog waiting for an instant of inattention when it might tear you apart. It was his need in some fundamental way to possess everyone he encountered. At times, he felt more a contagion than a human being. It was as if—as Ray had warned—he could enter you and once he was inside you would never be rid of him.

This physical revulsion was so strong that when I had to go to the toilet I would use the bathroom two floors down to avoid the one he frequented. And it was returning from the other bathroom that morning when I saw Gene Paley walking towards me in the corridor. Often, he didn't even stop, only nodded a greeting, but now he halted, asked me where the book was at, and went on to say, in a formulation that I found irritating, that 'no pressure' but the response from the booksellers following the announcement of the imminent publication of the Heidl memoir had far exceeded expectations.

So, have we turned a corner then, Kif? he concluded.

I said we had. And even added the word *Several*.

And Siegfried? We're getting good things from him?

I said we were.

Gene Paley seemed not quite convinced.

I suggested Pia Carnevale was pleased with how it was coming together.

This annoyed Gene Paley.

Pia's a wonderful editor . . . but a little *fragile* sometimes. Don't you think?

I didn't think it. It had never occurred to me, but I agreed in any case, because it was Gene Paley's point of view and when in the company of Gene Paley there was no other point of view.

No longer annoyed, Gene Paley assured me that although Pia Carnevale was no Max Perkins, she would be *more than adequate* in doing the necessary shepherding work on the book, and that I could have every confidence in her.

But the thing is, he went on, we need to know. How the scam worked. How he defrauded the banks of so much. Seven hundred million! As I was saying, it's impressive. And the CIA? What things have you got out of him about that?

I said a few. Enough. I may have again used the word *Several* in the form of a question.

But the thing is. Do we have a book? Are we *in the game*?

I said we were in a game.

Great news, Gene Paley said, his face a determined grimace. Wonderful. Look. I know I said forget the outline and just finish the book. But! Sales and marketing are chasing me. They want to know the rough direction the book's taking. A draft by Thursday? Think you can do that?

I could think of nothing to say. It was Tuesday. I had two days.

Jez Dempster, Gene Paley went on, has a theory of writing. The Alpha Omega Program. You've heard of it?

I hadn't.

Begin at the beginning and end at the end. That's the alpha and omega of books. Okay?

Okay? I repeated, as if learning an unknown word in a new language.

Hold that thought, Kif. Thursday it is. I look forward to it.

And he did his click-wink thing, leaving me feeling as if he had stapled me to a vast blankness of unfillable paper.

5

Just a minute, Heidl said when I returned to our office, raising a silencing hand, then dropping it to continue undoing the sleeve buttons on his red and white striped shirt and fold his sleeves back a strange one-fold while he continued talking on the phone, as though it were some theatre of rolling up his sleeves, of getting down to the work he spent the rest of the day evading. The moment he hung up, his smiling face transformed into a scowl.

That fucking maggot Knowles. Five thousand to have him blown away. Cheap at ten times the price, eh?

This strange interplay between Heidl's seductive calls to media—backgrounding, seducing, dealing, cajoling, bargaining—and his now almost daily theatrical talk of having Eric Knowles murdered, was, to say the least, frustrating. But to my shame it also exercised a strange power of compulsion. Still, I must have seemed shocked.

Look, Heidl said, scowl vanishing, dreadful smile appearing before me like that of a fun park clown, you should listen to what I am saying more carefully. You believe the world is good, Kif? That most people are good, that the world improves because of those good people and good things? Yes?

I made no reply, obeying my rule neither to talk about myself, nor be diverted into opinion.

Goodness is like God, Kif, the worst lie. You think you are kind and good and you will be rewarded. If not with money, then with the good life. But look at the world. Do you think millions die of starvation, of war, because of the good? Many of them, maybe most of them, are good people. But they suffer, and they suffer terribly, and they die horribly.

I wouldn't be drawn. He continued, his tone suspended between a newsreader's monotone and a sportscaster's jubilation.

Look around you, Kif—sickness, war, the poverty that makes people savage, the riches that make them worse. Do you think the evidence of the world is that the good are rewarded? Oh no! They're punished. They're beaten and tortured. They have the skin peeled off them and they're left hanging in trees to die. The evidence of the world is that the world is evil. Cheats and liars win out, Kif. Money wins out. Violence wins out. Evil wins out.

I refused to say anything.

Think about it, Kif. The evidence of the world is with me.

I said nothing.

What is it Tebbe says?—the long arc of justice breaks beneath the blow of history's hammer. Make your choice: be a fool, lie to yourself that the world is good, and go with the good. But you will lose.

I walked over to the window so that I didn't have to look at him.

Everyone and everything is destroyed in the end by evil. You can choose good. Or you can be like me and accept the world as it is.

Heidl stood up, came over to the window and stood next to me. He pointed to the street below.

See my new Cruiser down there?

I realised he meant the LandCruiser Ray chauffeured him around in each day. At the time they were a very expensive car, and Heidl's was loaded with every bit of boy-bling going: bull bars, roof bars, lights—a lot of lights—radios, winches and assorted toys.

I prefer it to my Porsche. More fun. Because when I am gone I can get nothing. Why deprive myself of anything, that's what I think. Would you like a car like that? A woman? Money? You would, wouldn't you? What do you drive—some shit box, I imagine. A ten-year-old Valiant? A beaten-up Corolla?

A Holden.

A Holden. What sort?

A twenty-eight-year-old EH Holden. I swapped a pushbike for it. I do better than most on depreciation.

He left the window to browse a bookcase—anything but return to the desk and the possibility of working.

You can choose to drive something else, Kif. But you think, I'll choose goodness and drive a shit box. Because it's the right thing. But what if there is no right thing? What if there are just good cars and bad cars? What if there is just what you can take and hold and enjoy? he said, taking a book down from a shelf. What if that's all there is? Here, he said, proffering me the book, across the cover of which was emblazoned its title: *Six Stepping Stones to Success: Free Yourself Now!* Have this.

I'm fine, I said.

Because it will destroy you, Kif, he said as he put the book back. It will destroy me. It destroys us all. In the meantime, I'll take what I can get—the money, the good times, the fun. And when it comes for me I'll know I lived my life. Will you be able to say that?

And with that he sighed, and, reaching up for a collected short stories of Jez Dempster, asked if I would prefer that.

It was a large, heavy hardback, perhaps seven hundred pages, perhaps more. I felt not so much defeated as exhausted by his logic.

We need to work, I said.

Jez Dempster! They say he's like the Great Barrier Reef. Maybe you've never looked at a word he's written, but it's great to know he's there.

Your time on the run, I said wearily. Tell me a little about that.

I am not an evil man, Kif, Heidl said, stuffing the block into his briefcase. Please don't think that.

He went on about how he was an ordinary man who just happened to see the world a little more clearly than other men. And, almost without pausing, he began reminiscing about the times he and Ray had had choppering about Cape York Peninsula, the wild jungle below, landing on a beach with not a footprint or human being within a hundred kilometres.

Though I tried to deny it to myself, to push it back down, I sensed I was jealous—after all, I was broke, isolated and self-isolating, with a family I couldn't support and a dream I couldn't realise. All the things that I valued suddenly seemed lustreless and worthless. All my ideas, all my beliefs, appeared sentimental, naive, and, worse, false. Heidl's reasoning left me confused, but I would not surrender. The book! I told myself. The book!

ASO's early days, I pleaded. The book keeper. Brett Garrett. A good man?

Any fool can endure being killed, Heidl said. It's enduring killing that takes something else.

And Heidl continued heidling: how goodness wasn't the game, that the game was all life was, to enjoy playing the game or don't play and be miserable—your call! Because it will destroy you, he said, almost gleefully. It will!

He reached up into the bookcase and pulled out *The Koala Kid*, the Australian children's classic. In a gesture that felt in equal measures touching, insincere, and implicating, he handed me the book, saying it was for Bo, to make up for his having stolen her dad away for so long.

I don't want it, I said.

He put the book down on the table next to the Mac Classic.

She'll love it, he said.

Your mother, I begged. Please tell me what she was like?

But he was already calling someone, his lawyer, a journalist, another hitman, perhaps God or perhaps the Devil, and he had to go, he said, to a meeting with his legal team and would be back later, and a moment later he and Ray were gone, vanished, as if they had never existed.

6

They returned late afternoon. Ray seemed odd, even upset; he said he wasn't feeling well, and left soon after. Heidl was strangely calm. He said nothing of his own volition, yet if asked a question he seemed—for perhaps one of only two times I ever saw him—to be seeking to answer it honestly. And following Pia's advice I decided for once to go with him rather than against him. And so I asked about the murder threats he claimed were being made against him.

What will they do, eh? Heidl told me. Everyone will know it was the banks that killed me. Just like Nugan Hand all over again.

Meaning?

Roger that. Who did kill me? That's the question.

I told him he was far more likely to die in an old-age home with a box of remaindered copies of his memoir under his bed.

But the possibility of not being, of cheating the courts by

dying before trial, all these things not only interested Heidl but seemed to come close to thrilling him. To say nothing of the melodrama of mystery that might accompany his passing.

I'm not taken with old age, Heidl said. And in some heidling of near Tebbean intensity, he went on to say how dying of old age was unnatural to the point of being wrong; men, he argued, had since the beginning of time died at any age, but mostly not old, no; they had died from disease and misadventure, tragedy and stupidity, war, crime and accident. These deaths gave life its meaning; old age to the contrary proposed a settled flow of events, a progression. The idea of life as a movement upwards, as a career, he loathed. Ads for pension schemes, retirement villages and funeral plans drove him to fresh rages.

I'd rather be murdered, Heidl said.

I said that maybe I'd do it for him if we didn't get the book done.

To die of old age, Heidl continued, is a rare, singular, and extraordinary death. It is the last and extremist kind of dying. It encourages people to lead a life devoted to not dying, which is really another way of not living. To know death is coming and coming soon, to die soon, is to live better now. And isn't that what we all want?

He meant it. He meant every word of it. But I knew it couldn't be true. It wasn't possible to believe him; it was impossible to disbelieve him. That was what was so confusing about him— what was genuine? What was fantasy? What was fact? All I knew was that whatever or whoever he was, I was fed up with him.

How do you think the book will go if I'm found dead? he finally asked, as if it were a question that genuinely preoccupied him.

Exhausted by his unbelievable laziness, his lies, his greed, his selfishness, his lunatic melodramas, I felt my frustrations transform into a wild hatred.

It will be a bestseller, I said.

How big a bestseller?

A number *fucking* one bestseller.

It felt cruel to say, but it felt good saying it. And besides, I thought it was true, but truth, I was learning, was never really a defence for anything.

The idea, far from angering Heidl, seemed to calm him and almost delight him.

A great career move, I said.

Exactly what I thought, he said.

Heidl smiled. His cheek ticked harder than normal. I had pleased him, and somehow I was pleased that I had. I felt an unexpected complicity, a strange warmth, almost an intimacy. And in all this, there was an inexplicable happiness.

7

In my notes there is a question Heidl then asked me: Why do you want to be a writer, anyway?

I don't recall what I said, but I do remember thinking I couldn't exactly say what being a writer meant to me, or why it seemed so important. And that was odd. After all, no one had compelled me to be a writer. My mother still had hopes I might become *a good plumber.*

Because you have a brain, Heidl went on. Really, the bankers I dealt with—you'd run rings around them. I respect writers. Writing matters. But is it fun?

In truth, so far it hadn't been.

So much fun, I said.

Because if you don't have some fun, then what's the point? I know you think the ASO was a racket—

—I don't say that.

Ray told me that's what you think.

Ray didn't tell you that.

So you said it?

So you lied about Ray?

We made something. And we were the best. Ask Ray. The best. As good as the US Seals. As anyone. And it was fun. You want to know the real rackets? The banks and corporations that financed us. Maybe every now and again someone just has to be sacrificed so that they can keep going. And I am that sacrifice.

He leant back in his chair and rolled a pen between his fingers. It was as though he were offering me a promotion.

You should give up writing, he said. Have some fun while you can.

His cheek seemed to be twitching double-time, triple-time, almost trembling. I never forgot that. That, and what he then said, and how he said it, as if it had just happened out on the street and he was describing it to me, as though it were the most matter-of-fact thing on earth.

Before you're sacrificed.

He went on, I can't remember exactly what, and though I tried to concentrate on what he was saying, seeking to glean some sentence or phrase or idea I could use, they were increasingly sounds without sense, and the more they and his life blurred, the more my life came into focus with all its attendant poverty and pointless struggle. And everything Heidl said to me—even his lies and evasions—somehow proved to me what a fool I was for thinking my life was one worth pursuing.

After Heidl had gone I picked up *The Koala Kid* from the table. It was a handsome fiftieth anniversary edition, of a type I could never afford to buy Bo. As I absent-mindedly leafed through it, I thought of how thin and small my world seemed—Suzy, our damp, decrepit tenement with my poor attempts at home handiwork, the limited, limiting lives of remote islanders. For while Heidl talked I had begun to see that my life was not the thing I had thought it had been, that it was not full or rich, but somehow mean and pinched; that in choosing to write I was closing myself off from the world.

For the world was in Heidl—strange, perhaps undivinable, beyond good and evil—and I found myself both resentful of it and jealous and covetous as well. Biblical sins. I seemed to want to commit them all. And, though I refused to admit it to myself, I wanted in. Because the world had no need of me or my books, but I had need of it.

Now I think that was precisely the point of all Heidl's stories: to make me believe my life was based on illusions—the illusions of goodness, of love, of hope. And persuaded of that, I would betray something fundamental within myself and embrace his world as my real life.

Perhaps then I would be granted that great vision I knew Ray sometimes glimpsed in Heidl. I wanted to know it too, but it frightened me because I could see it breaking something in Ray. And though I did not wish it to break me, though Heidl filled me with an ever-greater dread, I wanted in. I can't explain it. With every passing day, more and more, I wanted fucking in.

I closed the children's book, put it in my backpack, and switched off the lights as I walked out.

12

1

YOU THINK YOU CAN BE something other than a two-headed, shit-eating Tasmanian, Ray said, when really all Tasmanians are two-headed shit-eaters and go back to doing what they were always meant to do, eating shit and eating it day after day after day.

We had arranged to have a quick drink that evening. To my surprise, Ray fronted. I told him about Gene Paley's demand for a first draft by Thursday, but Ray seemed elsewhere. Sullen. Angry. After his invective—although I wasn't sure if he'd even heard what I'd said—I felt he had a point. We didn't fit. We had drifted into that world of publishing and celebrity and were, we knew, in spite of my ambitions, likely to drift out of it at book's close, leaving only an evaporating shadow of ourselves as an after-dinner anecdote, a story that truncates over time into an aside, a joke, a dying laugh—nothing and nobody of consequence except to amuse the world of publishers, and then only for so long until something or somebody else amused them more. A half-life of a year, a month, a week, a night, a drink.

A drink?

No, Ray said to his empty glass.

Ray and I did not have whatever it was you needed to have. We did not have whatever it was that Gene Paley had. What Pia Carnevale had. What Heidl had. Was it some inner certainty? Something indefinable, but real? Some sense of equality, perhaps. But I recognised in Ray, in myself, even in Suzy some opposed emotion. We had only a terror. A Tasmanian terror. That we were nothing. What did Nietzsche or Tebbe or, for that matter, the world of publishing, know about shit-eating?

Nothing, Ray said, when I asked him what he made of Heidl being pleased with the idea of the book being a bestseller if he was murdered.

I said I thought it was weird.

Ray seemed at once uncharacteristically bitter and adamant.

It's fuckn nothing, Ray said. Okay?

How could I have known all that was playing on his mind? That he wasn't talking about my self-pity and my failure, but something far more serious, something terrible?

Fuckn nothing at fuckn all.

And with that Ray skolled his beer, stood up, and walked out.

2

When I got home I did what I could with what I had. In my original conception the book was meant to be twelve chapters but I had written only one and a half. In the manner of Christ feeding the five thousand with two fish and five loaves I set to work on my task of miraculous thinking. I cut and reshaped my one and a half chapters—with a little padding that later read as the best thing in those pages—to form three chapters. I next set to work on rearranging Heidl's own manuscript—chopping here, adding bridges and colour there, moving passages hither and thither until I had a further four vaguely coherent chapters. That made a total of seven. For the rest of Tuesday night I worked on a very rough draft of another chapter on the nature of the fraud. In this way, by three in the morning I had eight chapters done. But I still didn't have enough, nor anything like enough.

I made some progress Wednesday morning talking with

Heidl about his early days at the ASO before he vanished for the day. Over the course of the afternoon and that night, fuelled by instant coffee and some speed Ray had, I managed to put together three more chapters, combining rough outlines with passages I had cut from his memoir, hybrids of passages stolen from my notes, some descriptions of bridges that were yet to be written, along with some ideas taken from my novel.

By the time I had finished these, revised what I had so there weren't too many obvious contradictions or repetitions, dawn was a blurred grey rope over Port Phillip Bay as I drove to TransPac's Port Melbourne office. Despite my best intentions I passed out for a few hours on the office floor, to be woken by Heidl when he arrived a little after ten.

That morning Heidl was oddly loquacious on the matter of his escape across the vastness of Australia when ASO collapsed. I say odd, because in his stuttering, cryptic language he spoke so differently from his usual gush. It was almost as if he were striving for the truth, but the truth was impossible to know, as if something happened out there that puzzled him. I had asked him how he felt about the massive manhunt that was chasing him. He told me he felt nothing. In that era of computer freezes and disks corrupting, Gene Paley made me make daily print-outs of all my notes and drafts. Among the several boxes of resulting papers I kept from that time I found this transcript.

You know how it is out there on the Nullarbor, Kif? That road running straight through the desert for hundreds of ks. Sand. Saltbush. Nothing. I had this work ute. Holden V8. The more I gunned it, the further I went, the straighter the road became. The more the earth in front of me bent. You could see the curvature of the earth. Weird rising waves of heat haze. My head was sand. Felt if I kept driving I might fall off the edge of the world. So I'd stop the car. Get out. Throw myself in desert dust. Scratchy saltbush and empty beer cans and toilet paper. I'd dig my hands in dust. Trying to hold on. Lying there, you can feel it. The whole earth moving. Me on it. Riding it. Holding on. It was spinning faster and faster. Just holding on. Tighter and tighter. But I'd have to let go. It wasn't safe. I'd have to move on. A few hundred ks until I'd feel I was about to be spun off the planet again. Stop. Throw myself back in the dirt and shit and try to hold on. That's what I felt. Nothing. Just trying to hold on. The earth spinning faster and faster. Holding on, just holding on. But I'd have to move on.

Even now, I feel an eerie glow of recognition re-reading it. And listening to Heidl that day he seemed to be saying things I actually understood, almost as if I'd lived his life myself, or as if he'd lived something of my life, or was going to live my life. But that moment passed, he lost interest or me focus, I can't say which it was, but he was back on the phone, and not long after was heading out to yet another lunchtime meeting.

For once I was happy when Heidl failed to return. I had promised I would have the draft to Gene Paley on arriving that morning, then midday, then 5 pm, then 5.30. I *say* draft, but much of it was little more than notional outline, where whole sections were described in a paragraph, above which sat the italicised caveat—

Yet To Be Written.

In the space of that afternoon, feeling watery and tight and out of focus, getting by on more of Ray's speed, I managed to transform the morning's notes into a short draft chapter, bringing to twelve my total completed, albeit in the roughest form. I was wired and sick and began making things up, and though the writing seemed awkward and I felt both afraid and a fraud I kept making them up until I had another completed chapter. But when I scrolled through what I had, all I could see were gaping holes. By then it was five in the afternoon. In a panic I added another chapter composed of several unrelated passages linked by cryptic notes. To that I added the briefest descriptions of another four chapters, each of these papering over the worst holes in the chronology, so that it was now a seventeen-chapter book, of which perhaps two chapters could be considered close to finished.

All-in-all—explanatory notes and numerous caveats included—there was close to 27,000 words—less than half what was expected as a final manuscript—and these I had to abandon to Gene Paley in the hope that there was enough in them to satisfy him for now. He had, admittedly, made it clear he did not expect a final completed manuscript. But whether Gene Paley would find in my draft evidence of a book he thought worth publishing was a different matter.

Gene Paley had sent me a message saying that he would stay at his desk waiting for me to deliver. When—a little after seven that evening—I handed my typescript over to him he seemed pleased to receive it, though not as surprised as I was that I had actually managed to finish the draft. I felt intensely depressed and I had the shakes so bad I thought I might fall over in his office. He told me he would have it read by the morning and give me his thoughts then.

Although I was washed out and coming down badly from the speed and lack of sleep, I was too exhausted to say no when Ray, who was waiting for me outside, suggested we grab a counter tea at a St Kilda pub.

3

Over steak and chips we talked about old times, which are mostly free of rough edges, and we avoided the thing that had brought us together to drink in that city far from our island home. A band was playing, and the noise made for an odd intimacy. Maybe because I was feeling depressed, I confessed that I didn't like what I was doing, but when Ray asked me why, pointing out that it was money, I was hard pressed to answer.

I'm working hard to make him look good, I said finally. Maybe that's it.

So? Ray said.

A man robs, maybe kills—

Maybe, Ray said. He seemed unusually equivocal. But has he told you that?

Not exactly.

How do you know then?

Well . . . I don't, I said. He's a liar.

Ray snorted. So? Maybe he is, maybe he's not, maybe he's something else.

What does that mean?

Something worse.

Like what?

Fuck him. That's all.

I was irritable from the speed and exhaustion, and not really listening. I said I didn't know if I could do it any more, and even if I did somehow manage it, even if it were a good job, all I would have done is managed to make Heidl look a hero.

I dunno, Kif. I'd have to read it. You'd have to be pretty good to polish that turd.

I talked about how it would be impossible to get published if I failed with this book, though I had no idea if that was the case or not. Ray didn't agree, but as he admitted he'd be the last to know. He tried to be his normal cheery self, but he wasn't really cheerful at all, and when I asked him why, he looked around the bar room before fixing me with his eyes. He made me promise if he told me something that I'd tell no one, and, above all, never tell Heidl.

I asked why.

Because . . ., Ray said but his voice grew uncertain as he said it, as though he was repeating something he had learnt but never believed, *because* it's a secret.

And he told me.

4

Heidl had made Ray stop outside a sports goods store. They had gone in and Heidl had bought a Glock pistol, along with some boxes of bullets.

Why? I asked.

That's what I asked him. Why? I said, what do you want that fuckn thing for? Ziggy raves on for a while with that shit about the banks trying to do him in, how we needed protection now, but it was nothing to do with that.

Ray was oddly upset about something I felt wasn't so far out of character with someone as self-dramatising as Heidl. I asked when it had happened.

The day before yesterday, Ray said. When Heidl said he had to quickly meet with his lawyers and then we didn't come back for the best part of the day. We didn't meet any lawyers.

I'd worked that out before you left.

Ziggy was on a mission. First, he gets me to stop to buy the Glock. Next, he wants me to drive him to Bendigo. But an hour out of Melbourne, he gets me to drive us down some side roads until we end up in this patch of thick scrub. He tells me to pull over. He gets me to follow him into the scrub. We walk about ten minutes, and then he says, I need you to kill me, Ray.

I laughed, but quickly stopped. Ray didn't smile, and just kept staring at me.

I'm serious, Ziggy says. I'd rather you kill me, he says. I need a friend, Ray. You're my *mate*, he says. I hate how he says it. Like it's a leash. My best *mate*, he says. And he went on like that, that sort of shit—a real *mate* would do it; that's what real *mates* are for, the *tough thing*, the *hard shit*.

Ray was pouring Jack Daniel's shots into our beer, making the beer taste flat and sickly. We skolled them and ordered more, skolled them and drank some more. I didn't know what to say. We started talking about other things.

Then Ray said: he made me practise.

What?

Killing him. With the gun. Showed me how it had to sit in the mouth, what angle. That sort of shit. You fuck it, you blow half your brains out but you live.

Ray thrust an index finger into the front of his mouth in a vertical position. With a garbled voice he said, this way, you lobotomise yourself.

He slowly moved his finger down until—still in his mouth—it angled in a diagonal line up past the top of his ears.

Like this, Ray said. That's what Heidl said. Like *fuckn* this.

He pulled out his glistening finger and wiped it on his jeans.

For the first time I realised that beneath all the talk of adventures, of choppers, of the wild lands of Cape York, of hunting dugong with the Aboriginals, Ray was unhappy and his unhappiness had about it the nature of something tormenting and inescapable. I also realised that we had both ended up somewhere we should not be.

Why don't you just leave, I said. He can find someone else. You don't owe him anything.

It's not that. It's him. You don't get it, mate. You just don't get it.

Get what? I asked.

He dropped his hand from his face.

Him.

What?

Him! He doesn't, like—you can't.

Can't what?

Leave.

The band was noisier than ever, and I had to lean in.

Can't leave. He won't allow it. He says if you're really my friend, you wouldn't. If *mateship* means anything to you. If you're a *mate*.

Mate?

And Ray yelled—

You fuckn can't.

He leant back, his elbow on the bar.

Yeah, that's what he says. I know. It's weird. But if you leave him you wouldn't know what he might do to you. Come after you . . .

His voice trailed off. He ran his finger around the rim of his glass and when he looked up from his drink I caught his eyes.

Kill you? I said.

Ray looked back down, tapped the glass rim with a finger, but what he meant by this gesture I had no idea. I thought of the odd way Heidl said mate, with his strange half-American, part-German voice with its Strine overlay.

Mate? I said. He's no fucking mate.

Well. He thinks I am. I can't explain it.

You should fucking kill him.

Yeah. Don't think I don't think it.

And once more he put his finger in his mouth, angled it back, closed his lips around his finger as if it were a lollipop, and said, Boom! His face went into his maniacal, slightly cracked smile that he seemed to reserve for when he wanted to have his way, when he was drunk or stoned, and wanted to steal a car, or steal someone's girlfriend; only this time it vanished almost as quickly as it appeared.

Yeah. Don't think I don't think it, Kif. Don't think I don't think it all the time.

5

At 11 am on Friday I was in the office, Heidl-less, when the phone rang. With the hours I'd been keeping, the work, the speed, Heidl, the tension of not knowing if I was going to get the book written, I was fried. My head was mud. I had passed the morning seeking to make a chapter work but nothing worked, nothing connected, and I was lost again in the story of Heidl, defeated by his strange refusal to have a life, even on the page. I picked the receiver up. It was Gene Paley's secretary.

In his office, TransPac's CEO apologised for having troubled me to produce a draft manuscript under such extreme pressure. His manner felt ever more an unsettling combination of simpering deference and casual brutality.

But you see I have to know, Gene Paley said.

He lifted my manuscript off a side table, placing it on his desk and pushing it towards me as if he were returning a defective toaster to the shop.

What you and Heidl have been up to. To see if you can deliver us a book.

I may have flinched but it might have looked like a smile.

There's some fine writing here, Gene Paley said.

I may have smiled but it might have looked like a flinch.

Kif. A book is a mirror. If a capuchin monkey stares at its pages, Albert Camus isn't going to stare back.

I mumbled something.

You need to reveal the story to the reader.

I have, I said.

You haven't yet.

I will.

Kif, for the moment I think you've gone as far as you can with Siegfried. You're flying back to Tasmania tomorrow?

Tonight.

Don't come back till next Thursday, Kif. Stay at home, flesh this draft out. As much as you can. And then use next Thursday to check it over with Siegfried. That gives us a bit over a week after that for you to rewrite and edit. Okay?

Having run what felt the equivalent of the three-minute mile, I was now being ordered to run a sub-two-hour marathon. I may have nodded in despair.

One question.

Yes, I said.

What is the story?

It's straightforward, I said.

He slowly tapped his marsupial-like fingers on my manuscript. What is it though? Gene Paley asked, tiny pale digits drumming.

A story of the future lost? I ventured.

The way you tell it, Gene Paley said, he's the coming dawn. The new tomorrow.

He's a parable, I said, or perhaps just hoped.

There are no numbers in parables, Kif. They don't sell. Unless it's America. And there they package it as self-help.

And here?

Well, here in Australia we like hanging calendars—you know, defiant confessions of crimes. Given from the gibbet. Yo ho and sorry lads, but fuck the power and then the power fucks you. We want them punished, but we like them proud.

The dying game.

Exactly.

So what do you want? I asked, because I really had no idea what he was on about.

How he was CIA. How he ripped the banks off. How he's not repentant.

No?

No. Australians like their heroes bad. Unrepentant. That's the point.

He's German, I said.

He told you?

No. He said he was Australian.

Mmm.

My eyes dropped a little. I noticed the starched ghost image of an underarm sweat stain on Gene Paley's white shirt.

Kif, there's interesting things here. *But you need something to happen.*

Something does, I said.

Not yet.

But it will, I said. I am sure of it.

13

1

A FEW HOURS AFTER SPEAKING with Gene Paley, I flew home to Tasmania. Disembarking at the airport in the winter dusk, the undertow of weary passengers washed past me, walking through the rain towards the terminal. I stopped on the wet tarmac and stood alone. Inside the terminal, Suzy was waiting for me. She too would be standing alone, ready to meet, and not meeting.

And I wondered: who was she? For that matter, after three weeks with Heidl, who was I? And the hardest question: why were we *we*?

I had no idea.

We just were.

For our island and our time, all of it now too far away, we had been old for marriage. Suzy was twenty and I was twenty-three, and we knew with the fatalism of our world that now was the time when we must go on, and go on we did, ready to meet, and not meeting.

Our marriage consequently was a mystery to us both. It was what you did, and, having done it, we went on doing it. We did it and we did it and we didn't question it. There was a great determination tempered by a great pity that bound us together. There still prevailed on our remote island the custom of the unarranged marriage, as arbitrary and doomed, as hopeful, as absurd and oppressive and liberating as its corollary, the custom of the arranged marriage. The belief was it ended well when it did not end badly—at which point there had to be a villain, the bad man or bad woman. But of the custom itself there was no questioning or criticism.

I made my way inside to find, in defiance of even my imagination, Suzy was bigger than a week earlier. As the airport's sole luggage carousel groaned into life and began its elliptical labour, we both had to bow awkwardly to reach over her huge stomach to hug. Suzy seemed more than ever a stranger, a country I had once known now changed out of all recognition—her body, her smell, her softer voice, a slight blurred emotion in her responses, a vague smile in speaking—about what? whom? why? Did we feel something less? Or something more? I don't know. Sensing the danger of unravelling, I said the book was coming together.

The book and the twins—triplets! Suzy said.

Yes! I replied. A trifecta!

That's how we talked, or how we tried to talk. Going on, getting on. Cheerfully. I wasn't always so cheery, but I accepted my lot, or, at least, accepted that I should accept it. And Suzy never ceased trying, and I admired her for that. Our world was one of labour, and marriage was understood as another aspect of work. Suzy was a hard worker in all things.

Suzy was thirty-eight weeks gone, and we had had drummed into us by doctors and midwives and a murder of birth professionals—knowing, slightly irritating people who smiled too much when making their points—the many reasons twins always came early and the often distressing consequences of premature birth. But the doctor's warning about the possibility of pre-eclampsia hadn't seemed to come to anything and our twins continued happily ensconced within, by all measurements still healthy and growing.

Other than lethargy and the difficulties of manoeuvring

her improbable body through doorways, in and out of the EH's front seat, between furniture and people on the street (Homemaker? More like an icebreaker, she said, after knocking over a vase and two chairs with her belly), Suzy seemed to be having no physical problems—no bad back, no varicose veins, no wild emotional rides and, other than occasional heartburn of a morning, no discomfort. And so, after reading Bo her favourite fairytale of wolves and woodcutters, I returned that evening to my tiny writing room and Suzy to the sofa in the lounge room.

At my desk I stared dully at paper, empty screen, blinking cursor. From downstairs I heard a record playing softly, songs of innocence from the '70s. I went back down to the lounge room, lit now by only one low side lamp. For a song or two Suzy and I danced, the four of us making of our awkwardly aligned bodies a slow shuffle.

I'm sorry about the money, I whispered into Suzy's ear. I didn't know when I took the job that I'd get nothing upfront. I'll find us a second cot.

We still only had the one cot I'd scrounged from the tip and fixed up myself when Bo was born.

It'll work out, Suzy said. We'll be fine.

Writing this now, trying to recapture the mood of that night as we gently held each other, it is not the softness, the sweetness that I am astonished by. No. It is our lack of doubt. Our terrifying lack of doubt that tomorrow could be better than today, that things would turn out well. Knowing me, knowing you, as the song went. Round and round we went, knowing we were safe, knowing we had each other, knowing—knowing—knowing—knowing nothing at all.

2

The screen froze.

I swore at the computer, unbent a paperclip and with it forced the ejection of the floppy disk, switched the Mac Plus off and on, reinserted the disk, and then waited for an interminable time as the machine chugged away, making a harsh noise not unlike a choked coffee grinder as it booted back up. I looked around my writing room—more a wardrobe than a room, with its narrow walls that each night seemed to press in a little tighter—stretched my arms, and yawned. It was past midnight, but I had made unexpected progress since arriving home that evening. Finally, the machine once more running, I opened the file in which I had been writing the latest chapter.

None of my changes was there. That long evening's work was gone, all wiped by the screen freeze. I sat there feeling not so much angry as nauseated. I had so little time left and was now half a day further behind. The calamity only reinforced my growing sense that the book was an empty farce—that there was no book, and, worse, that there was never meant to be one.

And that, in turn, brought a painful question to my mind— had this always been Heidl's plan? After all, he had too many lies to cover, too many untruths to square to want a writer who might make sense of his ludicrous life. And coupled with that he had a criminal's disinclination to leave any record, no matter how devious and untrue. It all amounted to evidence. Was his growing confidence in me not as someone who would write his story, but as someone *who never would*? A front, a fool he could use to con the last of his advance out of Gene Paley? Was that why he chose me?

The mist outside my window left night-time Hobart wet smears of yellow on black. My hopes for myself as a writer were a joke, my failure as a family man unable to bring any money home a joke. And the most bitter joke of all was that Heidl had picked me out of obscurity because he knew I was incapable of writing the book.

I threw the manuscript pages into the corridor. I hated every word. I hated the computer on which I worked, I hated the table I had fixed up on which the computer sat. I looked at the scattered pages on which was written not a book, but the mounting evidence that I could not write a book. How stupid I had been! I told myself that I could have had a hundred other jobs and careers—though when I thought on exactly *what* job or career none immediately came to mind. Perhaps, I thought, that was what a writer was. Someone for whom writing had once been a passion and now it was the only thing they knew how to do.

Except, I realised with horror, I didn't know how.

3

I went to our bedroom. I needed the comfort, the oblivion of Suzy. She was awake, the twins were moving inside her, and she was unable to sleep.

You should be at your desk, writing, Suzy said. Not here with me.

And with that all my feelings of tenderness, of love, transformed into hate. It was becoming a familiar fall: sometimes it was enough for her to pour a cup of tea or put a fork to her lips for me to hate her. And, sometimes, I hated her even more for insignificant things than important ones—the way she did Bo's hair, or, for God's sake, how she arranged the kitchen utensils in a drawer. Love and hate were with me becoming so close and so strongly entwined that they sometimes felt the same thing. And this reassured me: for even at my worst, I consoled myself that this hatred perversely proved that, surely, some love must remain. What I began to fear was what suddenly seemed far worse, a moment when there might no longer be hate or love, a looming moment when I might feel *nothing* for Suzy.

Suzy would sometimes fight back, but in a way that was measured and reasoned, and that only angered me more. She would say she understood me. That she understood my fears. And that was the worst.

Because if I didn't understand what was happening to me how could she? If I couldn't name the dread that I felt surrounding me, soaking into me, rising within me like a silent scream, how could she be so confident she knew?

At times I could see how much Suzy was suffering from my outbursts, and I would be satisfied. But only for a short time. After, I would be horrified at what I had done and who I had become, and I would not understand myself. And amidst the growing rubble of my life, Heidl appeared before me as a guide with his nostrums about a world that one could only sample and exploit, but never take root in.

The evidence is with me.

It was. And I was terrified.

Go back to work, Suzy said.

I exploded. Bo was staying a few nights at Suzy's parents in order that Suzy might get some rest, and with the restraint of a child sleeping nearby gone, I now heard myself yelling at Suzy, What the fuck would *you* know about writing?

I watched her crying with a sense of desolate satisfaction. When I left the house she was still sobbing. It was pleasant to walk the cold streets and feel the chill wind on my face blowing off the mountain snow far above. I found a dingy, late-night bar. And as I downed drink after drink, I told myself that it had been necessary to make clear to Suzy the many burdens I bore as writer.

On going to the grim outdoor toilets, I walked into a spider's web freshly spun across a doorway corner. I was seized by an odd panic. I brushed and then tore at my cheeks, but when I returned to the bar I could still feel the sticky threads as if they were enshrouding me. And suddenly Heidl didn't seem a job, or money, but somehow inescapable like the spider's web, something enclosing and claustrophobic. As my fear grew my anger evaporated and there arose in me a sense of Suzy as my only refuge. I had to admit that Suzy had not meant anything by what she'd said, while what I had said began to seem to me so unnecessary, because, really, what was unbearable about being a writer if you were writing and your writing was about to be published?

And, for some reason, as I scratched at my sticky face I became convinced that the only way to escape these wretched threads was to go back to tell Suzy how much I loved her. And then I remembered how I'd made her cry, how hurt she had looked. When I thought how vulnerable she was, and how bullying I had been, my pride soured into shame because I had been cruel. I realised nothing could justify what I had done, and without finishing the drink I'd just paid for, I rushed home to apologise.

But when I got home our bed was empty. Suzy was gone.

4

On the kitchen sink I found a note from her in a jerky hand. It said her waters had broken and she was driving herself to the hospital. Overcome with guilt for all that I had done, horrified by my cruelty, and worried for Suzy in labour, I rushed to the hospital in a taxi. But when I finally found Suzy lying on a gurney in a corridor, she was oddly peaceful and relaxed, and it was as if I had never abandoned her when she had needed me.

She took my hand, an uncharacteristic gesture, and told me she was in the early stages, her contractions occasional and not much worse than a bad cramp. Mercifully, she said nothing about all that had passed earlier. I was too ashamed and too addled with drink and remorse to apologise. I sat on a plastic chair next to her and she abruptly fell asleep. I stared at the waxiness of her closed eyes until mine closed also, thinking of Heidl and trying not to think of Heidl. Instead, I tried to focus on how I might get a second cot, a new washing machine, and as time passed, Heidl became less real and the world of the hospital, its fluorescent lights, its smell of disinfectants, its constant clatter, became more concrete and finally grew comforting.

I woke to Suzy pacing the corridor as a fresh set of contractions came and went. I rushed to hold her and as I did so she looked through me and moaned. I felt a stranger. Fearful, I went to get help. At the far end of the corridor I found some nurses chatting at a ward station. I asked them to do something. But what was frightening for me was everyday and mundane to them. When I begged them to help Suzy, a chubby-faced midwife fobbed me off, saying that they would send someone down shortly.

Defeated, I returned to Suzy. After what felt to me an eternity, a nurse came with two orderlies and wheeled Suzy to a four-bed ward—dimly lit, hushed, empty—a peaceful haven in which to await the birth. Not long after, a young girl in labour was brought in. No more than fifteen, she could not stop sobbing.

Her cries of loneliness and desolation were unbearable, but still she kept on, sometimes a low whimper, sometimes a stretched moan. A middle-aged woman arrived with a boy who appeared to be the prospective father. He had some fluff under his nose, a cigarette pack poked out from under his rolled-up flannelette sleeve, and with his spindly sticks of torso and limb he affected the slightly arthritic swagger of the older man. He didn't know what to do or what to say. Not once did he touch her. Perhaps he was born the same way, falling first into this same terrifying void, and perhaps, thereafter, the fall never ended. After ten minutes of awkwardness he left, and after half an hour so too the middle-aged woman. The child-mother started to sob once more.

Her howling grew terrible, the wretched lament of a child lost and alone. On and on it went, sometimes a screech of despair, sometimes a dull whimpering of terror. Sitting in the dark, listening to her cry, I thought people are not even born equal. They are born in misery, they are born in sadness and despair, they are born in terrible fear. She was right to be frightened, to not be grateful. The world was only beginning for her, and every day it revealed itself as crueller. I thought again of Heidl's dark visions of the world, and shuddered. In the morning she was taken away to a birthing room and I never saw or heard of her again.

5

As public health patients we were not entitled to any specific doctor. An older white coat told us everything was going perfectly well, but his successor, a young white coat, decided Suzy should be induced. He dismissed me with a wave of the hand when I told him his predecessor's opinion, and when I pointed out that Suzy was already in the early stages of labour he shook his head. He told me this was about the health of my wife and two unborn children and we weren't going to play games with that—*were we?*

A tall nurse appeared with a stand from which hung a sack of clear fluid. She inserted a cannula into Suzy's arm, connected the sack, set the machine, and the drug began to drip. We were transferred to a birthing room. For some time nothing happened. We wondered what the point of it all was. But when the contractions began to come like blows of a sledgehammer, we knew. The slow, gracefully building tempo of the body was gone and in its place Suzy now had to ride a chemically induced catharsis in which the pain came too quick and too hard.

Suzy began journeying deeper into her solitary world of torment, her mottled face drained of all emotion, silent and exhausted beyond imagining, before her screams started all over again. Yet, other than her growing cries, which were accepted as commonplace and unimportant, a perverse serenity reigned in which all was good and as it should be. Around Suzy people smiled, even joked and discreetly gossiped.

But in her screams I began hearing his laughter.

Making an excuse that I needed the bathroom, I rushed outside to get away from it all: Suzy's screams, Heidl's laughter. In the abruptly bright corridor outside I found another world where life was lived as ever; some nurses were laughing about a fading rock star's plastic surgery while two doctors were arguing about a Middle Eastern war. So different was it that I caught myself looking at my watch wondering if I needed to reset it for a new time zone, a different place where it was unexpectedly morning or evening, but never what you understood it to be. Yet just metres away, separated by a thin wall, I knew there was another country.

On the other side of that wall so many wondrous things were happening and accepted as part of the process of birth that it would not have surprised me if a swarm of blue butterflies had filled the room and covered Suzy's face, or if Suzy was to be found floating upside down from the ceiling, and all these phenomena would be drolly dismissed as everyday and normal and part of what I was told was *the birthing process*, and all was fine as long as they observed their natural and correct order, and the blue butterfly swarm came at this time and lasted for so long, and not less and not more, and Suzy floated in the air this way but not that, and so on and so forth. Everything was miraculous, and yet any indication that each miracle was anything other than ordinary and everyday was dismissed by the professionals as the hapless naivety of the father.

6

Hours became minutes and minutes days. At some point it was night and at another time morning and then night again, or perhaps it was always night or always day. And yet in all that long time, some thirty-six hours as I was later to learn, I secretly struggled with myself. The room seemed full of such goodness, of people seeking to bring life into the world, yet I kept hearing Heidl's voice saying the world was not good, that it was evil. And to drown out that voice in my head I mopped Suzy's brow, consoled her, rubbed her back, worried and fretted for her.

No matter how much I tried *to be there* for Suzy, through the beeping of heart-rate monitors, the murmur of low conversation, through her screams, I kept hearing Heidl, and, as ever, he would not shut up: *There is no right thing. You will lose.* And my growing terror was that Heidl was right; that none of my emotions was genuine, that my real instinct was at best a vague physical curiosity and at worst a morbid indifference, that I was simply playing a role—the husband, the father, *the good man.*

And suddenly unsure of who I was, every gesture I made seemed despicable, every word I uttered seemed false. My anguish for Suzy became muddled with my terror as to who I might be, and I almost felt her contractions as blows to my own body.

At times, her suffering came close to overwhelming me. Suzy was in such agony and yet everyone understood that the only path out of that agony was the birth. And so, to that end, there could only be more pain and more suffering. Suzy was offered pethidine, I begged her to take it, but she wouldn't. Perhaps she feared that losing some physical sense of pain might mean losing her babies. I don't know. I realise now it was just one of so many things we never talked about.

She began crying but her tears were overwhelmed by the next set of contractions that left her groaning in agony.

It hurts, Suzy growled in a register so low it was hard to believe it was Suzy. *It hurts, Kif.*

Her lips had grown thin, her face flushed, her eyes, usually dreamlike, were now bright and hard, starkly intent. She was becoming something else, something fundamental. And I understood she would not give up, that her whole being was summoning up and concentrating all her agony and strength to push.

The birthing room had begun to fill with a new tension and more and more white coats: two obstetricians, two pediatricians, assorted others, one for each twin. And though nothing was said I became aware that all that had previously been good had somehow become bad. Suzy, who had been in pain but strong, was now, I realised, in worse pain and growing weak. In the rippling whirlpool of contraction and rest, Suzy's moments of coherence were fewer and fewer until she was not even aware of my presence, but seemed to have sunk to another place where I could no longer reach her.

7

A strange hiatus settled upon us. We were all now waiting. I sensed the diminishing smiles and conversation, and I understood whatever it was that was happening was no longer something preordained to end happily, but a moment where everything lay finely poised between life and death. A doctor, an athletic young man, walked up to me, and, looking at me as if I were the doorman, without introducing himself, said, tell your wife to push harder. Fresh contractions were hitting Suzy's body with a rising violence, the breaking of which were marked by long, low moans of exhaustion. The doctor sniffled.

She's trying as hard as she can, I said. I was defensive. But more than that I was, for the first time, frightened for Suzy.

If we don't see some change in the next ten minutes we're going to have to do an emergency caesarean, the doctor said, and sniffled again.

I asked what exactly was happening. Wiping his fine aquiline nose with a crumpled red polka-dotted handkerchief he told me they thought the twins' limbs had become locked together in the birth canal and they were jammed. The longer it went on the further down the birth canal the babies would be forced and the more inextricable the jam would become, making a natural birth impossible. Getting them out might require *a major procedure.*

He spoke softly, quietly, as if he were a teller advising me my bank account was overdrawn. He added the usual caveats, that this was only their opinion and a natural birth remained possible. However, to wait any longer than ten minutes might mean babies and mother would all be risking *grave consequences.*

When we go in, he said, we'll be going in with the mother's life our first priority.

And the babies?

He wiped his handsome nose again. Behind the crumpled handkerchief I saw a grimace.

We'll do all that we can, he said.

I walked four very long steps back to Suzy, lost in her agony.

Suzy, I said. Please. Please listen. This is serious.

It sounded false; worse, an insult. Yet Suzy's eyes finally fixed on me, looking at me with an almost infinite trust, as though I alone might rescue her from her suffering. It seemed wrong to ask of her what I now did.

You must try harder, Suzy.

I *am* trying hard, she stammered, and I knew that I had upset her and, equally, that she was disappointed with herself. As hard as I can, she whispered, her voice scarcely audible.

Try harder, I said. I felt such shame asking it of her.

I can't, Suzy was saying in guttural gasps as a new wave of contractions slammed into her. I can't, Kif! No! she suddenly cried, Please don't! Please! No!

She began a low moaning, a strange animal sound, and I was again losing her; she was tumbling into some void as her body heaved and convulsed. Her face was scarcely recognisable. I leant in close, telling her again that she could do it. But it was becoming clear she couldn't. I felt a tap on my shoulder and turned to see the handsome doctor. I walked with him to a far corner of the room.

Your wife is exhausted, he said, sniffled, and continued. The babies are increasingly stressed. We have to operate.

Five minutes, I begged. Just five more, that's all I'm asking.

8

I went back to Suzy. I pointlessly wiped her face once more, and once more I begged her. She was very far away. Her whole being seemed caught in some primal struggle that was not hers to share. She suddenly screamed in a way that I had never heard before, deeply, terribly, as much an unrooted gasp of horror as a primeval cry. It was as if from somewhere deep within she was finding a strength additional to all that she had spent, summoning some will to push her exhausted flesh further.

And as that awful screaming continued—a sound suspended between a moan of death and a plea for pity, an acceptance of what life was and a rage against it—as a mood of terse attention took hold of the room, everyone continued on as if it were everyday work, which it was also, and still measurements were taken and still vital signs were checked, and still people chatted softly.

Suzy reached for my hand. It seemed an insignificant thing. Her grasp was not strong, hardly a grasp at all; rather it would be truer to say she rested her hand in mine, no more than that. But when I tried to place her hand on the bed, her body jolted, and her grip tightened into a lock. She was adrift in some vast elsewhere and I understood I was not to let her go.

An excited sound cut through the room's hushed babble. I looked up from Suzy to see a sudden interest among the white coats.

She's crowning, I heard the plump-faced midwife say.

Suzy's hand fell away from mine as portentous faces crowded somewhat comically in between her spread thighs and then parted for the midwife. In spite of all the expertise massed in the room, she seemed the only one helping Suzy give birth, while the others contented themselves with occasional stares and the stern murmuring of expert opinion.

I rushed around. Between Suzy's bloody thighs an orb of greasy hair was appearing and receding in powerful pulses. There was blood and fluid everywhere. Each time, the greasy hair would emerge a little more, then vanish within, as if taunting the world, as if unsure whether to arrive or to depart. A hush came over the room.

Get ready, a voice said.

And in that hush, as the moment of birth grew close, I heard Heidl.

The evidence is with me!

A head that seemed vastly oversized had begun to form out of Suzy—so much bigger than anything I had ever imagined possible. It was in its blood-slubbed state far more reptilian, even amphibious, than human.

And again, that wretched voice.

Take what you can! Before it destroys you!

The midwife grew serious. The doctors all deferred to her now as she talked Suzy through the final stages. As she softly spoke, telling Suzy to slow down or speed up her movements, to push this way or that, to relax or to strain, a dance between the two women began.

Suzy travelled further into her agony, screaming, writhing, begging God. The blue hospital smock fell away, leaving a nipple exposed; she didn't care, no one did, we were all beyond such things, and yet I covered her and watched it fall away once more. Suzy looked up, wet-flecked hair stuck to her sweaty flesh, lost eyes searching me for some answer I didn't have or direction I couldn't give.

All we understood was that in that crowded room so full of expertise Suzy was alone with her body. So terrifyingly alone. She was on the gas now, I don't know for how long she had been on it, she had a thing against the gas as she had against the pethidine, but now she sucked on it greedily. I couldn't get Heidl out of my head. Suzy stared at me from some great distance, as if I were a stranger, a monster, and her face began to contort and then broke into a scream as another contraction took hold.

Good girl, the midwife said as the head began to protrude, good girl, push harder.

I *am* pushing hard, Suzy pleaded and then she cried out from the bowels of her being as slimy shoulders appeared, followed in a tumble by arms and froglegged torso, bloodied, bunched up and buttered in vernix; and in a final shuddering convulsion legs and feet suddenly slid out.

The baby was taken off to be weighed and measured before I even saw it properly. From a far corner there came a cry, almost a quack, hot dry air rasping still-wet lungs. Through a wall of white coats I saw the baby, stick-like legs kicking as if erratically pedalling a partly seized crank, penis wobbling below a pear torso. And I felt such a tumult of so many things: gratitude, fear, wonder, emptiness, and a confusion as to why I was allowed to be part of such a thing.

I heard Suzy groan. Turning back to her, I saw her now partially deflated belly was convulsing.

Slow her down, a white coat barked. It's too soon.

But it was too late. Something was wrong. I had forgotten that there was another child still inside.

9

Once more, the mood in the room abruptly changed. The midwife urged Suzy to try to ease up on her contractions, but her contractions were all that Suzy now was.

My God! It's crowning already, the now red-faced midwife said. It's coming so quickly—

And she had just got into position when I saw Suzy open once more. Out of her there flowed a translucent egg, which the midwife accepted in her cupped hands as if it were a gift.

And inside the egg there floated a tiny being.

There were cries of astonished delight at the pink- and blue-hued globe as the midwife held it up. We all gazed in wonder as a ginseng root-like creature, serene in its perfect world, rolled within the amniotic sac's limpid clutch. I gasped as the midwife pushed her thumb into the caul to rip it apart. As if it were a magician's sleight-of-hand trick, the miraculous bubble vanished in a flood of water, leaving revealed in the midwife's cupped hands a baby boy.

He had blue eyes, an unearthly china blue, large and open as a summer sky. For no more than a moment or two, in the dimly lit ward, those eyes gazed steadily and calmly at me. The enormity of it, the insignificance of me, everything at that moment suddenly made sense and was as it should always be.

And then, once more, I heard Heidl. Something had happened, and yet what was it? All I could see was my family yet all I could hear was Heidl, Heidl, Heidl. I wanted them safe, but were they? I feared Heidl coming for them, for me, for us. Everything was as it should be, everything was good, and I knew it would not get better. I had thought I would finally know some truth of life and that it would be liberating, and for a few moments it had been so.

But almost immediately it all vanished as the miracle of the amniotic sac had, dissolved into a bloody puddle, and my euphoria was overtaken once more by Heidl's talking. Everything that had been liberating was revealed to me as imprisoning, and all that had been joyful suddenly grew desolate.

I saw before me two strange animals, wobbly limbed and puce-faced, grimacing creatures with spastic movements, almost aliens. I felt worthless on this earth unless I was capable of doing something that was equivalent to their birth. Yet other than death what was equivalent to what I had just witnessed?

I desperately wanted to feel something, to feel anything, yet my mind was filling with Heidl's words, the madness of Heidl's thoughts, a terror was on me, and much as I fought the sensation I couldn't escape the sense that what he said was true.

The world is evil.

I traced a finger on our firstborn twin's cheek.

You will lose.

I cupped the secondborn twin's tiny warm head with my hand.

Be punished. Be destroyed.

I suddenly felt so many things. Yet Heidl had all the words.

Look around you, Kif. The evidence of the world is with me.

You're lost for words, the midwife said.

There is no right thing.

No, I said, unsure, Heidl's voice like a tinnitus of derangement in my ears. It's . . . it's just *not* what I expected.

There was fluid everywhere and still it poured out of Suzy.

It never is, she said.

And there came the placenta, a huge liver-like organ, which half-fell and half-flopped out into a stainless-steel kidney dish, and after it more blood and fluid.

And, with that, finally, it was done.

14

1

ENCRUSTED IN THE SHAGGY SEAT COVERS of the Melbourne taxi was the Melbourne taxi smell of burnt plastic and stale Melbourne vomit. I opened the grubby Melbourne street atlas to show the Melbourne taxi driver what route to take through his city of Melbourne to get to Port Melbourne. It was that sort of city. Maybe it still is.

What did you say you were again? the cab driver asked.

A writer, I said with little conviction.

Would you be a Jez Dempster man by any chance?

I wound down the window to get a mouth of fresh exhaust and tried to think through how I might deal with Heidl on this, my last day working with him. I had just nine hours to surmount the insurmountable.

I was astonished to have got this far. When, after the twins' birth, I was on the verge of ringing Gene Paley and tossing the whole thing in, it had been Suzy who had urged me to go on, saying I couldn't give up, that we needed the money. How else were we to pay for the firewood? The bassinet? The baby seats?

Not that she liked it either. She had come home the previous day with the twins, was exhausted beyond measure and needed me, and I was in my writing room. But as she said, what choice did we have? We were in too deep. We both understood that it was no longer about my literary ambitions, or any ambitions, that it wasn't about vanity or art but only cash, the cash we didn't have, the cash we so desperately needed to keep our mortgage payments going and our heads above water.

And so, following the twins' birth, Suzy still in hospital, Bo at Suzy's parents, I went straight back to work on the second draft, preparing a special manuscript with my concerns tagged and highlighted. I drew up a list of highly specific questions to deal with the major confusions in Heidl's story that I had never been able to reconcile, and which Pia Carnevale was now insisting had to be resolved one way or another. I even had printed out a schedule to show him. It broke down the scant few hours we had together that day into the pressing matters of the manuscript, showing—if we were to get the job done—how many minutes we could spend on each concern before moving on to the next. It was ludicrous. But it was also the only hope I had of ensuring Heidl might do what had to be done.

In addition to this not inconsiderable task was something simpler. Having grown nervous with Heidl's ever more apparent lack of interest in his own biography, Gene Paley now wanted me to get Heidl's signature on a document drawn up by TransPac's lawyers that said my manuscript was a true and accurate record of his life.

As my taxi pulled up at TransPac's offices, I saw Ray in his now familiar sentry position outside the main entrance, leaning on the concrete planter box. It was a heavily overcast day, with a storm constantly threatening but never arriving, and Ray seemed similarly lost in some interminable waiting. He was so absorbed in thought or memory that he didn't notice me arrive, and never saw me until I was standing next to him, calling his name.

He raised his head slowly, still looking at the ground where a few rain spots would fall and vanish, as if he had spilt his thoughts on the ground and couldn't see where they had fallen.

Ziggy's lost it, he said.

What?

Completely fuckn lost it. Someone tried to kill him last night.

Who'd be bothered?

That's what he reckons. He thinks—

Ray shook his head.

I dunno what he thinks. He's got choke marks around his neck, that's all I know.

He looked at me.

But who knows? You? Me? Ziggy?

You've seen him, I said.

Me? Ray asked, genuinely bewildered by where his talk was leading him. You've talked to him. You know his whole shitty story so you tell me—what does he *fuckn* think?

Let's go up.

He says I should have been there. That I let him down.

Come on, Ray.

But he gave me the night off. Said he didn't need me.

Let's go.

I can't, mate.

Cmon.

He's ordered me to stay here.

For what?

To keep a lookout.

For fuck's—

For whoever tried to kill him. In case they come back. I dunno.

Well they can enter over there, I said, pointing to a distant entrance. Or over there—there's access from the rear at the end of that drive.

Tell him! Ray suddenly shouted. Fuckn tell him! I can't protect him down here! I'm better up there with him.

I'm going up, I said, and left Ray to his strange, pointless post, a job that for some reason troubled him so much he hadn't even bothered to notice me. I caught his reflection in the glass as I entered TransPac, standing there almost as if he were the assassin waiting to strike, while all the time posing as the body-guard who was meant to take the bullet.

<h1 style="text-align:center">2</h1>

In the executive's office Heidl was for once not behind the executive's desk but pacing the room.

Siegfried, I said.

He glanced at me, shook his head, and kept walking back and forth. But this day of all days I had resolved that I would keep my cool and not be drawn into his games of evasion. Not be provoked, not be diverted, not be misled. Nor would I lose my temper, nor my interest, but keep to my schedule of tasks. One way or another I would by the end of the day have made coherent, if not accurate, all that I had written, and—above all other things—have the release signed. I sat down, arranged my manuscript and notes on the table. Heidl took no notice.

Ziggy, I said. I realised it was the first time I had ever used the familiar form of his name, though whether it was out of contempt or a growing intimacy, or both, I have no idea. Fuck you, I thought. Fuck you.

You see anyone out there? Heidl said. He was pointing out of the window at the city. Sitting in a car?

He seemed different than I had ever seen him: agitated, flushed, almost deranged.

Ziggy, we need to get through a lot today—

As you drove in? Maybe half a block back? Maybe a whole block?

He waved his hand towards Europe, towards Mecca, towards Houston and Langley and Laos, towards the South Pole and the North Pole and the past and the future and everything that spun in between.

There, he said. Did you?

I hated the shape of his mouth at that moment, his gap teeth, his whole aftershaved and lolly-striped shirt look. I wanted to ask him: are you a mid-level accounts manager presenting half-yearly results or a con man with some fucking criminal pride?

Instead, though, I patted the pile of paper that was my manuscript in the splayed hand, flat-palmed manner I had observed of Gene Paley, hoping, perhaps, to project a certain executive élan and suggest a good job nearly done.

We just have to get these last queries sorted, I said with a fixed smile of a type the word *determined* is sometimes used. And then the book's done.

Well, *you* wouldn't see anything, Heidl said. Would you, Kif? What do you know? There it is—that's the thing.

But what was *the thing*? That was perhaps my fundamental problem. I had no idea what *the thing* was. Nor did Ray. Heidl, on the other hand, had too many ideas about *the thing* and not one of them was useable. All I could do was offer up the illusion to which I had devoted my life.

The book, Ziggy.

The book wasn't the thing either though. The book, as I'd come to realise, wasn't anything.

Heidl went back to the windows that faced the street, and drawing his back tightly up against a rough-rendered concrete pillar that separated two of the windows, he twisted his head and scanned the street, as if a sniper might be out there. His gesture struck me as absurd and melodramatic, and it only infuriated me more.

The book? Heidl said. You really think I want to talk about that?

I said I did.

The book? Heidl hissed, half-question, half-astonishment, as if it were a trick or a curse or some inescapable destiny, or a fatal trap combining all three. He shook his head. Today's emotion, I guessed—it always felt a little like bad charades—was despair.

I told him, yes, that was right, that it was the book, that it was his book, and because of his book we were there.

How do you think this happened? Heidl said, turning to me and pointing at his collar. *Tell me!*

With a sudden jerk he pulled his collar down to reveal two shocking bruises that ran around half his neck, disturbingly large blue-black welts.

3

Obscene and inexplicable, I avoided looking at the bruises any further by returning my gaze to the monitor and clicking a few keys.

Look! he hissed.

I said it was time to work.

Heidl leaned in, adopting a posture and tone at once angry and conspiratorial.

I'll give you an idea, he said.

I agreed an idea would help. I said it might even amount to a novelty.

The banks! he stage-whispered.

I asked if he had got hit by a bouncing cheque, as a test to see if he was listening.

The banks, he yelled, *the fucking banks, Kif, want me dead!*

He wasn't listening. I felt this wasn't a bad approach for me either. I walked over and passed him his copy of the typescript and schedule and explained our timetable for the day.

Two men tried to garrotte me, Heidl said.

I said I wouldn't blame them, but we had other things to think about.

He thrust himself off the pillar and, coming in close to me, started yelling, brandishing the typescript and schedule as if they were damning documents for his case.

Kif—someone tried to kill me last night! I was walking back to my hotel from a restaurant when two men grabbed me and pulled me into an alleyway. One began strangling me, then—

I asked the obvious question: Why?

Why? You ask me why? Maybe for the same reason they killed Frank Nugan.

I was falling: Who? I asked.

Frank Nugan. He knew too much. I know too much. I showed the world how stupid they looked. They don't like looking stupid. Seven hundred mill! If I tell you all the things I know about them, about how they work, naming names, you know, if I tell you all those things then they'll want to kill me. I'd want to kill myself, because it'd be easier.

And still I continued to fall and still I couldn't help myself, and Heidl had me as he always had me: falling and falling.

Kill yourself, I said, or tell the truth?

Both. That's why they're out there. They probably think I have written it all up, everything, and that's why they want to kill me.

You're saying the banks paid these men to kill you?

My God! Heidl cried. They tried to strangle me, Kif. I am no hero, but I knew it was the end if I didn't do something. I managed to trip one over, slip out of the wire they had around my neck, and run like hell.

The bruises were real, but who could say what had happened? If it was a wire, I wondered, why then were the bruises wide rather than narrow? Was it a mugging gone bad? Some rough trade turned too rough? But I didn't bother saying any of this.

Why would the banks want to kill you when they can get you locked up for years? I asked. They'll win in the court, that's all they care about.

What if I tell the truth in the dock about them?

For God's sake, Ziggy—can we just work?

I'll tell the truth, he said.

It'd be a first, I sneered. You've given me nothing, not truth, not even half-decent lies. I've written my book in spite of you, and now all I'm asking is one thing; just one. Just help me correct any obvious errors in the lies I've made up on your behalf.

Even as I heard myself saying it, it made no sense. Errors in lies? My book? I thought of his memoir as *my* book?

What do you mean lies? Heidl said. His tone had altered. Being with Heidl was like eating an ice cream that turned into underarm deodorant that turned into an echidna. *Lies?* Heidl repeated.

Lies? That's all I have—

Lies? Heidl interrupted, his tone one of incredulity. I fought off two men who were sent to murder me, but it's not the end of it, I know. And you say I am a liar? A liar! he said again, this time shriller and louder. This is *my* memoir, Kif!

Just tell me what you can and can't wear. I can fix the rest.

Heidl was mumbling something about needing to call Phil Monassis, his lawyer, as he picked up the phone, hit a few keys, put it back down, and walked over to the window. He swore under his breath.

Where the book has an accidental collision with known facts, I said, can we just make sure that it's a successful hit and run? And if not, that I can't be found out as being wrong?

Heidl glanced at me, and then looked out the window at a blue-black sky of darkening clouds and below them the cheerless concrete bunkers of Port Melbourne.

And if there's anything you want to add, I said, tell me.

Once more there was that odd moment where Heidl looked at me blankly, as if searching for the next emotion to wear, and then his face turned to anger.

Anything I want to add? hissed Heidl. You and Gene Paley listen to nothing I say; you've gone ahead and made up that pile of lies. You want me to put my name to it? I should never have signed with such a disgraceful company.

And then he threw in the kicker.

I should have got a real writer.

He was crazed, impossible. I was exhausted by him, angered by him, insulted by his continuing idea of me as one more credulous fool who would believe any garbage he spun.

You are a liar, I said. But I don't care any more. We just have to get through these pages today.

You're the *fiction writer* and you're saying *I'm the liar*?

No one's going to murder you, Ziggy, I said. Other than me. But the banks? They're locking you away for a very long time. That's their vengeance.

They want to kill me.

They want to do you slowly. That's why they pay lawyers, not hit men. Now can we work?

It's just like Nugan Hand.

Ziggy, can we work?

They killed him.

Who?

Frank Nugan. They killed Frank Nugan.

4

I'm flying out at seven, I said. The cab will be here at five-thirty, and we have to have a signed-off manuscript that I can then finish back in Tasmania over the next week. That gives us a bit less than five hours.

Heidl's back remained turned to me.

You don't need to read it all, I said.

My panic was a tennis ball in my throat. It was already past midday and still not one fact checked and not one step closer to Heidl's signature on the release contract.

They can do what they want, Heidl said to the glass. He brought a hand to his bruised neck and rubbed it. Cut me up into little pieces, he went on, post me in a box to Dolly. They're out there, Kif.

Who?

Maybe I am the goat. You with me?

What are you talking about now? I asked.

They barbecue people for less, Kif, he said, and turned around. That's what I mean.

What?—Who, Ziggy? The CIA? Hungry Jack's?

Maybe. Maybe it's the banks. Maybe it's the banks *and* the CIA. Maybe it's not. They'd know I'm here. Talking. Writing.

I wish—

And they have a common cause. I can see you're with me now, Kif, and that's what matters.

What matters?

Who killed Frank Nugan. That's what I'm saying.

To write I was overwhelmed is an underwhelming way of describing my state of being at that time. I was exhausted in every way, and I was out of ideas on how I might cajole or trick or persuade Heidl to finish the book. I had been on the job, day and night, non-stop for over four weeks now, except for the day and a half when Suzy had given birth to the twins. I needed to rest a moment, to go with him while I thought of some other ruse to get him back to the book. I ventured a nod.

You're getting it now, Kif, Heidl said.

But I've never heard of Frank Nugan.

Exactly my point, Kif. Nugan Hand Bank. You've heard of it?

I said I had, because it was easier than saying I hadn't, but other than Heidl's occasional comments and a few mentions in the clippings file, I hadn't really—something of a scandal, conspiracy theories about the CIA bringing down Whitlam's left-wing government in '75 in a more sober manner than they had Allende in Chile or Manley in Jamaica. I had been too young to take any real interest.

It was an Australian merchant bank, Heidl said. Set up in Sydney in the early '70s by an alcoholic Australian lawyer, Frank Nugan, and an American ex-Green Beret, Mike Hand. Except it wasn't really an Australian bank, was it? And here's the kicker—

It's nearly one, I said.

It was a CIA front.

I wanted to ask about the date you—

It was full of CIA people, Heidl interrupted. Enough spooks and ex-generals to take a small country. Bill Colby, ex-head of the CIA, he became the legal counsel of this little Australian bank. Strange, eh? There were lots of others. Buddy Yates—he was a US admiral—he became the bank's president. Unusual? Dale Holmgren. I knew him, good guy, back in Laos. Ran the CIA airline there.

So what? I said. Pol Pot wasn't that great either, but if the debt collector repossesses my car it doesn't make the Khmer Rouge responsible. Now, on page forty-seven you'll see that what you've said contradicts what you say on page—

Laundering heroin profits out of Indonesia, Heidl went on and over me, oblivious as rain is to sun, as sea is to sand. And where did that go? Straight into the CIA's account in Tehran to run special ops there.

I held up a page as if it were an incriminating document Heidl was compelled to answer questions about.

Now, I said. When Tantalus Bank set up your second line of credit for thirty-seven million dollars, was it May 1988 or—

But on Heidl went, ignoring my pleas, evading my questions, detailing how Nugan Hand had *lines* into money laundering and tax evasion through Nugan, and through Hand, who had worked for the CIA in Laos, *lines* into the drug business and gun running.

Ziggy, it's past one. We've got a bit over four hours—that's all.

Nugan Hand was everywhere, Heidl said. Selling bomb timers and plastic explosives to Gaddafi. Arms to Angola, spy ships to Iran. Then 1980—bang! Frank Nugan, shot dead in his Merc in Lithgow. Mike Hand vanishes from Australia, never seen again, all the money funnelled out of the bank over the previous few months, and nothing left except fifty million dollars of debts. You get it?

Ziggy, how has this got anything to do with the book?

Well, if you can't see what I am saying here, Kif, I can't tell you.

He returned to staring out on the dismal Port Melbourne industrial park on that dismal winter day, a gathering catastrophe of tilt-slab concrete building and tilt-slab concrete-coloured sky. His voice was soft as he spoke.

They'll understand when I am found dead.

I was worn out with Heidl. I wanted to kill him, but as far as I knew I was the only one. Sadly, it was a job even the loyal Ray wouldn't do for Heidl. I sensed at heart the idea of his death was just another illusion he was inventing for us all to live in—a game that involved the near murder the night before, toying with the idea of suicide, homicide, the Glock, imagining with relish the posthumous mystery, the grand conspiracy theories . . .

I couldn't stomach the falseness of it all, the toying with people it involved, the perverse curiosity of placing people in extreme situations to see how they might react. I couldn't explain the bruises, but I was sure the truth was far more mundane than attempted murder. And I didn't care. I simply understood his purpose with all his stories was to divert me from finishing the book. And as he kept on talking, I loathed him more than ever.

5

Shut up, I said.

I pushed my Francis Bacon tub chair back and stood up. I felt something breaking inside of me, or perhaps it was several things—some tolerance, some balance, some acquired decency unravelling, transforming into one thing: rage. I walked over to where Heidl stood at the window.

Please, Siegfried, I said. Please. *Just shut up.*

Heidl spun around. He stared at me for some time with the snap-frozen intensity of a lizard with a fly. Then he became suddenly energised, and seemed almost pleased. All traces of his fretting and fear vanished, and he spoke with a new voice, sonorous and soothing, the voice of an HR manager sacking someone he particularly despises.

Why all this negative energy, Kif?

Shut the fucking fuck up! I heard myself yelling.

I have noticed this anger you carry.

Can we just get the work fucking done?

You can get help to manage these emotions, Kif. Perhaps they have someone here you could talk with. I can mention it to Gene—

I held out a shuddering hand. I warned Heidl I had had enough.

Somewhere there's help, Kif. Never forget that. It's a beautiful thing, an important thing. It would do you and Suzy—

And then I was yelling that he was lazy, so fucking lazy, so fucking unhelpful, but now, just for once, he had to fucking work.

Heidl froze, as if his mind were rebooting. And after a few moments, as if putting on another coat, he reappeared before me cloaked in righteous anger. He began yelling back in a manner almost identical to my own.

Fuck you! he cried. I thought you were my friend! I trusted you—and now. Now! This! Fuck you!

I wanted to hit him. Actually, I wanted to hurt him. He moved away; I followed. We circled each other. I was full of a great violence that needed release. If he came close enough I was going to hit him. Hard. And not just once. I was ready. He had no idea.

Or he did, as he made sure to keep out of my reach as I advanced on him. For an overweight man he was surprisingly light on his feet. I would not have been surprised to learn that he was a good dancer.

You arrogant shit, Heidl shouted, as he circled around. I gave you your big fucking break! Who do you think you are? You've done nothing in your life. Thirty-one calling yourself a novelist but there's no novel.

I felt my face tighten.

Is there? I'm right, aren't I? And Suzy? Poor thing. She supports you, doesn't she? While you pretend to yourself and the world that you're a talent. That you're going to make it.

I lunged at him, but he managed to dart out of reach.

But you're not, are you, Kif?

He scurried behind the conference table, across which he now shouted.

And I introduce you to Gene Paley! Vouch for you! I gave him my word that you were up to the job. But what have you done? This pile of shit—I have read it. It's a disgrace. What am I to do?

You lazy arsehole! I yelled. You haven't read it. Even now you can't be bothered to read it—can you?

Heidl used the table to keep his distance, yelling and cursing. But his rage didn't seem real. Nothing about him was real. I yelled at him all that I thought: about his cowardice. His laziness. His lies. His greed. His manipulation. His *shit*. About how we now had less than half a day to sign off on the book or there was no book.

But I knew now that his cunning was so much greater, so much more determined and wily than my patience. We kept circling each other, screaming and shouting at each other, me ever wilder as his imitation of my rage grew more ludicrous with each passing minute. He imitated my anger, but he couldn't mimic my madness.

I finally managed to scruff him by one of his lapels. My other arm was flexing with a fist balled ready to punch him when his blue double-breasted sports jacket—when not in disguise he dressed as if for drinks at a yacht club or a Rotary dinner—fell open. Beneath his coat and tucked up under his armpit I glimpsed a black leather shoulder holster.

And in it was a gun.

6

My grip loosened. There must have been some strange alteration in the balance of power between us. Heidl looked up from my fist with his wet dog eyes, his wet dog lips.

He saw my gaze.

Maybe he saw that I worried he might use the gun on me. Because I now feared he was crazy enough to shoot me. And I felt as if I had been caught in a net, or a trap, but like all traps it was not clear to the trapped how they might escape. For a moment I wondered if my only problem was that of the reader—of not knowing, of impatience—whereas if I was patient, if I just turned a few more pages, if I just went a little further on, everything would be revealed and a path of escape become clear. But with a growing terror I began to see that the pages before me had a purpose, that the gun had a purpose, and I began to fear Heidl was the author of these things, and all I knew, all that I wished for, was that his ending now not include me.

Heidl's face, which was still close to mine because I was still scruffing him by his jacket, returned to its more normal impassivity. Once again he seemed to be taking stock.

You're a monster, I spat.

Whoever fights monsters should see to it that in the process he does not become a monster.

For God's sake, can we just get this—

And when you look long into the abyss, the abyss also looks into you.

What are you on about?

Aphorism 146, he said.

Is that your beloved fucking Tebbe again?

His disciple, Nietzsche.

I don't give a fuck about Nietzsche, I said, pulling him back into me, I don't give a fuck about Tebbe, all your pretending to your German fucking darkness, all your crap about being hard done by, all your shit about the CIA and Laos and Frank-fucking-Hand. You're just a low-life who got lucky, and you're lucky again with me, because I only get ten grand but you get two hundred and fifty, and I have to do all the work. All you have to do is approve what I have written here, sign off, and then we're free of each other.

But I knew I was defeated. I looked away and I shouldn't have. I should have stared his blank face down. Like you do a dog. But instead I let go of his lapel and stepped backwards.

His mood transformed again. He was abruptly calm. He was possibly happy. Certainly he smiled.

What sort of smile?

The worst: benign.

The worst: knowing.

For once he said nothing. His tongue darted out, licked his upper lip as if it were an envelope being sealed, and vanished.

7

At that moment there was a knock on the door and lunch was brought in to us by Gene Paley's secretary—cold spanakopita, Greek salad, rolls, and cakes. And strangely, bizarrely, amazingly, we sat and ate in peace. It was as if the spanakopita was an armistice we had signed announcing a cessation of hostilities. Yet, Heidl, who seemed to enjoy meals, ate little, nibbling at the spanakopita's edge, before filleting a chicken roll of its chicken and tomatoes and then leaving the roll on its plate. Over the meal, I again asked him to sign the release form. Heidl said of course he would, just as soon as he had answered all my questions thoroughly. He then spent half an hour on the phone to Monassis.

Sensing the effect of the gun—or so it seemed to me—his manner was now almost serene. We still were terse with each other, but some element of madness had passed and my behaviour felt to me almost as theatrical and as insincere as his.

I went back to work, reducing my ambition to resolving eight of the most ludicrous errors. When Heidl finally got off the phone, I pleaded with him, pointing out that without a signed release there would be no further payout on the advance. But for once even money failed to move him. He fobbed me off with a Tebbeism ('Creation is the correction of errors in order to make a larger mistake') and seemed preoccupied with some other, more pressing matter. But whatever that matter might have been was a mystery to me.

Your book is beyond repair, he taunted. You'll have to answer for that now. But as I'm here, ask me whatever is worrying you. I'll tell you whether you're right or wrong.

Yet again I asked questions and yet again Heidl failed to answer in any meaningful or even vaguely sane way, and in this manner that long day dragged on, a single moment of exhausted defeat extended over several hours. I failed again and again to get his take on this or that contradiction in the story, all of which he argued were simply further proof of my incompetence rather than of his cosmic deceit. Instead he continued bravely shaking his rattle bag of lures and diversions—everything from ASO's management philosophy to Nugan Hand resurrecting the Tonton Macoute. But even on these, his most beloved obsessions, I felt he spoke coldly and wearily. It was as if it had become too much even for him, valiant as he was. Finally, even Heidl seemed to tire of heidling, and at three-thirty the game was up.

He made yet another phone call, and when that ended he announced he was off to meet Monassis for a pressing meeting. After that he was returning home to Bendigo to prepare his speech for the auditors' conference he was addressing the following day. He wished me the best 'tidying up' the manuscript.

I am not finishing anything, I said. There's nothing to finish.

I was done with him, but he wasn't done with me.

But you must, he said, as he went to a bookshelf and picked out some books to steal. How else are you going to do your job?

And with that, Ray opened the door, and, looking at me, shook his head as Heidl put several books into his briefcase, snapped it shut, walked past me and left.

I sat in that dismal office alone. Outside, the storm at last broke and wild rain slashed at the windows. I went to his desk and noticed sitting on it the release form. It was unsigned. I picked it up. I stared at it until it blurred. I looked at my carefully annotated manuscript, so much hard work, and all of it now for nothing. Without the necessary corrections, without the signed release form, Gene Paley would be unable to publish the manuscript. There would be no book. There would be no ten thousand dollars. Nor, now, would there be a future for me as a writer. For the first time since I had dreamt of becoming a writer at the age of—what? seven? twelve? I couldn't remember—I felt my dream vanish.

I was finished.

8

I stood up. I just wanted to leave. But first I resolved I had to see Gene Paley to tell him there was no book. Grim as that would be, I also knew it would be for me a relief and a release. I wanted to go home to Suzy, to Bo, to the twins, to a new beginning, as soon as possible.

Making my way along that walk of shame that was the corridor leading to Gene Paley's office I could think only one thing: it was over.

Gene Paley's secretary greeted me with a bright smile.

Kif, she said, I was just about to call. Your flight's been cancelled because of the bad weather.

It seemed a cruel final blow, albeit of a piece with the slow ritual death the whole day had been.

That's the last tonight to Tassie, I said.

I *know*, Kif! the secretary said as if it were a source of wonder. I tried, but the earliest flight I could get you on is tomorrow evening at seven-thirty. I'm sorry! She winced a smile. Do you want to see Mr Paley? I am afraid he's in conference at the moment, but if you come back in, say, an hour, he could—

No, I said. It's not important.

I went back to the office. I gathered up my papers and disks and left. Outside was a deluge. I drove to a pub, bought a beer. And as time passed, I bought another beer.

And another and another.

The same bleak thoughts went back and forth in my brain. There was no agreement signed by Heidl so there was no book that could be published. There wasn't even a book to publish if an agreement was signed as I didn't have anything like the material I needed. I didn't wish to admit defeat to Gene Paley, take my five-hundred-dollar quit fee and go home. But what choice was there?

That night I found myself alone at Sully's home watching the TV. Sully was away visiting old friends. In a bookshelf, on top of a yellowing volume of Michael Dransfield's poetry, I found an opened bottle of cheap gin, but there was nothing to cut it with other than orange cordial. It tasted like hand cleanser mixed with sugar snakes. It tasted like my life, and it did the job. A late-night news item came on about a bad car accident in which a vehicle had plunged off the Great Ocean Road near Lorne earlier in the day. Its sole occupant, the reporter continued, was well-known Melbourne businessman Eric Knowles. He had been rushed to hospital but died shortly afterwards. I poured myself another glass of gin and orange. So that was that, I thought, or tried not to think. The same stubborn thoughts made their sluggish circles in my defeated, befuddled brain. The phone rang. I ignored it. I resolved to get further drunk, sleep in, and see Gene Paley on my way to the airport with the bad news and to collect my five hundred dollars. I'd plead for five thousand, on the basis of work done in good faith, and I knew Paley would simply press his flat palm on the contract and remind me of what I had signed.

And then it would be done.

The phone rang again, I poured another gin and topped it with gin, drank it and pondered my future life. There was nothing to ponder. I emptied the glass and was pouring another gin and gin when the phone rang yet again. I went to the hall table to answer it.

It was Ziggy Heidl.

9

Ray gave me your number, he said.

I took a long slug of the gin.

Told me that storm shut down the airport.

I refilled my glass.

Can you come tomorrow?

I felt no need to say anything, preferring to fill my mouth with gin.

I'm at the homestead, Heidl said. I think working here would be so much better than that office. We'll get some things done and your questions properly sorted.

He went on, but only a little. It was all uncharacteristically direct. Almost helpful. He even gave detailed directions, in that way, I felt, that he always used the truth of detail as a cover for some larger lie. But I was beyond such games and just wanted to put myself out of my own misery.

I told him I wasn't coming.

We argued.

He: money, obligation, promises made.

Me: indolence, impossibility, pointlessness.

No, I said, finally.

As a friend.

No.

I need your help as a friend to finish the book.

What about the auditors' conference? I thought you were speaking at it tomorrow.

Oh—*that!* Forget it. I have. But this matters, Kif. It's been very hard for me, you know—coming to terms with what my life was, what it is.

So you're not going?

Going? Where? No. The thing is, Kif, I think you, of all people, you understand my situation. I know I've not been easy, but it's not been easy for me. Please come here, and let's finish the damn thing.

I'm sorry, I said, and hung up.

All about the book were confusions, dog-ears, missing pages. Nothing felt clean and straightforward any more. Out of habit, though it was forlorn and dead, I went back to the dining-room table that I had worked on of a night these past crowded weeks. I looked at my notes, returned to the pages of the latest manuscript, and, though a little under the weather, I began cutting here and adding clauses there, writing one or two new sentences and then runs of a few paragraphs. Some dreamlike mood took hold of me. The more I invented Heidl on the page, the more the page became Heidl and the more Heidl me—and me the page and the book me and me Heidl. For the first time in my life I sensed the terrifying unity I had always craved as a writer but had never known. Everything was growing ever more ambiguous—his life, the book, my sense of who I was and what I was doing. My first novel, I was aware, had suffered from being autobiographical, but now I feared my first autobiography was becoming a novel. Everything blurred and then dissolved, and when it finally came back together it was to discover myself in the Nissan Skyline, driving through the dawn to Bendigo.

15

1

SOME EARLY MORNINGS ARE MESMERISING with their light and their clouds and, above all, their odd sense of departure. On Port Phillip Bay a few tinnies trickled like black ink drops over a brilliance of broken glass. What a book should be. Looking at that light, those clouds—if only for a few moments—I felt free. I felt I could write a hundred books and still not have caught a fraction of the feeling that overwhelmed me in those few seconds.

And for once, as I travelled through the long urban villages with their falafel shops and cafés and Vietnamese restaurants, their bakeries and groceries blossoming on the street with plastic buckets of floral bouquets, nothing mattered. I made my way past beaches and palm trees and entered a less colourful nether world of industrial parks, peopleless and quiet, that gave way to the silent farms and broken bush, the rising sun leading me off the highway, along a country road and finally, after some hours, up a long gravel drive past a neglected native bush garden poking out of an eroded paddock like springs and horsehair out of a broken sofa.

I didn't recognise myself in the man now getting out of the car to greet Heidl in front of a sprawling '70s white concrete brick house, low slung as slander, with its mission-brown windows and burnt-orange tile roof, smiling, saying how I was looking forward to working with him at his home.

I felt something running along my calf and glanced down to

see a blue Siamese cat, back arched, pushing into my leg and purring. Heidl, who rarely seemed to touch other humans, put his hand on my back and held it there for some time. Smiling, he told me how much we were alike.

And as it was good to agree, I agreed with him. Hadn't we, after all, little by little, in our clashes, our fights, and our necessary communion of work, both begun to change? Weren't we slowly coming to resemble each other, as the coloniser does the colonised? It was as if a door I had been pushing on forever had unexpectedly opened and I was falling through it into a void on the other side. Perhaps I was trading some part of myself as a human being for another part as a writer; some dignity or pride, or something even more fundamental. Whatever it was—whoever I now was becoming—that morning in Bendigo the trade felt as if it might just be successful.

Now that we are *mates*, Heidl said.

His German accent, however acquired, meant that rather than emphasise the beginning of words in the Australian manner, he always accentuated their end. *Mates-ss*, out of his mouth, was serpent-ribboned. Something went wrong with the word *mate* in the 1980s, as with so many things. Some criminal complicity, some implied threat, some shared guilt. I am not sure what, but it wasn't good. Yet his sibilant 's's no longer unnerved me. For the first time I felt an ease, almost a serenity about Siegfried Heidl.

And this, in turn, calmed me.

2

I want you to help me, Kif, Ziggy Heidl said as he led me into a cathedral-ceilinged pine kitchen, all cheap knotted timbers slimed with polyester gloss as glistening as cling wrap. Wherever the seven hundred million had gone it hadn't been lost to interior decoration. Maybe that was why that unremarkable house felt to me one more disguise. Heidl pushed a small ginger cat off a pine kitchen table, inviting me to sit down.

As a friend, Heidl said.

Sure.

It's a very large thing, he said. Not difficult. Just, well, it may seem . . . unusual.

We talked a little while about nothing; me, a few pieces of meaningless personal trivia I felt safe in sharing about how Sully had gone away for a few days to the Blue Mountains to see old friends; he, about taking the kids to school and how Dolly was gone for the day seeing an aunt in Castlemaine. He was bubbly in the way of a bottle of spumante left undrunk, something not to be entirely trusted.

I waited for him to take the conversation to where he always did: toxo, Tebbe, Laos, *the* company. But that's not what happened. He was attentive that day and silent on many things. He poured coffee from a drip filter machine. Morning light fell through the back windows beneath which lay several more cats. He seemed, in a way I had never seen him to be, happy. Almost peaceful. And that's when he fixed me with his dog eyes and asked me if I might do him a favour.

As a friend, he said. As a mate.

Of course, I said, passing on the coffee he offered me in a mug marked DOLLY.

Kif, he said as he poured the coffee down the sink and put the mug in the dishwasher. I want you to kill me.

When, after some time, it was clear I wouldn't reply, he sat back down and spoke again.

I haven't much time left, Kif, he said. They're coming for me. And they will get me, Kif. That's the thing. I can't escape them. You know what they can do. The other night I was lucky. I might be lucky again. Maybe I'll be lucky two or three times. But I have to succeed every time. They only have to succeed once.

I remained silent.

So will you do it? he asked, as if he meant would I go to the corner shop to buy some milk.

Do what? I replied, as if I just wanted to check the order.

He reached inside his red baseball jacket and pulled out the pistol I had glimpsed the day before. With its stippled black plastic grip it looked almost a toy.

A Glock, I said, as if it was of no concern, as though it were an everyday thing to work with people who drew revolvers over morning coffee.

Roger that, Heidl said. I didn't know you were a gun man. But I knew nothing of pistols and I was only guessing it was the same gun with which he had made Ray practise killing him.

I guess you know all this then, he said, taking a clip of bullets out of the grip. He held the gun up to me in the theatrical way of a magician about to perform a trick, and slid the barrel back to show me the chamber was clear of bullets. Pointing the gun at the ceiling he pulled the trigger to show it was safe. These dramatic gestures seemed to please him.

Now, he said. Let me show you how.

With his dreadful dog eyes fixed on mine and mine with nowhere else to go, Heidl turned the gun away from me and onto himself.

3

He slowly slid the ugly square barrel into his mouth, angling it up towards the back of his head. Obscenely posed he sat before me, his face a vertiginous emptiness greater than that any desert or any ocean ever presented.

After what was probably no more than a few seconds but felt so much longer—minutes, years, decades—he took the Glock out of his mouth in an easy movement, black metal barrel glossed with spittle spume.

Don't worry, Kif, Heidl said softly.

As he wiped the gun with a tissue, he began laughing. At whom or what, at me or him or the world, I still to this day couldn't say.

No, I said.

A simple refusal seemed inadequate, and felt almost acquiescence.

No way, I said.

But he could hear that my voice was unsure, that my voice was betraying me; I could feel myself giving in to what Ray had tried to warn me against, the danger of *letting him in.*

No *fucking* way, I said as Heidl continued laughing.

But that only sounded worse.

Are we friends, Kif? he said. We *are* friends.

I nodded in a way I hoped was evasive and non-committal, but felt, as my head tottered, passive, even accepting.

We need to get to work, he said, his smile one of enormous good cheer, eyebrows arching, mouth ballooning wide as a fun park entrance, his newly found good humour intolerable.

Kif?

Yeah?

Friends.

Sure, I said, opening up the box folder that held the manuscript and the unsigned release form.

Mates?

Mates?

Mates, Heidl repeated.

Sure, I said. Sure, we're mates, Ziggy.

Why did I say that? I wondered. And yet having said it,

each further agreement seemed to make me weaker and him stronger.

Help me, then, Heidl said.

If you want to kill yourself, I said, almost stammering, kill yourself.

Please, Kif.

Why involve me?

Because I'm afraid I'll botch it, Kif, Heidl said. Simple as that. I'm afraid at the last minute I'll point it the wrong way and just wound myself terribly, end up with a mess, die slowly, or not at all. Maybe live as a vegetable. I'm a coward, Kif. I'm terrified. Here, he said.

He held the Glock out to me, lying flat in the palm of his hand.

It's okay—look.

He pushed the awful thing right under my face. He showed me the safety built into the trigger's centre as a separate lever that had to be simultaneously pulled to fire the gun.

Like this, he said.

With his repellent puffy index finger, he pulled the trigger.

Off, he said.

Squeeze, he said.

The trigger clicked.

He repeated the action, showing me how to pull the trigger and safety together, slow, constant in the pull.

Again, he said, off.

Squeeze.

Click.

And when he proffered the gun the second time, a tissue over its incriminating stippled grip and trigger, I slid the release contract over to him.

Sign the release, I said.

4

Thank you, he said, his voice now quiet. Thank you, Kif.

If I hadn't known him as I did I could have almost thought him genuine. And he looked at me with such gratitude that it was pathetic, as if I had already killed him.

Let's practise, he said.

No, I said, but somehow it was as if he had managed to make me agree, and though I'd agreed with nothing I was now holding a gun in my right hand.

Now, he said, taking my hand and threading my finger through the trigger. Like this.

It was mad beyond words and even madder that he would want to be killed. Maddest of all was that Heidl thought I would be his murderer. And yet everything I said seemed to somehow more deeply implicate and involve me with his insanity.

Not today, Ziggy, I said, opting for diversion, passing him the gun back. He seemed to take it well enough, placing the gun on the table between us.

Oh no, he said softly, it has to be today. Dolly and the kids are away; I've given Ray the day off; you said your friend is away, and so no one knows you're here—right? So what could be better? And if you don't do it who will?

Ray, I said and immediately regretted saying such a monstrous thing.

It can't be Ray, Heidl said. He would be their number one suspect. The prime suspect. And then Ray would suffer, he would go to jail for murder. I don't want that. You don't want that either. But you? No one knows you're here, no one will ever suspect you. The ghost writer of ghosts, he said, and laughed. The book will be a great success now, you know.

The whole thing seemed to make him rather jolly.

Well, of course *you* know, he said. You told me!

He reached across to where a box of brightly coloured latex gloves sat, and passed to me a translucent blue pair. Here, he said brightly, let's practise with these.

I looked at the blue gloves.

Please, Heidl said. It's the next stage.

The release, I said. Do you need a pen?

Let's just practise this first, he insisted as I pulled the blue gloves on, and he went on about how once I had shot him, in a detail that seemed to be lifted from a bad movie, I was to put the Glock in his hand and place the shell at a point Heidl would show me before his death. After, he explained, I was to immediately drive back to Melbourne, leave the car that evening at the publishers as I had arranged, and fly home to Tasmania. No one would ever know I had been with him.

So you're sure no one knows you're here? he asked.

I've already told you—

The publishers? Gene Paley?

I told no one at the publishers.

Pia Carnevale?

No one.

Wonderful, he said as he picked up the Glock, and, head lowered once more, demonstrated how to place the gun in his mouth with the correct angle, as if he were a whitegoods salesman demonstrating an electric toothbrush.

Wonderful, wonderful, he murmured cheerily. Now your turn.

He got off his chair and onto his knees in front of me. And for a third time, I did what he wanted because it was easier than not doing it, and because I thought it bought me time. I took the gun.

Here, he said, pointing with an index finger up into the back of his mouth.

No, I said in shock, looking around the kitchen. Not here.

And again what was meant as refusal sounded like agreement.

Oh no, he said softly. No, not *here*. That would be too awful.

We'll do it elsewhere, where Dolly and the kids will never see the mess.

No, I said, this time more firmly.

You don't like me, do you, Kif?

And I had no choice but to reply: Of course, I do, Siegfried. It's just—

Do or don't?

I mean, I said, we're friends, but I just don't feel comfortable—

A real friend?

Heidl was cruel like that. The little sorcerer wasn't just toying with me but with death, the stakes were infinitely raised, and yet the game continued on in the spirit of a game—daring, taunting, bluffing, serious and, at the same time, not beyond a wink, as if he were letting me in on the private joke the whole thing really was. In this spirit, we played on.

Because if you're a real friend this is what you do, Heidl said, kneeling before me. You are my friend, Kif?

More out of embarrassment than anything else I now brought the gun to his lips and slid it into his mouth. Something brushed up against my leg and purred. I recalled what Ray had told me about the barrel placement, and, without being told, as best I could, I angled it up until I felt the resistance of his meaty palate. He brought his hand up to adjust mine a little. His touch was unpleasantly warm. I pulled the trigger so he would let go.

Click.

We played out this pantomime over and over—

click

click

click

click

click

—until I pulled the glazed barrel out and Heidl asked if I'd like a cup of tea.

5

His calmness was terrifying. But his certainty about the day I didn't dare agree with.

I'm fine, I said. And reaching into the box folder I pulled out my annotated manuscript as if it were a lifejacket.

He dried the gun and holstered it back under his arm.

Ziggy, I said, just a few questions.

Please, he said, wiping spittle from the corner of his mouth with a handkerchief. But as he made the tea he was much more fixated on the details of his actual death than those of his fictional life. He filled his mug, on which was written SIEGFRIED. A large grey Persian cat began a strange wailing by his side as he assured me that his death would be understood as suicide. As he sipped his drink, he told me how he had already written the suicide note, everything was thought through, really, I was just assisting him with his death, an act of mercy, he'd always thought of me as merciful from the first time we met, he'd always seen me as a good and merciful man.

On and on he went, why the banks would kill him anyway now or kill him in jail, on and on about how much better it was to die free—did I not believe in freedom?—to escape, to have a friend rather than an enemy help him die, how he did not believe in suicide, how it had to look like suicide to make others question their persecution of him . . . on and on and on, an ever-thickening confusion of arguments, bewildering, illogical and logical, coherent and incoherent, and the more I listened the more those ideas seemed reasonable, incontestable really, part of my own thinking even if in my own heart I didn't agree with any of them.

I reminded myself of why I had driven to see him that day. While he drank his tea we managed to get through a few pages of manuscript and even resolve several major confusions with what felt neat deceits.

After a good hour or so—a near geological time span for Heidl to concentrate—he stood up and walked over to the sliding glass doors at the back of his house, gazing out, with a clowder of cats swarming around his feet—small, large, old, kittens, cats of all colours and types.

There's a magnificent view from that hill up there I'd like to show you.

As Heidl spoke the cats all began softly purring, though whether in expectation, or gratitude, or just hunger, it was impossible to know.

It sounds crazy, but when I'm up there I feel I have all Australia spreading out below, radiating out from my hill. I'd love to show you.

I just kept scrawling on the manuscript, evading the implication. Heidl sighed, turned his back to me and told the sliding glass door that we were due for a break and a walk would do us good.

The ironbarks up on the hill are amazing, he said. The bark they drop fixes nitrogen in the soil for the next generation of trees, he said. You can hear the rings forming, he said. You can see a currawong's wing holding the sky, he said.

Ziggy Heidl had, as far as I knew, neither interest in, nor feeling for the non-human world, so his riffs about the charms of the forest, an unhappy melding of the faux scientific and cod poetic, felt forced. I refused to go for a walk, and he was for once oddly amenable when I led the conversation back to the manuscript.

We worked for a further two or three hours. It was remarkable for him to show such patience and the work was almost pleasant. We were finally getting the book sorted—at last, I thought, at last! Heidl relaxed, and, after a time, so too did I. The bizarre pantomime of murder was not spoken of again, and I felt he was seeking to put it behind him, a mad manifestation of some terror. He was helpful in a way I had never known him to be, at one point going to a filing cabinet and returning with some amusing letters from bankers about the probity of ASO, and at another giving me his own well-thumbed copy of a book on 'hot' money, so I might better understand a point he was making about laundering dirty cash.

Only later did I see the combination of intrigue and luck that allowed for the events of that day and all that was about to happen. Ray's day off; Dolly visiting relatives on Heidl's advice, 'to get away from it all'; the auditors' conference he was meant to be speaking at that day—had it ever existed? And I too had been manipulated to come on that day of all days. But Heidl couldn't control all things, and I am sure he knew it. It was a grand risk haphazardly built on the accident of my missing my flight, and at such moments he thrilled to bending reality to his way.

While he made a late lunch of toasted sandwiches for himself—I wasn't hungry—a fat tabby cat turned and eyed me from where it sat on the kitchen counter. Afterwards I couldn't draw him back to work; he kept insisting we take *the walk*, as he called it. His use of the definite article should have been a warning, but I put it down to his odd English. He tried to cajole me, pressure me, and beg me. He talked of the walk being nothing more or other than a walk, and though I felt his idea of my murdering him was some strange fancy that had now passed, I still wasn't eager to be alone in the bush with Heidl and a gun. I told myself I didn't think he would kill me.

But that wasn't exactly true. I *did* think he might kill me, and everything up to this point was all some elaborate ruse to that end. So I can't really explain why I agreed to go for the walk. Perhaps even at this late point I still bore the arrogance of the writer: after all, I carried the presumption he was my subject, not me his. In my heart I had no idea of what he was truly capable. He was set on the idea of the walk, he had been so helpful, sweet even, and it seemed a necessary part of the dance.

Besides, as he once more pointed out as he slid the glass doors open, it would do us both good and refresh us for an afternoon's work.

As he zipped up his red baseball jacket, he told me we could sort out a few of the larger manuscript issues while we walked. He brightly promised he would attend to the other issues, sign the release form and any outstanding paperwork I needed him to deal with when we returned. For once he seemed free of his fears and worries, and his mood was almost joyful.

Following him, I made my way through a throng of milling cats at the glass door, their purring now a blood crescendo, and we headed out.

6

He led me through a back paddock that crumbled into a bastard bush arisen from the devastation of a gold rush a century and a half before. We picked up a fire trail. Walking along it—the winter light vivid and strong, the air fresh, the day alive—he was talkative.

You know what your problem is, Kif? he told me as we made our way along that eroded gravel scar into a broken country of crabbed redbox and twisted ironbarks that felt hard as a shattered axe.

You want to live without enemies, Heidl said, that's your problem. You think if I am good and kind and don't speak ill of others I won't have enemies. But you will, you just don't know it yet. They're out there, your enemies, you just haven't met them. You can seek them out or pretend they don't exist but they'll still find you. Trust me. You want to be like a dog that everyone likes, but there's not a dog alive someone doesn't want to kick or kill. You want everyone to be your friend. Why? Why bother?

His monologues grew stranger, and all leading to something that began to feel inescapable unless I turned and fled. And yet I continued to walk, to listen, and with every step go further with him into the enclosing ironbarks, their sinuous black trunks writhing and wrapping around me, brushing past clusters of round redbox leaves softly jiggling in the slight breeze, so many little blue-green pendants that somehow felt too many, and too familiar, wanting to touch me at every turn. He led me off the fire trail, onto another path, and deeper into that increasingly claustrophobic and oppressive woodland.

People aren't afraid of dying, Kif, he was saying. It's living that terrifies us. We're afraid that as we die we'll realise we've never lived. Death is the revelation of our failure to live as we should. I won't die that way. We are allowed a small moment to glow yet we forget.

A fiery and deranged winter light began to take hold of the day, banishing the blue light of the foliage to shadow. It fell between the ironbarks' black trunks making them blacker and stranger yet, as if they were so many upright, incinerated corpses. It freckled our faces, flecks of light dancing with darkness. Heidl looked up, the sun fell directly across his fleshy face as he smiled, and the tic in his cheek seemed to be strobing.

I stole the sun, he said. Souls, I stole souls. I ate them whole and no one saw. I am eating the world. I am eating myself. I don't understand what God wants from me.

He seemed to be trying to climb onto words, as if he were a drowning man and words bobbing jetsam that might save him, yet with each word grabbed he only succeeded in sinking further into a deep ocean of meaninglessness.

I walk, I eat, I drink, think, feel. I want, I know, I fear, I dream. But is it me, Kif? Is it? I want myself.

His talk was now little more than a tone, but what that tone was I can't describe. I tried to commit it to memory as best I could, hoping there might be something to later steal. Like everything of most interest about him, none of it was to prove useable.

As the hill steepened, I do remember him saying how he never sought to control anything. His idea was to let everything out of control and see what happened.

And what did happen? I asked.

Some chaos, he said, but less than you might expect. People repeated themselves, reinventing all the old orders and hierarchies. I hoped for more, and after a while it impressed me how people always tended to be less.

For the first time the thought occurred to me that he was insane. His floundering grew more desperate.

I want grandeur, he said. To shit grandeur. At another point he said, I die you. And giggled.

We had reached the hill's summit and he stood there before me in his magnificent derangement and a red baseball jacket.

Look at me and love me. I have been dying since I was born.

And his head jerked strangely, he looked at me shocked, as if I had appeared out of nowhere, as though I were the aberration, and he murmured,

Is it strange to be you?

7

He turned back to look out over hills, scrub, farmland.

He said, It's beautiful.

I said that we should go back to work on the manuscript.

Roger that, he said.

But he may well have just shaken his head. His method of agreeing when he disagreed was always formidably played. There was about him at that moment some cosmic despair that was also a form of terrifying patience. We stood there saying nothing more for five or ten minutes. Maybe longer. I worried if I stayed too long he might just start again with all that weirdness about my killing him. I waited perhaps one or two minutes, perhaps twenty—it was like that, everything slowing down and speeding up at the same time.

The book, I said.

He was troubled by something or many things. He looked at his watch several times. He made no attempt to answer me.

Rain spat the dry earth a little.

Somehow it was over.

I knew I had to leave. He terrified me. In truth—and in that eerie silence I only had truth to be confronted with—in truth I believed if I stayed I could be dead by nightfall. I gave up trying to reason with him about the manuscript. It wasn't that I had enough material. I didn't have close to enough. But I knew now I never would. I thanked him for his time and hospitality and told him I was going.

This news seemed to break him. He spoke of how lonely he was; how much my friendship mattered to him; how he was sorry he had scared me so with the gun and his talk, his silly, mad talk. But he was frightened, he said, so terribly frightened, of what jail might hold for him. Of course, he didn't want me to kill him. Never, not really; no, not that. *That* was just his fear talking. Nor would he kill himself. But he was so afraid of death, of *the people* who were coming for him. He began to weep. I knew better than to indulge him. He began talking in an ever more disconnected way about a vision he had had.

The dream, Heidl said, the dream—I saw it, Kif! Just for a moment, I held it—I was it, wasn't I, Kif? I was. All the rules, all the morals, all the mysteries, they didn't apply. For a short time I flew above them, beyond them. I was the world and the world was me, Kif—you with me, Kif?—because I was, Kif, I was, and

288

I wasn't them and I wasn't bound by the need to obey. Not their rules, not their morals, not their anything. I hid in plain sight pretending to be less, when all the time there I was, more and more, and more was never enough for me, Kif. Never.

He talked a lot of shit like that.

He pulled out the Glock from his jacket as casually as if it were a pen. I thought he was going to shoot me, that this was it. The end.

You see, Kif? he said, waving the gun around. I know you see, I know it, I know you know. I am all there is, Kif. God is the hangman's hood, Tebbe says. Maybe. But I am the noose. Everything they pretend to hold dear I trampled beneath me. You'll have your end Paley wants to the book, me dead, and buried with me all wickedness. But we know it's not really so. *We know.* I'll go on.

His back was to the north and the late afternoon winter sun behind him lit him up, a strange red-haloed black silhouette.

Hell swarms with the ghosts I've sent before me and I'll send after me, he said.

He dropped his hand and held the gun at his hip in a noncommittal way. Threat or invitation or both it was impossible to know. The sun was lost behind a cloud, the light behind him faded, and I saw his eyes were looking at me but they glistened and seemed to be focusing on something far away, so distant it perhaps hadn't even yet been born.

The world will burn. And why? Because of me, Kif.

I couldn't take my eyes off his arm, his hand, his finger resting on the safety of the Glock.

Because I placed myself at the centre, Kif. Me. I am the way, the light, and the centre. And it frightens me, Kif.

I said I had to go.

I'm terrified, Kif.

He was trembling.

16

1

I FLED. I DIDN'T RUN. I turned around and walked away, and hearing nothing from Heidl, I kept on walking. And as I walked I was waiting for the sound of a shot that might mean my death or his. I tried to remember my high school science. If I heard it, did that mean he had missed me or did it mean that he had shot himself? Could you ever hear the sound of your own fatal bullet? But I heard nothing other than the blood-thud in my ears.

I feared he was coming after me to kill me. Making my way down the hill, I sneaked furtive looks behind. There was no one. Halfway down I'd had enough. I stopped, turned around, and waited. Again, no one, nor sign, nor sound, of anyone. As I stood there scanning the bush for any movement, I thought that perhaps he was going to kill himself. Or that he had. Or that he was waiting for me to come back to kill him.

I told myself that to kill another human being was loathsome, revolting, abhorrent. I told myself I wouldn't kill him. Yet having practised it I won't pretend that I didn't think about it. Now that killing him was no longer a possibility it was a possibility that I could entertain. Of course, part of me had recoiled from the act not so much in horror but in fear—of being found out, of being tried and jailed, of losing my life to his madness. But, in truth, every time I thought about killing Heidl there had come such a feeling of excitement—the prospect, I suppose, of entering his world, that world he had taunted me with and held out to me as a hope, as a promise.

As the future.

I couldn't decide whether I hated Heidl or admired him, if I was his friend or his enemy, if I wanted to save him or kill him. I was trying to hold on to some idea—of myself, of life, of something, anything—but what was the idea? I tried to steady myself by holding on to the book instead. I tried to think that the book remained possible. Yet all I could think was that Heidl was going to kill himself and I would be left with nothing. I had to keep Heidl alive because it mattered to me to get paid my ten thousand dollars. And for that to happen the book had to be finished and the release signed.

Sensing a way of thinking that excluded the factor of Heidl's character and my loathing of it, by putting self-interested concern ahead of hate, I found myself running back up the track, through the ironbarks and towards the top of the hill.

The thought that he might be dead somehow hastened me and I ran harder. I had to know. Yet as I came close to the summit I lost all haste, my dread vanished, and was replaced by a fear of it all being an elaborate trap on the part of Heidl. I slowed and concentrated on quietening my breathing, on walking softly, watching that I didn't crack sticks underfoot.

As if they were frames of aged technicolor film the black-trunked ironbarks broke the world into countless near-identical images, through which I glimpsed a flickering red figure. I dropped to my knees behind a clump of redbox.

Heidl slowly shaped out of the striated Australian light like a mirage or heatwave made incarnate, walking back and forth. He would halt, turn, and take a few steps in another direction with as much purpose and concentration as if he were pacing out instructions to the site of hidden treasure or a secret grave.

After a minute or two I began crawling slowly towards him,

circling around as I did so. When I was perhaps a hundred metres away and hidden behind a bush, I halted.

He continued pacing back and forth for some minutes before stopping. He was talking to himself, waving his arms around, though I was too far away to make out what he was saying. At last he seemed to have found the spot marked X. He stopped pacing and talking, stood still, and looked out on such view as that small hill afforded of what he imagined was Australia.

It is hard to say what he saw—hope, failure, a land that in the end confirmed to him his own meaninglessness? Or perhaps he saw something beyond all that, all that was moving through the clouds and the restless land itself. Whatever he saw, it wasn't enough. Maybe he wanted more. Maybe he saw more. Maybe he saw tomorrow. Who can say? The great deceiver stood before me, alone, unknown to all, even those who presumed to know him, most particularly me. Maybe even himself.

He dropped his head, reached inside his red baseball jacket and again pulled out the Glock. He stared at the gun as if it were some object he had never seen before, something that had just magically appeared in his hands and for which there was no explanation. He rolled his hand this way and that, examining that strange weapon and the new power it bestowed, as though only now he understood that it was not metal and stippled polymer grip, but something else, something greater. He straightened up, and stretched his gun arm out straight, his other hand steadying it beneath his elbow. In a single movement of grace—perhaps the only movement of grace I ever recall him making—he pulled the gun up in an arc and placed it inside his mouth. He tilted his head backwards, eyes skywards, and adjusted the angle.

Something cracked.

With a cry of astonishment Heidl jerked up and back. His legs buckled. For the briefest moment his collapsing body took the form of an inverted question mark, before falling to the ground.

He beat around in the dirt for several seconds, thrashing and convulsing, an Australian berserk. Abruptly he stopped, and his body was still.

I forgot how much I hated him. Maybe at that moment I loved him. I wanted to run over to him. I didn't move. I could hardly breathe. I was frightened it was some sort of test or trap; if I ran over to him would his corpse stand up and shoot me dead? And I was terrified that if I didn't move he would jump up and walk over to where I lay cowering behind a scrubby bush and gun me down like a dog. I wanted to run away and yet I didn't; I feared also that if he came over to shoot me I would be unable to move, and that I would die as meekly as a goat.

He made no movement.

My confidence grew.

After ten minutes or more, I slowly and carefully began crawling towards Heidl. From forty metres out I could see flies were collecting over his head, dipping in and out of the grey matter and blood that was forming a grisly porridge on the bark and eucalypt leaves.

I rose from a crawl to a crouch, and as I came closer from a crouch to a hunch, ready to hide, to drop, to run, should Heidl suddenly rise and start firing at me.

From twenty metres away I saw the shocking exit wound that had previously been obscured. The blood, the spilling brain, that violent void, jagged and bloody, in his head—the head that was no longer a head, a part missing, as if there were a jigsaw piece that I might be able to pick up and place back to make it all right again.

And then I was standing above him, half-torn Adidas Vienna at his head. Small black ants crisscrossed the red-flecked gruel near his ear. There was a smell of shit. I forgot the book, the money I was owed, my rage at his laziness and lies. Overhead a black jay was circling.

And that's the worst part.

His eyes were moving, following the bird above.

He was alive.

2

A gust of wind lifted the leaf and bark litter and moved the eucalypt branches overhead in a rising hush. And in the momentarily
whispering and moving dirt Heidl lay mute and still as despair,
and all the while the ants continued with their immortal labour,
devouring the spilled brains of one more thing waiting to be
reborn, patiently now taking on the burden of the toxo, Tebbe,
the CIA, and homicidal banks, bearing it all back to their own
nest. A bit of blood dribbled out of his mouth, but not so much
as you might expect from the movies. The afternoon sun rested
on a clutch of eucalypts not far away. It was peaceful and the
beauty of the day was overwhelming.

Why would he not die? He made no noise other than what I
came to recognise as a growing struggle for air that slowly transformed from a quiet, leaky rasp to a strange and terrible whistle.
There were intervals of silence when I thought him dead only
to be proven wrong when the rasping and whistling resumed.
Sometimes his breathing would alter to a sort of snoring, except
his eyes were open.

His awful gaze remained fixed on the circling black jay, as
if determined not to arouse the anger of his wound, of his
appalling, spilling head. His face—more a mask now, really—was
childlike, plastic, unformed. There was nothing there. His whole
life had been a lost search. It was as if Heidl had never found
his true métier, a grandeur or passion as endless and uncaring,
as intoxicating and as indecipherable as the vast lands below
that fatal hill, spreading away from where he lay to places more

distant than Moscow is from London but which were still also Australia, an invention as absurd as himself, a country that he continued to claim to the end was his birthplace.

And perhaps in some fundamental way it was. It was a land not infinitely perfectible, just infinitely corruptible. There was nothing of itself it wouldn't sell, and always cheaper than last time. In such a land he should have gone a long way—all the way, really. He must have wondered why it was ending this way.

I wanted to talk with him because it seemed rude at such a time not to, and it seemed ridiculous to think that talking would now mean anything. I knew that, and I also knew he must have too many things to say, or not know how to say even one simple thing.

It's a dream, I wanted to say, because it felt to me that way. And I felt the terrible emptiness of things, an emptiness that we can only defend ourselves against by being with each other. But I couldn't tell him I was with him because he might yet misunderstand and kill me, and he couldn't tell me he was with me, because really he wasn't. What was a dream and what was real, that was the problem, that was the question, and we needed to ask each other about these things, because maybe he knew the answer dying, or maybe I knew the answer in watching him die.

He said nothing, and he just kept on dreaming or thinking, or dreaming he was thinking or thinking he was dreaming. It was hard to say and impossible to know. A mosaic of sulphur-crested cockatoos dragged a winking pattern of white wings across the sky and Heidl's eyes with them until the moment the flock vanished and the blue void returned.

It was then that I heard a barely audible voice croak. Looking down I realised with horror that it was Heidl. I stared at his eyes gazing at the sky, his lips scarcely moving, more trembling really, each word wet, slurred, slow and mucusy with something—saliva? blood?

Shoot . . . me, he murmured.

I did nothing. I just watched. I hated him. As I stared into his eyes I needed him to know it. I am not sure he did, or if he did that he cared. His body made short choking noises then halted.

Finish me off, he said, or I think he said.

It was hard to know. His voice was that faint. Each sentence was a rasp of breath, a goat bleat. He started choking again. I could have run back to the homestead to get help. Maybe saved his life. At the least I could have consoled him.

I didn't want to console him. I didn't want to save him. I wanted him to die. To break the spell. To be rid of him and be free.

Please, he begged.

I felt things but I understood I had to conquer my feelings.

You bastards with your books! he suddenly shouted, his voice momentarily strong, spitting out the words. You're the worst! You have no pity!

His right arm jolted up, a blue palm stretched outwards, fingers outstretched and taut, shuddering, reaching for something—a final hope? a curse upon us all? somebody to salute or strangle? The gesture was incomprehensible and terrifying.

His arm dropped back into the dirt. His dog black eyes wore a fierce varnish; his nostrils flared angrily, in different rhythm to his twitching cheek. His voice trailed off into babble and incoherent grunts. Perhaps threats, or curses. Perhaps prayers, though I doubt it. Perhaps nothing. But the effort seemed to exhaust him and he fell silent. I held my gaze. He continued to exist. I let him look deep into me and know all that I felt. His mind seemed confused, lost in shadows.

Suddenly his head shuddered in a terrible spasm as though he had had some dreadful premonition, some intolerable vision.

It's coming! he hissed. *It's coming!*

I strained to hear what else he might say. But that was it. Ten, fifteen minutes later—maybe longer, I can't say—his eyes stopped moving. His cheek was still.

And I knew.

Even dead I didn't trust him. I waited, not daring to move. But my body was ahead of my mind. It slowly turned, took one step, then another. And I kept going, walking slowly, weary beyond imagining. No shot, no sound came. I began running and I didn't stop.

3

Night threw itself over me like a mugger's coat. Night filled the world into which I rushed headlong with tar and headlights and the rushing wind of trucks and cars passing by. Heidl's wailing angered the universe; air horns sounded warnings to the heavens as I overtook on blind corners and careered through black space towards the city and the publishers' car park and the sea over which I flew a few hours later, buried in the clammy gut of the night sky as behind me jets of fire hurtled me to my destiny.

Seated, belted, contained, I was amazed to discover the world was no different, that those dozing or reading around me were perfectly content to sit with a man such as me, and that the plane and the seat I was sitting in now, the trees, the bitumen and road trains and sheep in the paddocks I had just fled past, the deep chasmed creeks I had bridged and the bleak ravines of concrete sound barriers I had descended into as I made it to the city were all just the same as they had been earlier that day.

Rainblear, cloudink, wingstutter, breath mist on porthole plastic.

So much was so much the same that it stood to reason that so too was I, and it seemed for long periods afterwards that nothing had happened, that nothing had changed, but every time that feeling began to form itself into hope another stronger feeling took hold of me. *Everything* was changed. Because I had changed. Because it had happened.

Headspun, soulfucked, lifelost.

And yet *what* had happened was unclear to me—had I gone back to help him live, as I was still trying to convince myself, or to make sure he died? Had I killed him, or had he killed himself? Or had I gone back because he wanted me to know that finally *he* controlled me and I had killed him as he had wished?

The plane shuddered earthwards.

There was a sickening fug of fresh glue in the taxi I took from the Hobart airport. The car radio was on. A newsreader was saying Siegfried Heidl had been found dead with a gunshot wound to the head.

I wound down a window. As the air gusted in I gulped. I gulped and I gulped. It was as if something had taken hold of me, somehow enslaved me, and I couldn't even vomit it away.

There's a bloody story for you, the taxi driver said.

The police were asking for help with their investigation, the newsreader continued, and were keen to talk with anyone who saw Heidl in his final hours.

Who'd do that? the taxi driver asked.

That's me, I said, pointing ahead. Just past the crossroad, thanks.

I kept hearing his terrible final whisper, those two meaningless words full of some incomprehensible foreboding, hissing over and over in my ears. I wanted to say something more in reply, but I felt sick from the flight, from lack of sleep, from fear, and when I opened my mouth to speak it just filled with rushing air. I tried to remember the word Gene Paley had used the first time we had met, and as we pulled up at my home and I took my bag from the taxi driver, it finally came to me.

Nègres.

17

1

TWINS SLUNG OVER MY SHOULDERS, wailing, I walked back and forth in our lounge room watching the late-night TV news while Suzy dozed on the couch. It was all Heidl and Heidl was all. In the middle of footage of the ASO—choppers, fires, Heidl receiving his Order of Australia, passing-out parades of young uniformed men, Heidl in handcuffs running a media gauntlet after being captured—the phone rang.

I thought it would be the cops, but it was Gene Paley. He told me my identity was being kept a secret so that I would not have to deal with any unwelcome media intrusion and I could get on with my writing.

He went quiet, waiting for me to answer. I didn't. In the background I could hear the reporter saying that the police were at this stage ruling nothing in or out. I wanted to be reassured, but I wasn't. I felt resentful. Confused. On edge. Guilty. Frightened. I felt too much.

Excuse me a moment, I said. I went over to the TV and switched it off. Gene Paley seemed to misunderstand my leaving the phone as hiding some grief. I wondered what grief I might be hiding. I had no idea what emotion I was even feeling.

I know this would be very hard for you, Kif.

I thought Gene Paley knew, but, of course, Gene Paley knew nothing. He meant only the book. He was a publisher. He only ever meant the book. I was immensely relieved. Then I was disappointed that he didn't know, that he didn't even suspect, that he wouldn't ask. Me, I wanted to say. *Me!* What a fool I felt Gene Paley was with his wispy arms and horrible red-moled flesh, all raddled and wrong, white as death.

It's fine, I said. I'm fine.

But all I could see were his lips trembling, his eyes, the circling black jay overhead. Trying to steady the phone with my other hand, I noticed the dirt still under my fingernails from crawling through the bush only a few hours before.

A good writer needs dirty hands, Kif.

It *is* going well, Kif? Gene Paley asked.

It's coming, I said.

I was feeling something in me changing, something growing both cruel and pitiless in a way that frightened me.

How much is locked in?

Maybe a third.

And the rest?

He's *dead*, I said.

Gene Paley went quiet a second time. I was angry, as if he had somehow made me do what I had done and was now forcing me to confess that there was no book.

I'm sorry, Gene Paley said. Kif, I know you are—were—fond of . . . Siegfried.

Fond? I said, feeling something I worried I might not be able to control coming up through my chest into my neck and shuddering my mouth.

Siegfried . . . Gene Paley said, coughed, and went on. Siegfried . . . never cleared—*anything?*

Maybe because I felt I needed to offer some hope for us both, or just me, I sort of said he had. I certainly didn't say he hadn't. I don't know why I lied, but I did. Maybe I just wanted Gene Paley off my back and off the phone.

He signed the clearance form? Gene Paley said, his voice

rising, insistent. The form saying there was a final manuscript and the final manuscript was true and accurate?

My world was heavy and I was irritated with so many things. What did I just say? I said.

Well, that's the best, Kif, the very best news.

The problem, I said, isn't that there isn't a document authenticating the final manuscript as true and accurate. It is that there is no final manuscript to authenticate.

Kif, I understand that. But you have a signed clearance.

There's no one now to say what his life was, I said.

Death isn't a full stop, Gene Paley said. It's an em dash with an empty page below.

That's the problem.

There was a short silence.

See it as an advantage, Gene Paley said. Fill the page.

2

By the morning Heidl's death was front-page news everywhere. Throughout the day he remained the lead on the radio and TV news bulletins as the connections and comparisons he had for so long craved and tried to promote were finally made by others— commentators, academics, experts and journalists. They used all the words and phrases he had wished for: *Nugan Hand, murder, CIA, spy, Allende, conspiracy, Whitlam, assassin, Cold War, clandestine ops.* They went on and on about *the inexplicable nature* of so much of the ASO and its activities and its paramilitary trappings and fuck knows what else. And knowing, I realised, nothing. Gene Paley was everywhere, being quoted as saying Heidl had left a tell-all memoir, full of sensational details which, when pressed, Gene Paley refused to divulge.

As well he wouldn't.

I was still trying to make them up in Hobart.

Each time I read or heard something more about Heidl, I felt annoyed with Gene Paley for ensuring the media would not talk to me. For didn't I alone know the truth? Shouldn't I be the one to share it with the nation? And then vanity was abruptly over-taken by panic. The police, the police! It could only be a matter of time before they came for me—and what would I say? A brick caught in my throat. I ran a thousand different stories through my mind, and realised I had to stick to the simplest—the one I'd told Suzy, the latter part of which was true: that I'd spent my final day in Melbourne at Sully's place working on the book, dropped the Skyline back at the publisher's car park in the evening, taxied to the airport and flown home.

You'll have to call Gene Paley back and say something, Suzy said when I explained the situation to her, or at least some of it— the unsigned release, the unfinished manuscript, the unsolved death, almost certainly suicide, which she fully understood did not move me—as we had breakfast coffee, she relishing it for the first time since she was pregnant.

The good thing about Suzy was that I didn't need to lie to her except when I had to lie. I had meant to tell her. But time passed, time dammed, time eddied and formed deltas that blocked, time kept moving on as the truth, once urgent, receded and soon somehow seemed as unnecessary as it was pointless, lost far upriver. I wanted to tell her everything. But the longer I went not telling her, the more impossible that seemed. And, in any case, what was everything? What had happened? It was unclear. It was *just* . . . unclear.

Out of habit rather than with purpose or hope I had gone upstairs to my narrow closet–study that seemed to grow smaller and more claustrophobic with each passing day. As far as Gene Paley and the world was concerned there was a book. As I climbed over my desk and eased down into my chair to start the work I had to finish as soon as possible, I realised the few days I had left to complete the final draft weren't nearly enough to say all the things I wished to say. And yet what those things were that so needed saying became vaporous. When I tried to think of even one I couldn't.

I reached into my backpack. When I had fled the day before, I had grabbed all my papers from Heidl's house to make sure nothing incriminating was left there. I took out the manuscript along with the book about dirty money he had given me. On top of the manuscript was the unsigned clearance form.

Why had I been so stupid to deceive Gene Paley about Heidl having signed the clearance form? It made no sense. However much it might have pleased Gene Paley, it now doomed me. It had been a lie, and, worse, a stupid lie, an unnecessary lie. I had now also lied to Suzy, an even worse lie, a lie of omission. But around my lie to Gene Paley others would need to be quickly invented and, henceforth, lived, encrusting like salt crystals. For a short time it frightened me to the point of feeling physically sick.

Yet I also felt an opposite emotion—almost a joy in doing something that felt both dangerous and liberating. And sitting there jammed between ever tighter, closer walls, this combination seemed to me strangely thrilling, offering the possibility of unknown freedoms—of a life differently lived, which, I suppose, must have been the appeal of such a life of lies to Heidl.

Still, the manuscript in its oppressive pile looked too depressing to start work on. To divert myself I opened Heidl's parting gift, the book on dirty money. On the right-hand top of the title page, handwritten in a slightly childish, clumpy-dumpy cursive, was his name. I leafed through the book but there was nothing of any interest or bearing in it. I returned to my manuscript.

A few minutes later I reopened the book at its title page. There before me were the same two handwritten words. Except now they seemed illuminated by God. I picked up a pen. Beneath the slackjawed gaze of Caravaggio's Goliath, copying the roly-poly script as best I could, I wrote—

Siegfried Heidl

My first attempt was a botched copy.

Siegfried Heidl

My second was better. I could almost feel something entering me. I thought of that voice, the pleasure of writing a name not your own—

Siegfried Heidl

—as your own. I pulled some matted cat hair off my coat sleeve, threw it away, and held the paper up to the light. It was beginning to look passable.

Siegfried Heidl
Siegfried Heidl
Siegfried Heidl

I took the clearance form, set it down carefully on the desk, dated it two days earlier, and where it read Signature, I signed myself—

Siegfried Heidl

3

I bundled up the manuscript, stowed it in my backpack, and walked down to Salamanca. The world felt quiet and glorious. I walked those streets marvelling at the beauty of gutters and trash. The people I passed seemed particularly kind to each other and there was about the day a wholly unexpected serenity and joy.

I went into Knopwood's tavern, empty as it mostly was at eleven in the morning, and ordered a beer. I drank it down, gratefully, feeling something leave me as something else found me. I ordered a second beer, sat at a table in the corner next to the sticky chess table, got out the manuscript, and put it to one side of the table in a neat stack.

I opened a notebook in front of me. I re-ran my calculations. I had 30,000 useable words, and needed another 45,000 to have the minimum for a book. Allowing two days for final revisions, that left nine days, which, divided into 45,000, meant I had to write 5,000 words a day. And understanding what my job was and who I had become, I began.

I skim-read what I had, making notes as I went. When it wasn't just obviously contrived, or simply obvious, everything I had hitherto written seemed dull beyond reckoning. Once more, I began to despair. And with Heidl gone, I could see no way forward to finish it. All I could see were the questions I needed answered—from the matters of small detail to large story I needed Heidl to tell me what had happened. But he would never tell anyone anything now. I had none of the real information I needed, nor was there time to interview his wife or close friends who, in any case, probably only knew different lies.

On top of these difficulties, what little I had didn't neatly fit any of the conventional tropes that the memoirs I knew of dealt with. Heidl couldn't be made over in the image of the Corporate Leader, the Con Man or the Redeemed Criminal. Nor was he the Guilty Good Man or the Wronged Prophet. He was none of these things yet at various times he seemed to be serially—or concurrently—each of them. My problem was my task: to create a single, plausible human being out of a man who on any given day could be Princess Di, Lee Iacocca, or Papillon. Or all three in one sentence.

For Heidl wasn't so much a self-made man as a man ceaselessly self-making. He had many births and many parents, and his origins were as mystical and protean as the gods of old. Each incarnation more mysterious than the last, Heidl begat Heidl who begat Heidl.

Or was he—as I was to discover some years later in a TV documentary that may have been more or less accurate—always the same man but with different names and stories? The program was a story of perennial metamorphoses. It began with the Bavarian fraudster Heinrich Froderlin who, as a transport clerk in late 1960s Munich, defrauded the Bavarian department of main roads of several million deutschmarks, and vanished, only, it would seem, to beget the Viennese huckster Friedrich Tomek who, in turn, begat Tilman Frodek, who begat Karl Friedlson, who begat Siegfried Heidl. It was like *Alien*, only worse, and who knew out of whose chest—yours? mine?—the next incarnation of the monstrous parasite might burst and what and who it might look like?

That Siegfried Heidl—who, at the point he became Siegfried Heidl to take up an appointment as a safety officer with the Australian Safety Organisation, a superannuated charity that had been staggering on since the 1930s urging the use of hairnets for lathe operators in a series of posters and (briefly) training films—that whoever he was might once more colonise one last identity and morph into someone else was at that time still inconceivable to me.

The ASO's total staff at the time of the arrival of Siegfried Heidl numbered five. Heidl's job—in that era before the rise of obsessive work and safety rules—was to travel to factories and workshops where he would give short talks advising the safest ways of using stepladders, lifting heavy weights, and operating lathes. Prior to this documented existence of Heidl there was for Heidl no Heidl history, only his Heidl stories as he, Heidl, chose to tell them, reinterpret and reinvent them, week in and month out.

Perhaps that's how it is if you live in a state of constant transformation, but his utter lack of interest in even the few incontestable facts of his past was trying for me as his biographer.

Life is permitted chaos, but books have to fake the idea life is order.

There were some strands that seemed true—or, at least, not demonstrably false. For example, his claim that the year prior to joining the ASO he had worked as a book keeper on an Aboriginal reservation in the Kimberley seemed to be attested to by a photograph from the *Northern Territory News* (though the caption that might have revealed his name had been torn off) and some blurry Instamatic photos of him standing on red dirt roads bounded by low-riding saltbush, alongside solitary boabs, or amidst lush tropical rainforest leaning on his red and white 55 series LandCruiser.

In any case, every story partly denied and partly complemented the last, only to be obliterated by a new story. All that remained was the dance of telling, the game of seeing how long he might get away with it. And in this, he recognised the gifts of others for self-deception and wishful thinking were infinitely greater than his own for lying.

I am not even sure if he was that much of a liar. For his story was never *his* story, but manias he invited you to share—the ASO, Spaceportal, Nugan Hand. Heidl, the great story maker, like God, was everywhere present in his creations but nowhere visible. The desire for belief was what he had so assiduously cultivated in others. It was this that led to his theft of seven hundred million from the banks—or, viewed another way, their gift to him. And perhaps, I sometimes thought in my darker moments, worse crimes. He certainly alluded to murder, but I found it hard to believe.

Still, he could surprise. About much he seemed ignorant, but occasionally he would give odd evidence that he wasn't. When once he pressed me for details about Suzy and the impending birth of the twins, I had told him that was personal.

I remember Heidl replying that the Latin root for person is *persona*, meaning mask.

Is that what a person is, Kif? he asked. A mask?

His own mask—when he could be bothered to invent it for me—was dreary beyond belief, a cloying tale of an *average* man who loved his family and worked hard helping others, a *decent* man who in the course of his labours built an empire on the back of selflessness, industry, and the common-sense insights of an *ordinary* man in a world of large-scale folly. For one who had created such spectacular lies for others, his own invention of himself as so dull a man was one of his most audacious achievements.

4

I bought a beer, necked the froth, wiped my lips, and, having no other idea what to do, began work. I took the first page, put it down in front of me, and in the margins started to rewrite the book. I worked as I had learnt as a brickies' labourer, without pleasure or misery, without hope or despair, devoid of ambition. Though I had nothing to say, I had read enough Australian literature to know this wasn't necessarily an impediment to authorship. As word was mortared up alongside word, as courses and walls and corners came into being, something unknown to me slowly began to arise, something formed that was not just a pile of meaningless sentences. Here some new words had to be cut and fitted; there, other words removed or reworked; yet others, more and more others, had to be invented and, in their invention, demand and summon into being even more words. In this way—in the odd dedication to industry—came the slow surfacing inspiration, strange and sweet, of simple labour.

When I went up to the bar for another drink, the barman asked what I was up to. I told him.

A writer, eh? the barman said. Never met a writer. I love Jez

Dempster though. There's a book I can read. That's a book *anyone* can read.

I worked as if in a rising fever at the pub table, stopping only for a counter lunch and an occasional beer, leaving only when the pub began filling with tradies late in the afternoon. I went home, cooked tea for Suzy, but she was feeling nauseated and couldn't eat. I changed the twins, cleaned and washed one set of nappies, hung out some others, and read Bo her favourite bedtime story of the wolf and the woodcutter.

That night I inserted some bright orange ear plugs I'd bought at the chemist to block out the junkies' quarrels and took some of Ray's speed. Withdrawn and wired, I stayed up late reworking the handwritten passages that now covered the printed manuscript into a new file on the Mac Plus, growing more excited as I began to see connections and patterns that had hitherto eluded me.

The contract I felt I had with the truth and with the way Heidl wanted his story told was, it seemed to me, over. It had always been absurd anyway. The truth of him was unknowable. I resolved to act in the spirit of Heidl by simply making it up each day, as best I could.

For the first time, I found myself free to write, and though the words came awkwardly, they came, and, after a time, they came more easily as I found within me a man without morals, who could pretend to any feeling that was necessary in order to gull others. Like Heidl, I tried on emotions, wore them for so long as they were useful, then changed into something fresh. And I was struck with the force of divine revelation by the simple understanding *that to write about Heidl I had no need of Heidl.* And finally freed of him, I felt I could at last tell his story honestly though every word was now invention. When I could work no more, I word-counted the chapter. I had written 6,452 new words.

I finally understood what Gene Paley had meant when he had said to see the lack of Heidl's life story as an advantage. His death was a liberation, allowing me to make something singular and recognisable of a man who was neither.

5

In the days that followed in a blur of coffee, heartburn, and a strange flow of words I knew was finite but which for a short time seemed unlimited, I simply let one word join the next. It wasn't in the large aspiration but the small detail that I found the book danced; not in the overwhelming ambition but in the simple determination to have the sentences good and strong that a story sang.

And with each passing day I found myself with more of the book written. I didn't think it great or even good. And I didn't care—I couldn't care. If I had lost ambition, that didn't worry me. *It was a book*, something far greater than I had ever achieved. What worried me was only this: that things worked, or, if they did not, how I might fix them so that they did. That was all. That was, I discovered, everything.

I don't wish to make too much of this. It was not life as Borges or Kafka. It wasn't Joyce poking at offal at the Polidor or Tebbe tebbeing or doing whatever Tebbe did when life rose beyond alliterative aphorism. It was life as life; the full catastrophe. As well as writing at an impossible pace I was rebuilding broken cots, scouring second-hand shops for twin strollers and bassinets, answering ads for baby capsules, and trying to ease Suzy's situation by taking over the cooking and cleaning.

I slept when and where I could—a few hours of a night with Suzy before the twins, who tag-teamed with their crying, took over the bed; on an air mattress next to the bed after eviction; head on my desk or lying beneath it of a day when I was too exhausted to write another word. Suzy tried to care for the kids while I worked but in practice it wasn't possible, and with a rising panic, sensing every minute lost to writing with terror and resentment, I helped. People asked in wonder how we did it. The answer was badly, but there was no other way, and do it we did.

I could take no pleasure in what should have been the supreme pleasure. I found myself irritated by Suzy's talking about the baby boys and even more ashamed for being irritated. Her face was drawn, she wasn't sleeping, and she had lost weight feeding both boys. She was exhausted beyond measure, but other things filled my mind, obsessed me if you like, visions of ants crawling, birds circling, the smell of damp earth and bark. Much as I wanted them gone, these things excluded all others. And the more pleasant Suzy was with me, the more she tried to humour me, or to ask where I was with the book, the more she took on the burdens of the home and the babies to help me with my writing, the more sullen and spiteful I became, because I could not tell her what it was I was thinking. There was not, in any case, even words for it.

We fought—under such circumstances how could we not? And then we just had to go on, washing, cleaning, feeding, and in my case writing all day and long into the night and, when I could, into the early morning, cranked hard on speed and desperation and overriding it all our dire need for money, until it was hard to know exactly what it was that drove me on.

Ray rang late one night from a public phone in Port Douglas to say he'd got work on a prawn trawler and I might not hear from him for a while. The line was bad and sounded the thousands of kilometres away that it was. He told me the cops had interviewed him twice, that he had said nothing about the Glock, or Heidl's desire to be killed. The cops had seemed happy with his story, so hopefully that was that.

And in between all this I waited for a phone call that never came. I was a little shocked by what I took to be the laxness of the police. My anxiety was terrible. At times it took an almost superhuman act of will to overcome my terror and type another word. But I was never called, never questioned, the matter of my being there at Heidl's home that day of his death never raised, because—as I had to constantly reassure myself—no one knew I was there.

Still, not an hour would pass without my worrying that the police would call. And to forestall what seemed inevitable, to get ahead of the game, I found myself several times picking up the phone to dial the police to tell them . . . *something*. To say I was there but . . . *what?* To say that I wasn't there but . . . *why?* And I would put the phone down. I must have done that a dozen times. Picked it up and put it down. Thinking I had some truth to share. But what was the truth anyway? And other things would return to me and I would return to them, relieved. There was almost a joy in the escape.

And then the police said that they were confident that there were no suspicious circumstances. Over the succeeding days, the fascination with Heidl began fading and other stories blossomed in its place. As if it were a mathematical progression from celebrity to anonymity, Heidl's story slipped from page one to page two, and then page four, and each day each story was half the size of the story of the previous day. One day I came across a small column, buried mid-newspaper at the bottom of the page, speculating on what Heidl may have revealed in his forthcoming memoir. Above it sat an advertisement for washing machines and next to it a much larger item about a Melbourne contract killer. It was the photo that caught my eye: Bertie's Pizza 'n' Pasta Takeaways, Glen Huntly. Its owner, an Alberto Ricci, had been arrested and charged with four murders. His front had been the pizza shop, where messages were left on an answering machine. I didn't read beyond the second paragraph.

6

Things grew molten. I had thought the point of writing was to fix words with their exact meaning, but the fun seemed to be in freeing them to perform outrages and miracles, watching them commit acts of indecency and being surprised by their unexpected moments of grace and revelation. I had been told words were a mirror, but I found them a moon that let everything in their quicksilver light turn into something that always hovered on the edge of mystery. Nothing held. More and more I let myself slip with them.

I had thought it was about writing what I knew, but after a time I discovered the more I acknowledged all that I didn't know, the closer to some truth I seemed to get. I loathed Heidl yet I was now condemned to writing an entire book in his voice, hoping to lead readers to the point I had reached: that this man—who was Heidl and yet not Heidl; who was me and yet not me—was evil. And I had to do it in a way that might keep them reading until the last page.

He kept dying before my eyes every day and every day on every page I perversely resurrected him in vengeance, in triumph, in amazement. No, the son had not forsaken the father, nor yet the father damned the son; did it any longer matter who was who? For we were now a holy trinity—subject, book, author—undivinable and indivisible.

Heidl wasn't stopping, he wasn't done with invention, not even now he was dead—perhaps more so, now he was dead, when I didn't have to check his inanities, his outrageous and preposterous stories with him, seeking somehow to reconcile my new lies with his old lies. Now he was dead he could live more than ever through me, my story veined with the odd rhythms and pompous kitsch he claimed to be; that marvellous creation that had at once been him and the invention of him, and was now my invention and the invention of me.

I was St Paul on the road to Damascus.

Gone was the confusion, as well as the anger; all that divided me from him evaporated, and with it all that separated me from the truth about myself. I could see and hear and think, but not as I had once seen and heard and thought. I had passed my whole life in a valley of mist and now the mist had cleared, and the deepest reality of the world was finally clear to me and it was nothing like the world I had formerly thought was real. The book I was writing was my story and, no longer myself, I was finally me.

In this way, eleven days and twelve nights passed.

And then it was done.

I took out my bright orange ear plugs. Outside the rain was smashing on the roof. I should have felt euphoric, but really, I just felt nothing and that felt good enough.

I posted the disks; two days later the second-hand fax machine in my writing room–wardrobe began to shudder as it dropped a long toilet roll of paper covered in an unpleasant gloss coating that smelt of burning chalk, and on it the first of the many pages covered in Pia's copyedit. Within a week, as per our schedule, the editing was done, and four days later I flew to Melbourne to discuss some final matters—the proofed galleys would be there ready for me to sign off, and we would close on cover copy and internal images.

18

1

PIA AND I MADE OUR WAY down the corridor, past the executive's office in which—for a short time that had seemed such a long time—I had felt imprisoned forever. But that was a death ago, already another world and another life. The door of the office was open. Inside I glimpsed a large, possibly obese man being photographed carving a ham that sat on the desk behind which Heidl had so recently attempted to fabricate one last empire of illusions.

Jez Dempster, Pia said. Photo shoot for his new cookbook.

I thought he wrote fiction?

He writes cheques and we cash them. If he did anal imprints we'd whack them in clapboards and set to work flogging them as a book.

A book!—in the end Heidl had failed even to make that. And no longer having Heidl to deal with I felt partly relieved and partly triumphant, because somehow, I too, like Jez Dempster, had written a book of which, for a short time yet, I felt proud. Glimpsing that office again, that desk, the Francis Bacon screaming chairs, the view beyond the windows of an infinitely replicating despair, my old feelings of incarceration and dread seemed already a distant memory. And I felt an emotion the opposite of mourning, a joyful rebirth. I was writing an autobiography whose author was now dead, knowing I only had to answer to the logic of a book, not the madness of its supposed creator.

Chin tucking the carousel into her chest, Pia used the slide projector she carried to push open the door to a windowless conference room.

Nice new shoes, she said, pointing at my feet as we went in.

I thanked her, and while at one end of a long meeting table she set up the slide projector, I found the switch that released a screen from the ceiling. As she clicked the slide carousel into the projector, Pia explained how Heidl had left the carousel and some other photos with her his last day in the office. She spilled a large manila envelope full of snaps onto the table.

Dreary shit, Pia said.

And dreary they were: a melange of conventional shots of Heidl and his family, so redolent of the '70s—HQ Holden wagons and auto tents, tight shorts, terry-towelling caps and peeling skin, old four-wheel drives in the bush.

We picked those images that promised the best hope of reproduction and moved on to a second envelope's contents. These were of his time working with the ASO—promotional stills, professionally taken black-and-whites of the paras jumping, marching, training; a uniformed Heidl watching, ordering, smiling. Corporate glossies of the ASO board as well as of Heidl with dignitaries—police chiefs, local and national politicians, ambassadors, and CEOs. We culled the least incriminating. Still, for a book that needed photos there was little of real interest. I crawled under a side table, found a power point and plugged the carousel projector in. Pia switched the conference room lights off.

In the darkness it took Pia a few moments to master the machine. Once underway, the colour slides were as unenlightening as the stills we had just looked at—the same unpromising mix of amateur family snaps and the sharper but no more interesting pictures taken by professionals of ASO paras leaping out of planes, climbing oil rigs, and fighting fires.

Your book, Pia said, does make him sound more interesting than I think he was.

And maybe it was true, I thought, as Pia kept clicking on with the wired remote, as the carousel kept whirring and clunking as unremarkable image morphed into unremarkable image. Other than cleaning the banks out of seven hundred million it was possible to believe that Heidl was as dull as his pictures.

At least he did some work putting this together, I said. They tell a kind of story.

And they did. If they were banal, they still had a coherence Heidl rarely managed in his conversations with me. They progressed from genial family man to employee at the ASO, to man of action, to man at the centre, the action CEO.

I know he got off on the idea of evil, Pia said. But maybe it was a shroud to cover up the fact he was just a dirty little con man.

She clicked and the screen shone bright white. There was no slide. Dust particles danced in the cone of light.

Show's over, Pia said. No more slides.

I stood up and went over to take the carousel off and pick out the few slides we had chosen for possible reproduction in the book.

I think there's one left here, I said, pointing at the carousel. One empty slot and then a slide.

Pia pushed the remote again, and in my mind something clicked and rolled forward with the slide carousel. I felt I finally understood Heidl, Heidl who had for so long troubled and disturbed me, Heidl whom I had to shower away every night, Heidl who was now, I realised, so much less than I had ever thought. He wasn't evil. That was too grand an idea when his truth was much more mundane. He was just pathetic.

I looked up from the carousel to see a blurry image of dark trees appear on the screen. Pia jiggled with the focus, the trees reached forward and as quickly fell back, before forming into the soft image of a rainforest with a tropical tree at its centre from which something was dangling. I turned to Pia.

You're so right, I said. Heidl, the dirty little con man.

Kif—Pia began, and halted.

She was staring straight ahead at the screen, playing with the focus with a sudden intensity, perhaps hoping it might somehow airbrush away what she was seeing and make it morph into something else.

I looked back at the screen.

It did no good. No amount of focusing would. I walked towards the end of the table in disbelief.

Oh my God, Pia whispered.

On the screen a naked corpse was hanging from a tree.

I am the forest.

I stood close to the screen, staring.

And a night of dark trees.

It was oddly bloodied. After some moments I realised why.

He has no skin, I said.

We stared at the picture of the flayed corpse, repelled, fascinated, sickened, silent. There could be no doubt: the corpse's skin had been peeled off his body. On the far left of the image I could just make out what I first thought was a large tropical bush, but what on closer inspection seemed to be the blurry red and white bonnet of a 55 series Toyota LandCruiser.

We could have put things together. But we didn't.

I think about that even now. Why? I suppose we had a job to do and that wasn't our job. And for us, who had the vanity of believing we were creative people, it was a reality too hard to imagine. What if it was just one final con from beyond the grave, a last joke on us? Maybe it too was nothing, just one more empty container. We were trying to reduce something to the smallness of a book, not open ourselves up to the largeness of life. That's

what I tried to think anyway. We wanted it ended, not opened;
our prejudices neatly confirmed, not laid bare.

Heidl's dead, I said.

2

Pia pressed the remote as if in silent agreement. The shutter
dropped. The carousel awkwardly rolled forward another place.
The screen went white. The room around us was lit in its lunar
reflection, stark and austere in a way that was still then new and
yet to become ubiquitous.

In its functional surfaces, its lost cables disappearing under a
side table, its off-white tones, it spoke of a future of cosmic emptiness. In that mercurial light, it was—in its pure functionality, its
powder-coated matt black steel, its melamine and Laminex and
fireproof industrial carpet that dissolved into almost complete
abstraction—a place where the gravity of the present was
growing weak and that of the future was growing strong.

I had travelled a great distance from my wretched study,
somewhere even beyond the faux teak bookshelved office, to a
floating realm, a vertiginous world that was at once somewhere
and nowhere, both that morning so long ago and the future.
The windowless void in which we sat fixated on the hanging
screen seemed only to exist to have shown us this one image. It
was as if we were to travel through that void, an empty infinity,
forever after.

Alone, so alone.

We felt these things, but we ignored them. We talked instead
in hushed voices, professional voices, about what our final cull of
photos for the book would be. Neither of us spoke to the other
again of the slide of the flayed corpse. Maybe it was too much to
take in so soon after Heidl's death, or too hard to acknowledge

what it might mean if we did. The book had reached its end and an end was an end, right?

If the image before us didn't fit with what I had written or what we thought, well, it simply didn't make the cut. Another dud image. It took too much imagination, would cost too much pain to conceive of it as anything other than a curious accident. But the book we had with such care cobbled together from his inventions and my own now clearly was—I could see—just one more evasion, another untruth.

And once more, Heidl somehow seemed in that room with us, taunting us, or worse. My good humour gave way to a clammy tightness. Was it his photo or someone else's? If it wasn't his, where would he get such a photo? After all, this was 1992, there was no internet, and it wasn't exactly easy to get hold of a slide of a hanging flayed corpse. A machine for piping a sewer line of all the world's horror into your home wasn't yet viewed as progress. Why, at the end of the story of his life, would he want to put that picture of all pictures in the carousel? To prove that he was, after all, a killer? That he had been Iago all along?

My dreams were for a time haunted by that hanging corpse whom I recognised variously as Pia, as Heidl, as myself, or, sometimes, as me and Heidl somehow morphing in and out of each other. Perhaps, like all dreams, it was something there and not there at the same time, something that I thought was transitory, whereas it was what we were all becoming.

Pia would go on to survive the clearfelling of publishing companies that proceeded apace over the next few decades, finding at each point in the ever-diminishing forest another, higher tree which to climb. She ended up working at Penguin Random House in New York, the last of the great publishers in the last of the great European cities and all the things we once thought mattered.

She had risen far beyond even the wildest aspirations of Gene Paley, was bound to publish famous authors and hack writers, accumulate prizes, publishing divisions, libel suits, unearnt advances, bestsellers, spreadsheets and corporate memoranda, and at the end of it all die not of the dementia she feared, but of stomach cancer at fifty-six, miserable that life had never amounted to more than a corporate table strewn with paper and, later, a monitor, with emails and messages and alerts that metastasised over her screen and spread into her soul and gut where, released, they killed her. Her manuscripts, once her love, were finally a misery to her, and then no solace at all.

And me?

I am still alive.

I would go back to Hobart and wait for a moment that would never come with my novel.

3

On the way out from the conference room we ran into Jez Dempster. Pia introduced me to the great man. It was the first time I had ever met another writer as a writer. I was flattered, and I was appalled that I was flattered.

You must try my jamon, Jez Dempster said, ushering us back into the office I had last stood in staring at Ziggy Heidl's revolver. I have a farm in the Otways, he continued, his manner so pleasant, so easy after Heidl. Wessex saddlebacks, he said. I feed them the Spanish way—only acorns—and this jamon is the result, the first in Australia.

Jez Dempster was a man as ahead of the times in boutique agriculture as he was in girth, as he was in so many things. A neatly trimmed beard sat on his spreading cheeks like cracked pepper on pork rind waiting to be roasted. Although the cook-book was purportedly by the great man himself, the recipes in the book were those of his anorexic Andalusian chef, Jez Dempster told us, adding, in a voice sonorous with sincerity, that the chef had been rewarded handsomely for his anonymous efforts.

It's the best book I've never read, he confided.

He wanted to talk about his pig farm and invited me once more to try his jamon. With a long, flat-bladed knife—so thin it bent like paper as he cut—he sliced for me an impossibly thin piece of jamon. He held it out to me on the flat of the blade. I stared at the cut flesh as fine and pink as skin.

Once you try it you'll never go back, he said. They live in a beautiful dark forest and have a lovely life and a quick death.

It was as if it were a sacrament.

Did it suffer? I asked, because it suddenly seemed to matter. Somehow in my mind's eye the corpse we had just seen dangling from a tree and images of pig carcases dangling from an abattoir rack merged into one.

Jez Dempster smiled benignly, as if to suggest life was too sweet to think such things.

I was upset. The pig, I said, because at that moment I sided with the pig against Jez Dempster. Did it? I asked again.

Ignoring my question he went on to instruct me how to taste the meat, where to place it in my mouth as I chewed and sucked.

People don't rate the saddleback for jamon. It's impossible with such a pig! they said. But that's because the Spanish never tried. Never! It's like our literature—the Europeans, the Americans, they say we should abide by their rules, their ways—but I never let it define me. We must have our own Australian letters, don't you think, Keith?

I said nothing, feeling only an incommunicable horror. At that moment, I sided with the pig against even literature which, after all, had done many brilliant things but had done nothing for the pig or all the dead pigs; I was on the side of all the dead pigs against Australian literature, against all literature, against publishers' numbers, against what was as bad or worse, my own wretched ambition that had led me to a moment of shameful complicity in something larger and broken and wrong.

I needed to know: had it suffered? Why must we—pigs, people—suffer? Why do we do this to each other? But, of course, I said nothing.

I'll give you one word for the coming century, Jez Dempster said, face shiny and ebullient, knife and pink flesh still held out before me. *Charcuterie*.

4

Lying in bed with Suzy that first night home, the memoir done, half my ten thousand dollars paid, the other half only three months away, my immediate future assured and a finished novel now within my grasp, smelling Suzy's warmth, I wondered what was this feeling that then came upon me, that filled me? Her soft breathing as she slept, the smell of her back . . . what was it? It seemed everything yet I felt a wanting, but what I wanted I had no idea. It was everything yet there was a life beyond our experience, and whatever that was, I wanted it. Already I was drifting outside of our unity, staring down at us.

And even now that I have a life outside of Tasmania, far from that wretched island that ate us all, I think of us two, held back by bonds neither of us ever really understood—loves that were also resentments, families that punished as well as loved, freedom that also jailed, beauties that deformed and tormented. There was a power to the island, or perhaps a weakness in us, such that we thought we could never make the break from it, or shouldn't, that to leave was somehow to betray. And perhaps it was, and perhaps it is.

Maybe it was jealousy or envy, greed or hunger, ambition or dissatisfaction on my part; maybe it was my ignorance of all things that were not books. An insufficient lack of attention to what is real, you might say, to what matters—to all those things that people like Suzy carried within them, within their hearts every day, all the things at best only alluded to and described, but never named.

It was hard for me to reply when earlier that evening she told me she loved me; there was such a look of suffering on her face, and at that moment love didn't mean that much to me and I wasn't sure if it ever really had. I was both of her world and already becoming of another world, Heidl's world, and perhaps she sensed that I was leaving her even then for that other world, and that other world was a wedge, an axe, a blockbuster that forced things apart, that broke things and broke people like us.

Still, she thought it was books at first and at first I thought the same—that world of books, *Fuck it!* I said. I don't care, I said. As though it were some choice. As though we were through it, as though it were over. But it wasn't books. It was Heidl's death. That was the other world.

I will do anything for you, she said. Until I die. I know that.

And I couldn't doubt it, and I knew I would never be offered so much again, and that it was also not enough for me, that nothing was enough for me now. I went to say something, but stopped. We all say too much. Things we don't feel, things we don't think, looking for reasons and signs where there are none. We build worlds of causes and effect, thinking that will explain and we will understand, terrified of a world where chance and chaos rule. Trying to persuade others and convince ourselves. It should be otherwise, we think. We think and we think but there is no wisdom in thinking. We know and we know but there is no peace in knowing. And when we can find neither wisdom nor peace we are told to accept and be serene in acceptance. But what if there is no knowledge, no acceptance, no serenity? That's what haunted me.

A few days later she said what I realised I had never wanted her to say.

Go, she said. Life's too short.

There was no comfort in it. Though it would take other things, we were undone from that moment. But we were breaking from the beginning.

5

When the book finally arrived I hated it. I had not expected to hate it so much. On receiving my carton of twelve finished copies, I set it down on our kitchen table. I paced around the table for a good hour or more, occasionally going outside, then coming back, and staring at it with an emotion that I finally recognised as fear. This seemed shameful. I cut the packing tape and opened the box. Packed in shredded newspaper were the books. I lifted one out. It made me slightly queasy to look at it and hold it. Perhaps it was a nausea of unavoidable familiarity—the inescapable taste of the off-chicken that remains in your mouth as revolt grows in the gut—that I had much of the time I was with Heidl and led me to take those long showers every evening at Sully's home, seeking to wash him away, to steady my stomach.

I hated the book's cover, with a newspaper photo of Heidl's face torn in half, a face that even in death was there and not there; I hated its uncertain design, half-thriller, half-memoir; I hated the whole look of it as uncertain, as nebulous as he himself had been. The one thing—the only thing—I liked was that which I had fought against most strongly—the relegation of my name as author from the cover to the spine where it existed only in near illegible type—SIEGFRIED HEIDL with Kif Kehlmann.

My relief quickly gave way to panic when I felt that my name, no matter how small, would still however be associated with the book—a book I had only a short time before wanted to own in every possible way. I worried I would be inescapably shamed by such a cheap and mediocre work about which everything was of the cheapest and most mediocre quality—the soft cover, gloss treated, with its faux thriller design; cheap paper stock as coarse as kitchen paper; the large amounts of white space in the margins and breaks to bulk out a thin implausible tale to make it look a large convincing drama. It looked exactly the sort of book it would immediately become—worthless, ephemeral, disposable. *Forgotten.* The only notable publicity it received was to come from an organisation called Don't Buy Books by Crooks, which in other circumstances I might have found offensive. They could have saved their breath: no one would buy the book anyway.

Telling wasn't selling, or perhaps it wasn't even really telling at all. Flicking through the pages that had cost me so much effort, I now saw only a mish-mash of his lies and my inventions never once convincingly turned by me into a plausible story. My writing—I was vain enough to still worry about such things—was by turns dreary and evasive, here a dulled recording, there a failed affectation, my aim of making Heidl compelling enough to carry the reader through to the end revealed as a delusion. The book, in short, was a failure.

I put the book back in the box. Bo was watching cartoons. The twins were crying. Suzy, who had just fed them, was exhausted. I changed both twins' nappies, strapped them in their baby capsules, put them and the box of finished copies in the EH Holden, drove to the McRobies Gully tip and threw the box of books on the tip face. Seagulls rose and fell like startled ash from a dead fire.

When I arrived back home, the twins were asleep. I carried them inside in their capsules and put them in front of the wood heater, though the fire was out. Suzy had taken Bo to the park.

Spring was coming. I didn't know that I never would be a writer. For that too was over, and what had begun, I couldn't know.

In an hour at the most, the twins would be awake. I fetched some kindling to start a fire, but it was damp and wouldn't take. I cleaned the kitchen, returned to the lounge room where I sat down, watching over the twins in front of the cold firebox. Watching and watching, terrified of the hurt waiting for us all.

6

With the money from the Heidl memoir we managed, by living carefully, to buy me six months' free time to write. I told myself that now I, and not Heidl, would be the author of my own life. But I was mistaken. It was as though from the grave he was still writing my story, my fate a tale foretold that people could read in a book, flicking past this moment to the end, and then throw away.

While the junkies next door went on another bender, I put the ear plugs back in and practised the discipline I had learnt writing Heidl's memoir in six weeks. Words and pages began adding up, and soon enough the novel was starting to take its final form. But these words of my novel were nothing: they said nothing, meant nothing, were nothing. I finished my book in a defeated mood. All that I had wished for was done. And none of it gave the slightest satisfaction.

I printed out six manuscript copies and tied each one with a green cord that was lying around the house, finishing each off not with a bow but with a barrel knot—an obscure, complex knot known to very few, taught to me by my father, a crayfisherman. I entered one manuscript in a national prize for unpublished novels and sent the other manuscripts off to publishers. Top of my list was Gene Paley.

Three months later the shortlist and winner of the unpublished novel prize were named. There was no mention of my novel. Still I believed, though in exactly *what* was less and less clear. After several more months, with no replies from any other publisher, and three unanswered phone calls made by me to Gene Paley, I received a short note from a TransPac editorial assistant thanking me for sharing my manuscript with them. While my novel was not one suited to their publication needs, she wished me the very best with it.

I wrote a letter to Gene Paley. To my surprise, he replied. In addition to a slightly arch variation of the normal publisher's formula of the time ('much as we admire your writing, we cannot see how we might find a way to publish it in a manner that might be commercially remunerative to you as writer and us as publisher'), he added the more revealing sentence; 'This novel does not fit into any recognisable school of Australian literature'. It was written in a kind tone that somehow only left me more despondent.

Some weeks later a parcel addressed to me in my own hand arrived. Not until I opened it and saw my manuscript did I realise what it was—my failed entry in the national unpublished novel contest returned, as manuscripts were in those days if you enclosed a self-addressed and stamped envelope. I put that sorry pile of paper on the table. Only then did I notice that the manuscript was tied up with the same green cord I had used.

As if it were an unexploded bomb, I carefully picked up the manuscript, turned it upside down and returned it to right-side up, stared at it suspiciously from a dozen different angles, and put it back down. It was impossible to believe what I was seeing.

I ran a finger along the cord until it reached the barrel knot—the *same* barrel knot with which I had bound the manuscript when I sent it away. I squeezed the knot between forefinger and thumb.

It took me some moments to process the full implication.

And then the bomb went off, turning my world to swirling dust. No one had ever untied the knot. No one had read my novel. No one would read my novel.

A writer is someone with readers.

I was not a writer.

I still have the typescript somewhere, though I am not exactly sure where. Still tied up in the same cord and knot, the cord and knot that have far outlived my dreams. Perhaps one of my children will find it going through my effects when I am gone and read a page or two before giving up. Or not. I can see now that its story—a drowning man having visions of his life—was not something of any originality or appeal. It was a young man's book. And death—Heidl's, or a character in an unpublished book—well, death is just death. Not a novel. Just a full stop with an empty page waiting to be filled by a stranger.

I went out to a local bar. I tried to drink myself through it, under it, over it, around it. It did no good no matter how many beers I had. I was finished and I knew it.

7

Ray called. Or maybe he didn't call. When I think about it I don't remember Ray being in touch again for maybe the best part of a year. No one knew where Ray was, until one day he just turned up. It was early in the evening, he was standing there at my front door with a flagon of Penfolds port and a pack of chocolate biscuits. Bo was bouncing on the tramp, Ray and I were once more drinking, once more watching her. We were like an old married couple who didn't remember their spouse's name; we were like strangers who had nodded to each other for a lifetime and knew nothing whatsoever about the other person.

He had fled north and spent six months working in the Gulf on a prawn trawler with a couple and their pet corella called Sandy, whom he had befriended. Its wings were clipped and when the seas blew up it would seek to fly from shoulders and railings, and inevitably, he said, go skidding on its arse along the steel decking, leading to an often-ruptured anus that he treated with Vaseline. Beyond this anecdote, he said nothing much apart from prawns had happened. He hadn't wanted to talk, and kept to himself. His dreams were terrible. Heidl was there, but it wasn't Heidl. It was a green slime that covered all his body and which—no matter how hard he tried—he could not clean off. He met a girl in Margaret River, and she was sweet; she was kind. One night he dreamt he was flying through mountain passes and landed in a beautiful green paddock. But in the end she had wanted him to talk too, she had kept asking questions, so, he continued, he had cut out of that. Why do people want to talk so much? Ray asked.

She sounds okay, I said.

She was okay, Ray said, if she just didn't talk so much.

It's not the worst, I said.

What's to tell? Ray said. There I was, finally starting to feel a fuckn sea eagle but every time she made me talk I was back being a corella with clipped wings and a busted arse.

She sounds a good woman, though.

She might have been a good woman, he went on, only she talked too much and so I cut out of it.

Why don't you just stick to one woman for a while? I asked near the bottom of the port flagon.

She wouldn't shut up with her questions. I used to say to her your problem is that you think there are answers.

And he told me about how his father would get drunk and beat his mother, how he used to tie them up at the table and beat Ray too. And when he was sixteen his father came home drunk and started once more hitting his mother and Ray took him on.

I creamed the cunt. I thought I was going to kill him. I wanted to kill him. He never touched her again.

And now? I asked.

I don't want to end up my old man. That's all. When I get in too deep, I move on before I become him. Before I do what he did.

You never told me, I said.

Maybe it's wrong. Maybe that's all life is, isn't it?

I never knew, I said.

He looked at me as if I was the biggest fool on earth.

What's to know?

His eyes were manic, the live electrode inside his brain once more sizzling.

What's to fuckn tell?

And I could smell it.

19

1

ONE WAY OF TELLING THE STORY of what ensued would begin
with a dog running into our yard, grabbing Suzy's pet parrot,
and killing it. Suzy loved that parrot as much as I loathed it, an
Indian ringneck cock, a luminous green bird that every time I
went near would bite me so hard I would bleed. With Suzy it was
as peaceful as a puppet. She would fold its long tail feathers into
circles and it would give her nibbling kisses. It would roll a ping-
pong ball across a table for her when she asked. It would run its
beak up and down her hair, gently grooming her while it sat on
her shoulder as she watched TV.

After I wrested the dead bird's strangely passive body from
the dog's wet jaws Suzy began to cry and could not stop. I held
her in bed that night, but she was inconsolable, cracked open
by a grief that seemed to me disproportionate. She had clipped
the bird's wings so that it could wander the garden and not fly
away. She kept thinking of the flightless parrot seeking to escape
the dog with its pigeon-toed hopping, then finding itself in the
dog's mouth, and she blamed herself. Trying to sleep, I felt her
slow, violent shuddering through my back. The death of the bird
seemed to have summoned up all the sadness of the world in
her, and there was nothing I could do to calm her.

We'll get another bird, I said into the darkness.

It's just—*I don't know*.

We can tame it up, I said.

Us, she said.

Her body jolted with more sobs.

For God's sake, Kif! *Us!*

Maybe it was then that a wild disorder of my inside began, a turmoil, an aching of the guts, a heaviness in the bowels, which would not leave me alone. At times it affected me so severely I found it hard to breathe. Where it came from I have no idea. I would have to stop and concentrate so that I might not fall to the floor. And some force, some weight would push in on my chest on all sides, crushing me, as if the world had grown too heavy and too powerful to keep out a moment longer. And it would no longer be me looking down into the eyes of the dying, but my eyes staring out of my collapsed body, my defeated flesh, looking out at the living. I would just have to hold on as thoughts, dreams, hopes would rise within me like stones I'd have to vomit out or they'd choke me. And I would rooster some sour slime into a sink or toilet and stagger back to whatever chair or sofa I could find.

What's wrong? Suzy asked a few nights later as she took me by the arm, the body, and wanted to lay me down. My God! Kif, what haven't you told me?

What's wrong? I thought. What hadn't I told her? What was it that was untellable? And my tongue would shudder in my mouth trying to find words that would explain a collapsing question mark, grey gruel, ants, rustling bark, trembling lips—

You must tell me, Kif, she'd say.

But just trying to find words for that circling black jay was beyond me, because the more I saw it the more I was caught in its spiral.

Or it will kill you, I can see it, Kif! It will kill you!

And I would try to hold on, for her, for me, for us, but all the time my grip was growing weaker and Heidl's stronger. I would look through her. I would see Heidl looking at me. And I would tell her nothing.

Later that night I woke in an empty bed. On searching I found her in the backyard where she had fallen asleep in a sleeping bag on the lawn. She suddenly awoke and seeing me there smiled.

Look, she said, and pointed above. I can't believe the stars tonight.

Because she did believe in them. Suzy believed, it's fair to say, in what she called the *loveliness* of things. It was her defence against a world that in so many other ways had offered people like her little—little education, few prospects, declining hope. It was a reconciliation I was possibly incapable of. There is a sweetness in things that can be intolerable to the less well disposed, that can irritate the more ignorant, who dismiss it as lacking some gravity or weight. And among their number I perhaps count myself. Suzy's soul was transcendent. Maybe that's what I couldn't bear. I was full of wanting what she had, but it wasn't possible.

The stars, Kif—can you believe them?

I never could. She carried summer within her, and now summer's gone.

2

Another way of telling it would be to say that I had become a liar, that I neglected and abandoned Suzy. And that would also be true. But maybe we just couldn't *hold*.

I could begin this version by saying that for a time I raged, but that other realities were overtaking me, foremost among them the need to make money. I had gone back to labouring, but through a chance phone call from a television script writer who knew Pia Carnevale I got a break. He was researching the background for a possible television series set in Tasmania.

We met for a drink, he liked my ideas, he suggested I write a treatment for him over the weekend for his drama series. I had no idea what a treatment was. Instead, I wrote a short story which, while never used, made a small impression.

This led to that. Here and there—through his recommendation—I came to be offered hack TV work. I took it. It paid better than labouring. I even enjoyed it. I still entertained the lingering notion I was a novelist, and that once cashed up I would return to novel writing. But I had less and less conviction. Perhaps a novelist without conviction *is* a TV writer. Claiming to be the conscience of their nation, writers are more often just courtesans of cash, and I—I guess—was just one more. Besides, I sometimes asked myself, what was a book next to a dead man? That seemed to me an achievement of sorts, and I had no other. When I hadn't known life, I had attempted to write books perhaps in order to know it. But now I knew. Or I knew enough not to bother.

In any case, there were natural limits to any Tasmanian wishing to be taken seriously as a writer, as a head writer made clear to me on the first day in her writing room.

A Tasmanian writer, she snorted, oxymoron or just plain moron?

And I understood that there would need to be serious disguises effected if I was to make it through unnoticed and unremarked upon as a fraud and a phony. Television, as it turned out, was the perfect camouflage.

I worked my way up, from writing gags for late-night shows to fill-in work on soap operas that were for a time Australia's greatest pride. Once more, one thing led to another, and soon I was head writer in Sydney working on a long-running soap, and from there moved onwards and upwards to scripting mini-series.

I awoke one morning in my newly purchased, overpriced Bondi apartment—exclusive, ridiculous—to the realisation that my great talent in life was a certain mediocrity that meshed perfectly with Australian television of the time. I had found my métier. TV was a tyranny and the tyrant was money, and I was happy to live in its velvet prison. It was work that offered everything a young man or woman might want—plenty of money, enough sex, a certain celebrity, the oblivion of industry.

In those days television was about advertising, which aspired to art, while television aspired to advertising. I discovered in Australian television of the 1990s a lack of conviction even greater than my own. We talked—how we talked!—of wanting to write great, ground-breaking television. Our real skill though was meekly adapting our ideas to the programming conventions demanded by advertisers through their agents, the executive producers and commissioning editors, all of whom had *droit du seigneur* over any script. We made rubbish, and, in the Australian way, the more mediocre our work, the more awards and the more praise with which we garlanded ourselves. There was no end to our conspicuous self-celebration.

Still, if the work was in equal measure gruelling and ridiculous, I was also learning. Within two years I had moved into production, where I've more or less—well, mostly more— stayed ever since. You probably have seen and forgotten several of my shows. That's okay. I've forgotten them too. Unlike my memorable novel which didn't fit into any recognisable school of Australian literature, I worked hard to ensure my shows were always recognisably Australian and immediately forgettable.

That's not the dispiriting revelation it reads as. Rather, it was liberation from ideas of immortality and genius that I associated with books. TV was the art of turning money into light and light into money. It was a more magic circle of money than Heidl ever dreamt. With TV, I was able to bring to bear so much that Heidl had taught me. I am not saying though that what I did was a con. I am asking the question: what is not? Where is the border at which your job, your business, crosses over into the badlands? Where is it? Because I'd like to know. I really would. Heidl knew, or he knew that much. I've had the vanity of thinking similarly. But not too often. Because I'd be wrong.

At the time I wanted to succeed, and I had thought that life was about success. Later I came to a different point of view. Living is about being wrong, as Ray once said. But hopefully getting away with it. To live *is* to be defeated by ever greater things, and it may be that you learn from your defeats, but mostly you are defeated by what you learn. Perhaps the sole purpose of life, I came to think, is learning to understand the measure of your own particular failure.

3

The kids stayed with Suzy in Hobart. They understand—as I do—that I was freed of their gravity, that gravity which is perhaps another name for love, many years ago. What remains is something: fondness, certain memories—mostly invented—friendship, I suppose. Or hope. The deep dark things though, *those things* that pulse thick and hard through the wrists and heart and wake you drumming terrifying death marches in your ears in the night, that won't stop screaming like torn flesh and crumpling metal—they cannot be carried together. They are not us. This understanding transcends bitterness on my children's part and sadness on mine. We cannot be father and children. I don't say that there are not worse possibilities—a Christian student in north Kenya, say; a Sumatran orangutan in a logging zone, or a Muslim refugee anywhere—but sometimes I see a young man playing with his kids and that joy—*that joy*—fills me with a sense of loss so large I feel I might fall into its infinite void forever and never stop falling.

As for Suzy—though I'm told that there were one or two *flings*—she never ended up with anyone, in contrast to me, who couldn't stop falling in with partner after partner. As Tebbe says, only the invalid stays put. I had a need in me, childish, initially appealing, finally appalling, for comfort, company, a passenger to share the daily journey through the night and all its attendant terrors.

To be held, I guess. To be—

But I am increasingly unsure.

I admired Suzy's strength, her courage, the neat contours and open generosity of her ordered life which seemed at once stronger and wiser than my own. That people pitied her and envied me after we split was comic. That they felt sad for her, thinking it had worked out for me and not her, was touching. In truth, my celebrated homes, my beach houses, my bathrooms, kitchens, serial partners, my *décor*, familiar to readers of architectural and celebrity magazines alike—all kept changing in order to fill the void I felt.

But the void remained. The void only grew larger, blacker, more terrifying. I was like Ray's turtle. Even with my limbs hacked away, with all hope gone, I couldn't stop living.

4

The millennium came and went, the Twin Towers fell to a fiction made murderous reality, and I rose in reality TV production making fiction. *TV Week* hailed me 'the genre's *sui generis* genius'. I worked on the whole tragic series, from housemates to renovation to cooking and weight loss, while the world made of petty fictions great wars and wars' terrible reality cursed ever more people. Over the years, I progressed from script development to project development, from project development to production, from production to executive producer, from executive producer to partner in a production company, to my own company, and, finally, when I sold out to the Americans, director of the Australian arm of ZeroBox Entertainment.

I continued growing older, but the women in my life—some serious, some not, and these days none so serious—have steadied out at a median age of thirty-five. And that seems as right and as empty as everything else in my life.

Tebbe again: there is about our passions something inexhaustible; we love one unto death only to discover in life the capacity to love so many more. We fear that this makes us fickle and shallow; we do not grasp it may be what is infinite and best within us.

Or that's what I try to think when I find myself having to think about such things. The good thing about making television is that it is rarely conducive to self-reflection.

The latest left when I forgot her thirty-eighth birthday.

Who are you? she screamed in our final fight. Who?

I had no idea. It was two in the morning, I was typing, seeking to answer that very question by writing this memoir, and so I said nothing.

Who? she said, reaching to shut the laptop lid before I stopped her.

Who indeed?

I want so badly to trust you, Kif, she said. I don't think I can trust anything you say. I love you, she said. My sweet man. Why won't you tell me what happened?

I already have, I said.

I read what you wrote.

That is . . . *that's* what happened.

But is it? she said. Your story keeps changing.

No, it doesn't, I said.

You wrote that Heidl asked you to shoot him. That you stood over him as he died, and he watched you. That's what you wrote.

But you always told me that you went up that hill to spy on him and he never knew you were there.

What I wrote is what happened, I said.

I watched her pull back a long curtain from a window that rose from the floor to the wood-lined ceiling far above.

I don't believe you, she said.

Moonlight ran over the sea in front of her, and onto a car and some outdoor furniture beneath a statuesque eucalypt to her side; each was lit silver bright on one side and duplicated on the other in powerful black shadows, images larger, more real than the silvered objects themselves.

I thought I knew you, she said. But I don't know you at all.

In front of me there was one word on the screen: Heidl.

I deleted the word slowly, letter by letter.

Heid

Hei

I want a child, she said.

He

Our child, Kif. What I wanted from the beginning.

H

Kif!

|

I sat back, looked blankly at a blinking cursor, and my hands returned to the keyboard.

Who are you? she asked, and I could hear the rising panic in her voice.

Heidl, I typed once more.

Who? she was insisting. *Who?*

—*through this inadequate labyrinth of twenty-six symbols, I ask only one thing.*

Did you kill Heidl? I wouldn't blame you.

Remember me, Kif, your enemy, who ate your soul.

But I wish I could trust you.

But I wasn't hearing anything. I'm a writer. I looked at the monitor as words, patterns, lives formed before me.

Our baby, Kif, she said.

I continued murdering memory, trying to learn to live again.

Our first battle was birth, I wrote.

20

1

I RODE OUT THE GOOD YEARS, the golden decades, rode them hard, had fun, made money, and lost most everything else. It was pleasant enough and I can't complain. I don't judge myself, which is wise, for I would appear as rather lacking. Occasionally these days I am taken by the most terrible pain—when another woman drifts away, but less and less so; more and more so on the rare occasions I see one or both of the twins. They have a goodness about them. Forgive me—but the goodness—their goodness—it astonishes me, moves me. I tell myself that it comes from their mother, that kindness, that selflessness, and the thought comforts me.

But after they've left I sometimes have a crushing tightness take hold of me. I am without strength, it is all I can do to sit and not panic, I can't say what it is but I hear the blood pounding once more, as if it's pushing to escape me and be free, as if my body or I have become some wicked prison, and I fear above all that their goodness comes also from me, that I once too had something good, and then lost it, or spurned it, or traded it, or somehow let it go and with it something fundamental. You can do that, you know. Lose some fundamental part of yourself. And you cannot have it back. Ever. There's just a hole, like a cancer survivor minus their limb or liver or breast. But the hole has no name. Or it has, and you don't dare even whisper it. Something good. And then it's gone. Like the stars. Like a bird in a dog's mouth. Like a child eaten by a wolf in a fairytale.

2

Whatever was human in Heidl by the time I met him had long ago atrophied as it has now also in me; in the mirror when I force a smile it *is* him smiling back. Sometimes, if only for a moment, I even worry my cheek is twitching. Destiny, like TV, favours repetition, all stories demand similarities, patterns, the music of symmetries and juxtapositions, and I realise now that in my life I have done little more than repeat Heidl's own. In my own humble way, retailing lies as reality, I see I have become just another con man.

In the production meetings and over the elaborate lunches, I would sometimes cease to listen and simply look around at the hucksters and boosters, the driven bankers and the resilient producers trying to pitch yet one more cracked idea, and I would remember Ziggy Heidl.

His grotesque personality was a monstrosity, something almost deformed. Yet I am convinced that beyond all his endless talk was a larger silence about things of which he would never speak. I sensed a horror born out of a despair and a loneliness so terrifying, so absolute, so universal, that it amounted, for him, to an evil he could not escape, but had to accept with a clarity and humility that was breathtaking. When necessary he spoke at length about goodness, ethics, morality, but in a cold and withered way. There was an infinite weariness and surrender about his absurd words at such times, like grace before an orgy. Later, I met men and women who echoed him, but they lacked something—belief? desolation? desire? madness?

Sometimes I wonder if Heidl was the only real thing I ever knew.

I tried to free myself from Heidl decades ago, yet as I have grown older I find myself less in the tapes and now digital copies of my old television shows, and more in him—in what he told me, in what he taught me, and most particularly in his crimes which have now also become mine. Perhaps the two, his crimes and my programs, are the same thing. I moved on long ago from his memoir and made so many new things—entertainments so delightful I sold the idea of them around the world—bulimia races, real-life cancer competitions, and so on—but all these things are really his invention and I can see now he came to own me like no other.

Take my latest *succès de scandale*, *Dying to Know*. Filmed in China where neither normal codes nor laws of any recognisable variety entirely prevail, it is my biggest rating hit. *Ever*. The idea is simple enough. Those who wish to die and those who wish to assist their loved one to die sign up to the Black Ace Club. Each episode begins in a gaming room, redolent in its decadent fixtures and crepuscular lighting of the pre-war Shanghai Bund's dives. There six players play the game of release. Whoever receives the two black aces—of clubs and of spades—are condemned respectively to be the euthanised and the euthaniser. There's more to it, but that's the essence, and I must say even I've been pleasantly surprised by the viewer interest and the advertising it's attracted. These words aside, it's the closest I've ever come to autobiography.

3

Two years ago I found myself gossiping with Pia Carnevale. I was visiting the US on work and it was the first and, as it would transpire, last time after that morning in the conference room I would ever again see her.

The thing is, Pia said, I have this hairdresser. A lovely man, gay; Cherry, he's called. I go to Cherry once a week not because I really need to, but just for the—*well*, it's embarrassing.

Go on, I said.

Pia had taken me to a cold and for New York rather empty restaurant near the Hudson. Somewhere past the Village or next to the Village or behind the Village—I don't know. Maybe it was Brooklyn. I never really got NYC geography and the infinitely fluctuating social gradations in which it imprisoned itself. Pia leant across the table.

To be touched, she said.

She laughed, and leaning back on her chair she looked away and then furtively back at me.

Ridiculous, really, isn't it?

Is it? I said.

Pia had lost her younger, fuller figure and in her middle age was now very skinny after the New York professional woman model, a stick, hair now dyed black, her iridescent teeth prominent. Her bright, slightly kaleidoscopic wardrobe had ceded to dark clothes of better quality and taste but less character. But as she chatted her manner remained as I remembered it.

When he shampoos your hair he holds your head so softly, he takes all the weight you carry. And it all goes away, and he *knows*. I don't know how, but he does.

I thought other, less generous things. I said, That's special.

The kindness of touch, I guess. For a few minutes each week I don't have to carry that weight.

Cherry's popular?

Well, I'm not the only one. There are a lot of lonely women in this town. Sometimes something happens in your life and you wake up one night in the dark and you know that this is it; that you're alone, and now you'll always be alone.

This is an awful drink, I said.

I think I've had too much, Pia said.

Really awful.

Do you ever feel that way? Pia asked.

I did. Often.

No, I said, and smiling I beckoned a waiter for another two drinks. Pia put her hand over her glass.

So lonely, Pia said, paying someone to touch you?

Now it was my turn to look away, at the bar, the already dated subway-tiled trim, the faces, the swirl of people.

Do you, Kif?

I was momentarily overwhelmed by the babble of strangers, but Pia's voice cut through.

I think some days I want to be dead, Pia said. At peace. I think how glad I'd be to be dead. Dead as only the dead can be. With a vengeance.

A woman who turned out to be one of Pia's writers sidled up and said hello, saving me from awkwardness. Her name was Emily Coppin, and after she moved on to talk to someone else she knew at the bar, Pia whispered how she was *connected* with the Brooklyn set.

We bill her as one of *the voices of her generation*, Pia said. Hoho.

I said how lucky Pia must be here, though I didn't exactly mean it, how many extraordinary people she must meet. She replied that it wasn't exactly so, that while she met many people and knew some, she would have to be honest and say few were extraordinary and none were real friends. They have a word here, she said, *transactional*.

Pia cackled heartily, throat throttling.

People are your *transactional friends*, she said, and this time we both laughed.

What does that mean? I asked.

She told me it meant they used you and you used them. It's not really a word, she said. It's a horrible idea. It's so horrible that no one can see how horrible it really is. People don't even have the courage to use an honest word for it.

Robbery? I said.

Consensual rape, she said.

Like that.

She paused and looked around and seemed to be considering something. After some time she turned back to me and fixed me with a gaze that allowed no relief.

4

Pia wanted to talk about what had happened back then, but about what had happened I had ever less idea. Luckily, Emily Coppin returned with a friend, a bearded young man whose role seemed to be to agree with Emily Coppin in all things, and for Emily Coppin all things were all things Emily Coppin.

I asked her what she wrote.

Autobiography. It's what everyone writes now. Knausgaard, Lerner, Cusk, Carrère. All the best writers taking literature somewhere new.

Pia politely interjected to say how the third volume of Emily's memoirs was in this week's *New York Times* bestseller list.

Congratulations, I said. That's incredible.

Why did I come to a dead end writing novels? Emily asked.

She talked as if giving a TEDx presentation. Direct looks, definite hand gestures, questions that were only pretexts for moments of extended faux thought.

Because, she continued, like, as a *mode of narrative* it's dead. I mean, we all know that.

Emily Coppin was perhaps late twenties, with that strange face of the striving class of New York—an elemental erosion, preternaturally aged yet aping adolescence. Down her left upper arm ran the tasteful tattooed half sleeve, razor-wire spirals sprouting red roses, an adornment to an unspoken privilege posing as its antithesis. She appeared to have an agreement with the world that she was attractive, even if, on closer inspection, her glamour was the groomed cuteness and big-eyed stare of a palace's pet capuchin monkey. I say these things, but perhaps she was beautiful and at that moment I just hated her. Certainly, she understood her own limited experience as the full extent of the universe. Perhaps she had no sense of the fragility of things. It was hard to say.

It's fake, inventing stories as if they explain things, Emily was saying. Plot, character, Jack and Jill going up the hill. Just the thought of a fabricated character doing fabricated things in a fabricated story makes me want to gag. I am totally hoping never to read another novel again.

Novels disempower reality, the beard said.

Emily mimed putting two fingers down her throat and made violent choking sounds. The beard laughed heartily. Emily turned and stared at him. A fruit fly buzzed around her head.

Whatever, Luke, she said, trying to swipe the fly away.

The beard went quiet. For the first time I noticed her eyes, the dull colour of old snail shells, as she returned to her theme.

Everyone wants to be the first person. Autobiography is all we have. I mean, isn't that what you do in reality TV?

I don't know what I do, I said. I just go in each morning and make it up.

That's where we're different then, Emily said. I don't *make it up*. I hate stories. We all hate them. We've heard them all before. We need to see ourselves.

It sounds like literary selfies, I said.

What's wrong with a good selfie? Emily said.

The beard laughed again. Emily Coppin turned her gaze on him as if he were a natural history specimen in a museum.

Luke's a successful narcissist, she said. Great sex for him is me watching him jerk off. He's got a lot of followers. He tells them all about it. The more he tells the more likes he gets. The more likes the more he tells.

Pia tilted her head towards mine.

Luke's life is to Mark Zuckerberg what the bison plains were to the railway barons.

The beard brightened. Post. Share. Die, he said, and smiled.

I've learnt a lot from Luke, Emily Coppin said. She waved a hand at the fly.

Somewhere, somehow, over some acrid mojito that wasn't really a mojito but a slightly rancid concoction called the *house specialty* because mojitos were passé, the conversation wandered on to the recent disappearance of two young sisters, one four, the other six. Someone used the word evil. I don't remember who.

Evil? Emily said. Hey, don't tell me you believe in evil?

She shook her head and smiled. Emily had many strong opinions on many things. I was no longer sure what I thought about anything.

It's not a question of belief, I said.

I totally get it, Emily said. *Not.* But it doesn't exist, right? Evil is an idea, that's all. But what is evil? You can't see it, you can't touch it.

The beard agreed. Emily Coppin nodded sagely.

And that's the thing, she went on. I feel there's, like, environment, reasons, a lack of respect. Right? Like, biology? Neural elasticity. But neural elasticity's not evil. It's terrible if it happens to you, but, you know, a serial murderer? Crazy. But that's what it is, a chemical imbalance, some misfiring of neural transmitters—a malfunction of brain soup. Can you call a bad minestrone evil?

No, Pia said. You call it lumpy ketchup.

My point exactly. Thank you, Pia.

I wanted to tell Emily Coppin about seeing a flayed corpse. About what you can become. About reading stories to Bo. But it was inexplicable. Unknowable. Unsayable as autobiography. All I could manage to say was that I didn't agree.

Evil's a relative notion, Kif, Emily said, fixing me with the determined gaze. Her snail-shell eyes were duller and more distant than ever, pavement-hued vortices.

You think so?

The science is in. Evil is just a construct of the old Judaeo-Christian order. What you talk about when you talk about a white god—a black devil.

The beard smiled. Emily smiled. She was after all an American writer, her purpose was uplift, answers, certainty, knowledge, characters whose origins and psyche were all reducible to neat explanation and final judgement, one more moral grammarian.

And what could I say? That I had been frightened, that I was still frightened, that something happened, that something changed for me and nothing was as it had been? That something had broken in me and me with it?

What would I know? I said, smiling, hands opening out. I'm just an Australian reality TV producer.

It wasn't the *moving epiphany* I presume Emily wrote so well, but something I could see she sensed as even better. Having made of a conversation a contest and having made of the contest a victory, the natural order of things had been restored. The beard's hand shot out, grabbed at the air, and opened to drop a crushed fruit fly. Emily laughed, and together they left us for the far end of the bar and a group that had formed around a well-known actor telling stories.

5

1992 seems so close, I said, glancing at the far end of the bar. But there are people running the world today who weren't even born then.

The way I remember it, Pia said, time suddenly, crazily sped up back then. Crazy fast. Suddenly everything changed. People were insanely optimistic; they said they knew that time was racing towards something. They didn't really know towards *what* but the thing was that it was going towards *something*. If you pressed them they'd mumble words like democracy.

Freedom, I said.

Pia smiled. Yeah. Those sorts of words, she said. The main thing was that everything was going forward so fast that time itself was about to stop. The end of history.

One of history's better jokes.

Sure, Pia said. The thing is we thought we were gaining the world when really we were losing something fundamental. Do you remember that slide carousel? Sometimes I think of it going backwards, looking at Heidl's life in reverse.

The washed-out Kodachrome colours came back to me, and I too could see the flickering images of the parachute jumpers giving way to an ever-younger family, hair growing on Heidl's head, the bonnet of a red and white LandCruiser in front of which his family posed for the camera.

Maybe that was what was happening, Pia said. No one could see that it wasn't really progress at all, but regress. No one could see some breakdown beginning, or returning, some universal collapse of values that was also the beginning of the acceptance of a new violence and a new injustice.

You need to see Cherry twice a week, I said.

Pia fixed me with her editor's eye: she wasn't done; she needed me to listen, not speak.

What was so shocking, Kif, wasn't the violence, not the injustice, but the acceptance of the violence and the injustice as natural. And with it all a culture of solipsism, a pandemic of loneliness, a politics of hate; an invitation to join in making up murderous stories that finally robbed us all.

I didn't like thinking about the past or present the way Pia did.

It was a coma, Pia said. A coma that lasted for decades.

I didn't understand why we couldn't just swap stories, laugh, and enjoy an evening together. I didn't like the way she was so worked up. I tried to take the conversation back to Cherry.

Fuck Cherry. I want to talk about what haunts me, Kif, Pia said. If the world could have dreamt its future as one man, do you think it would have dreamt Ziggy Heidl?

But I didn't agree with what she was saying. I couldn't. I had to believe he was just a man. How do you compare the crimes of a petty criminal with some breakdown, some collapse so immense that even now its contours remain unclear? Some terrible violence that was coming to us all. Maybe I didn't want to believe that there had been any sort of collapse. And so I said no, that what she was saying seemed an American sort of idea and Heidl's wasn't an American story but an Australian one.

What's an Australian story? She laughed. Or German? Or American?

No, I said again, I don't agree, and I said nothing more about it, because maybe she was right, or maybe she wasn't, and I just made some jokes and ordered some more drinks.

And then Pia asked if I remembered the last slide.

6

The image came back to me in an unpleasant rush—the harsh light that made the musculature particularly pink, the striations of subcutaneous veins an awful blue.

I remembered we looked at that swinging corpse for a long time, not because we wanted to but because we were too shocked not to look at it. Of course, the corpse was not swinging—how could it, a frozen image, do such a thing?

Pia remembered a feeling she had in the conference room—as if something else in that room was moving. Or the room was moving, or even something beyond the room.

I knew what she meant about that feeling of something large moving—history perhaps, the future, or our souls, or all these things—and feeling sick with a momentary knowledge that vanished almost as quickly as it was granted me.

We observed it closely, Pia was saying, I remember you up there at the screen staring at it.

I ordered Aperol spritzes, which I find always help to rescue me from such conversations. But Pia had things she wanted to say, had perhaps wanted to say for a long time, things that grow calluses around them in another country and we carry unspoken, until we find another person from that distant time, that faraway place—that other country—and mistakenly think that with them at least—at last—we can communicate the incommunicable.

But we can't.

Still she continued, head bowed slightly, a strange and singular determination I hadn't recognised in her before.

I was hoping, Pia said, that what we were seeing was some trick.

The waiter returned to say that they didn't do Aperol spritzes, but that they did do their own *artisanal* take on a negroni.

Pia said how at first she wondered if it was the fault of the projector or our eyes, and thought it would transform into something else, something benign and unobjectionable.

Two non-negronis, I said to the waiter.

I wondered if it was some waking dream, Pia said.

And I thought how perhaps it was—of a world where something had ended and something else, something unimaginable, was beginning, against which we were powerless to act, but could only observe, waiting to wake up and scream, never knowing that we were in fact being condemned to a waking nightmare that never ended, a world where not one heart knew how to touch another.

Pia looked up at me with a look that was full of tenderness. The sort of look people give when they know they're losing someone. The sort of look that is wrongly confused with love. She leant forward, and put her hand on mine.

I saw that she wanted to say something; that it was important to her to say it, and nothing I would say would dissuade her from what she was about to tell me.

Can I say something, Kif?

Of course.

I don't care, I really don't. I might have done the same thing in your place.

Pia leant further in, her eyes gazing at me with an odd intensity. It was a moment before I recognised what she felt. It was, in equal parts, admiration and despair. I noticed there were tears catching in the wrinkles around her eyes. She tilted her head back and blinked two or three times.

I think you killed him, Kif. But you can't kill *it*. Can you?

I saw that Pia believed this implacably; that it was important to her to believe it.

No, I said. You can't kill it.

21

1

EVERYONE I MET THAT NIGHT was a stranger. They claimed to know me, they greeted me affectionately as an old, dear friend. But I had trouble recognising them. Their cruelled bodies were a battle of bloat and collapse, their faces strangely slackened. At first they all seemed to be wearing masks—oddly set things often with a look of fixed astonishment. Everything that was superfluous had eroded. Something had happened and they had not known it and now it was already done. As if a final judgement, virtues and vices reduced and were wrought as drooping face, dull and watery eye, crusted skin. Their arms they put around me were flabbily fleshed, their cheeks sunken and strangely dry, and there was in them all a mood, an attitude, that I can only describe as weary acceptance. And when I saw myself reflected similarly in the pub window that night it was with horror that I realised that time had claimed me also, that it had made its judgements about me as well as them, that it had condemned me as surely as everyone else in that room. Too many years had passed and I now was someone else.

There is no going back.

On looking across the bar, I didn't recognise the almost albino figure shuffling towards me, smiling brightly and holding up an arm in greeting. Even allowing for the decades that had passed it was almost impossible to recognise him. He was shorter, rugged up in a scarf and a ski beanie. He had no hair. But neither did he have eyelashes or eyebrows, all lost to the six rounds of chemo he had so far undergone. Even in dying, as in living, Ray remained a man of determined excess.

2

I had flown down to Hobart for this night. Old, hard, shitty Hobart. Ray's farewell—his billing—was in a brightly lit beer barn, the only redeeming feature of which were the pool tables. Outside, sleet occasionally gravelled the windows, blurring the traffic into dissolving rainbows.

Ray looked like a dying turtle—bug-eyed and carcinoma-faced, his great chest now a mandolin shell. But none of that was what was surprising about him. What was shocking was his gentle good humour.

I'm a much nicer bloke than I was, he said. Which is nice for Meg.

Meg was his new partner and his only concerns were for her. And with her, he seemed to have found himself.

Meg looks after my weight, he said. I lose it and she feeds me these awful protein shakes to put it back on. So I am a few kilos lighter but still as fat in all the wrong places.

He laughed, and as he laughed our eyes caught for the first time. If his mood was remarkably upbeat, his understanding was clear. His oncologist had sent him to a counsellor who had wanted to discuss with Ray his worries.

I don't have any worries, Ray told the counsellor. I'm going to be dead in six months.

He called the cancer Tassie.

It's a lazy shit of a thing, he said. Meant to be highly aggressive. Oncologist has never seen a case like it. Tassie tumour, I said. Only works once a week, and even then not very well.

The six rounds of chemo were, he told me, purely palliative. He wanted to live for as long as he could, but he was still going to die. They had given him till December.

I think I'm going to do better than that, Ray said. Maybe another four months. Maybe even more. But I am gone.

The living is only a species of the dead, and a very rare species.

He laughed. He laughed a lot that night—about hospitals, about doctors, about himself. He talked too, mostly about Meg, with whom he had moved in a year before the diagnosis.

Do you know what really does my head in? he said, and not waiting for an answer he went on. The goodness of people. Bad shit I understand. But Meg?

And he couldn't stop laughing about such good fortune as he clearly felt was his at meeting Meg, at life's wonder and its cheating nature, at what was allowed him and what was so soon to be denied him forever. It was as if facing death, he had somehow transcended it.

As Ray laughed I smelt his foul breath, a reek of chemicals, with an under-scent of a cloying putrefaction. Each time he muttered *Meg* a stale and metallic odour escaped his mouth.

He smelt wrong. But perhaps it's just my ageing nose. Things smell differently when you are young. People smell different and the young smell different. Late of a night now I download songs from my youth. I hope in listening to them I might again, however fleetingly, smell those same scents of people and places and times—of love, of joy, of jealousy and fear and confusion— that now seem important, that now seem, well, *my life.*

Why this relationship between sound and smell I can't say. But there it is. I listen not to hear things, but in the hope of smelling them. It rarely happens. Still, these smells—on the rare occasions I manage to successfully conjure them up from my past—would, if I could communicate them, be a far more accurate and complete reconstruction of that time than these words.

You would understand how young I was. And other things, besides. Suzy would be a strong smell. A tree after a storm, maybe. Our kids' wild wet animal odour. Everything smelt, and every smell was a universe. Even the road outside our front door of a morning, even that bitumen and spilt oil smelt intoxicating to me.

Meg told me she even liked that smell of the chemo oozing out of me, Ray said. Because, she said, when it's gone, then . . .

But Ray didn't go on. He turned his face away, and when he turned it back he was smiling.

You know what keeps me going?

No.

When I'm really fucked up?

No.

I imagine a set of tits in front of me, Ray said.

And he laughed, because it was both true and a ridiculous lie, because it was a vision of beauty and a vulgar joke, and because, really, what fists could he now oppose the world with other than his laughter?

Do you think Meg dreams of cocks? I asked.

I hope so, he said. As long as it's mine.

He winked, his eyelid as obscene as white salamander skin.

When I'm going under, Kif, he said, you'll know what I'm seeing.

And just for a moment I thought I could smell Ray once more as a young man.

3

When I went to leave half an hour later, lying that I had a conference call with cable executives in Los Angeles, Ray was unexpectedly emotional.

You came! I can't tell you how much it means to me, mate.

He was genuinely moved. I don't know why. Our lives diverged after Heidl, or maybe my life snapped or broke or went somewhere else. For the past decade I had only seen him once, and that was by accident walking down the main drag at Bondi Beach. And now he looked at me with such openness I had to keep looking away. He had somewhere acquired an old man's capacity for candour, and, worse, trust. There's no other way to put it: I felt awkward there with him.

I think of those years I had with Heidl, Ray said. We were doing things. Real things.

Yeah, I said. Real things.

We were standing at the hotel entrance. The room was somehow stuffy and cold at the same time, and as the front doors swung open and shut the blasts of chill, sharp air blew in.

He had a vision, Ziggy did. Not many people have that. That's what's important. These fuckn idiots now—what do they know?

No idea, I said.

Exactly. Ziggy knew, mate. Ziggy *knew*.

I saw Ray and Ziggy Heidl together once more, Ray alert for the assassin, not knowing I was already there.

We loved him, Ray said.

Yes, I said. People loved him.

You knew him.

I invented him, I said, but it's not the same thing.

He felt something for you—I could see that. He wouldn't have kept you on otherwise.

What choice did he have? I said.

You just don't fuckn know. You knew him as well as any of us. Maybe better. Didn't you?

It seemed a frightening possibility that might just be true. I tried not to think about it. I tried to say no, but Ray's gaze—those mesmerised eyes mesmerised when? by whom?—seemed to be intently focused on my lips, compelling them to dance to his desire, to his bright-eyed belief.

I couldn't, I said, searching for some anodyne formula of words, but those eyes kept boring in. *Help* . . . but to . . .

Admire him, Ray said.

Admire him?

Was it so bad? Ray said. That's what I say when people ask me. What's wrong with creating jobs, employing people, saving lives? You can't disagree with that.

No, I said.

I felt something close to panic—the wretched room, the fluoro light, the cold, the heat, the others there, chiding each other as they played pool, what did they know of it all?

No, I said. You can't disagree with that.

What he was doing, it was the sort of thing, the attitude we need now.

His lashless eyes were unnerving; they had about them a wet gleam, a desperation, I suppose, to hold on to anything—some meaning, some hope—when nothing held; a reason to live, or at least to have lived.

Yes, he said, you can see it! I know you can, being in TV and all that. Look at politics! It's a disgrace.

It is, I said, but I had no idea. As I had grown older I was increasingly amazed that you turned a tap and there was drinkable water, that you flicked a switch and there was power. These seemed not inconsiderable achievements given what human beings were, and deserved, I felt, no small measure of gratitude.

We need a man like Ziggy now, Ray continued. Someone who does, someone who gets it done. Not for himself. For others. For us. So he fucked some banks over—all the banks fuck us over. Maybe they should be fucked over some more. People looked up to him, you know. You just had to look at all he achieved.

To realise it wasn't for himself. If you had seen his home, it was nothing flash.

I saw a photo at the end, I said. I was shocked by what I saw.

There you go. That's why people were attracted to him. They saw themselves in him.

You think so?

Absolutely, Ray said. Didn't you?

In him?

The best, Ray said.

Yes, I said. The best.

See? Ray said. You know! He was a great man.

And as he continued on about Heidl, his slow, slightly slurred voice was becoming confused in my mind with the sound of a black jay's wing cutting the air above—

It was an example, Ray was saying. He was—Ray was searching for words here—*an idea*.

And perhaps to keep my attention, he said, An idea—like you writers have.

But what writer ever boasted such achievements? I wondered. The great books were but the works of amateurs compared to the inventions of Ziggy Heidl. With them, he mesmerised financiers, torched merchant banks, consumed law courts, and fascinated a nation. And yet the writers' names live on while his is forgotten, and even the annals of ignominy have long since dispensed with the story of Ziggy Heidl for the simpler, brutish and more banal tales of thugs and killers, vanities of those with nothing to teach anyone.

An idea, yes, I said. I suppose he was.

Sometimes it's like it's now. Like he's standing here right before me, Ray said, raising a hand, before dropping it. I can see him. Pedro Morgan reckons he saw him last year, alive, coming out of a Bunnings store on the Gold Coast.

I wanted to get away.

Pedro said he'd lost a lot of weight, Ray said.

I am sure he had. Do you want a drink?

I can't drink.

I'll get you another Coke, I said.

If I drink any more of this I'll piss myself, he said, holding up a half-empty pint glass of cordial. He put it down and, fixing me with a strange look, said, Sometimes I wonder about his death.

Ray's grotesque eyes, globular and opaque, stared at me. The blasts of night air were cutting them into tears. He didn't seem aware of this, or if he was he ignored it.

About how he died.

4

I guess he died as he wished, I said.

He went out free, Ray said, as if that mattered, his cheeks glistening.

I have no idea.

You saw him at the end, Ray said. You saw it.

I suppose I did.

You remember it? That last day in the office?

I am not going to forget it.

So you know the truth.

The truth?

He could have been a great man, a leader. We believed in him.

He could make people do things, it's true.

It's rare, Ray said. It's a gift.

Ray. I've got to tell you something. I think Heidl—

I halted. But there was no way to say it except by saying it.

—that he, like, killed the accountant. Garrett. Brett Garrett.

The book keeper, you mean?

Yeah, the book keeper. I think Heidl killed him.

That's not true.

How would you know, Ray?

Because I did.

We caught each other's eyes.

I shot him.

It would be untrue to say this filled me with many questions. Rather, it felt like an answer I'd always feared. Ray was looking straight at me with complete trust. It was an awful thing.

That's how it is mate, he said. His voice was very soft.

Why? I asked.

There is no why. I just did. Heidl wanted us to go pig shooting. Ziggy said Garrett was holding him back. Blackmailing him. I dunno. He had all these stories. I'd never been pig shooting.

And after?

What do you mean after? After, Heidl said he'd fix it with the body. I left him to it. I don't know why it happened. You know how he just sort of led you step by step until you couldn't see where you'd come from or where you were going?

I shuddered.

Just to see what he can make you do, how much he can control you?

I shook my head.

Like that. It was my first time in the Gulf Country. Weird fuckn jungle. Fuckn rain. Fuckn mud. I felt shit, nothing. Worthless. What he always said.

Who said? Heidl?

No, Ray said, incredulous. The old man. He always said I was a loser. And Ziggy made me feel . . . *good*. You know? That I was someone. But he scared me. He said he needed me to do it. For him. You understand, Kif. You know how he kept at you.

I said if we stood any longer in that freezing doorway, Ray might die of the cold instead of cancer. He didn't seem to hear.

He kept at me. All that *mate* shit. Like I had to do it. Like it helped him. You want details? I can give you details. But you don't want details. No one wants details other than cops and nosy women. What do details mean anyway? I shot him, he fell in the mud, he got up covered in this green mud, I shot him again. That's it. I left and flew home that afternoon. The point *is* when I pulled the trigger it felt—

Ray's lips began trembling, and his face, now little more than a tear-glazed snout and hairless eyes, looked as if he had seen a ghost and the ghost was him.

It felt *good*, he finally stammered.

He was shaking his head as if in disbelief or horror or despair, the deep lines in his harrowed face etched silver with moisture. He kept talking.

It did, Kif. It felt good. I always wanted you to know. It felt like this weight was finally off me, that something had changed, that I was finally free, like I'd finally stood up for myself. But I had fuck all. That's what I realised after. Fuckn fuck all. And I realised he would kill me too if I ever told anyone. I started feeling worse and worse. And I really thought about killing Heidl, I wanted to kill him but to kill him was what he wanted. So I wouldn't do it. Not after Garrett. Does that make sense?

I didn't know what to say.

If I killed him or helped kill him, he'd own me forever.

It was as if Ray was describing my life.

I don't understand it, Kif. I don't really think about it, except talking now. You feel so good then you feel so guilty and after a while you really don't feel anything at all. Nothing, really. Garrett was dead before I shot him.

I wanted to flee Ray, to run out of that wretched hotel bar into the sleet outside, to fly home as soon as I could.

I was just a tool, Ray said. Like a gun or a bullet.

I felt such guilt, but it's hard to say why.

I still remember all the good things Heidl did, he was saying. And maybe that's what's really important.

I couldn't tell Ray what I had done.

You're the clever cunt, Kif. You tell me. The good things, that's what matters. Isn't it?

I left not long after. Was my silence Heidl's curse too? But then, even all these years after, I'm less and less sure myself of what I did. It's too hard and I can't hold it together and make a picture of it. And, all up, I find it better if I don't try.

That night I didn't sleep well. The airless hotel room, I suppose, or the pillow. I awoke, or dreamt that I awoke, terrified, the sheets wet, a fetid musk upon me. Around me crowded a desolation of wounded birds, dying animals, corpses in trees, beneath cars, corpses on bark and leaves. In their pitiless derangement, seeking their vengeance, they pressed in, they folded over me, they dragged me further into their darkness, they pushed me down and under, smothering me, staring dully ahead as they did so.

22

1

FINALLY, I WAS FULLY AWAKE, and in the particular blackness of a hotel room I could only think of Heidl, of how maybe Heidl was in his way a leader, a leader of the future, a leader of a coming age and its dawning obsessions, and like all great leaders he had a certain humility about himself and always concentrated on the task at hand—survival, robbery, fraud, imposture, perversion and domination.

I dare say some of these things will be reckoned crimes—certainly, the courts of the day were readying shopping trolleys of words to prove them so—but I thought that a thin and inadequate way of reckoning him, though how you might ever reckon him properly is beyond me.

In my darker moments that night I wondered if I wasn't his greatest challenge, his last and perhaps most extraordinary achievement. To persuade me to do what I did but to take the credit for his own death—what questions that poses! About who we are and what we might yet do? And what a final victory for him!

He was the closest thing to a man of genius I ever met.

But I've always been inclined to vanities, and perhaps this was just one more. Maybe he just knew the game was up. Maybe he was a coward. It's hard though not to see in what his life was and with what my life became—the repetitions, the skills and tricks, the conceits—a certain continuity. It's not too much to say everything about me has changed, that in those days I was a different person, and that what once seemed another's life I now see as my own. In any case, he stays with me—perhaps at a certain point he became me, and perhaps, worse, we him. Who can say?

Perhaps a genius is the man closest to being himself.

He swindled the banks of seven hundred million, but soon enough the world would be swindled by so much more, the racket disarmingly the same taking and making money out of shipping containers that were so empty they didn't even have a physical existence—junk bonds, no doc loans, derivatives. The shipping containers had names like Enron, Lehman Brothers, Northern Rock and Bear Stearns. Along their walls were stencilled the bills of lading purporting to show what was being transported within: trickle-down economics, the rising tide lifting all boats, inspirational opportunity, aspirational economy, and democracy for all. And so on and so forth, and every one of them impressive from far away, the promise of *good things*.

And up close empty, rusting black holes.

Heidl's philosophy had about it a resonant truth that no one would dare name in the coming decades. His bemusement at the utter need of others to believe—his determined pursuit of that need perhaps in curious experiment to see at what point such belief might finally break, to see what will break such belief, only to discover the great truth: *it never breaks*. Rather each mad test of belief, as the jihadists were later to discover, even when fatal— even more so when suicidal—only strengthens belief.

At some point, a fire started that was to engulf us all. Time tires of all things, perhaps even itself, and it may be that our malicious future was already with us. Homes, towns, lands laid waste; the unlucky tortured, the innocent slain, the children drowned, the bewildered mourning, a world of compounding fear. And maybe that was Heidl's real mistake—the one we all make: thinking life is a sprint when it is a marathon. If he had just jogged along until the new century he might have brought whole countries down rather than just his own business and a few investment banks.

Oh, I know he was not the first and very far from the greatest of corporate criminals. Still, I feel I am not alone in thinking he deserves better—more, if you wish to put it that way. Mankind is incapable of dreaming collectively, but if it did, would it—as Pia had wondered—dream Ziggy Heidl? Who can say? Who can answer? But of everything that came after Ziggy Heidl I can say this much: nothing surprised me.

2

All I could see were Ziggy Heidl's dulling eyes looking up into the sky, but when I lifted my head and stared upwards there was nothing there, and when my eyes returned earthwards, to Hobart, to Tasmania, to my life, all the people I had known, all the laughter and the friendship, the kindnesses and the love, all that too had long ago vanished along with all the subservient stupidity and hate, the idiocy that ruled Tasmania as its fiefdom, the island of stupidity. There was nothing here; there had never been anything.

I was sitting in my hire car the day after Ray's farewell, wanting to leave, but that's the thing about a prison island, and that's why islands are such wonderful prisons—you can always move on but you can never escape. I had some sort of brightly coloured sports convertible, it the sort of car and me the sort of driver I would have once derided. But I never claimed to be consistent. I had rung Huw, one of the twins, but he was busy and didn't have time to catch up, while Henry, he said, was out of town. We have a cordial if distant relationship, cordial because it is distant. Bo—

Bo died.

Have I mentioned it? I think I have mentioned that. I never talk about it. I can't stop thinking about it. A car accident when she was twenty. It was nothing I could have done anything about. We hadn't spoken for some years, I don't remember how many. I have her hairbrush. I blame myself entirely. Eight years ago she died. Her hair: black and glossy as bird feathers.

Sitting in that rented car I felt the intolerable weight once more of all the dead things gathering around me, pressing down on me. And so, flight postponed and having a morning to kill before the next plane out, perhaps seeking the greatest expanse possible so that I might breathe again, I drove to the top of the mountain that looks out over Hobart and beyond to much of the south of the island. Or maybe I drove there because the roads on which I found myself seemed to lead that way and I followed them; but really, I wasn't seeing roads, or shitty Hobart shittier than ever, another small ugly building boom having left some more small ugly eyesores, as the road rose out of the city. I was trying not to see anything.

When Ray and I were young we had often walked and sometimes run up remote tracks to the mountain top. Run! It was inconceivable now. The joy, the wonder of it all. The beauty that was our gaze. Everything we saw sparkled in its glory. The loveliness of it, the sweetness of it. We could not believe that such beauty was ours. We had nothing and we had this. It was beyond explanation. We did not know the beauty was us.

We had made a philosophy out of our world as we had experienced it—the beaches, the sea, the rainforests, the wild rivers and the mountain that was our path to the sky—the sky that seemed to draw out of the rock its monumental uncaring and the stones that brought down from the sky the tender indifference of its brilliant light. And in our wild world we found we were not, as we had been led to believe, passive slaves of destiny, defined by our history as forever less. No. We discovered that we were free to choose with every step and every decision, and all hope was ours, all hope was within us, for so long as we never forgot.

Why had we forgotten? What had happened? Why did we trade our freedom? Were we dizzy with it, were we lost with it, were we unequal to it, were we frightened of it? I don't know. At twenty we had decided to live. And later? Later we chose differently.

All we could do was run hard and laugh and run harder and harder, over the rocks, up those boulders of the Zig Zag Track as it grew steeper, wilder, more forbidding, in heat, in snow; running, panting, barking, burning, rising and running and never stopping running. The wildness we felt all around us was powerful, almost overwhelming. Beyond the mountain peak there lay a wild land that extended all the way to the island's west and south-west without the interruption of road or settlement, and it was possible to walk for ten days and meet no one and see nothing other than that world until you finally reached a wild sea. We ran and we ran and we were somehow nothing and yet of everything. It was incomprehensible. It was incommunicable. You could run it and laugh it. But you could not describe it. Words were and are inadequate to all that we felt, all that we knew, all that I have lost. Words were part of it, but they were also cages in search of a bird.

And we were the birds flying, higher, quicker, harder.

3

I drove. But it was not the same thing. The wildness was gone. Some unremarkable large trees gave way to some unremarkable smaller trees, then shrubs, then, as the car climbed higher, stones.

Not far from the car park at the mountain's summit was a decaying viewing platform looking out over Hobart and beyond. No platform looked in the opposite direction to the once great wild lands, some partly logged and napalmed by woodchippers, the rest in torment as they dried up and burnt in the new age, as the incinerated rainforest gave way to the future: a damp desert, moss and tundra and wet, charred gravel.

In the bracing cold, I wandered over to the platform along a stony path, slapping my hands as I went. The only other people there were three Chinese tourists with a selfie stick, and a short man with a three-legged greyhound. The platform's celebrated view was tawdry and ordinary. I looked at the mundane interpretation panels with scenic features outlined and named, seeking, I suppose, to fill the void that was so apparent.

Bo and I never spoke after her seventeenth birthday. I don't know why. An argument—but about what I can't remember. Suzy, her, me—I guess. What you have to understand, Suzy told me after, is that it's not personal. It's just how they are.

Some people are free. I had been, and I had not known it. I had been free, and I had traded it for something else. Why could Ray and I not keep running? Why could I not sit again in that little kitchen with Suzy, Bo and the twins? Why? Why was Bo dead and me alive? Why was it all gone? Vanished? After she died I needed some meaning to go on. I begged for a purpose, a reason, an explanation, an idea. And there was none, and I went on. That's the horrible truth. On and on and on.

Far below me spread a town, a past, a future, an airport. Down there my sons would have nothing to do with me. Down there Ray was dying. Down there my daughter was dead. I wanted that torment of a wild world at my back, more wounded than we, to rush past me, tumble down the mountain side and overrun it all. I longed for that terrible uncaring world to roll over me, to crush me and destroy everyone else in its final agony. To take us back to some moment of humility. I wanted, above all things, to return, to be grateful and show gratitude and be comforted.

I waited for such a long time.

Dark clouds moved over the mountain top and gathered beneath me. I searched the darkening sky for hope. I longed to hear an almost forgotten sound within me.

I was Adam awaiting entry to His City.

And I knew I never would.

A black jay scavenging on a glacial moraine looked up, its head slowly jerking around as if answering to a great flywheel of divine clockwork. It trapped in its amber eyes a century broken before it began and screeched the end of time.

No one had told me I was dead.

4

Why?

There is no why.

I hardly even remember the how. The details I—well, perhaps I make them up. I don't really know any more. I only remember the last thing; those odd last words.

Looking back on it I often wonder though. Why did I agree to go through with the execution? Why, when he pushed the revolver into my hand did I not drop it, give it back, or put it down? But there is no why. I just did. I just did, and I did and I did, and at each point, the further along Heidl's path I went the more likely I understood it was that I would just do the next thing. Some bond of trust, or agreement, or understanding, something deeply human was growing between us, and it felt wrong to break with it—a betrayal, if you like. Maybe I didn't want to upset Heidl. It seemed bad manners to say no—I understood what Ray had meant—a rudeness to interrupt the steps to death just because it might lead to death. It was so much easier to agree, to say yes. It always is.

In any case, something had changed, I was no longer in charge, he was, and we were walking that rocky path to oblivion, him leading, me following; *me*: desperately wanting to break free and not knowing how.

I wanted to write a book. That's what I told myself. That was all. But writing that book was at that time also everything. And maybe I thought what I was doing that day would help me write the book. Or that it was *experience*, that most illusory of art's myths, the nonsense that we must go beyond ourselves to discover the world, when all the time it's only by going within ourselves that we discover the truth of anything.

Tebbe: the quest for experience is the lie that the life we have is less.

Fuck Tebbe.

What was coming? I sometimes wonder. And there's no answer. Or the only answer, I guess.

Mostly though I don't think about it. To be honest, I hardly think about it at all. I should say I have regrets.

I only remember his last words.

It's coming! It's coming!

I have no regrets.